A SUNDAY IN JUNE

Also by Phyllis Alesia Perry

Stigmata

a novel

A SUNDAY IN JUNE

PHYLLIS ALESIA PERRY

HYPERION NEW YORK

Library of Congress Cataloging-in-Publication Data

Perry, Phyllis.
    A Sunday in June : a novel / Phyllis Alesia Perry.—1st ed.
      p. cm.
    ISBN 0-7868-6807-4
    1. African American psychics—Fiction.   2. African American families—Fiction.
3. African American women—Fiction. 4. Psychics—Fiction. 5. Sisters—Fiction.
I. Title.

    PS3566.E7135S86 2004
    813'.54—dc22

                                     2003056681

Hyperion books are available for special promotions and premiums. For details contact Michael Rentas, Manager, Inventory and Premium Sales, Hyperion, 77 West 66th Street, 11th floor, New York, New York 10023-6298, or call 212-456-0133.

FIRST EDITION

10 9 8 7 6 5 4 3 2 1

*For my grandparents, Arcola Barr Johnson
and the Rev. Sterling Johnson*

⌖ACKNOWLEDGMENTS⌖

I would never have survived the writing of this book without the loving support of my extended family, especially my mother, Arcola J. Perry. I'd also like to thank all of the people who have helped me to nurture this book, including my agent, John McGregor, my editor, Leigh Haber, and all the friends and fellow writers who have honored me with their love and kindness.

A SUNDAY IN JUNE

February 1915

OF ALL THE JOHNSON CREEK FOLK who showed up at Frank and Joy Mobley's looking for the future, Etta Mae Early was the most persistent.

Almost from the time that the Mobleys' two youngest daughters learned to talk, Etta Mae had begun appearing at their back door, offering money, chickens, a smoked ham if she had one, her help with cotton-chopping or pea-picking or just about anything else. Other people had come in the beginning, excited by rumor, but most had listened to Joy's calm, almost amused, denial of little Mary Nell and Eva's reputed fortune-telling abilities. She told everyone how ridiculous it was. "Look at them," she would say, pointing to her children as they played in the yard. "Ain't nothin' in them heads 'cept silliness." And who could disbelieve that? They were always laughing, those girls. All girls, and all cherished by parents who were childless for years until Grace, the eldest, came along.

But Etta Mae had held on. After awhile, the Mobleys knew her knock, and Joy lost her patience. Every time Etta Mae came, Joy told her, "Ain't no heathens in this house." The last time, she had screamed this at the other woman, and slammed the door. She had stood, her shoulders trembling, as Mary Nell, who had been setting the table for dinner, stopped and stared. Grace had turned from the stove and waited. Her mother was still as a stone, as if she'd forgotten where she was. At first Grace thought her mother was shaking from sheer anger, until she turned and the girl saw that dread had stroked Joy's dark features. Then she moved again, glancing around the room and saying, "What y'all lookin' at?"

That moment came back to Grace now, as she stood at the dusty counter of Johnson Creek Store noticing, out of the corner of her left eye, Etta Mae standing just outside the door, staring at Grace with a look of desperate determination.

It was the middle of February, but Etta Mae was sweating. She had walked fast; her exhalations clouded the cold air like steam from a train. Then she was coming in, all two hundred and more pounds of her, and Grace was caught between her and old Mrs. Johnson, who skimmed the shelves, not at all sure she had the five-pound bag of flour Grace had asked for.

"Grace Mobley!" Etta Mae said, between puffs. "Ooo-wee! I'm glad I caught you. How you doin' gal?"

"Fine, Miz Early. How you?" Grace spoke to her over her shoulder, keeping her body turned toward the counter and her attention on Mrs. Johnson, who was poking at the stacks of flour sacks, mumbling.

"Oh, I wish I could say I was good," said Etta Mae, "but—"

"You say you want the five-pound, Grace?" asked Mrs. Johnson.

"Yes, ma'am."

"Well, I'm gettin' low, down to my last three five-pounders. Sure you don't want a ten-pound?"

"No ma'am. I gotta tote it home." Mrs. Johnson shrugged and began tugging flour sacks off the shelf. She looked like she might hurt herself, and Grace wondered if she should help her. But you never knew with white people; it was better to stay quiet unless asked, so Grace stayed quiet. Etta Mae leaned on the counter.

"No, I ain't doin' well atall," she said. "I don't know if you heard, but my boy Jeremiah—"

She paused as several bags of flour tumbled down. A white cloud rose from the floor behind the counter. "Can I help you, Miz Johnson?" Grace ventured to ask, but the old woman glared at her and flopped a bag on the counter.

"Thank you, Miz Johnson," said Grace, digging in her pocket for the coins her mother had given her. When she turned to go, Etta Mae turned with her.

"I gotta get on, Miz Early," Grace said gently. "Mama wants this flour and I still gotta get to school."

"Oh, I'll just keep you company," Etta Mae said, trailing Grace as fast as her thick legs would let her. Grace wondered why Etta Mae had gone into the store. Surely she hadn't come just to worry the devil out of her.

"Ain't you 'bout through with school?" Etta Mae asked,

stretching her neck a little to look up at Grace. "Ain't you too old?"

"I'm fifteen," said Grace. "This my last year. I didn't go for a while."

"I guess your mama needed you 'round the house . . . ?"

Grace gritted her teeth. Etta Mae made it hard to stay polite. She had no problem with digging as deep as she could in a person's business and no problem with spreading that business far and wide. The truth was, they hadn't been able to buy the books, slates and chalk to send all three of them to school last year. This year had been better.

"No ma'am," Grace answered. "She didn't."

She crossed the main road that ran in front of the store. That road split the little community of Johnson Creek, and the store was at the center of it all, hugging a curve at the top of the hill, guarding the crossroads. In one direction the road bent north toward Union Springs and in the other down to Troy, finally spilling out of Alabama and into Florida, if you had a mind to go that far. Maybe it ended at the ocean. Grace stood on the other side for a moment, thinking that if she tried hard enough, she could see all that big water from this very spot. But all she saw were the tops of the big tombstones in the white people's cemetery. She sighed and hit the hard-packed red clay of the smaller road, which only took you down to Johnson Creek on one side of the crossroads, and, eventually, to the Pea River on the other.

"I know your daddy had some money trouble . . . ," Etta Mae was saying, having crossed the road with Grace, even though her house was on the other side.

"Miz Early, I really do need to get home."

"A family like y'all's would be ready for trouble like that, I 'spect. And you know y'all coulda made a lot of money with them lil' girls. People would come to hear them. They would pay. I don't see how . . ."

"Miz Early!" Grace stopped suddenly. She asked God to forgive for the lie she was about to tell. "Mary Nell and Eva, they just two little girls. They ain't got no fortune tellin' in 'em. And all that talk 'bout them havin' second sight and all just aggravate my mama to no end."

"Maybe they got it, maybe they don't," said Etta Mae. "But even if they don't, who it gon' hurt for them just talk to me? Now, 'specially?"

Grace started walking again. "Now?"

"You see, Grace, it's my boy. It's my baby, Jeremiah."

"What's wrong with Jug?" asked Grace.

"I don't know why you chillun try to give him that name. That don't be his name. It's Jeremiah."

" 'Scuse me for saying it, Miz Early, but it's his head. And he had that name long fo' I came into the world. Jug—I mean Jeremiah—gotta be least ten years older than me."

"All the same, you oughtta call a man by his real name."

"He don't seem to mind," Grace said.

"When I woke up this mornin'," Etta Mae went on, frowning, "it was so quiet there in that house. I laid there trying to hear him breathin' but there weren't nothin' to hear."

"I hate to say this Miz Early, 'scuse me again, but everybody 'round here know Jug runs 'round in some dirty places. Him and Lou Henry Evans, they tear up the woods 'round here, tear up most all of Alabama, probably." Grace shifted the sack of flour to her right hip. She would ask Mama if she could have this sack to make into a washcloth. It had a nice picture of a lily on it.

"You sho seem to know too much for a young 'un. But anyways, I ain't dumb. I know he ain't no angel," said Etta Mae, breathlessly. "That's why I'm scairt. And just 'cause he wild don't mean he ain't worth worryin' 'bout. I'm his ma and I gotta worry, I 'spect." She stopped walking and leaned over, her hands on her knees, breathing hard.

Grace stopped and waited. It would be impolite to leave her. "You all right, Miz Early?"

"Yes, chile . . . thank you." She straightened. "He ain't been home for three days and that's long, even for him," she said. "Maybe he done just fell asleep in the arms of some bad woman and don't feel like gettin' up. But maybe, too, he done fell down a hole. Maybe somebody got mad at him, and hurt him. It wouldn't be the first time." Then her voice dropped. "Or maybe, he at the end of a rope or shot between the eyes, layin' somewhere dead or dyin'. Alone."

Her face wrinkled with fear and she pulled a handkerchief from her bosom and wiped her eyes. Grace waited, her face calm, her foot tapping quietly.

"I just want to talk to 'em," the older woman finally said, looking up at Grace.

Grace didn't know what to say to that so she just repeated, "I gotta get home. I'm already late, so I can't stop for you no more."

She hated to leave the woman there. It was rude, but she had to get home. Grace walked faster, listening to the sound of Etta Mae's shuffling feet getting fainter. Soon Grace heard only her own shoes scraping the hard-packed clay roadbed.

She shifted the flour sack again. There would be some kind of pie tonight at supper. Her mother wouldn't have sent her out before school unless she needed the flour to make something today. Grace couldn't believe how heavy that five-pound sack had become and she hadn't even passed the church yet.

She stopped and looked back the way she'd come. No sign of Etta Mae. She dug into her apron pocket for the clean handkerchief she'd put there this morning and placed it on top of her head. She lifted the flour on top of that, balancing the sack with her right hand. She'd just carry it this way for a little while. Joy always frowned when she saw women walking with things on their heads, "like they back in the slav'ry time." But when her mother wasn't around, Grace would practice, balancing schoolbooks, sacks, baskets and bundles.

She remembered asking her mother, long ago when she was small, why she didn't carry her clothes basket on her head like so many of the other women did.

"This ain't no Afraca," Joy had said.

Now Grace took her hand away from the flour sack and balanced it, straightening her neck. She felt taller than her already lanky five feet, seven inches. She felt light. She imagined whole nations of African women walking together, running together with the weight of their world on the crowns of their heads and not worrying about a thing falling down.

"Hundreds and hundreds," she murmured.

She couldn't begin to picture them, those African women. Her mother had said they just ran around half-naked in the hot sun, not caring about turning themselves blacker than black, a sure sign to Joy of their ignorance. She had spoken of them with a charitable pity. Her own face was always shielded with a hat, and she had lovely smooth skin, but God had meant for Joy Mobley to be black, no bones about that. She looked like her own mother, while Grace and her sisters carried the inevitable stamp of their father's Indian family, the Creeks whose souls still seemed to live there among the trees.

There was a picture above their fireplace of her grandmother Bessie. She'd died before Grace was born. As a little girl, Grace had asked her mother dozens of questions about her. Joy never said much about Bessie, but once she had been standing there with the picture in her hands as Grace came in from school. Grace had come to stand next to Joy with the usual questions in her eyes.

"She was a kind woman, very sweet," her mother had said softly. "And strong, too. She made it from Afraca to slavery to freedom. She and Papa bought they own land, this land right here under our feet."

Bessie was from Africa. After that news, Grace would often go and stand by the fireplace looking at the picture for long stretches of time, trying to see her grandmother there. In Africa.

But she couldn't. And Bessie Ward just looked back at her, remaining the rather plain-looking woman she'd always been, wearing a white headrag and a soft smile.

Nowadays when Grace looked at that photograph, she no longer felt as if Bessie's smile was a happy one. Her mouth was a little twisted, Grace could see, as if she was tasting bad fruit. And in her eyes was a deep longing that Bessie seemed to be giving to Grace with just that glance. It had gotten down into Grace, so much that it sometimes hurt to breathe. She didn't know what she was wishing for exactly. There was pain in that feeling, utter helplessness, and an anger that she sometimes thought would drown her. It would sometimes follow her around for hours, come upon her at the oddest times, like when she passed Bessie's old house, which stood alone among the ever-encroaching woods not far from their own. Like now, as she walked the familiar road with her bag of flour, moving through cold air that held the rumor of spring. She felt it coming, a deep, old hurt that she couldn't shake, and she tried to walk faster. She tried to think of something else, like her arithmetic lesson. She should get home.

Grace began to feel out of breath. She stopped and let the bag of flour slide down, resting it on the ground and leaning over to grasp her knees through the wool of her skirt.

Someone else was moving, stepping lightly, but swiftly, along the road. As she bent there, Grace saw the movement of small, bare feet on the ground ahead of her. Who in their right mind would be out here without shoes in this cold? Even as she thought this, the feet stopped moving. Grace slowly unfolded her body, her eyes following the line of those feet to the hem of a brilliant blue skirt, and finally seeing all of her. A girl, perhaps twelve, Mary Nell's age, but thin with a round, brown face. She was close enough for Grace to see that she didn't know her, but too far for her to really see the expression on the girl's face.

The breathlessness Grace felt didn't go away, and she knew that it had nothing to do with how fast she'd been walking. The girl didn't move and neither did Grace for a moment.

Finally, Grace shouted "Mornin'!" with more energy than she felt. The girl didn't answer and Grace took a few steps closer, lugging the flour sack with her. She could see now that the girl was smiling softly, that she was dressed in blue, wrapped in it really, from chest to toe. It looked like some kind of strange shroud. It was so bright against the late winter landscape of gray-barked oaks and sweetgums, of dull green, drooping pines. Grace walked toward her, shivering in her dark brown wool skirt, her old shoes, and the long, frayed coat that had once belonged to her father. But the child stood there, bare-shouldered and barefoot, her head wrapped in the same cloth that she wore. A basket was on the ground beside her, filled, Grace saw, with more colorful cloth. As Grace approached, the girl picked up the basket and turned as if to go.

"Wait!" Grace opened her mouth to form the word, but nothing came out. She had only thought it, yet the word seemed to hang there in the cold air, as her breath became mist.

"Wait!" said someone behind her, and Grace knew without turning that Etta Mae had caught up. She didn't take her eyes off the girl, though, who looked ready to run or to fly back to wherever she had come from. She wasn't anybody Grace knew, and Grace knew everybody.

A hand clutched at Grace's coat, and Etta Mae stood there bent double, breathing hard with the water streaming down her face.

"You ought not make a old lady run so," she said. "Just give me a minute. . . ."

"Miz Early—" The strange girl looked straight at Grace without seeming to notice Etta Mae. She was waiting. "Who that girl? You know her?"

"Girl?"

"There," Grace pointed ahead. She turned to look at Etta Mae, who wasn't gazing ahead, but at Grace, with a frown. Her mouth seemed to be wrestling with a question.

"I don't see nobody, Grace Mobley. You see somebody?" Her voice became a whisper and she let her hand drop from Grace's coat.

Grace looked again. The girl's gaze reached across the clay

and gravel of the road and held Grace inside the circle of her ever-widening smile. She said something. Music came out of her mouth. No, Grace thought, shaking her head. Words. Words, like she'd never heard before.

Grace lowered her arm. "No ma'am," said Grace to Etta Mae, even as she watched the child turn and start walking away, carrying her basket. "I musta seen something on the side of the road. Deer maybe."

Grace could feel Etta Mae's eyes on her, but for once she didn't really care what the woman thought. The blue-clad girl glanced over her shoulder and put her basket on her head, and Grace found herself hoisting her own burden. She knew she shouldn't follow. Best to let that, whatever *that* was, just turn the corner and leave, she thought. But even as she thought it, the girl picked up her pace, and Grace nearly broke into a run to keep up, leaving Etta Mae staring after her, her bottom lip hanging.

The gravel flew from under Grace's feet, and she thought that in a moment the two of them would be flying as well. But the faster she went, the faster her strange little friend went, too. The rocks in the road bruised the soles of her already worn shoes, and she couldn't keep the flour sack on her head. She had to take it down and cradle it like a baby, and even then could barely hold on to it.

The girl disappeared where the road curved just before passing the church, but Grace thought she saw her, just a glimpse of the blue, farther up. How'd she get that far away? Just around the corner, just around there and she should see her.

She came to a bend in the road, only to see a flicker of blue disappearing around the next crook. No matter how she picked up the pace, she couldn't catch up, and the girl wasn't running like she was, but walking. There she was ahead, just on the other side of the bridge. Grace hadn't seen her *on* the bridge, but there she was on the other side of Johnson Creek, walking in a swaying, leisurely way that for some reason made Grace nervous. By the time Grace made the bridge, the girl was gone. She'd looked away for a moment, down at the swift swirl of water, and she was gone.

Grace slowed down, thinking how stupid it was to be running. She was coming pretty close to home, anyway, and it seemed as if this strange person had disappeared into the morning air. If she'd not been so silly, following strangers, she could have taken the shortcut, the older road that ran behind the church, and been almost home about now.

Here the road plunged between old fields where young trees had sprung up. There used to be fields right up against the road, Grace knew, some of them worked by her grandparents. Their house now stood empty, but her father still planted a field behind it that backed up to his other fields. If you stood on Grandmama Bessie's back porch, you could see their bigger, newer house. In summer you could only see the top of it over the rows of corn and sorghum. They owned all of it, almost seventy acres and the two houses. No other black family had as much land. It used to be Ward property; most of the land around there still was. Most of the rest of it belonged to the Johnsons. A good portion of the people had once been owned by the Wards and the Johnsons, too.

Grace was coming now to a narrow drive that turned off and led to the old house. She was wondering if the girl had gone this way, and was casually scanning the ground for signs of her feet when she glanced down the drive and saw a flutter of blue.

She came to a dead stop. She let the sack of flour slide to the ground. The house stood gray and quiet. She hadn't been here since Christmastime, when Mama had gone in to clean up. She kept it clean, always. Four times a year, with every season, the old place was swept out and the floors washed and the curtains washed and rehung. Papa would come and clean up the yard, front and back. Mama kept a few old things in there, and she always said that those things, some of which had belonged to Bessie, deserved someplace clean.

Grace didn't even want to think about what time it was. School prayers had been said and her class was already well into history about now. But she found herself there with one foot on Bessie's front steps, looking back at the flour sack drooping there in the road and then in front of her at the house's dark windows. The girl had been here. She didn't see her now. But she had been here. Somehow.

Nervously, she smoothed her skirt. She didn't know why she was nervous. There wasn't a thing in the house, couldn't be. They'd all been born here, but it'd been empty since Papa had built the new place. For breathing space, he had said, after Eva came. Papa had built it with some neighbor men. A new house with a kitchen on the enclosed back porch. Daddy had wanted to use boards and things from the old house for the new one, but Mama had gotten upset about her mama's house being torn up, so he'd just left it. Bessie had breathed her last here, her mouth filled with African words, Mama said. Grace had cried the day they left here.

The old house looked a lot like the newer one, just smaller. There were only a few things inside. Two trunks. The cradle they'd all slept in as babies. The curtains at the windows that Grandma Bessie had made.

Tiptoeing up the front steps, as if not to disturb the quiet, Grace went across the porch to the door, looking through the front window and rattling the padlock at the same time.

She went back to the steps to pry up the loose board that lay on top of the key.

The morning light through the windows made golden squares on the floor of the front room. The trunks sat up against the back wall. An old iron pot hung in the fireplace. The curtains moved slightly as Grace came into the room.

If that girl had been in here, there was no sign. The fine layer of dust on the floor was undisturbed. Grace sat down on one of the trunks, turning the key over and over in her cold fingers. Her mother was going to have a fit about her missing even one minute of school. *And* she was home waiting for that flour.

She shifted her weight and almost slipped off the trunk. The lid rattled under her. She tried to remember what was inside. Cloth, maybe? It wasn't locked. Hadn't she seen Mama turn the key in the lock the last time they were here? Mama kept some things of Grandma Bessie's in that trunk. Old things from old days. Mama didn't like to talk about the past, but just the same, she kept the trunks.

Grace slid all the way off the trunk and knelt in front of it, opening it and propping the lid against the wall.

It was full of quilts, beautiful thick cascades of color that looked nearly alive against the rough, graying floorboards. She took them out one by one and stacked them on top of the other trunk. She counted five quilts and under the last one more cloth, loose in the bottom, and under that, a bunch of papers. Grace assumed the quilts were Bessie's. She could see that they weren't Joy's work. Her mother was a good sewer, but her efforts were fairly plain. She made quilts quick and thick and wore them out washing them.

An expert hand had fit the pieces of these quilts together

with tiny stitches. The colors came together in a kind of dance, right there in that old house, as the weak February sunlight shone on them. Except one. The last quilt in the stack was dark blue and gray and was made in a pattern that angrily tumbled and whirled.

Grace unfolded each one, spreading them all around. She took the blue and gray quilt out and held it on her lap. She ran her fingers over the tiny stitches. Bessie had sat in this room in front of the fire, before Grace was born, guiding the needle through the cloth, conjuring this music and—Grace closed her eyes and held the gray and blue to her chest—these storms.

Chilly air brushed Grace's cheek and she opened her eyes. The hems of the curtains moved, lifting slightly and then lying still. She stood up suddenly, the quilts sliding away from her. "Draft," she murmured. "This place got so many cracks.

"This a crazy mornin'," she said. She remembered school and the flour. "I better get on."

She began hurriedly folding the quilts. As she put the blue and gray back in, her fingers brushed against the stack of papers lying in the trunk bottom. Writing careened across the pages.

She dropped the quilts and kneeled again. The pages were dated and well-loved names leapt out at her: Joy, Frank, Bessie. Carefully sliding out the first page, she read:

Mama dont move round much these days. She sits and sews. Christmas fine Frank ate a lot and Sam was here with his wife and young uns and Mama make a big fuss over them but after they went home on down the road she sat for a long time lookin after them out the window.

It was her mother's handwriting. Grace gathered up a handful of sheets and sat down on the other trunk, thumbing through, and then going back to the first few pages, covered with Joy's spidery scrawl.

Bessie ain't my name she said. My name Ayo. Soon as she said that her voice fell low. She stop and look over my shoulder like she werent even in the same room with me. Like she saw somethin off on the edge of the world . . .

My name mean happiness she say. Joy. That why I name you that so I don't forget who I am and what I mean to this world.

Grace stopped reading, staring down at the writing until her vision blurred. A diary. Her mother's, judging by the writing. The curtains still moved now and then and she shivered. She knew she should put them back. Instead, she stood up and tucked the papers inside her coat.

"This a crazy mornin'," she said again.

LIKE ALWAYS, THE THREE SISTERS TOOK the old Indian road home from school that afternoon. It left the churchyard, crossed the creek as two wide planks laid side by side, and cut a narrow, deep path through the pine and oak forest that once had been fields. The road was a very old path, hardly wide enough to be called a road. Worn down by the feet of Indians and slaves, when you walked down it, you looked up from the bottom of a rocky trench at closely huddled trees. At one end was the back door of the church, the school during the week, and at the other the back door of their house. The road ran right up to their place, before petering out a little farther on. Then the trees took over completely, growing down in the trench. There weren't any other houses on it, and Papa kept the road cleared from their house to the church.

They walked fast in the chill air, but Eva complained of the cold; Grace had to stop every few steps and bend down to warm her little hands between her own. Mary Nell would stand tensely, waiting. "You such a baby, Eva! Come on! We coulda been warm by now if it wasn't for you!"

"She's younger than you, Mary Nell," Grace said. "You 'spose to take care of her, not make fun." She was down on one knee in front of Eva, pulling off her mittens and rubbing her slender fingers. Eva had wrapped her scarf all the way around her head, leaving just an opening so that she could see. Even so, looking down into those large dark eyes, Grace could tell that Eva was smiling.

"I wasn't such a baby when I was six," Mary Nell said, pulling her own scarf tightly around her thick braids and looking up nervously at the silent trees. "It's gettin' dark, too. I'm leavin' y'all!" She flounced off, breaking into a run. Eva stuck out her tongue at Mary Nell's back, and Grace laughed.

"Come on, silly," she said, pulling Eva's mittens on and tugging her forward.

Her head was bent as she talked to her little sister, who was just nodding. They were walking between their father's fields now.

"Uh-oh," said Eva suddenly, her voice muffled by the scarf. She had slowed and was looking toward the house.

Grace flinched when she saw Etta Mae sitting on their back porch. Mary Nell was already sitting on her knee, talking loudly.

Mama opened the back door a crack and called out, "Come on in here you girls and help me get supper." She gave Etta Mae a hard look as the girls climbed the steps past her. "Miz Early gon' be leavin' in a little while."

Etta Mae said nothing.

"When she show up, Mama?" Grace whispered, as she stepped inside the door. That morning she had finally run home from the old house with her sack of flour, grabbed her books and rushed out again, with her mother's scolding following her and those mysterious, handwritten pages tucked into the back of one of her schoolbooks.

She could see that it wasn't a pie, but a cake, that had needed flour. It sat cooling on the table. Her mother was stirring sugar and butter in a bowl for frosting. Grace didn't bother to tell Mama how long the flour sack had sat around on the ground that morning.

"Not too long after you left here for school. Just planted her big ole self on our back porch."

"In the cold?"

Her mother shrugged. "I asked her in."

"She wants to find out what happened to Jug," Grace said.

"She tole me. Same thing that usually happen to him, I 'spect. Done got drunk and in some trouble somewhere. She gon' kill herself worryin' 'bout that no-gooder. And Eva and Mary Nell can't ease her mind. Even if they did have the sight. And they don't."

"Mama?" Grace put her books down on the table.

"Yes?"

"Why you don't let her talk to Eva and Mary Nell? What's that gon' hurt? Then maybe she'll see that they ain't got nothin' to say."

Mama stopped stirring. Eva was at the door, wrestling with the handle.

"Stay inside today, Eva," Mama said, looking at Grace, who

was still waiting, and sighed. "You know why, Grace. If I let her then every fool in the county will come 'round here botherin' us. Ain't no such thing as seein' the future, but them kind of ideas die hard. In this house, we gon' kill 'em."

"You tole me once that Grandmama Bessie could. Maybe they got it from her, you think?"

"I tole you that Grandmama Bessie *thought* she could. And them two ain't got nothin' but big dreams. Y'all are the dreamingest chillun! And them two," Joy gave a little snort, "they make up all kinds of stuff. It's just playin', and I don't want nobody thinkin' that talk is for real. 'Cause it ain't."

"Why can't it be?"

"Be-cause it ain't," Mama bit out between clenched teeth. "Them girls goin' to school and learn to be teachers or somethin'. Mary Nell say she wanna be a nurse. What kind of nurse gon' be goin' 'round talkin' hoodoo? They ain't got time for that mess and you don't neither."

Grace watched her mother bent over the mixing bowl, watched the muscles in her forearm contract with each flourish of the wooden spoon. She had plenty to worry about, Grace thought, without me throwing my piece of fat in the pot. The wanderings of strange children with baskets on their heads would have to stay secret.

She looked down at her little sisters, who were staring out the window at Etta Mae. "Come on y'all," she said, going over to take each little girl by a shoulder. "Chores to do."

"But Mama said not to go out—" Mary Nell started to say.

"It's all right," Joy said. She was looking intently out the kitchen window over the girls' heads. Through the scratched glass, Grace could see her father coming, his long legs eating up the road. She felt something inside her body relax as she watched him. He always looked straight-backed and strong, even now, at the end of a day at the sawmill, with his head down and his battered brown hat pulled low down over his eyes. He still had plenty of work ahead of him at home.

When he saw Etta Mae, he stopped in his tracks. Grace saw his chest move up and down in a deep sigh. But then he continued, greeting Etta Mae with his customary smile. He pulled his hat off. It was when his face was fully visible that people knew he wasn't a colored man. With his ruddy brown skin, he could have passed for colored, but the shape of his coal-black eyes and his strong nose gave it away. That, and the dark, dark hair that lay thick and straight around his skull. The only pure-blood Indian around, though there were plenty of mixed-bloods here and there, some of them related to Frank Mobley. The white folks didn't make too many distinctions. They were all the wrong color, as far as they were concerned. Once Grace had asked, "Papa, do you ever miss your people?"

"Why should I?" he had said with a smile. "I'm with my people."

"You know what I mean."

But he had only continued smiling.

Grace stepped out on the porch just as her father was saying, "Now Etta Mae, most folk gave up years ago. Even Willow."

Etta Mae just sat there, her battered black hat cocked to one side and her chin resting on her knuckles. "I know," she said.

"Now, if you done come by to say hello or to help Joy with somethin' or to bring us news—how's your boy?"

"Well, that's what I come 'bout, Frank. He—"

"I hope Joy done offered you a drink of water or somethin'. Maybe coffee. It's chilly. Why don't you come on in?"

"Yes, she been most kind. I do believe she went in to finish supper. She asked me to come in, but I just as soon wait here. She tole me it wasn't no way she'd let the young'uns talk to me, but that I could wait and ask you 'bout it if I was willin'."

Her eyes widened hopefully as she said this last bit, but Frank just shook his head once—no. She sighed, getting slowly to her feet, and he turned away toward the house, locking eyes with Grace there on the back porch. But even as he turned away, Etta Mae said, "Tain't no gettin' 'round it, Frank Mobley. Them little girls got the sight. Eva told me . . ."

"She told you . . . what?" Frank halted at the bottom step. Grace held her breath.

"They could be helpin' folk. It's from God, that gift, and I say it's a sin to waste it all!"

"What Eva tole you, Etta Mae?" A frown marred his usually cheerful expression.

"Now I know you didn't want them to do any fortune tellin', but every once in awhile the girls do give me a little look ahead. And the other day I saw the little one—Eva—after school let out and she say—" She stopped as his expression grew darker.

"She say what?"

"My baby, you know my boy Jeremiah?"

"I know Jug."

"Jeremiah," she said firmly, thrusting her chin in the air and drawing herself up to her full height of five feet. "Anyway, she say she saw Jeremiah in a noisy place in the middle of a bunch of people and automobiles. He was standing there, dressed for the cold, she say."

"So? It's cold. That don't mean she got the sight," he almost growled.

"It don't mean she don't. Everybody know how she and Mary Nell been seein' things for years. Willow Davidson tole me . . ."

"See, now," he started to come down the steps again toward her, "that's what you get for listenin' to an ole root woman. She liable to tell you any damn thing. That's her trade, talkin' crazy like that. She don't come 'round here no more neither, 'cause she know better."

"Don't you cuss me! You know what I think, Frank Mobley? You just scairt. Scairt of your own chillun."

"I'm too tired for this mess!" he said, stomping up the stairs past Grace and into the house. "Eva! Mary Nell! Come on out here."

"Scairt, that's all he is," Etta Mae whispered, looking at Grace.

The two little girls came out, each holding their father's hand, and he led them down the stairs to stand right in front of Etta Mae.

"Miz Early wanna talk to you girls," he said.

Mary Nell looked up at her father warily and he looked back steadily. She leaned across him and said something to Eva, who giggled.

"Eva, baby," Etta Mae said, coming closer and bending down to look right at the girl. " 'Member what you told me, 'bout my boy? 'Bout Jeremiah?"

Eva shook her head and took a step closer to Frank.

"Yes you do, baby," Etta said softly, urgently. "You told me. You saw him, didn't you? Not here. Some other place?"

"She ain't seen nothin'," Mary Nell said loudly. "You leave her 'lone! She ain't seen nothin'."

"You see? You see, Etta Mae?" Frank smiled and let go of the girls' hands. He patted Etta Mae on the shoulder. "Jug done got into some more trouble somewhere and probably be wanderin' on back once it's over. Let's just hope it ain't no white-man trouble."

Etta Mae was in tears. "Frank—"

"Now go on home and rest yourself. You gon' worry yourself into the grave."

With one more mournful glance back at the two little girls, now standing there holding hands, Etta Mae lumbered away down the road, her head down.

"I think y'all got some things to do," Frank said. "The dogs fed?"

"No, suh," Mary Nell said.

"No, Papa," Eva chimed in.

"Well, like I said, y'all got things to do." He went into the house.

Mary Nell strutted all around the room, her hands on her hips, such hips as they were.

"Now, Frank," she said with mock tears in her voice. "My boy Jeremiah, I'se gots to know . . . my boy," and here Mary Nell pretended to break down into a crying fit. Eva, sitting on the bed, fell over laughing.

"Y'all better stop that. I'm gon' tell Mama." Grace was on the bed, too, frowning over the diary pages she had just pulled from under the pillow. She squinted at the erratic writing, holding the papers closer to the kerosene lamp that was perched on a crate beside the bed. "That ain't right, doin' that. Mockin' Miz Early that way."

Mary Nell poked out her bottom lip, but she took her hands off her hips and sat down heavily on the bed with her sisters.

"She need to leave us 'lone, then, if she don't want to be talked 'bout," Mary Nell said defiantly. "She don't really wanna know what *we* know, no how."

Grace stared at her little sister. "What you mean?"

Mary Nell was silent, and Eva looked at Mary Nell.

"Girl!" Grace grabbed Mary Nell's upper arm. "What you mean by that, she ain't gon' wanna know . . . !"

Mary Nell set her lips in a straight line.

"What's goin' on in there?" Mama called from the other room. "Y'all better be gettin' ready for bed!"

"All right, Mama!" Mary Nell called back, jerking her arm out of Grace's grasp and putting it around Eva's shoulders.

Grace stared at her, the papers clutched in one hand.

"He dead," Eva said quietly.

"What?" Grace looked down at the little girl. "What you say?"

"He ain't dead!" Mary Nell said, frowning at Eva. Then she looked down at the floor. "But maybe he gon' be. And not 'cause of old age, neither."

"He bloody," Eva said, her eyes staring at the space around the bed. "Blood all around. And peoples lookin' down at him."

"Oh, Lord," Grace said, as she put a hand over her mouth. She looked again at Mary Nell, who just nodded.

"We can't be tellin' Miz Early that, she'd fall down and die herself," Mary Nell said.

"And you was mockin' her!" Grace said. Mary Nell just shrugged, but Eva started crying softly.

"If Mama and Papa heard us talkin' 'bout it, then we might

as well wish we dead our own self after they get through with us," Mary Nell said.

Grace sighed. Her little sister sure was right, but she shivered as she remembered Mary Nell strutting in mockery of Etta Mae, when the little girl knew the woman's son was about to be dead. What was this thing that had her sisters laughing one moment and crying the next? Mama was right. The sooner they forgot about their so-called gifts, the better.

Eva wiped her tears with the back of her hand, staring again straight ahead. Grace found that she was still clutching the papers of the diary tightly.

"Blood," Eva murmured. "Every which way. All over."

"We ain't gonna talk 'bout Jug no more," Grace said, relaxing her fingers and laying the papers on the bed. "And Mama and Papa won't be hearin' 'bout it from me." She leaned over and gently removed Mary Nell's arm from Eva's shoulders. When the two little girls were no longer touching, Eva slumped down on the bed and curled up into a little ball. Mary Nell climbed off the bed and went to get her nightgown off the peg by the door.

"Baby?" Grace reached down and fingered one of Eva's braids and then stroked her forehead. "It's all right. What you saw ain't really there, you know."

Eva nodded, but closed her eyes, a little frown furrowing her forehead.

"Come on. Get ready for bed."

"You see it, Grace?" Eva whispered her question.

"See what, baby?"

"That boy. Layin' there on the ground. That blood . . ."

"Nah, Eva. I don't see it."

. . .

Grace squinted, trying to read by the lamp with the flame turned down low so she wouldn't wake her little sisters. It had taken them a long time to fall asleep, especially Eva, who wouldn't even think about closing her eyes until Mama came in and told her a story.

The diary pages were safely tucked under the pillow while Mama spun her tale about Jack and the Devil, and finally the little ones' eyes began to close and Mama had warned Grace that it was just about time for her to be sleeping, too, as she left the room.

Mary Nell and Eva slept with their heads at the foot of the bed. In their sleep their toes wiggled, with Eva's tickling Grace in the ribs as she tried to read.

I remember lookin back cross the water and when I got close to the rail I climbed on top and the person next to me bump hisself on the edge of the rail. I was hangin there both feet over holding the rail with my hands trying to figure out how to jump without takin this other poor critter with me when one of them white men on the ship cam and jerked me back. He got hold of the chain that was hooked to the chains on my wrists and pulled so that I fell back headfirst on the ship. I just lay there for a long time and the sores open up again.

Grace held the papers limply, afraid to read further. She wasn't sure she understood the words on the paper, but still they were frightening. She shuffled the pages again. They were mixed up, out of order.

I am Ayo. I remember. This is for those whose bones lay sleepin in the heart of mother ocean for those whose tomorrows I never knew who groaned and died in the dark damp aside of me. You rite this daughter for me and for them.

It wasn't her mother talking about chains and blood, it was Grandmama Bessie. Ayo, she called herself. Rolling over on her stomach, she felt her fingers go slack, watched the papers fall, scattering across the rough-cut floorboards. She could still read one of the pages, lying on the floor by the bed.

I watched the blood run down onto the wood planks that soaked it up like the ship was thirsty. Drank it up. Drank it right up.

Tears stung the backs of her eyeballs. She hardly blinked as she stared at the floor. She was expecting it—the dark red pool, the thirsty wood.

Still, when she saw the blood, seeping up from the cracks in the floor and staining the edges of the diary pages, her head snapped back.

Mama and Papa murmured in the next room and her little sisters breathed softly beside her, but she was immobile for a moment, unsure if she was breathing herself.

I'm dying, Grace thought. Because surely she had no breath, she had no heartbeat; her mouth was open, but her scream gave up no sound.

There was no sound at all. But she could see everything. The water went on and on. The ship moved under her. They were all—the black bodies surrounding her were a sea unto themselves—together in hell, bound there by iron and water. Like Grace, all of them had their mouths open. There was no sound.

The vision faded but the terror stayed. Still, she didn't move or sleep. The papers remained where they'd fluttered down to the floor, unmarred by any stain.

"Time to rest!" her mother called cheerfully as she came into the room. Grace lay with her face in the pillow.

"Sleep with the lamp on again," Joy laughed to herself softly, bending down to pick up the papers that were scattered about. "You gon' burn the house down."

Grace stirred, sitting up abruptly and wiping her eyes with the back of her hand.

"Mama . . ." Oh. She took air into her mouth and nose, breathing deeply, glad to be alive again.

"Oh, honey, you need to put your gown on now," Joy said, smiling. "Don't sleep in your clothes and wrinkle them up." She began straightening the papers in her hand, only glancing at them after they were neatly in a pile. Joy quickly read the top page and then looked at Grace, who was making no move to get ready for bed.

Joy frowned. "You been in that trunk?"

"Yes ma'am."

"What for? What you got this for?" She shook the pages.

Grace didn't say anything. Joy sat on the bed, putting the pages in her lap. "Grace, I ain't saying you was wrong to look in there, but I just wanna know what the reason was."

"Mama, I thought somebody went in there. In Grandmama Bessie's house. And when I went in there wasn't nobody there."

"Who you saw?"

Grace forgot that she had decided to keep her vision to herself. Her mother sat with her hand over Grace's. She was real, and these visions were not, so surely it was all right to tell her.

"I don't know. A girl. A girl with a basket on her head, dressed strange. But I thought I know'd her, couldn't put my finger on it, but I know'd her."

"When was this?"

"This morning, after I left the store. I was talkin' to Miz Early, tryin' not to talk to her, I guess. After I left her behind, I saw this girl ahead of me on the road. And I tried to follow her. I thought I saw her at Grandmama's and when I got there, I thought . . . I thought she might have gone in the house. But wasn't nobody in there."

"So, that's what made you late for school. You wanderin' all around after some strangers . . ."

"No, not strangers," Grace said quietly.

"And this?" Joy asked, holding up the papers.

"While I was in there at the house, I looked in the trunk and got them out to read. Just curious, I reckon."

Joy looked long at her daughter, who sat with her chin nearly on her chest and her eyes on the floor. There was a slight trembling in her body, little ripples of movement that seemed to invade her from head to toe, making her hands shake a little.

"How much you read?" Joy asked.

"Not much, Mama. Really."

"And not no more, neither. Not now, anyways." Joy went over and took Grace's nightgown off the hook by the door, tossing it to her. Slowly the girl began to undress.

"It's too hard a tale for most full-grown folk, and you . . . well, you almost grown, I guess, but . . ." Joy sighed, sitting down on the bed again, putting her arm around Grace's shoulders. "Grandmama Bessie had a hard time her whole life, you hear? She had nothin' but horror to tell. And I heard all of it. She made me write it down for her. And when I was done writin', I never looked at it again. The tellin' of it lifted a burden from her after she was old, but for us now, it be best to forget it all. That slav'ry stuff ain't nothin' to dwell on." Joy looked down at the papers in her hand. "I don't know why I even kept this. But Mama she . . . it was so much for her to tell me all this, I couldn't just throw it away. You can have it, later when you older maybe."

How much older I gotta be? Grace thought, but she only nodded and put her arms around Joy and kissed her cheek. " 'Night, Mama."

"Good night, baby. You don't think 'bout all that old time no more. Your grandmama wouldn't want you to be in no pain 'bout it."

Grace woke up clawing at her wrists. It was still deep night, nowhere near morning when she sat up in bed, her head still going around and around. She thought she could still feel them, the things on her arms. The blood was warm on her skin, making a little path down from her wrist to elbow.

It took a moment to recognize, through her tears, her own room in her parents' house in Johnson Creek, the small bodies of her sisters beside her, breathing softly. Just a moment ago she had been there on the ship again with the blood staining the wooden deck. Just like Grandma Bessie had said. She had hit at the manacles with her fists, knowing they wouldn't come off, but not being able to help trying to tear the iron away from her skin.

For one long second she thrashed around in the bed, even as her eyes took in the familiar contours of the room and the objects in it. Then Eva, lying beside her, moved, whimpering a little in her sleep and then opening her eyes and slowly sitting up to look at Grace. She watched Grace without moving, as the older girl still ravaged her own skin at the wrists. Eva watched the movements of Grace's hands become slower and slower as she realized she was no longer there, she was here, safe.

"You bleedin'," Eva whispered, sitting up and touching the

little drops of blood on Grace's wrists, where the skin was broken by her fingernails.

"It's fine, lil' bit. I'm fine."

Eva scooted up beside Grace, sneaking an arm around her waist. "You had a bad dream. I had one, so you must have had one, too."

Grace smiled a little, even though her breath was still coming in fast through her lips. "I told you, Eva. People don't share dreams." God no. Don't let the baby see these things.

"I dreamed 'bout Jug. I saw him again on the ground. That what you saw?"

"No. Somethin' else. It's all right now. You go on back to sleep." Grace slid back down under the covers, taking Eva with her and tucking the quilt underneath her little sister's chin. Eva snuggled up to her, nestling her head under Grace's arm and putting her own arm around her. Her little fingers tickled Grace's stomach.

"Stop that, now," Grace said. "Go to sleep."

"Grace?"

"What? Go on to sleep now, girl."

"Mary Nell say our dreams mean the devil is here, tryin' to do his work. But it don't feel bad to me. Magic. Maybe you got magic like us. I don't think it's bad."

Grace just stroked the little girl's cheek. "No, Eva. I think maybe Mary Nell got it right this time. Maybe not *the* devil, but something. God cain't mean for us to be walkin' around with these burdens. Nah."

But Eva had already slipped into another dream.

3

MARY NELL WISHED SHE HAD SLEPT without dreaming. She wished she was deaf and dumb. As she stood at her bedroom window, her feet like rocks inside her borrowed white shoes, the stems of the little blue and white flowers she clutched were being ground into mush in her sweaty fist.

If she leaned out of the open window, the two women talking just outside it might see her. If she left, she wouldn't hear the worst. This is not a good day for crying, she thought, even as she chose to stay, trembling a little in Grace's crisp, white linen dress, pressing her back against the wall beside the window.

She knew those voices that floated on the warm air.

"I can't believe Joy and Frank would 'low it," said Janie Freeman, her words barely more than a whisper. "That poor chile. Uh, uh, uh. Lou Henry Evans already got two bastard babies. Who knows how many mo' we don't know 'bout? From here to Florida, I 'spect. How they let her go and marry somebody who they know gon' hurt her, I just don't know."

"Well, he have been rather quiet lately since he took to talkin' to Mary Nell," said Etta Mae Early. "You know, since he got back from the war."

"That sorry thang ain't been to no war," Janie snorted. "I'd bet money. He was always goin' off. Goin' and comin' all the time. He probably think he can just come and spin any old story he want and think folk ain't gon' know what he done and what he ain't done. Ain't even from 'round here really. Ain't his folks from Pike County?"

"Um-hum. I wish to God he'd stayed there."

"Mary Nell?" said a voice from the doorway, as the quilt hanging there moved aside. "You 'bout ready?"

Beside the window, Mary Nell shook her head in warning as Grace came through the opening. Frowning, Grace covered the width of the bedroom in two long strides. Mary Nell put a hand on the other girl's arm to pull her back away from the opening.

"Peoples do change you know, Janie," Etta Mae was saying softly. "He a young man and you knows how they can be, runnin' all over. And when he decide to do the right thing and settle down with a sweet, respectable woman, here we are—and everybody else too—talkin' 'bout him bad. 'Sides . . . you know them Mobley girls got the sight. If Mary Nell saw trouble ahead, she wouldn't be marryin' him now, would she?"

Grace and Mary Nell locked eyes. Grace lifted an eyebrow.

"Huumph!" said Janie. "Sometimes folks like that can see everything 'bout everybody *but* theyself. Anyway, they might not have it no more. Grown out of it, I 'spect. And I don't need no sight to tell me that if she think Lou Henry Evans gon' take good care of her, she in for trouble. I'm tellin' you, she is in for it with that run-around. How can you think that he gon' be any good for her? After what happened to Jug? Your own son? I still ain't so sure Lou wasn't mixed up in all that somehow. And I believe them Mobley girls knew what was gonna happen to Jug and they wouldn't tell you. So why you so nice to them, I don't know."

"Listen Janie—" Etta Mae said, as the quilt over the bedroom door moved again and Eva barreled in, plaits flying.

"They 'bout ready!" she said gleefully. "You should see, you should see the cake and all the food—!"

"Eva, shhh!" Mary Nell said. But outside there was silence.

"Let's go down here," Etta Mae said after a moment.

They moved away, and Mary Nell now only caught a word or two. She and Grace went up to the window and saw the two women walking away from the porch between the smooth white rocks that lined the walkway. Etta Mae waddled really, struggling to pick up speed. She glanced back at the window and Grace glared at her. A spasm of fear passed over Etta Mae's cherubic face. She quickened her step even more, hiking up her skirt with one hand and pulling Janie along with the other.

"What y'all lookin' at?" Eva asked, and Mary Nell turned around, almost tripping because Eva stood on the hem of her dress.

"Girl! Look at that! You got your old footprint on my dress!" Mary Nell put a hand on Eva's shoulder and pushed her down on the bed before stomping over to the washbasin.

Eva sat quietly on the bed in the exact position she landed, watching as Mary Nell threw the flowers down on the washstand. She grabbed a still-damp washrag and began to attack the dirt.

"Mary Nell," Grace said softly, turning her back to the window and half-sitting on the sill. "You know them two just talkin'."

Mary Nell said nothing, still rubbing, while Eva looked back and forth from one to the other.

"No call for you to be upset over that," Grace continued. "It's your wedding day. You look so pretty. Though," she grinned, "I guess my dress and shoes got somethin' to do with that."

Mary Nell sighed and straightened, holding the cloth limply. I want to believe you, she thought, looking over at Grace, all long legs, arms and neck topped with a beautiful face and that head of shiny black, half-Indian hair. She was her name. It was easy to see her father in Grace and Eva. It was only Mary Nell's ruddy-brown skin that marked her as one of his. Otherwise, she was their mother, short, pleasant-looking, but somewhat plain, blessed with a surplus of curves.

Lou Henry loved those curves. Lou Henry loved her. He had told her she was beautiful the first time he spoke to her. And even though Grace at the time had warned her that he was just trying something on her, Mary Nell couldn't stop herself from being happy about it. Grace was used to men falling all over her, but before that day a year ago, nobody had ever called Mary Nell beautiful. And after that day, Lou Henry said it all the time.

She sighed, relaxing her grip on the cloth. She was, after all, the first one of them to get married. Grace seemed like she was going to string George Lancaster along forever. He had asked her to get married more than once, but Grace didn't seem in a hurry.

Eva might well get hitched before Grace did. Eva was already walking around Johnson Creek with that same nonchalant beauty. Mary Nell would be an old married lady by the time those two caught up. Mary Nell smiled at the thought of her sisters coming to her for advice on how to handle their husbands. She was going to be happy, she didn't care what her mother or anybody else said.

"Do Lou got babies, Mary Nell?" Eva asked. Grace gasped softly. Mary Nell's smile fell clear off her face.

"You best stop lis'nin' to things you ain't got no business hearin'," she said, quietly. She had rubbed the smudge away, but now resumed rubbing furiously at the dress.

"I wasn't lis'nin'," Eva replied. "I was just standin' out there on the porch."

"Silly," Grace said quickly, taking Eva by the shoulders firmly. "You need to go and help Mama put the rest of the food out and I'll help Mary Nell finish gettin' ready, all right now?"

Grace pushed Eva to the doorway.

Mary Nell bit her lip. I can't go out there crying, she thought. What I got to cry for anyway. I'm getting married today. Lou Henry say he done left all that craziness behind. He has promised me. We'll have our own babies. Etta Mae and Janie just talkin'.

It wasn't the first time she'd heard such talk. It probably wouldn't be the last. But Lou said he was walking away from all that to be with her.

"I ain't never asked you 'bout all that," Grace said from behind her.

Mary Nell quickly wiped the dampness away from her cheek. "Asked me what?" She examined the hem of the dress. Fine. It was fine. No dirt showed.

"Don't do that, Mary Nell. You know what I'm talkin' 'bout.

Janie and them may be just wonderin' about you and Eva and prophesizin', but we know that a lot of the time what you and she see comes true in some way or the other." Grace sighed. "Even if Mama and Papa don't like it."

"Well," said Mary Nell. "We sees a lot, me and Eva. Sometimes it mean somethin'. Most of the time what we see don't make no sense at all. And sometimes they just dreams—plain ole dreams."

"Y'all had any dreams 'bout you and Lou?"

"Well, no. I mean, we sees a lot. Cain't always make no sense of 'em."

"So you have seen somethin' 'bout him . . . ?" Grace stepped closer; she was just behind Mary Nell, her mouth bent to her ear. "What?"

"Nothin'. Get 'way from me, girl!"

I need to get out of this room, Mary Nell told herself. Before I say somethin'. Maybe if I don't say anything—

"You know I can go ask Eva," Grace said, her voice quiet, but hard.

Mary Nell thought she'd burst if she didn't cry. Go up just like a firecracker. But if she let the tears come, maybe they wouldn't stop. She let one slide down her cheek. Just that one and maybe I'll be fine, she thought.

"Sometime dreams is just dreams," Mary Nell whispered. "Cain't always make heads or tails of 'em." She tried to keep standing, but her knees buckled just a little, then a little bit more and she found herself perched on the edge of the bed.

Grace sat next to her. She laid a hand on Mary Nell's arm.

"But one of them dreams got you worried," she said.

"Eva and me dream together all the time," Mary Nell said

quietly, staring out the window. Outside her mother was talking to her father on the porch. She looked up at him with her hands on her hips. He put on his good hat, hiding the shiny black hair shot through with gray, and smiled down at her. Mary Nell would never tell Mama and Papa about this dream or any other.

"Just 'cause we colored don't mean we got to be like that," Joy often said. "We got to look in front of us, not back there. They was nice women, your grandmamas. They was strong and smart. But some of them things they did weren't right. They weren't true Christian things."

And when Mary Nell and Eva had come to her with their dreams, she had shut her ears and told them no, her daughters were more respectable than that. On more than one occasion she had beaten the respectability into them. But even the strap and the switch hadn't stopped those stories from visiting them in the dark, though Mary Nell had tried so hard to make them stop. Eva was the problem. Eva had learned not to talk about what they saw, but she never tried to make the dreams stop. Not the way Mary Nell did.

"Don't be scared to tell me, Mary Nell," Grace was saying. "Just tellin' it don't make it come true."

"How you know that?" Mary Nell asked, watching her father walk down the steps, going to the church. The time for the wedding was close. Mary Nell stood up to leave, but Grace's hand was heavy on her arm.

"Please, sister," Mary Nell said, but she stayed where she was. Grace waited.

"Eva and me been having this one dream since we was real little," Mary Nell finally said, softly. "One of them dreams we have together, you know."

Grace nodded.

"We walkin' down the road, the Indian road." Mary Nell sat down again on the bed. "And when we come to a certain place we can't move no more. We just stop. There's something happenin' farther down where we can't see . . ."

She closed her eyes, and it was as if a conjurer had waved a magic stick and there in front of her eyes was that road. And she and Eva were on it in their dream.

But who knew if the road of their dreams led to the same place? In the world of sleep, the road began where they stood and curved away into the unknown and she and Eva would be standing on what seemed to be the edge of creation, holding hands. Their Sunday dresses would be crisp and clean, their shoes faintly gleaming in the light of the dreamtime sun. As they looked down the tunnel of trees, the underbrush and low branches would begin a noisy thrashing and the woods would groan as if suffering from some long and painful affliction.

". . . and the trees are whipping 'round and 'round like they in a storm," Mary Nell said now to Grace. "But the sun is shining, something is shining. There is light."

She felt Grace next to her, leaning close; her hand on Mary Nell's arm tightened. But Mary Nell watched only her memory. Even though Mary Nell felt the bed sagging under her, felt the sun coming through the window and kissing her face, fear crept up and into her throat, cutting her voice down to a whisper.

"We heard somebody callin' from the direction of the church," Mary Nell said. "And I turned to Eva and said 'We just dreamin'.'" She remembered her fingers tightening around her little sister's and craning her neck to try and see the road ahead.

"We can't go that way," she said.

"What?" asked Grace.

"That's what I told Eva," Mary Nell said faintly. "'We can't go that way,' I said. And I couldn't go forward and I couldn't go back. Then we just woke up and sat straight up in the bed and we was holding hands just like in the dream."

"That don't sound that bad to me," Grace said quietly.

"You weren't there. You can't know how it felt. You know it ain't real, that place you in, you know you dreamin'. But you still so scairt you can't breathe. And a few times, we done seen that dream when we was awake."

"What?"

Mary Nell opened her eyes then, blinking to adjust them to the real sunshine that streamed in the windows. Grace stared at her, her nose wrinkled in confusion. "You remember that time when we was late for Second Sunday and you had to pick up Eva and carry her because she had stopped in the road . . . ?"

"You mean that's what y'all were doin'? I was so mad I coulda spit! We was late for church anniversary service and there the two of y'all are standin' like two rocks in the road . . . !"

"We saw it then."

Grace started. "What you mean you saw it then? In broad daylight . . ."

Mary Nell nodded. "I know. It was more like we heard it, though. Bushes rustling. Wind. And somethin' else, too. Somethin' or somebody cryin' and whimperin' like a hurt animal or somethin'. We'd had the dream the night before and then there it was right in front of us when we was wide awake." Her voice was a hoarse whisper. "And we couldn't find you, Grace. That dream or whatever it was dropped on top of us like a blanket and you wasn't there no more. It was like I didn't know what day it was. We was just standing there, wherever there was, scairt and alone. We've seen it since, too. Usually in the dream again. We ain't never had a dream so many times as that one! And it was always the same and we always look the same in it until just 'bout two weeks ago."

"You stopped?"

"No, no! But it changed. We was there again on the road. But this time, instead of stoppin', we keep goin' on the road and we meet Lou comin' the opposite way. He look like a wild man. Like he been fightin' the devil. I ain't never been so scairt. As soon as he came, we'd be back to ourselves again. Awake. And Eva would be cryin'.

"They only last, maybe, not even a minute, but . . ." Mary Nell turned to face her sister, and Grace silently wiped away the tear trickling down Mary Nell's cheek. "It scares me, Grace. I can't figure out what that mean, 'cept I know when we walk down that road I know we walkin' into what's to come."

"How many times you seen this last one?"

"Twice recent. And Eva say she seen it once while she was by herself. Just walkin' down the road and it come on her and she cain't move for a long time."

Grace turned and walked the length of the room and then back again. "I wish you'd told me this befo'."

"You think somethin's gon' happen to Lou, Grace? You do, don't you?"

"You can tell better'n me 'bout that, don't you think? I ain't got no fortune-tellin' in me. I'm crazy for sho, but I ain't that kinda crazy."

"What you mean you crazy?"

Grace shrugged. She walked around and around the room,

and Mary Nell sat on the bed, the white dress making a nest of starched cotton and frayed lace.

Finally, Grace plopped down again beside Mary Nell and took her hand.

"What do *you* think, Mary Nell? Down in your gut . . . what do you know deep down that you don't know in your head?"

"I don't know. Somebody gon' be hurt, I 'pose. Don't mean it's gon' be Lou that's hurt. Could be somebody else. It work like that sometime."

Mary Nell stood up and went to the window. "Like that time me and Eva saw Etta Mae's boy Jug—Jeremiah—in a dream. You remember?"

"Yeah."

"I wish Eva hadn't said anything to Etta Mae that time. Nothin' we could have done to stop what was gon' happen. And all we could say anyway was that we saw him, shiverin' in some cold place . . ."

"She don't blame you 'cause he dead."

"I can't live just waitin' for stuff that could happen, might happen," said Mary Nell. "If somethin' gon' happen, it just is. Lou and me, well we done already talked 'bout that old crazy stuff he used to do. He through with that now." Her words sounded confident, even to her, even though there was a knot in her stomach. But who could be really sure about anything in life? Might as well go on anyway. Might as well go on before Lou Henry got tired of waiting and went somewhere else with all of his passion and yearning.

"And them babies of his?" Grace asked. Again her voice was so soft, Mary Nell barely heard her.

Mary Nell looked at the floor. "They not his."

"Oh, you better be sho 'bout that, sister," Grace said gravely.

There was a knock on the door frame, and this time when the quilt was pushed aside, it was their mother who looked in, smiling.

"Where the bride?" asked Joy, coming all the way in. "Everything just 'bout ready, baby. Is you ready? Oh, you look so sweet!" She came over to Mary Nell and slipped something in her hand.

Mary Nell held up the pair of delicate lace gloves, crocheted with tiny blue flowers around the wrists. "Oh, Mama . . . !"

"Don't get excited, now," Joy said. "They your Grandma Bessie's. She gave 'em to me years ago. Now, since you the first of my girls to get married, I thought you'd like to have them."

"Oh, Mama. I ain't never seed nothin' so pretty!"

"I have. This right here . . . !" Mama kissed Mary Nell's cheek. "Let's go then. Everybody here."

Grace stood up slowly and went over to the washstand, gathering up the half-wilted bouquet. She pressed it into Mary Nell's hands as she met her eyes with a question. Mary Nell nodded and Grace kissed her gently on the cheek.

IN ALL THE STORIES EVA HAD ever heard about witches, they were old, bent and ugly. They stirred big pots that bubbled with unmentionable things. They could sicken you with a mere touch. But Willow Davidson, though old, was neither bent nor ugly. In fact, she was tall and straight and had a gap-toothed smile that could light up hell. And the only big pots Grace had ever seen her standing over were the ones in which she boiled white folks' clothes clean.

In the golden light of late summer, Willow looked almost angelic as she parted the crowd that had gathered in the Mobleys' front yard after Mary Nell's wedding. Gray kinks peeked from under the bright white cloth that covered her head. Her clothes were white, too, and immaculate. Her two grandsons, Clay and Eddie Adam, trailed after her, dressed just as perfectly in starched white shirts, brown pants, and what looked like new suspenders. Eddie Adam, the younger of the two, clutched a guitar.

The old woman climbed the porch steps to where Mary Nell, Lou Henry, and Eva stood with Frank and Joy. Joy's left arm slipped around Eva's shoulders, drawing her closer to her side.

"Well, Mrs. Evans," Willow said softly, grasping Mary Nell by the shoulders and embracing her briefly. "I wish for you a lifetime of happiness and good fortune."

Willow turned to Joy, and Eva felt her mother stiffen.

"Joy," she said. "You and Frank must be proud. Proud of all your girls."

"Yes, 'course we are," said Joy. Eva thought she was about to say something more and she remembered how many times her mother had warned the girls not to be too friendly with old Willow. Her mother swore up and down she was some kind of witch. "Or at least tries to be one," Joy would say. "I ain't sayin' she don't do good by tryin' to do healin' things. It's the other things she do that a Christian woman ought not to be doin'."

"I know you don't like me comin' 'round here," Willow said. "But—" Grace came out of the front door at that moment, carrying a quilt, and stopped in mid-step. Willow nodded at her and continued. "Bessie was my friend, like a sister to me. I felt I ought to be here. When I asked you befo' 'bout helpin' the girls, I was only thinkin' of protectin' them like I knew she would."

Willow's voice was calm and quiet, but her words carried easily across the yard. Though her face bore ample evidence of her many years on earth, her lean body seemed to be held up by some kind of strength the rest of them didn't have. Her voice vibrated with that power.

Most of the people in the yard stopped chattering and turned their attention to the scene on the porch.

Joy's expression didn't change, but she clamped Eva to her side with an arm of iron. "Protectin' our own is me and my husband's business," she said. "If you wanna work roots and do hoodoo or whatever it is you do, then that's *your* business, Willow. But you ain't gon' come 'round here tryin' to turn them into hoodoo women, too."

Frank gently grasped Joy's right wrist, then slid his hand into hers. Eva felt her mother let out a long breath. She looked apprehensively at Mary Nell, who clutched Lou Henry's arm. Eva's belly churned. There was a whole storm in there. Eddie Adam, perched on a step behind his grandmother, briefly met her eyes before looking down at his shoes.

Then her father stepped forward while keeping his hand in her mother's.

"Willow," he said, doffing his hat and bowing slightly. "It was kind of you to come. Please go on and help yourself to somethin' to eat."

Even after Willow left the porch, they didn't move for a while. Then Lou whispered something to Mary Nell and went off to talk to someone. That seemed to break the spell. Mary Nell sank down on a chair. Grace tripped down the steps with her quilt and went to talk to George Lancaster. Eddie Adam and Clay drifted away, too, and Eva went to sit on the edge of the porch. She let out a breath that she seemed to have been holding in. Only her mother still stood there, watching Willow as she talked and laughed with people.

Frank went down the steps to shake the hand of the Rev.

Thaddeus Jenkins, who was among the last group of guests trickling in. A week before the wedding the reverend had asked her father whether they intended to do some dancing. Frank's enthusiastic "yes" had killed the idea of having the reception outside the church. Not a good thing, the reverend had said, to have dancing on church property. Now Frank greeted the preacher with a laugh and a pat on the back, even as the music—played by three boys with only one guitar between them—began floating out over the treetops. It was Eddie Adam and his brother, along with their friend Isaiah Jackson, trying to get people moving.

The people swayed with the same rhythm as the trees, shaking things loose, just as the trees shook off their leaves as gifts to the wind. Their voices rose high in the air.

Eddie Adam, sitting in a chair near the porch, picked out a lively song on the guitar, which was only slightly smaller than he was, while Clay and Isaiah, who everybody called Son, sat on the porch singing, accompanying themselves with hand-claps and foot-stomps on the porch boards. Son, at sixteen, had just developed a boomer of a voice, which he wasn't ashamed to let loose.

"Now, boys," a gravelly voice said. "Don't be giving us none of that wild stuff. We done just had a wedding. It ought to be a love song or at least somethin' slow."

The dancers stood aside to let the speaker through. Lucius Turner came tottering forward, his left hand gripping the neck of a well-worn fiddle and his right waving a bow like a sword.

"I 'pologize for being tardy, Miz Evans," he said, coming forward and bowing to Mary Nell. His face looked so weathered that sometimes it was surprising that he could move his features. But he winked at Mary Nell as he unbent himself, which was a slow production for a man who had grown into adulthood before the

Civil War and rejoiced at emancipation and wept so many times since. He often seemed to weep into the fiddle, making it cry at funerals and weddings, at picnics and dances. He talked all the time about the parties he had fiddled for.

"Used to play for all them big-time white folk way back," he would say. "Them dances they had. They had them so many dances! I played for all of them, all over the county. Then after the war, nobody wanted no music no more. No use for me then. All they wanted was folk to grow the cotton. So that's what I did. But that's all right. 'Cause after the war, the music was just for me and my own. No music for them no more."

He sat down on the top step leading up to the porch and stretched out one leg, laid his hat to one side and tucked the heel of the fiddle under his chin.

"The bride and groom gets to dance now," he said solemnly, and drew his bow across the strings.

Lou Henry met Mary Nell at the bottom of the porch steps. She smiled, though she looked like she could begin crying at any moment. He drew her in, wrapping himself all the way around her. They fit together well, Lou Henry being not much taller than Mary Nell, with a thick, solid body and lively feet. He took her hand, his honey-colored fingers intertwining with her earth-brown ones. With her other hand, Mary Nell removed his hat and threw it on the steps.

"Aw right, now!" someone called out and the crowd laughed. Mary Nell slid her palm across his cheek.

Eva thought he was a good dancer, as she watched them spin slowly around the yard, circling past the smiling faces of friends, relations, neighbors, drifting along with the sweet whine of Lucius' fiddle.

Mama came out of the house, wiping her hands on her apron, watching the two of them make circles in the dirt yard. Eva sighed regretfully as they disrupted the last of the whorling patterns that she had carefully raked in the dust that morning. But Mary Nell looked happy enough, so she didn't really mind. Mary Nell tried to hold up the hem of her dress, but sometimes she let the fabric fall as she clutched at Lou's arm for support. Because Lou began to move faster and faster, out of time with the fiddle, which continued to cry joyfully under Lucius' chin.

The slow dance became a runaway ride as Lou Henry laughed, spinning, and Mary Nell clung to him. All around them everyone clapped and laughed, except for Grace and Eva, who kept their eyes on Mary Nell's face, and Lucius, whose eyes remained closed as he moved the bow with assurance.

It was he who ended the dizzying ride by drawing the last note against the strings, and even then Lou Henry continued to circle his bride around the yard for a few beats more. Mary Nell's smile had faded, Eva noticed.

"You better sit me down," Mary Nell said.

She watched from the porch as Lou continued to dance. Eva came to sit beside her and their mother brought out cake and lemonade, which Mary Nell waved away. She pressed her palm against the slightly sweaty linen at her waist and closed her eyes.

Lucius whipped up a faster beat for the dancers, who now moved together across the dusty yard.

Eva moved until she was touching Mary Nell, her arm brushing against her. Mary Nell had had her eyes closed, but now she opened them, smiling down at Eva. Eva thought it was a strange smile, one that didn't seem to reflect any emotion at all, and Eva knew Mary Nell was afraid. She questioned her with her eyes, but her sister merely continued to smile like that, giving a little shrug.

Eva started to just ask her outright what was wrong, but almost at the same moment that she opened her mouth, she was pulled into the fast-moving dancers by Lou Henry. He dashed up the porch steps and lifted Eva off her feet, setting her down again and dancing around her. Eva laughed and Lou put one arm around her and took her other hand trying to teach her the step.

But he was too close, his grayish-green eyes, the strangest color eyes she'd ever seen on a colored man, too large in her vision. Every time she pulled away to try and see what his feet were doing, he very easily kept her within an inch or two of his body. Like Mary Nell, Eva felt her smile turning into something strange, then falling right off her face as he spun around and around.

She tried to catch a glimpse of Mary Nell as she whirled by, and saw that the bride now leaned forward. She frowned down at them, not in anger, but in fear. Eva knew her sister's face mirrored her own and she became aware of a terror growing up through the bottom of her stomach and into her throat. She heard the high-pitched wailing of the fiddle, Clay and Son Jackson clapping and shouting, laughter singing in her ears. Inside that tight knot of fear she struggled, feeling the inevitability of being held in that hard grip until Lou Henry decided to stop. She tried to wiggle away and he laughed. His laughter was almost musical, too. It became part of the music. He teased her about being shy.

"You ought to learn to dance if you wanna make as fine a catch as your sister," he said.

Everything moved in a blur around where they were spinning, and Eva closed her eyes. Mary Nell's fear reached across the yard and touched her tentatively, and then Eva felt as if she was right beside her, holding on to her and passing that small, growing uneasiness from her body to Eva's. Eva saw the two of them as they were in one of their dreams, standing on the old Indian road, holding hands as a storm rushed to meet them. They weren't little anymore. They seemed to be full-grown women, older than they were right now.

We can't go that way, Mary Nell was saying.

But Mary Nell, ain't but one way to go, Eva said. *Ain't but one way to get there.*

And then Mary Nell's voice came again. "Stop that now, Lou. If you make that girl lose her wedding cake by spinnin' her, Mama'll never let you hear the end."

Eva opened her eyes, even as the whirling dance thankfully ended. Mary Nell had left the porch and though she stood there frowning mockingly at Lou Henry, Eva knew she was still scared. Eva pulled away and stumbled to the porch steps.

"You all right?" her mother asked, but didn't wait for an answer. She called to Mary Nell. "Mary Nell, you better eat! Ain't no use being so jumpy you don't eat."

"I'm fine. I can't eat nothin' right now." Mary Nell turned and came back to the porch, trying a smile. "My stomach *is* jumpin' 'round somethin' crazy."

Eva climbed the steps with her head down, not looking in their direction. She folded herself into the rocking chair, hugging her arms around her body.

"Ooh," Mary Nell said, and Joy looked at her with concern. "I think I really need to get out of this dress. It's startin' to feel tight."

"It is hot out here, ain't it? And you been goin' and goin' since early mornin'," Joy said. "I forgot that dress is a little smaller

on you than it is on Grace. Come on in the house and put somethin' else on. I guess everybody done seen enough of the bride
today."

She got up and, seeing Eva curled in a ball, said, "Oh, no,
don't tell me you feelin' bad, too." She pressed a few fingers to
Eva's forehead.

"No, ma'am," Eva mumbled. She felt like crying, but she
pushed it down. She didn't want to have to try and explain the
inexplicable.

"Well, all right, stop lookin' like an old sad hound dog then."
Joy went into the house, and Mary Nell started to follow. Eva
looked up at her, her eyes tearful, and Mary Nell leaned down to
grasp her fingers. Eva tried to draw her body into an even tighter
ball, but Mary Nell pulled her gently out of the chair, wrapping
an arm around her to hug her as close as possible. Eva curled an
arm around Mary Nell's waist and went without resistance, her
eyes still closed. Glancing over her shoulder, she saw Janie Freeman looking at them with fierce curiosity.

Grace waved a hand with a piece of wedding cake crushed
between her fingers. Crumbs fell as she talked. George Lancaster,
sprawled next to her on the quilt, was laughing so hard that he
had to hold his stomach.

"If you just wanna marry somebody, George Lancaster, why
don't you just go on? You so ready to get married. What difference it make if it's me or somebody else? Anybody?" Grace gestured dramatically around at the clusters of people assembled in
her father's front yard, flinging cake.

"See, now, you don' gone and twisted my words, like you
always do, gal," George said casually.

"That's what you said." She switched to a gruff voice. "'I'se a man. I'se gots to have a woman.' Well gon' have one then! I ain't stoppin' you!"

George fell over laughing, his hat tumbling off and landing in the grass as he stretched his long, gray-clad legs out full length.

"You'd pitch a fit if I even looked at another gal!" he said, after he'd recovered somewhat. "Why you gotta be so worked up all the time, Grace?" His smile faded into a weary grimace. "A fella can't even love you without you gettin' all up in his face, like you mad."

He was beautiful, she thought, feeling embarrassed at thinking it. A man shouldn't look like that, with smooth cheeks and long lashes that surrounded unblinking brown eyes. Most men she knew, even the young ones like George, had lost any sign of innocence. George worked as hard and played as hard as any of them, but though his hands were the hands of a farmer, his long, graceful fingers were gentle as he brushed cake crumbs from her nose and her cheeks. When he flicked a forefinger over her mouth, she almost jumped out of her skin. He seemed not to notice her staring at him. His hands had left her face and now he pried open her fingers and let the wedding cake, a tight ball of compressed bread and icing, fall.

"What's that that come outta your mouth? Love?" she asked in as hard a tone as she could muster.

"You know'd it already. And don't pretend you don't love me, neither."

I know that, dammit, Grace thought. She watched Mary Nell emerge from the house, no longer in white linen, but dressed in her own best skirt and blouse. Lou pulled her down beside him on the swing.

"You scairt," George said. He wetted a napkin with water from the jar he had been drinking out of and took her hand again. The stickiness and the crumbs came off as he rubbed, but even after her hand was clean, he still held it, tracing the lines in her palm with his thumb.

"You ought to be the one scairt. You think you know me." Grace slowly, reluctantly withdrew her hand, and turned to give him a cool stare. "You don't even know nothin'."

"I know you love me, Grace Mobley." George smiled, resolute.

Grace looked away again and out across her papa's fields. The sun was beginning to hang low and the tops of the cotton bolls were turning gold. It looked beautiful, that cotton. But not long from now they would all be out there picking and getting scratched like the devil.

"I can almost hear your heart beatin'," George said softly.

Grace snorted. So he was beautiful and sweet-talking, too. How could she *not* love a man like that? She wouldn't be able to say no to him, not while she was here, sharing the same air. But somehow pretending that there was still a chance to save him from her made her feel more in control of the situation. I can still leave, she thought. Before I hurt him.

She felt his gaze on her, felt it move over the skin of her neck. She continued to look in the other direction. Anywhere else. She looked out at the people assembled on their blankets and quilts. Their bent heads with their oiled and gleaming hair. Their blacks and browns and reds. The starched white of shirts and blouses becoming a colorless canvas for the rich earthy swirl of skin. She looked at the dancers.

Away from here, who would she be? Not Frank and Joy

Mobley's oldest, from down the way, from Johnson Creek, Alabama. Who would know her the way they knew her here?

And—Grace looked again at George, who had not let her go with those eyes of his—who would look at her the way this man did? With lust and longing, with some unmentionable yearning that she felt responsible for giving him? He is going to be hurt, she thought. He is going to be broke beyond fixing, either way. Either way.

Frank Mobley quietly puffed his pipe, shifting his weight in the porch swing so that his wife's body leaned against his. He liked this time, when the moon was rising, especially when it was still warm enough to sit out after supper.

The wedding had been exciting and all, but he was happy it was done. He stroked Joy's arm lightly, as she half lounged in his lap. The streaks of gray in her hair glinted in the faint light. He liked for time to move slow, because he knew now how little time there really was. Only a few heartbeats ago they were young, but now the days ran through his fingers like sand and everything was harder to do but easier to understand.

He liked sitting out on the porch with his wife, with no words between them, but he rarely got his wish on that one. Joy whispered, just in case the girls were eavesdropping.

"Maybe it wasn't such a good thing, Frank," she said. "Mary Nell and Lou. You know how that boy been known to run 'round."

He grunted and inhaled smoke.

"Suppose one of them other chillun of his show up one day, askin' for they papa. That would be humiliatin' for her. Terrible. That would hurt her so," Joy continued.

Frank exhaled with a sigh.

"I don't know," she said, without really taking a breath. "Guess I can't stand the idea of him doin' her like that after they married. Folk don't change, always, just because of a weddin'. They may try, they may want to bad, but some folk—the way they is, is the way they is. Nobody but God can change 'em. I don't think Lou Evans and God get along too well."

Then, for a moment there was blissful silence. Frank took his pipe down, hoping. He tried to think of something besides Lou Evans and his daughter. He thought maybe it was time to get started on the cotton. And maybe take the dogs out, get them ready for hunting. They'd been laying in the shade getting fat all summer. He didn't want to think of Mary Nell and Lou Henry. He watched the moon rise and hoped.

Then Joy said suddenly, "I mean it's lots of folk 'round here, white and black, that's got chillun born on the wrong side of the blanket. I know that. But all men ain't that way. Maybe she shoulda waited."

Frank stared down at the bowl of the pipe, then leaned over to the rail, shaking the ashes out into the flower bed. He reached into his shirt pocket for a leather pouch he kept there. He stuffed his pipe, inhaling the scent of tobacco.

"They wasn't gon' wait, you know that," he said. "If they hadn't a got married up, it would have been Mary Nell with a baby on the wrong side of the blanket. And she and that baby would a been talked 'bout just as bad as you all talk about them other po' chillun Lou done left scattered all over the woods. That what you want?"

"No." Joy looked down at her lap. "But I sho wish there was somethin' else for her. Someone else."

Frank clamped the pipe back between his teeth without lighting it.

"I could kill him and nobody would come lookin' for him," he said, surprised at how casually the thought skipped across his mind. He even saw, just for half a breath, him marching up to Lou Henry and pointing the gun.

"Frank!" Joy shot up from her half-reclining position. "I know you just makin' fun of me now!"

"I am?" He smiled briefly at her, then pushed her gently off his lap. He stood and stretched. "Maybe. He ain't got no people, least none that seem to care. He the only one of his family that showed up at the weddin'."

"You know you funnin'!" Joy scowled faintly.

Frank thought maybe he wasn't. But he said, "Anyway, it's done now, they married. We'll have to wait and see if it's right or if it's wrong."

Joy just nodded, and set the swing to moving slowly. He relit the pipe, enjoying the faint glow that flared up in the bowl, enjoying the quiet.

Summer 1919

IT WAS BECAUSE MARY NELL WAS gone that the bed felt differ-ent at night now. Until the day of the wedding, the three of them had shared this bed. There still seemed to be so much space; Grace and Eva might as well be in different states. Tonight Grace had taken the side of the bed next to the window and she lay curled in a ball, her face to the wall, one arm sort of wrapped around her head.

She didn't sleep. Her raggedy breathing filled the whole dark room. It was as loud as a storm wind, loud even to her. Her breath had holes in it.

"Grace, you all right?" Eva stirred beside her. It was going to take a moment to answer.

The air climbed laboriously in and out of Grace's lungs. Her head pounded. She was exhausted.

"Grace?"

"Yeah, yeah," Grace whispered. "My head hurt, that's all."

"Your wind is comin' out funny."

"I know."

"You want me to get Mama?"

"What for?"

"You sound like you need somethin' . . ."

"Just for you to be still and be quiet. That's all I needs."

"All right."

Grace shifted onto her back, her feet sticking out through the iron rails of the foot board. At eighteen, she still seemed to be growing.

"Grace?"

"Huh?"

"I heard Mama and Papa talkin' . . ."

"That's every day, ain't it?"

"No, I mean . . . the day of the weddin'. They said somethin' 'bout Lou's chillun."

"The weddin'! That was almost a year ago!"

"I know. But what they said been on my mind a lot lately. You think Lou Henry would hurt Mary Nell?"

Grace felt an ache growing on one side of her head.

"No, I don't think so . . . I don't know!" She regretted snapping at Eva, but the younger girl didn't seem to notice. "I thought the two of y'all was so hooked into each other. If you don't know, how you 'spect me to?"

"It's been different, you know, since she been gone. I used to know when me and her was sharin' things—dreams, visions, anything. And we'd talk 'bout things. Now I have the dreams and visions, but I don't know if Mary Nell is havin' them, too."

"I'd bet you money she is. She's fine, lil' bit. You worryin' 'bout nothin'."

"When I heard Mama and Papa talkin' 'bout chillun born on the wrong side of the blanket . . ."

"You ought to stop being nosy. Not supposed to be listenin' to grown folk. AHH!"

Grace sat up abruptly, putting both hands on the sides of her head against her ears trying to wrestle with the sharp pain that had just set off an explosion in her head.

"Grace! What is it?" Eva was up now, too. She put her thin arms around Grace's shoulders. "You sick!"

Grace murmured, smiling slightly through her pain. "Mary Nell would sleep through anything. But little Eva . . . I'm the one 'posed to take care of you, lil' bit."

Eva rubbed a hand over Grace's forehead.

"Just a headache," Grace said, wearily. "I ain't slept good in awhile." She lay back down, allowing Eva to curl up next to her. Eva slipped her hand into Grace's and started humming. Grace closed her eyes, trying to even out her breathing.

"You need to stop listenin' to grown folk," she said after a few moments, after a few deep intakes of air. "Whatever they was saying, well it ain't your business now."

"But Mary Nell my sister," Eva said. "So it's my business, too, 'bout her and Lou."

"That's one way of seein' it, I s'pose," Grace said.

"So he do have them chillun? Etta Mae was talkin' 'bout it, too . . ."

"Yeah, lil' bit, Lou used to do all kinds of things he didn't have no business doin'. Let's just hope the good Lord done cooled him down a little. The Lord and Mary Nell."

"Mama said Lou and God don't get 'long."

Grace laughed then, then regretted it as a sharp pain flashed through her head. Still, the headache seemed to be receding a little.

"Well, maybe Lou don't get 'long with God, but God gets 'long with everybody. And sometime He help you out whether you want it or not. So let's just say that's what He gon' do for Lou so's he stay at home with his wife like he s'posed to. Don't know what Mama and Papa might do to him if he don't. That Injun blood get to runnin' fast in Papa . . . whew! Be like the Creek Indian wars all over again! Let's just hope . . ." Grace laughed again, and Eva smiled, stretching out against her sister's considerable length. Her toes brushed against Grace's knees. Her eyes drooped.

"And you know, lil' bit, if somethin' is goin' on with Mary Nell, I expect you to tell me. If Lou hurts her, I'm liable to knock him in the head myself." Grace said this softly, feeling herself drift off.

Something—some sound—woke her. Maybe something outside the window. No, it was sort of a low twittering, as if a group of people were trying to whisper all at once.

Grace shifted against Eva's sleeping body, trying to change positions without waking the girl, telling herself that she didn't really hear anything at all. She wanted to sleep. She had prayed for one good night of rest and she expected God to give it to her. No 'rasslin' with ghosts tonight, she thought.

It had been years, it seemed, since she'd slept through the night. Not since she'd held those diary pages in her hands. Not since the girl in the blue dress had led her down the road. A door had opened for her that day. At night, she was often visited by strange dreams, too, but she didn't tell Eva. Grace wasn't sure what she was trying to protect her little sister from.

Often as she lay in this very room, Grandmama Bessie would come and show Grace her own birth. They would stand together in a room of the old house as night turned into day and Bessie's hand would be on Grace's arm as Joy sank down into the bed in the grip of a pain so deep that she could only whisper through sweat and tears. Willow sat by the birth bed, cool and still, her hands coming at the right moment to catch the girl child that fell down that day.

"From the lap of God," Grandmama Bessie would say to Grace, as they stood by unnoticed. "You know my name?" she would ask and Grace whispered, "Bessie."

"My name ain't Bessie," the old woman always answered, slowly shaking her head and smiling a child's smile. In fact, she now was a child, her smile radiating upward at Grace, who was now holding her hand. "My name Ayo."

Grace had dreamed this many times. She used to be frightened of her mother's pain, but now she hardly looked at the birth; she wanted to always, always look into Ayo's dark, moist gaze, wanted to see some bright future to come, instead of the heavy shadows that she glimpsed. And now she could see that the smiling girl-child was the same one she had seen on the road that day, in broad daylight, in a waking dream.

When awake, she sometimes heard muted voices, as if people were standing behind her whispering. Sometimes weeks passed without so much as a murmur. Other times they invaded her mind at the oddest times, and more and more lately at night. In the beginning, she strained to hear what they were saying, groped the air for their words until her head hurt. But now, she just tried to move through the day without being overcome by the sadness and fear in those voices. They had begun to suck the life right out of her so that she felt like a ghost herself sometimes. Somehow she walked around and did what she had to without crumbling into dust, though her body often felt like dry bones. Dry, hungry bones, walking and talking and passing themselves off as a living person.

Her headache receded. She felt sleepy for the first time in days. If she could just drop off before they got loud, she might rest.

Faint, gray shadows clothed the cold room; a crescent moon smiled through the window, riding high in the sky. Grace sighed, feeling her lungs expand and contract, her body sink into the cotton-filled mattress.

"I only want to sleep," she said aloud faintly.

Sleep. That for dead folk. Is you?

There they were. But this time the words were as clear as anything. Grace sat up abruptly. But the room held just the two of them in the bed and the silver moonbeams that slanted across the floor.

Is you dead?

"Not yet, God willin'. Not yet," Grace whispered. The voice stood out against the background of rising and falling barely uttered phrases and words that seemed to have traveled from far away just for the privilege of knocking up against her brain. The tension in her head returned, not as pain, but as a wall of sound that grew. For the first time she realized, as her head swiveled around and around the room, that these voices, these whisperings, these strange panting cries came from inside her own body.

It got loud. She couldn't hear Eva breathing beside her. She looked down, just to make sure Eva was still there, and put her hand on the sleeping girl's chest, which moved up and down comfortingly.

Peering again up and out into the grayness, she half-expected to see something right out of one of Mary Nell's and Eva's dreams. Still, they were alone. But the window beside the bed had moved to the opposite side of the room and the doorway was smaller. No quilt hung at the door, and the space beyond it was completely blank. No room on the other side. No space. No thing.

She wondered if she was asleep. If she was, then sleep was no escape either. She opened her mouth to shout in protest, but her lips didn't move.

Sleep ain't what you think it is, said the voice. It was female, familiar. Bessie.

It's only a place to wander. Sometimes a little trip teaches you something.

"I done finished with school. Don't need to learn nothin' else." Grace put her feet on the floor, trying not to jostle Eva in the bed.

Yeah, you do.

"I want you to leave me alone now."

I really cain't do that. Don't know how.

Grace stood up beside the bed, then turned around and around in that one spot on the floor. She smoothed her hands down over her nightgown and felt stiffness against her palms.

She held up hands that were no longer hers. Even in the faint light, she could see how dark they were. Black, in fact, with fingers a different shape than her own, the fingernails more oval, the veins disappearing into the darkness of the skin.

She opened her mouth again, expecting a scream, but not even an echo came out of her to compete with the wall of whispers being built in her head. She held up both hands and then brushed them against her night dress, which was not even a night dress. She was clothed in a dark blue something, much heavier than the well-worn feed sack gown that she had put on before getting into bed that night, the one with the little blue flowers. The designs on this cloth were different—swirls of light against the dark material. The dress had no sleeves or shoulders; indeed it seemed to be not on her at all, but around her, wrapped many times.

Eva stirred on the bed, stretching a little bit and kicking off the covers. Grace stared at her as the younger girl settled down more comfortably, looking perfectly normal except for the fact that the room they were now in wasn't their own room anymore. Could she have taken Eva into the land of the dead with her?

Grace felt her breathing stop. She had taken a breath in but there was no exhale. She tried to inhale deeply, but she felt no air moving into her lungs; she heard nothing except the whispers. Maybe she really was dead, like the voice said. She knew already who it was, even though she continued to search the all-enveloping gray light for a face. She knew it was Bessie, and didn't know how she knew. She felt as if she'd been waiting to meet her grandmother. But it was not a joyful anticipation.

"Why you want to possess me?" Grace tried to say out loud. She wasn't sure she said it; she couldn't hear her own words.

Why you want to possess me? Bessie echoed sadly. And this time Grace heard the words come up through her own chest and out of her mouth in a voice that wasn't hers.

"Listen, Bessie . . ." Grace said.

Name ain't no Bessie. Ayo. Ayo.

Grace felt her throat closing around the word *Ayo* and she ran to the door, moving easily in the long, wrapped dress, even though the feel of the fabric moving against her skin, winding around her body frightened her even more. She searched the nothingness beyond the doorframe, her voice reaching her own ears as an animal-like whimper. She looked out into a storm cloud that swirled and parted only to reveal more grayness beyond it.

"Lord, help me. Lord, help me. Jesus . . ." she whispered. "The dead should stay dead, you hear me?!"

No answer came, only Bessie-Ayo's fear on top of hers, smothering her. The mist from the doorway dampened her face and she put that alien hand up to her cheek to wipe away the water. Licking her lips nervously, she tasted salt, and as she stared out the doorway the misty clouds gave way to gray water. Wave upon wave of churning, leaping water. It lapped at her bare toes. It wet the hem of the blue cloth, and she stepped back, putting her hands over her eyes and breathing in moist air, every inch of her damp.

"Lord, Jesus . . ."

White man's god. He don't listen. The gods don't listen.

Ayo was there. Grandma Bessie. Sighing and crying and tugging at Grace from the inside.

I los' so much that day, Ayo whispered, sobbing softly. She seemed to be right there in the room, body and soul. *Ev'rything,* she said, and Grace felt Ayo's voice echoing inside her own chest cavity. Her body was empty except for that voice, and that deep, damp sorrow.

"Stay dead! Stay dead!" Grace said, putting a hand over her stomach and backing up, her eyes on the doorway, until the backs of her knees hit the bed and she had to sit down. She wrapped her arms around her body and rocked. She rocked for so long and so hard that she thought she was going to fall out. She was leaving the world. At any moment, she thought, I'll be gone. And Eva will wake up in the morning without me. Grandmama is taking me away.

I don't wanna go, she said silently, looking across at the window, where a faint light moved shadows across the floor. I don't wanna go.

"That's all right, baby. Grace? You not goin' nowhere. Come on, now, look at me. Grace?"

It was her mother's voice, soft and clear, but she couldn't see her mother's face.

"She was talkin', Mama," Grace heard Eva say. "Kept saying 'Lord, Jesus.' And she woke me up, just sittin' there rockin' the bed like that."

"Hush, Eva!" A male voice.

"Papa," Grace whispered. She thought her eyes had been open the whole time, but she was just seeing him now, leaning against the foot board of the iron bed, staring at her with intense concern. She continued to rock herself as she looked all around the room, finally meeting her mother's eyes. Joy rocked with her, had her arms all around her and moved with her.

"I don't wanna go," Grace said to her mother, quite clearly, quite seriously.

"Ain't none of us goin' nowhere. Not today." Joy smiled softly and Grace stopped moving, leaning against her mother's arms.

"Dreams can get the best of you sometime, don't they?" Frank said with a sigh, smiling nervously. "Eva got us up 'cause she was worried."

"You was rockin' and rockin' and sayin' things," Eva said, putting a hand on Grace's knee. "You was cryin'."

They all looked at her expectantly and Grace didn't know exactly what to say.

"What was it, Grace?" Eva asked. "A dream? Like me and Mary Nell have? What happened?"

Joy frowned and Grace quickly shook her head. "Nah, girl, I don't think it was a dream." She looked at her mother, whose worried expression was hardening into something else. "I ain't been sleepin' at all lately," Grace said, faintly. "And tired as I am, I guess it ain't no wonder I got a little bad off there for a minute."

Frank nodded and left the room, while Joy sat there not saying anything, just holding Grace's damp body. Grace shivered and licked her lips, again tasting the salty water, and ventured a look down. Her feed-sack nightgown was glued to her body by sweat.

Frank came back with a jar of water.

"You all right, now?" he asked, as she gulped it down. Grace nodded. He seemed satisfied with that, and left.

Joy took the jar and made Grace take off the sweaty nightgown and put on her other one. The flowers on this one were pink.

Eva was down under the sheet again, watching as Grace pulled the gown over her head. Then she lifted the cover and patted the space next to her in the bed. Grace slipped in, smiling as Eva pulled Grace's head down to her little chest, stroking her forehead.

After Joy turned off the lamp and left, Grace lay there with her eyes open, trying to forget the water lapping at her toes.

"It's fine for now," Eva said suddenly. "She gone for a while."

"You saw her!" Grace tried to sit up, but Eva clamped a hand firmly on her forehead.

"No," Eva said. "I saw you."

◈6◈

THE BAGS HAD TO BE CLEAN. They had to be sturdy. Something like that would be used for years, kept close to the skin, become damp over and over. She liked to use scraps cut from old work pants. They lasted longest. There were people in the county who had been walking around with Willow Davidson's little bags tucked next to their hearts for decades. It was good to have a supply of empty ones, ready to be filled. Somebody might need one.

This time Willow had used a pair of Ezra's work pants, the ones that had been hanging behind the kitchen door. She'd almost forgotten their existence. The rest of his things had long since been put away or given away, but yesterday she had closed the kitchen door and her dead son's pants, hanging precariously on that nail, had moved and brushed her cheek.

She wasn't sure they weren't haunted. But she didn't have the talent for seeing such things. Her friend Bessie, if she'd been alive, could have said one way or the other whether Ezra was still hanging around like those pants were, and Bessie'd be sure. If Bessie were here, maybe Ezra would still be here, too, because she would have warned him. She would have known where he should and shouldn't go.

And they would have worked on something just for him, even though her son would have laughed and scoffed at such a thing. A lot of people mocked such things in the daylight and then came creeping up to Willow's back door at night, needing her to help them get something. Some love, some money, some relief from fear.

"For protection charms," Bessie had said to her one day as they sat beside the creek, "you got to fill the bag up with sweet smelling things that calm 'em down. Put the herbs in, and you can say a prayer. Or write 'em down on a bit of paper and put that in." She had traced a symbol in the dirt on the bank. "Make it pretty. Put on your most serious look." Bessie had set her face in a mock frown and Willow had laughed. "It's believin' that works it. They got to believe it, and anybody that come to you lookin' for help with somethin' believes, even if they don't want to say so."

"I'm for healin' people, not puttin' nothin' on 'em," Willow had said.

"This healin', too," Bessie answered, smiling. "You think the heart and soul don't need healin'? That's the place that really do need it, 'specially in this place." Willow remembered that her friend's smile had faded then and she had mumbled something in a language that Willow didn't understand.

"What you say?" she had asked.

"I said, 'home ain't nothin' but a dream.'" Bessie's words were thickened by her strange accent.

It was only after Bessie died that folk started coming to Willow. And she had remembered what Bessie said and tried to help them as much as she could.

She fingered the cotton pieces laying in her lap. She had taken Ezra's pants down and washed the dust out of them. She hung them up on a tree branch to dry. Last night she thought about those pants hanging there in the tree, even though she couldn't see them from her window. In her mind, it was as if they were right there in front of her, twisting under the moonlight. Willow turned over a few times in bed, thinking about those pants, and then decided that they were just the right material for charm bags.

So now she sat on her overturned tin tub with her back against the shaggy bark of a twisted, ancient hickory tree that seemed to mark the spot where the woods began. The trees marched almost right up to her back door, and today they bent back and forth in the steadily growing wind.

Willow paid no mind. Storms were her favorite thing. With her ear close to the tree trunk, she listened to the hickory groaning from the inside out and continued to cut out the squares, measuring out the pieces to be about the size of her palm.

A few days ago, she'd been taking it easy, not even thinking about doing any doctoring or charm-making. And today here she was, with Bessie and Ezra on her mind, with the dead telling her what to do.

She hadn't thought about charm bags in a long time until this past Sunday afternoon. It being the second Sunday in June, the day Johnson Creek Baptist celebrated its anniversary, she had brought her dinner to eat on the ground like everybody else. She had been sitting there with her grandson Eddie Adam, Ezra and Dorothea's youngest boy, while he babbled about this that and the other. About baseball, about chocolate cake, and about something Eva Mobley had said to him. That's what got her to thinking about Bessie, she reckoned. Eva was Bessie's grandbaby, though the two had never laid eyes on each other. Bessie had been gone on by the time Eva came along.

She had looked across at the Mobleys, who were gathering themselves up off the grass in front of the church, shaking out their quilts and picking up the contents of their box. They were certainly the most striking family in Johnson Creek, the Mobleys. Bessie would have been proud of that. Bessie's daughter Joy was dark with a strong body and strong features. Her straight-backed walk reminded Willow of Bessie. They all walked like that, as if they owned every bit of ground they trod on. Even Frank, Joy's husband, had that. But that might just be the Indian in him. Eva and Grace were laughing together. Mary Nell and her husband were there, too.

"They gon' be somethin', them girls. Them women," she could hear Bessie saying, almost as clear as if the old woman was standing beside her. But Bessie had been gone for almost twenty years now. She had been just going as these Mobley girls, her granddaughters, had been about to arrive.

How she missed Bessie still. People had always marveled at how alike they were, as alike as mother and daughter. Bessie was twenty years older and had taken care of Willow when she was a child. Folks used to turn and look at the two tall, dark women whenever they walked together. Of course, Willow knew better than anyone that the similarities were only superficial. First of all there was Bessie's voice and that accent that crept into her words when she was sad or in pain. And few people ever saw the scars Bessie carried on her back or heard and saw the terror that crept over her at times. Times when she would sit staring and crying silently, sometimes whispering words Willow couldn't understand.

Both Bessie and Willow had learned about herbs and curing and midwifing from another slave, an old woman named Cassie, but it was obvious from the beginning that Bessie had something else. She knew things. She knew where to find the sickness in people. She knew what they were feeling before they knew themselves. She looked at people and often saw their lives before they happened. She tried to describe this to Willow, without much success.

"When I was a child, I once saw your face," Bessie had told her once. "When I was Ayo. Maybe in a dream. I don't remember."

And now, as Willow sat there under the increasingly windy sky, she thought about what Bessie had said: "My girls gon' be somethin'."

That was Sunday. This was Thursday, and a storm was brewing.

Willow's scissors split the cloth. If Bessie were here, she would have already taught those girls, if they truly had second sight. She wondered about Grace. She'd never heard anything about her.

Her grandsons weren't here and she was supposed to be getting on with the washing. Old Miz Scott's clothes weren't getting any cleaner and it wasn't like that frizzy-headed gal of hers was going to do it. Miz Scott paid good money.

I'm getting old, she thought, as she slowly rose from her low perch. No aches and pains, but I feel my life falling down away from me.

She lifted the large basket of clothes and left it on the back porch. She fingered the cloth squares in her right pocket.

That's when she saw Grace, obviously weary and worried, but still walking through the swaying trees like the queen of some undiscovered country.

EVA RAN AS FAST AS SHE could, knowing it wouldn't make much difference. The ball that she had slapped into center field a few moments ago was already in Eddie Adam Davidson's hand.

Even so, she rounded the bases with her legs pumping and her skirt whirling. Gravelly dirt spewed from under her heels. As the small stones dug into the soles of her feet, Eva fleetingly regretted her lack of shoes. But her only aim at this moment was to make it to home before Eddie Adam had a chance to throw.

Eva turned wide at third and almost ran right into a clump of plum trees beside the field, but merely brushed them as she twisted her body in the right direction and locked eyes with Son Jackson, who straddled that old piece of shingle that they called home plate.

Even as she ran, she heard Eddie Adam grunting as he threw,

even over the yells of the boys in the field and standing around behind home plate. He sounded like he worked real hard to throw that ball, and Eva risked a peek over her shoulder to see where it was.

She couldn't find it. Looking up, she couldn't see the dingy baseball against the curtain of stormy gray that was descending. When she turned her gaze again toward home, there was Son with the ball in his hand, outstretched toward her.

Eva tried to slow down. What was the point of scraping her knees when she was going to be out anyway? But her body didn't agree with her thought and kept going, plowing into Son and the ball and tripping up on the shingle, sending it skittering across the dirt, and Eva on top of it.

"Out! Out! You out!" Son Jackson yelled, dancing a little step and waving the ball.

Loud grumblings of disappointment went up from the boys on Eva's team. Eddie Adam came running from the outfield with his teammates close behind.

"That what you get for puttin' a gal on your team," Son Jackson crowed.

"Had to," said Saul, leaning forward and grabbing Eva under her armpits to haul her up. "Ran out of boys. I be glad when my brother gets back."

"When he comin' back?" asked Eddie Adam.

"I don't know." Saul frowned. "He say he may never come back. He still over there in France with the Army. Got through without a scratch."

"Even if he do come back, he gon' be too old to play with us," said Eddie Adam. "You can't be in the Army and come home to play with boys."

"Aww," Eva said, "I play better'n him anyway."

Saul laughed. "Well, if you could just grow you some longer legs . . ."

"You all right, Eva?" Eddie Adam asked, putting one hand on her elbow and brushing the dirt and gravel off her arm with the other.

"Fine," she said.

"Your ankle bleedin'."

Eva looked down at the slowly spreading patch of bright red on her leg. "All that, and I didn't even get to sco'."

"And you won't when I'm back here," Son said.

"Oh, hell, boy, Saul sco'd on you yesterday!" somebody yelled. "You better thank heaven Eva got short legs."

There were screams of laughter and Son Jackson screwed up his face. "Ha, ha," he said.

"We gon' play or talk?" Saul said.

"Dunno." Eddie Adam looked to the west. "I'm already late for chores. Maybe we oughta finish tomorrow. Look like it gon' rain anyhow."

The boys nodded, already drifting away.

"Three to nothin'!" Son Jackson called after them as they left the field. "Don't forget! Three to nothin'! And we up to bat! Eva was the last out!"

"All right, all right," Saul said, snatching his ball out of Son Jackson's hand and marching away.

"I'll walk with you home, Eva," Eddie Adam said, still trying to brush the dirt off her arm.

"Naw, I'm goin' her way," Son said casually. "I can take her back."

"Well, I said it first, so . . ."

"I don't need nobody to take me nowhere," said Eva, frowning. But Eddie Adam slipped his hand into hers anyway, and she, astonished, looked down at their fingers together and then up at him. He wasn't looking at her.

He started off at a fast pace, almost dragging her behind. Eva looked back at Son Jackson, standing with a slight scowl on his face, his long legs still straddling the shingle, his hands on his hips.

"You don't have to go so fast," she said, turning back to Eddie Adam. "Short legs, you know."

"Oh, sorry." He slowed down, but gripped her hand tighter. "They not so short, though. The boys were just sayin' that. You gon' grow into them legs real soon." He glanced up at the sky. "We shouldn't have let you stay so long. It's almost dark."

"It's all right, Mama know'd where I was. And Mary Nell's comin' for me."

"What?"

"She's comin' to get me." She was having one of those days when it felt like she and Mary Nell were in the same room even when they weren't. They didn't have many days like that anymore.

Eva heard footsteps behind them, the sound of long, drying grass being crushed underneath a heavy foot. Then Son appeared on the other side of Eva, seemingly in a hurry, but not breathing very hard at all.

"May as well walk with you," he said, looking at Eva and then up and straight out in front of him.

Eddie Adam frowned, but made no comment and they all walked along without speaking. It was uncomfortable walking between the two boys. Eva felt the heavy silence that traveled back and forth between them. Son glanced down at Eva's hand inside Eddie Adam's and she wanted to let go, but Eddie Adam kept tightening his grip.

They came to a little path that connected to the Indian road, the one that went past her house. Mary Nell was coming up the old road, Eva knew, and she was just thinking of untangling her fingers from Eddie Adam's so that she could turn off here, when he dropped her hand rather abruptly.

"Hey, Mary Nell!" he called.

She was on top of them almost before the boys noticed her. She was out of breath.

"I was just comin' to get her," Mary Nell said, nodding at Eva. "I was over at Mama's and she sent me." She looked at Eva. "Baseball, huh?"

Eva just smiled and Mary Nell shook her head. "You know you a girl, right? You a girl every other time, 'cept baseball time. You the most girly little girl, until you gets a baseball in your hand."

"She a good player," Son Jackson offered.

"That don't make it better," Mary Nell said, frowning. "Might even make it worse." She took Eva's arm, pulling her along. "Y'all better get on home yo'self," she said to Son and Eddie Adam.

Eva looked back apologetically at the two boys. Eddie Adam just shrugged and smiled. But Son stared after them so hard that she quickly turned around to face the road.

In the approaching darkness, the path was barely visible. The woods crept to the edge of the dirt and gravel.

"What you doin' at Mama's?" Eva asked, stopping to rub at the now-dried blood on her ankle bone.

"She wanted me to take some of her jars of apples. She got so many, she runnin' out of room."

"Maybe she gon' make a cobbler." Eva straightened immediately, and quickened her steps. She could almost smell the crust baking.

"Naw, girl!" Mary Nell laughed as Eva sprinted a little ahead. "You greedy thing! All you think 'bout is what you gon' put in your mouth. She ain't got time to make no cobbler!"

"Shoot!" Eva stopped, pouting, waiting for Mary Nell to catch up. They were about halfway to the house now.

"She got so many apples!" Mary Nell said. "I'm takin' some home with me to Lou. He eats them right outta the jar. Maybe *I'll* make a cobbler . . ."

"I'm eatin' at your house, then!" Eva said cheerfully.

"You sho eat a lot for such a skinny somethin'."

"I bet I can out-eat Lou," Eva replied. When she said that, she got a picture in her mind of Lou Henry at the table, with both elbows up, eating with two hands. He looked up, a strange expression alight just beyond his eyes, and Eva shivered. The picture faded and she hugged herself against a sudden chill. Both she and Mary Nell had slowed down, and when Eva glanced at Mary Nell, she saw an uneasiness flit across her sister's features.

They stopped, just at the same time. Eva moved a little closer to Mary Nell.

"Well," Mary Nell said quietly, turning around and around in one spot. "This a familiar feelin'."

Eva didn't ask what she meant. They knew each other well enough not to try and explain the fear that had abruptly poisoned the summer air. They had shared it before. Eva glanced back the way they had come, knowing that Mary Nell was looking there, too.

"Somethin's coming," Eva said.

"Yep."

"What should we do? Run?"

"Not back that way. We can't go back that way," Mary Nell said, taking Eva's hand.

"I think we have to," Eva shivered, pressing her body against Mary Nell's. "Let's run. Let's run home the long way!" She meant to start moving as she said this. But just like in the dreams they had shared about this moment, she didn't. She could only stand there, shaking.

"You know we ain't goin' nowhere. It's comin'. Maybe this time we'll see what it is," Mary Nell said.

"I don't wanna see what it is," Eva whispered.

Mary Nell put an arm around Eva and resolutely faced the direction from which they'd come. The wind began to pick up and Eva felt Mary Nell trembling. She took one or two steps backward and Eva with her. Everything grew close to the road here, and after only a few paces, they seemed to be surrounded by the woods and deepening darkness. Earlier it had just been a road with trees beside it. Now it was a room without windows. They seemed locked in by vegetation, by hard ground, by the night descending rapidly from above their heads.

Eva closed her eyes, and immediately cried out.

It was bright day again behind her closed eyes. She could see just ahead on the road, not more than ten feet. The back of a woman, or maybe a tall girl. She knew the tilt of the head and shape of the shoulders. Even before the woman turned around to look back, Eva knew she would be looking into her own face. An older face, but still hers. When the girl turned around, Mary Nell stiffened beside her, but Eva didn't open her eyes. Fear hung in the air all around them, a heavy shroud. It was such an odd contrast to the sunny day they saw. They held each other's hands, squeezed their eyes tightly shut, but still there was the sunlit road, the other Eva's swinging dress and even the sound of her feet crunching the gravel. She came to a place in the road and stopped, looking off to the right, into the bushes.

At that moment, a terror so immediate gripped Eva that she fell to the ground, taking Mary Nell with her. She was being ripped apart, and the sensation was so much more than physical pain that she couldn't breathe. A weight on her chest blocked all light and air. For a moment there was just blackness that she tried in vain to see through, and the sunlit road and the girl, the other Eva, were gone. But someone was screaming. From inside her body somewhere, someone was screaming.

A body lay on top of her, someone breathing heavily and erratically. Someone gripped her with fingers of iron around her arms and at her neck. Eva struggled to get the weight off, to make it stop. Make it stop. Make it stop.

Finally, she opened her eyes, and Mary Nell was there, having landed on top of her when they fell. Eva pushed her heaviness off her chest with both hands. One big heave. And then she lay there breathing hard and sobbing, drinking in the hard rain that was now falling.

Mary Nell stretched out where Eva had flung her, shaking there on the ground.

"That . . . dream . . ." Mary Nell gasped. "That was that dream we have."

"Yeah," Eva whispered, still choking on dry heaving sobs.

"But it wasn't like that in the dream. Eva, what's happening?"

"I'm so scairt. I'm so scairt . . ."

"It's gonna be all right," Mary Nell said, her voice thin and trembling. She sat up. "All right . . ."

"No, it ain't gonna be all right," Eva sobbed. "Somebody stole the life outta my body, seem like. I couldn't get no air atall. Was it you, Mary Nell? You were there . . ." Eva began crying again. "What is it? What is it?"

"I don't know." Mary Nell stood up and ran shaking hands over her own dress, trying to brush the dirt out. "Maybe it don't mean nothin'."

"How? How can somethin' like that be nothin'? Every other thing we done ever seen in our life meant somethin' to some-body. And this is me. This is us, Mary Nell!"

"Yeah." Mary Nell leaned down and took both Eva's hands to pull her up out of the dust. The younger girl still trembled and shivered in the hot, damp air. Mary Nell put both arms around Eva and looked again back up the path. But there was only dark-ness, rain and the voice of a summer wind.

GRACE SAW THEM COME IN COVERED in red mud.

She almost opened her mouth to say something, anything to divert attention from herself and the tension in the room, but she caught Mary Nell's pleading glance and stayed quiet. Mary Nell began surreptitiously brushing Eva's dress with her hand.

Grace turned back to the table to watch the old woman who sat there with her. She didn't have time to worry about what the little ones had been doing, not with the root woman there.

Willow smiled gently in Grace's direction, the papery-thin skin at the corners of her eyes crinkling.

"First off," she said, fingering the leather pouch that she had laid on the table, "you need somethin' to sleep. I got somethin' for that."

Grace's father scowled from a corner. Her mother walked back and forth the whole length of the small room, her hands folded in front of her, her eyes on the pouch.

"What is that?" she asked, almost angrily.

"Just some leaves for her tea, Joy. Nothin' that'll hurt," Willow said, still looking at Grace, still smiling. Grace felt loved by that smile. She let out a breath, not realizing she'd been holding it.

"This was a mistake," Joy muttered.

"'Course," Willow continued, not acknowledging the comment. "'Course, dreams many times come to tell you somethin'. Or your people—the ones that's gone on—will visit you there in the dream world."

Grace felt her body tightening as she recalled the ghost's words. *My name ain't Bessie. It's Ayo.*

"Ain't that what you said, Grace? Been talkin' to your grandma, I understand?"

"I don't know," Grace whispered. "It ain't like I see her exactly. But I hear her, feel her . . . in my head, talking . . ." She looked up briefly. Across the room Eva stared at her unsmilingly. Grace put her head back in her hands.

"Um-hmm," Willow said, finally opening the bag and raking out a handful of dried weeds onto a clean handkerchief. "Comin' to tell you somethin'. The old ones do that. I know Bessie wouldn't be hangin' around 'less she had somethin' important to say."

"We ain't gon' pay you to tell us that, old woman!" Frank burst out. "Any fool can say that . . ."

"You ain't got to pay me. I can see the young lady sufferin'."

Willow looked again at Grace, who hadn't moved. "'Sides, you ain't the one what came to see me." She nodded at Grace's bent head. "She did. But I didn't want you to think I was doin' somethin' behind your back, so I came back with her."

Frank retreated to a corner with his back half-turned.

"What Bessie look like in the dream, chile?" Willow asked. "I can tell you if it was her. She was my friend, your grandma. I know her face better than my own."

"Naw, naw," Joy said quietly but quickly, the words coming out in one big rush. "This wasn't the right thing to do. I'm sorry Grace got you here, Miz Willow. I know you got faith in this . . . root work . . . I know you do. But I'm gon' put my trust in the Lord. You can go on home, now. I don't know what I was thinkin' 'bout lettin' you come over here for nothin'. Grace just tired or somethin'. Can't sleep. Just like you said. She just gets that way sometimes. We don't need no hoodoo for that. Just some nice hot food in her. Some rest. She ain't slept in days. I'll take care of her."

Willow touched Grace's arm with one finger. "That what you want, baby? For me to go?"

Grace nodded. Willow shook her head as she rose slowly from her seat, gathering her skirt around her and picking up her walking stick from where it had slid under the table. She deliberately began putting items back in her pouch. Frank made a snorting sound and pushed past Joy to go into the other room. Willow paid him little attention, gathering up her things and closing the pouch before tying it on a string around her waist.

She was almost at the door before Grace saw that she had left the little pile of weeds there on the table. She looked up, thinking to stop her. Willow was there at the door, her hand ready to push it open. The old woman looked down at Eva and

Mary Nell and the two girls squirmed nervously. But then Joy came up quickly behind her and pushed the door open, saying, "I'm sorry for your trouble, Miz Willow."

While Joy had her back turned, Grace quickly swept the handkerchief with its pile of dried plants off the table and into her fist.

9

November 1920
࠵⌇—

MARY NELL HAD PRESERVES FOR THE little ones. Blackberry. Only two jars, because only the children and cook would eat it. The bag she carried them in knocked against the side of her right thigh as she walked with the early morning sun walking beside her. She would make it to the Wards' in time to give the children preserves on their biscuits.

"Preserves!" she could hear Mrs. Ward say with a smile. A low-down smile that said *how common, how low-class, how nigger of you to offer me blackberry preserves from your kitchen when I have mint jelly. Mint jelly made by my own cook. And why can't you, Mary Nell, just stick to what Cook has for them to eat?*

Mary Nell secretly fed preserves to the children on hot biscuits bathed in butter. Mrs. Ward never ventured into the kitchen when her two little ones were having breakfast. She never ventured into the kitchen much at all, at least not with her whole body. Her head would appear around the edge of the door from time to time to make some amendments to the detailed instructions she always left pinned to the door for Pauline, the cook, who pretty much ignored them and cooked what she wanted. Pauline didn't mind Mary Nell's preserves. Always took some home herself.

So Mary Nell would wipe the sticky juice off the children's pink faces, would sit at the kitchen table with them and listen to their adventures and tales, told in a slow, thick childish drawl.

She had hardly stepped in the back door, and Pauline had barely gotten out a "Hey," when Mrs. Ward stuck her head inside the kitchen about the same time the children jumped up from the table and hugged Mary Nell's legs. "Mary Nell, you are late. Now the children are in the kitchen howling from hunger and they wouldn't eat until you got here. You go on and give them breakfast. I have got a million things to do today, a million! I went ahead and got them dressed for you, but they have just been under my feet all morning and I really must . . ."

And before she came to the end of the sentence, she was back on the other side of the kitchen door. Mary Nell untangled herself from those little fingers and followed her out of the kitchen and into the hall, knowing better than to just stand there while the woman continued to talk. Mrs. Ward would claim she was being ignored.

Mrs. Ward swept the wood floor with the hem of her gray linen dress, then paused at the end of the hall to examine a bowl of fading fall flowers, which sat on a table underneath a large painting.

"Oh, Mary Nell, please do something with this," she said, pointing to the bowl. "Those things are just about dead."

"Yes, ma'am," Mary Nell said, but Mrs. Ward was already gone.

Mary Nell picked up the bowl. The bottom of the painting was right in her line of vision. She saw a pink dress with many, many folds and small feet in pink shoes just peeking out from under the hem. Almost against her will, even though she'd seen the portrait hundreds of times, she found herself looking up slowly. And she still shuddered when she encountered the face of the woman in the portrait. Mrs. Ward's grandmother looked out of the flat surface, sweet-faced, her rosy cheeks surrounded by black ringlets. Mary Nell looked at her smile and shivered, the petals of the flowers she held trembling.

"Mary Nell!"

Pauline gestured from the end of the long hall, halfway out of the kitchen. "Come and feed these chillun so's I can get 'em outta my kitchen!"

Mary Nell stepped backward down the hall, the glass bowl carefully cradled in her hands, the painted eyes following her all the way.

Pauline glanced back down the hall before letting the door swing closed behind them.

"Don't look at it, Mary Nell," she said. "Ole Miz Ward's picture. She the one what marked Miz Bessie. I hear she was mean as a dog her whole life."

Mary Nell put the bowl down on the counter. Grace had shown her her grandmother's description of that day, written on cheap paper in Joy's shaky hand. She didn't know if the picture was painted before or after. She tried to imagine that pink, hooped dress splattered and smeared with blood.

"Yeah, she the one," Mary Nell said quietly, looking at the two children seated at the table. Robert and Rose had opened the jar of fig preserves and were licking their sticky fingers.

Mary Nell understood that one day, sooner than anyone could imagine, those Ward children would wipe fig juice off their chins, step out of the kitchen and into the parlor, and never come back. She sighed, putting a hand to her belly, sitting down in a chair opposite them.

But by then me and Lou will have our own biddies to look after, she thought, pressing her hand against her navel. Might be a baby in there right now. About time, if that was so. Two years into the marriage and nothing yet. Most women she knew got babies right off. They came too fast. She had put off going to school, because she had decided to have children right away. She maybe could have been a nurse already, but she had put it off. She could have been working in a big town and Lou Henry could have gotten a job and they could have had a house like the Johnsons. Bigger than the Wards'.

"If it gon' be, it gon' be," Lou had said a few weeks ago as she bent over the No. 5 tin tub, scrubbing bloody rags. "Only God knows these things."

"What you know 'bout God?" Mary Nell had answered, looking down into the pink water. "Until we got together, you let yo' feet wander every place *but* in church. Now that you done had your behind in a pew a few years, you know 'bout what God want for me?"

God wanted her to have children, that's what. God wanted

everybody to have children, didn't He? That was just about all they were here for, to make new people. She thought about Abraham's wife, Sarah, in the Bible waiting and waiting and thinking herself barren. And then God gave her a child. Well, He didn't have to take so much time with her. She'd take her blessing right now. And she made sure He knew she was ready by walking her weary feet to church from Sunday to Sunday and sometimes in between Sundays. Sometimes with Lou, sometimes without.

Of course, her husband could afford to be unconcerned about such gifts from God as children. He already had at least two—two children that he pretended didn't exist. Two babies that should be hers, by any rule that was right.

The children wanted to know what Pauline meant by "the one what marked Miz Bessie."

"Who is Miss Bessie?" Robert asked when they went outside in the backyard after breakfast.

"My grandmama. She done passed on now."

"Oh, like our Great-Grandma Rose. She's in the big picture in the hall."

"Yeah, I know."

"Why did your grandma have marks?"

Mary Nell paused, putting down her mending and watching as he sat on the dying grass rolling a ball to his sister. The leaves on the trees whirled and fell, but the sun shone warm and steady, making those children's skin rosy and their hair shimmer. She had rocked them to sleep as babies. And some other black woman had rocked their mother, and some other their bullwhip-cracking great-grandmother. Whether they knew it or not, they were already sure of where she fit in their world. Well, maybe little Rose didn't have it yet, but Robert did.

"Somebody got to her with a bullwhip," Mary Nell said to him finally, resuming her sewing.

Robert stopped rolling the ball and stared at her.

"You mean somebody hit her with a whip?" he asked, his eyes round. "Like a horse?" His sister looked confused sitting there, waiting for the ball to return.

"She was a slave."

"But why did they hit her?"

"Because she wouldn't do what they told her to."

"Why?"

"Robert . . ." She sighed, wondering how far to go with it. He told everything. He didn't know there may be things that shouldn't be told. He didn't know that hearing the truth might make his mama and daddy mad. Or maybe he did and didn't care.

"See, my grandmama Bessie was new to this place. She was a young'un really and she didn't know how to speak like we do. You know how your mama talk in that there France sometimes. That's what it was like. Bessie had her own way of talkin' language, but the massas didn't understand her and she didn't understand them. So when one of them ask her to do something, she didn't know what they was sayin'. And one day they beat her with the whip."

Mary Nell didn't tell him that it was his great-grandma who had done the whipping. About how she'd splattered her pink dress with blood. She thought maybe she had said too much already and pursed her lips closed, hoping for no more questions.

Robert was quiet for a moment. He rolled the ball back over

the grass to his sister, and Mary Nell bent back over her sewing. She wondered what kind of scolding she would get from Mrs. Ward for telling Robert about that.

"Sometimes," Robert said, soft as a butterfly's whisper, "you've got to tell people what to do."

"What did you say? What you sayin' Robert?" she asked.

"Because they don't know where they're supposed to be or what they're supposed to be doing. They mess everything up. That's what Daddy says all the time." He gestured to his sister to roll the ball back, making big circles with his arm. He smiled at her when she did. "'Specially niggers. Need to be told what to do." Robert looked at the little girl, smiling, his voice calm. "That's what he says all the time."

Mary Nell tightened her jaw, but kept her voice as even as possible. "Is that what he say?"

"See," Robert answered, "she should have done what she was told and then that never would have happened."

"She didn't understand . . ." Mary Nell found herself saying, then stopped. Lord, she didn't want to get in an argument with the Wards' child about this. She didn't even want to imprint the conversation in his head.

"Oh, she probably thought she was fooling everybody," he said. "Pretending like she didn't understand. Lying to get out of working. Daddy says some folks are just lazy."

Mary Nell stopped pretending to sew, dropping her hands into her lap and wrapping her shawl more tightly around her body. She looked into his large brown eyes, at the little person sitting there who had come to her countless times, with his feelings hurt or his body bruised by some escapade, who had come to her thirsty or hungry or lonely or neglected, who had picked her flowers and brought her candy on her birthday. His lips curled so innocently upward in a smile that said everything she had ever known or heard in her life about white people. Even knowing where he got it from, it was still a revelation to see how quickly he learned it. It was still a pain that stabbed without ceasing.

Mary Nell again touched her belly, rubbing the palm of her hand over her stomach, hoping and hoping and hoping. Maybe this month. Maybe soon.

10

It's hard to know what the truth means, what real means when you look at somebody like Grace or like Mary Nell and me, Eva thought. She sat on the back steps of Mary Nell's house with a haze in front of her eyes. Lou Henry sang to the hogs and a familiar unease churned around in her belly. The pigs grunted as Lou approached. They ran and slid in the slippery muck under their toes. Lou raised his voice up over the noise, laughing intermittently as he watched them scrambling to the trough.

Eva's stomach flipped over and over, but she didn't move. She didn't react to it at all anymore. She sat with her arms propped on her knees, contemplating her feet. Lou's voice rose on a particular high note and a pain stabbed her abdomen, but she didn't bother to gasp. She just closed her eyes.

She and Mary Nell had talked a few days ago.

"It got something to do with Lou," Mary Nell had said, her face twisted in a knot. "Something bad. He ain't been nothing but good, Eva, I swear. Nothing but good to me since we got married."

"He is pain," Eva said, looking straight into Mary Nell's eyes.

"I know."

But the talk just went on like that with nothing to come of it. They were still no closer to understanding what they felt, except to know what real fear was. All these years of seeing and half-knowing misfortune in the making and they were still helpless in the face of their own.

"It's gon' be bad," Eva had said. "Maybe you should say somethin' to him."

"No," Mary Nell said. "Then he just gon' be scared. I know him."

He had been good, Mary Nell said. She would have heard in a little place like this if he were stepping to the side.

They hadn't seen visions in a long time. Maybe a year now. Just these ripples of fear, knots in their stomachs. It was much worse when they were together, which wasn't so much these days.

The back door was closed, but Eva could almost feel Mary Nell in the house behind her, sitting at the table with the mixing bowl in front of her, not moving like Eva was not moving. Eva had come out on the back porch for butter from the ice box, had handed it in to Mary Nell but stayed outside, needing to think, considering going home, despite her desire to eat some of the cake Mary Nell was making.

Lou Henry stopped singing. She no longer saw him from the back steps. The hogs sucked delightedly, their snouts in the troughs, huddled side to side for warmth. They would be dead soon, two of them at least. Eva wrapped her arms around herself, fighting a losing battle with the creeping chill in the air. It was cold enough so meat wouldn't spoil. Winter had finally opened the door. She got up and went inside.

Mary Nell sat still at the table. Eva went and stood next to the stove, trying to knock the chill off.

Mary Nell didn't look at her as she said, "I need eggs. Two. I didn't get enough for the cake." Mary Nell began beating butter and sugar together. Eva didn't move. Lou Henry was in the barn, maybe, where the chickens insisted on nesting despite attempts to build a chicken coop and yard that would contain them.

They snubbed the neat nesting houses and carefully nailed fence, flying awkwardly to the top of the posts and then down, toddling into the barn to assert squatters' rights in the hay. Occasionally, they toddled out and into the jaws of something—fox, feral dogs. They would go out for a morning strut, for a bit of warmth and light at the beginning of the day and die right there, in the midst of their joy.

Eva didn't move from the stove until Mary Nell said, "Two eggs. You get them for me, sister?"

Well, Eva thought. I could just go to the back door and yell at Lou Henry to bring them. She looked down at Mary Nell, but her head was bent over the bowl. Something was wrong, it was right there in the tilt of her sister's head.

Eva avoided Lou these days, because when she thought of him, she thought about going down the Indian road in a dream. She thought about seeing him in the dream running as if his life depended on it. She thought about she and Mary Nell, falling and struggling to get up and over their fear.

Sometimes now, she went alone to that place on the road, to

feel it again. She would take that route on the way to school. Or she would just go. If she went enough, maybe it would stop scaring her. The feeling she had there, standing under the trees, was always familiar, but still a little different every time. Often she felt nothing but the air moving the leaves, and she found her mind wandering so that she looked up and forgot why she was there. But sometimes, fear rushed at her as she looked down that road. Sometimes it whispered to her. And on days like today, those whispers followed her. Even to Mary Nell's house.

"Just two. Real quick. I need to finish this and get on with Lou's supper." Mary Nell glanced up with a smile that wasn't quite one, and Eva shuffled away from the stove. She grabbed Mary Nell's shawl from the back of a chair and pulled it on over her head and around her shoulders, winding herself in Mary Nell's scent.

"It's gettin' on to winter out there," Eva said, going to the door.

"Uh-huh."

The sun was no match for the wind and Eva tucked her hands under the hem of the shawl as she went again out on the porch, hugging herself hard. She didn't hear Lou at all now.

The chickens were gathered in a tight knot near the entrance to the barn, pecking furiously at dry corn. He had been there. Maybe just left there, since the chickens still had quite a meal spread before them.

The eggs had already been gathered once that day; there was only one and Eva only found it after she'd climbed up in the loft of the barn. She slipped it into the pocket of her blue-checked apron.

Her heel kept getting caught in the hem of her slip on the

way down the ladder, so that she had to keep stopping on a rung and free her foot. She was doing this, perched about halfway down, when she heard him come in.

It was hard to sneak through the hay; it crunched and moved underfoot. Even so, she could tell he was trying to be quiet.

"I just came out to get Mary Nell some eggs," she said, so he'd know she'd heard him, and again started down the ladder.

He didn't answer. Eva looked back and he was at the foot of the ladder, holding onto the sides, waiting, smiling. She stopped, and fear hissed inside her ear and balled her insides into a knot.

"Move on out the way now, Lou, I don't wanna step on your head," she tried to make her voice light.

"I wouldn't mind it," he answered, but he moved off to the side.

"Whew!" she said as her feet touched the ground. "Y'all didn't have but one more. I hope she still gon' make the cake." She let out a sigh as she reached the bottom safely, but Lou quickly stepped forward again, putting both hands on the sides of the ladder, making a cage of his arms.

"You right to be careful up there," he said, still smiling. Eva searched for malice or anger in that smile. She searched for evil behind his bright teeth. But it was just Lou Henry, smiling the same way he always did. "You ain't as light as you used to be. Not as little, either."

"I know," she said, nervously looking down to see if she could duck under his arms.

"Them boys gon' be after you soon. Already after you, I reckon." He leaned his head forward a little, breathing out moist air that lightly licked the skin of her neck.

"You watch out for them boys," he said, his breath lingering against her collarbone. "I been where they are. When they are. Think they grown now."

She looked long into his face, the familiar smile, the large, strangely colored eyes and honey skin. She didn't know what trick God was playing.

Eva let her knees buckle a little, then she squatted down and ducked under his arms.

He laughed. "Don't let me tease you now. Let Eddie and Son fight over you. You gon' be fought over, you know."

Eva kept him in front of her, walking backward out of the barn, through the dust outside and the chickens' corn and the chickens' shit. She tried to keep the fear from settling on her features, but she knew she couldn't.

"Oh, come on now," Lou Henry said, his smile going. "I'm just saying—" He stopped, looking at her, and shrugged. Coming out of the barn, he took a shovel that leaned against the side of the barn and moved quickly past her. "You so serious, gal."

Inside, Eva put the egg on the table. Mary Nell was on her hands and knees, cleaning butter and sugar off the floor. The white mixing bowl was upside down near her chair.

"I'm clumsy these days," she murmured stiffly. "Must have been stirring too hard."

"Just now?" Eva asked quietly.

Mary Nell grabbed the bowl and straightened up from the floor. "Don't know how that happened," she said.

Eva tried to get a good look at Mary Nell's face, although she didn't really need to look to know that fear had been here, inside the house, too.

"I'm going," Eva said, going over and putting her arms around Mary Nell.

"You should come back for some cake," Mary Nell said, patting Eva awkwardly on the back. She cursed softly in Eva's arms, her breath brushing the place on her neck where Lou's breath had touched her.

"No, I can't," Eva said. Then she untangled herself.

"Well, keep the shawl then," said Mary Nell, turning away and back to her bowl. "It's gettin' cold."

December

EVA WONDERED ABOUT RICH FOLKS' PARTIES. She supposed that they had a whole bunch of music, lots of musicians, and they played so loudly that they could be heard all the way into the next county. And the floors were so polished that the dancers' feet hardly made a sound. They whispered across glowing wood and there was just music and movement and whatever sound carefree people made when they danced.

Here, though, there was just music and movement and the sound that came out of work-weary people celebrating a moment's relief.

She tried to imagine that the church floor's squeaks blended with the music. But the music made by Eddie Adam, Lucius and

Clay wasn't loud enough to drown out the groaning floorboards.

Lucius didn't seem to mind Clay's bad playing on the string bass and Eddie Adam's amateur pluckings on the guitar. After awhile, Eddie Adam and Clay put down their instruments and left Lucius alone with his music, with just the dancers' clapping to accompany him.

The dancers circled the floor again and again, always at a good distance from each other, always acutely aware of the eyes of the church mothers, who sat and chattered in the corner, their mouths open and their eyes all-seeing. Since the reverend had finally consented to having such a function at the church, they were certainly going to keep everything decent.

Eva danced with Son Jackson. He held her at arm's length, his head bent, his eyes on his feet most of the time. Even though she was happy when he had come up and asked her, she was acutely uncomfortable now with his hand on her waist.

He mumbled something and she leaned forward.

"What you say?"

"I said you dance real good," Son answered. He looked up at her briefly and then down at the floor again.

"Thank you," Eva said, as she realized she'd never had a conversation with Son that didn't involve baseball, fishing or gossip.

Lucius played on and on, making that fiddle into a heavenly choir all by himself, but he was an old man and had to take a break sometime. As soon as the music stopped, Eva found that Eddie Adam was standing at her elbow.

"I gotta tell you something, Eva," he said urgently.

"What?" Son asked.

"This ain't none of your business, Son Jackson. I said 'I gotta tell you something, Eva.' I didn't hear your name no where up in there."

Eva paid no attention to either of them. Someone was waving at her; she could see the gesture out of the corner of her eye. Turning she saw that Lou Henry was motioning her over to where he and Mary Nell stood. As she looked, Eva saw Mary Nell turning to follow her husband's gaze. She looked startled, then frightened, and then Eva didn't know what to call that look because she'd never seen it before. It was a hard stare, as if Mary Nell was trying to look right through and into her, which was funny, Eva thought, because they'd never had much trouble figuring out what the other was thinking. But even as they stood there looking at each other, something was changing. Eva took a step back, away from the force of her sister's unwavering attention.

"Eva!" Eddie Adam almost hissed in her ear.

"What is it?" she asked faintly.

"Grandmama got something for you."

"Oh, Lord," Son Jackson said, rolling his eyes and throwing his hands up toward the ceiling.

Eddie Adam glared at him, but pressed on. "She say you need something she got and I'm to bring you out to the house after church tomorrow."

"Miz Willow? What she got?"

"Now you know how secret she is about her workin's. I ask her and she say to me, 'Ain't nothing for no man-child to be lookin' at.' Then she told me again that I should make you come tomorrow. All right?"

"All right," Eva said, forgetting that she wasn't supposed to be associating with Willow. That had been a standing commandment from her mother ever since she was little. But right now, looking across at Mary Nell and Lou Henry, she couldn't be blamed for not remembering. For several long minutes the three of them locked eyes, then Lucius' fiddle began again and Lou Henry took Mary Nell onto the dance floor.

"I gotta go play," Eddie Adam said. "Tomorrow, right?"

"Tomorrow," she answered, as Lou and Mary Nell whirled in front of them and Mary Nell's skirt sent a breeze that lifted the hem of her own.

"Good. All right." Eddie Adam smiled, and went weaving back between the dancers.

Son Jackson snorted and drew Eva again into the dance.

12

WILLOW SAT ON HER OVERTURNED WASHTUB, her long legs drawn up so that her knees almost touched her forehead. She considered the opened-out feed sack on the ground in front of her. On top of that, was a clean cotton cloth and on top of that, an assortment of objects. Leaves, sticks, bones. The fingers of her right hand, smooth and straight, were closed in a fist, holding something in.

Eddie Adam approached quietly, as always trying to catch a glimpse of what she was doing.

"Tain't for you to know 'bout," said Willow, not looking at him, but noting the sound of his Sunday boots scraping gently on the hard-packed earth of the yard. "This is work for womens, not men-boys like you."

She looked up at him then and smiled, just to let him know his curiosity didn't anger her. "Where she at?"

He gave a small shrug. "She says she had to go on home first, then sneak away. She had to go home from church with her folks."

Willow nodded, opening her fist and pouring a thin stream of dust over the linen cloth and the objects assembled on top of it. Eddie Adam peered at her, watching as she gathered the corners of the cloth together and tied the bundle with a bit of rawhide.

"Um, ain't you getting cold out here, Gran?" he said, his eyes on the bundle.

"No, chile. But if you is so worried, you can bring me a quilt. And then I want you to feed them dogs. They done started up making a fuss."

"Yes'm." The boy reluctantly made his way to the back porch and into the little leaning house.

"And just where is your brother?" Willow called as he got to the door. "He ought be helpin' you. He know better than that."

"I think he went to play baseball."

"In the cold?" She shook her head.

"Yes, ma'am." He disappeared inside, banging the well-worn door behind him.

Willow waited calmly, the little bag cradled in the folds of her dress, between her knees. Eddie Adam came clattering out of the back door again, a quilt thrown over his thin arms. He spread it out and approached her with his arms outspread, slipping behind Willow to drape the heavy cloth over her shoulders. Willow said nothing, and Eddie Adam, seeing the faraway look in her eye, didn't attempt conversation. He scampered back to the porch for the dogs' feed bucket.

She watched the woods that enclosed the house from all sides like a womb and soon she could make out Eva's dark dress moving among the trees. The girl stopped, but her skirts continued to dance around a bit in the wind. She stood with her brown arms wrapped around a gray-bark pine, looking around toward the front, then the back of the house. She took a step forward, away from the trees, but then stopped again, her hands clasped in front of her, looking back, as if thinking to turn around before she was seen.

Willow stuck an arm from under the quilt and started gesturing slowly, waving Eva over.

She didn't present the bag until the girl was standing in front of her.

Eva looked at the bit of cloth dangling from Willow's fingers and kept her eyes locked on the bag as she said, "You wanted to talk to me 'bout somethin', Miz Willow?"

"You know," Willow said.

"No ma'am."

Willow sighed, dropping the bag back into the folds of her dress. "Come here," she said, standing up to drag another bucket over and turning it upside-down in front of her. Out of the corner of her eye she saw Eddie Adam's head sticking out around a corner of the house. She only had to turn her head slightly, and he vanished. She patted the bottom of the bucket. "Here." Willow sat down again.

Eva sat down slowly, gathering up her skirts in both hands and crouching so that she was looking right down Willow's throat. She hid her hands in the folds of her dress, but not before Willow saw that her fingers trembled.

"Nothin' to be 'fraid of here," Willow said softly, smiling a little. "But there is fear in your life. Has been for some time."

Eva's eyes widened.

"Oh, chile, don't be scairt of me. I ain't got the sight. That's your gift, if you would just use it. But I see things. I see by lookin' at folk and how they are with each other. That's almost just as good as any special power or sight. I listen to the way they talk to each other and the way they touch and what they say. Who they try to get next to and who they try to get away from. I just keep quiet and look."

"Everybody say . . . you . . ." The girl didn't quite know how to put the question together.

"Everybody say I'm a witch, ain't that right?" Willow smiled wider, and Eva nodded.

"Well," Willow said, "it don't take no witch to know things. I had folk in my life, God bless 'em, just taught me some things. Yo' grandmamas—on both sides. Taught me some things about helpin' take away people's pain. The pains in the body and the pains in the heart. What plants did what. What things to use together and that sort of thing. It's just plain old learnin', like what you do in school. No magic involved. But people thinkin' I'm a witch, well, that's fine. Keeps folk from messin' with me."

"Some folk say you can come and go without nobody seeing you!" Eva blurted out.

Willow laughed.

"I just walk soft, that's all. I was taught how," she said. "Bessie, she showed me. In Afraca, she say, the women glide, like angels, no matter how heavy the load they might be carryin'."

Eva looked skeptical. "My grandmama tole you that?"

"I could teach you." Willow raised her eyebrows, casually smiling, gently hopeful. "See, I ain't got no daughter. My son, he gone. Kilt." She bent her head. "All I got 'round here is them old rusty grandsons of mine. I love 'em, but I sho was hopin' to pass on some things to a girl chile. That's why I was wantin' you and your sister to learn from me. Y'all already got more gifts than I'll ever have in this life, and with me teachin' you what I know, I could pass on happy. But yo' mama and papa wouldn't have none of it." Willow sighed.

"They say it be wrong," Eva frowned. "Root work ain't real medicine. Just a way to fool folk; get somethin' outta them. Money."

"Lot of folks wanna say it's wrong, but when they days get dark, and they hearts hurt, or they babies come too soon, they don't go runnin' for no white man doctor. They come to me first. Black folk and white folk, too. They all come, sooner or later. I done held all the babies of Johnson Creek right here in my hands." Willow reached for Eva's hand, closing her own fingers around the girl's little fist. Then she pried open the girl's fingers so she could drop the little bag in it.

"He got the devil in him, that man," she said, looking into Eva's eyes. "I seen it. He fightin' it, but the devil is there."

"What man?"

"Don't play. This here I'm givin' you is for protection."

"Protection?"

Willow frowned, searching the girl's face. Eva dropped her eyes.

"Powerful hurt is comin' to you if you don't pay attention," Willow said. "I coulda helped y'all girls use what ya got. I coulda helped you, I really could. Still can. You just say the word. 'Cause now God and the spirits tryin' to get your attention and you ain't got enough schoolin' on how to listen right." Willow looked hard at Eva, leaning so close that she almost slipped off her tin throne.

Eva leaned away from her and then dropped the bag at Willow's feet.

"Miz Willow," Eva said. "Beg yo' pardon, but I don't know what you talkin' 'bout and I got to get back home and help Mama with dinner. She gon' be mad at me fo' being 'way so long. Thank you for invitin' me." She stood up abruptly, smoothed her skirt and showed the old woman her back.

"Girl!" Willow called out, and Eva turned. "I seen it befo' you know. The sight. Ayo had it. Yo' grandma, the one they called Bessie. She could see back and forth and sideways. That power must come straight from over there. From Afraca. And it came with her, right there on that renegade ship they brung her on." Willow held out the bag once more, her face like stone now. "Ayo would have known what to do. Since she ain't here to help you, I am."

Eva just shook her head and hurried away, letting the trees swallow her.

13

ONCE OUT OF SIGHT of Willow's house, Eva's hurried walk turned into a trot and then a run. She didn't want to think about what was in that bag. Dead animal parts or grave dust or some other unspeakable thing.

Eva could still see Willow holding out the little bag, hanging heavy from the weight of something small and round. It had swung gently back and forth from the cord. It looked to Eva like it was swinging by itself, but that couldn't be true.

Eva slowed her run to a walk and then stopped altogether, bending over to put her hands on her knees and catch her breath.

She had almost taken the bag. Maybe she should have, just to see if it would work. She straightened and half-turned in the direction of Willow's house. She could see the old woman's white dress through the veil of pine trees, moving, floating toward her.

Eva put out a hand and felt rough pine bark underneath her hand. Willow's white dress danced among the trees like a lazy ghost out for a stroll, a spirit drinking in memories of life. That spirit trembled closer, Eva thought, leaning her whole body against the tree now. Surely she was closer. Surely Willow wasn't going into the house at all, but coming to Eva, who felt worn down trying to decide whether to stay or go. She had to do the right thing for herself and Mary Nell, and maybe even Lou Henry, as well. If she took the bag, that meant that she believed she needed protection from something, that maybe the gift she shared with her sister was a true one.

In all the times they had had their visions, she only half-believed that they came true. Even when she saw the evidence in other people's lives, it was hard to keep down, this idea that they were so different from anybody else. She wasn't sure she wanted to believe that it was more than a children's game that she and Mary Nell had somehow invented. That would mean that Mary Nell, who had been fearfully serious about it from the get-go, was right.

She felt herself shedding her childhood, right then and there in that grove of pine, knowing that she should just walk back home. But she stood still and Willow's spirit dress approached the little patch of ground where she was planted. The fear-filled dreams and the walks along the edge of chaos were things that could consume her. She saw Mary Nell on the road to destruction and because it was Mary Nell, surely Eva would have to go with her. It would push them down into the dust. Already, they were breathless with the weight of this thing they could not name.

A whisper, a flicker again of white. For the first time in her life, Eva was afraid of herself. She was afraid of all the things she knew, but could not uncover the meaning of.

"It ain't gon' hurt to take it," Willow said, from just beyond Eva's left shoulder. Something brushed against Eva's apron and her pocket grew heavy.

"No need for you to look at it right now. There ain't a thing in there that can hurt you. Oh, Bessie would haunt me for the rest of my days if I hurt you. I always try to honor her as best I can by tryin' to help anybody that need it. And you girls most of all."

Willow's usually strong voice grew raggedy and Eva sneaked a look at her, startled to find her standing rather close, leaning against the same tree with her head down and the white dress gathered all around her. Just a dress.

Eva knew she should move. "I should go," she thought.

But it was Willow who left her standing there under the trees, walking slowly and unsteadily back, muttering to herself. Eva shouldn't have let Willow slip that thing in her pocket. This wasn't a game anymore, where they had their little visions and then tried to figure out what they meant, watched for the signs and the events that would confirm their childish predictions.

Eva put her hand in her pocket and brushed her fingers against the rough cloth of the little bag.

She didn't take it out until she was standing in the front yard, watching Mary Nell come out of the house and down the steps. Mary Nell was pulling a shawl around her shoulders.

"It's a bit cool to be out. Where you been?" she asked, already looking past Eva, preoccupied with something else.

"Miz Willow's," Eva said softly.

Mary Nell was immediately alert. She clutched the shawl closer and took a step or two toward Eva. "What for?" she asked.

"She asked me to come by," Eva said. She imagined that she could feel Mary Nell trying to read her mind. There were some days when she could almost do it, but this wasn't one of those days. "What you doin' here?"

"This my mama's house, ain't it?" Mary Nell said in mock annoyance. Eva shuddered at the tone of her voice, different from what she was used to. "I came to get some thread." She stared at Eva. "What's wrong with you? Don't tell me Miz Willow put somethin' on you."

Eva's fingers groped inside her apron pocket.

"You got some kind of mood written all over your face and you know I can read you better than anybody," Mary Nell said. She planted herself squarely in front of Eva.

"I'm fine, sister." Eva pulled the little square bag out of her pocket. Mary Nell seemed not to notice, but then said, "Naw, you ain't. And that there in your hand ain't gon' make it fine."

"It ain't mine," Eva said. She pried Mary Nell's fingers away from the shawl and pressed the bag into her hand.

Mary Nell glared at her. Eva closed Mary Nell's fingers around the bag and pulled her hand away, stomping up the back porch steps just as Grace was coming out.

"You ain't stayin' for dinner, Mary Nell?" Grace asked.

"I reckon not, I done already started on it at home." She had her back to the porch and Eva couldn't see what she was doing with the charm bag.

"All right then." Grace turned to go back inside the house, but stopped, putting one palm against one of the posts that supported the porch roof. "Oh," she said very softly. And then she moved slowly down, her hand sliding along the post, her legs buckling until she was on her knees there at the top step.

"Grace?" Eva bent over her, her head jerking back when she encountered Grace's blank expression.

"Mama!" she yelled, as Mary Nell came bounding back up the steps, just in time to keep the falling-over Grace from hitting her head on the porch boards.

"Mama! Papa, come!"

Mary Nell took off her apron and put it under Grace's head. Grace lay on her side with her legs folded, her eyes unblinking.

"I can't believe you let that Willow give you somethin'!" Mary Nell glared at Eva. "How you know she ain't put somethin' on us?" She waved her hand at Grace.

"Where is it?" Eva whispered.

Mary Nell looked down at her hand, which was empty now. "I dropped that thing." She looked all around. Eva saw the little bag lying on the steps, where Mary Nell must have dropped it as she reached for Grace. Eva moved to pick it up.

"Give me that!" Mary Nell said, snatching it from Eva and slipping it down the front of her dress. "I'll get rid of it."

Joy came to the open door and looked out, her slightly annoyed expression slipping into dread.

"Lord, have mercy," she said, drying her hands on the towel she was carrying. "Lord!" She knelt beside Grace, drawing a hand over her cheeks and forehead, and then turning it over to stare at her daughter's sweat on her palm. She shivered there in the light of the cool fall afternoon. Frank appeared in the doorway.

"Get some water, Frank," Joy said. He took one brief look at Grace curled up on the porch and disappeared inside.

"What happened?" Joy said, tapping Grace gently on the cheek and then giving her a little slap when she failed to respond.

"She was just turning 'round to go back in the house," Eva said, "and she started fallin'. She just stop right where she was and drop down to her knees just like that."

"Grace? Chile? Lord . . ." Joy bent over the girl.

"Here," Frank said, as he came back out onto the porch with a full bucket. "Another spell?" Joy nodded.

"She gon' be fine," Joy said. Eva stared at her mother, wondering what she was thinking and Joy glanced up at her, frowning a little before dropping her eyes again. "She just must be a little tuckered, that's all."

"She ain't never fainted befo'," Frank said. "We need to get her in the house."

He bent down to pick her up, taking one look into her staring eyes and recoiling slightly. But he gathered up her long legs and went into the house with her.

She didn't move even after she was safely tucked into the big iron bed under the covers. She stared at the ceiling without blinking. Eva sat down next to her, picking up her hand.

"Fallin' out like that. I ain't never seen Grace that way before." Frank eyed her prone form. "You don't think she—"

"Hush up, Frank!" Joy said, pushing him toward the bedroom door with her fist in the middle of his back. "Bring me that water in here and a clean rag for her head. Go on, now."

Eva saw Grace's lips moving slowly and motioned to Mary Nell while Joy's back was still turned.

"What she say?" Mary Nell asked softly, coming to sit on the bed with her. Eva shook her head in confusion, leaning closer.

"Tain't no use. I'm lost now, truly lost . . ." Grace murmured, blinking once. "The gods done give up on me. Left me here to die. Surely, surely, to die . . ."

Eva felt Mary Nell looking at her, and she glanced up to see an angry kind of fear in her eyes. She took Eva's and Grace's hands, so that they made a circle, the three of them. Eva felt the tenseness in Grace's body increasing and she finally closed her eyes, crying out and starting to whimper. Joy whirled around, coming to kneel by the bed.

"Don't leave me here!" Grace wailed now, her grip tightening so that the tips of Eva's fingers turned pale, all the blood leaving her hand.

"Baby?" Joy put a hand to her head. "We ain't gon' leave you! What you mean? I ain't gon' never leave my baby . . ."

"She gon' leave you," Mary Nell said softly, looking at Eva.

"Don't you start that mess. She ain't goin' nowhere. She's gon' be right here for us to take care of." Joy was almost singing this now in a soft croon, and indeed, a few moments later she was letting a hymn loose from her lips as she stroked Grace's head. Grace sobbed quietly now, her body jerking. She never lost her grip on her sisters' hands.

Their father came in with a clean rag and a white enamel pan filled with water. He held it steady, his eyes sad, as Joy wrung out the rag and stroked Grace's sweaty cheeks. The room was silent except for her soft crying and they all seemed to exist outside of time in that place as Grace fought some unseen enemy that dared to launch an attack from inside her own heart. But after a long while, Grace's grip finally loosened and her hands fell away from theirs and the sobbing subsided to a little hiccup and then to silence and she slept.

Eva went to sleep that night with Grace's head heavy on her shoulder. She had not stirred the whole afternoon. Mary Nell had kissed her cheek and gone home. Eva had eaten a soundless supper with her parents, ever alert to any noise that might come from the other room. But Grace had merely slept and now she breathed quietly and normally there next to Eva, who dreamed of trains.

She had never seen a train for real. Just pictures. Her papa had described what they sounded like, the loud steamy huffing of the engine and the metal scraping on metal, clanking as the engine picked up speed and left the station, dragging cars and coal and animals and people behind. So good had been his imitation of those sounds, that she recognized them now, even through the haze of a dream, which she was sure she was having. And like so many times, Mary Nell was there, the two of them standing on a wooden porch or platform, straining their necks to see inside the car windows.

She gon' be further back, Mary Nell said, grabbing Eva's hand and stomping down the platform. Eva knew it was Grace they were looking for and she thought she saw her waving from the back of the train. She picked up the pace, but when she got to the back, the very back, there was no one there.

There she is! Mary Nell said, pointing back up the platform, and Eva saw her, wearing her Sunday dress, her shoes shiny and black, sitting on a large trunk with a child on her lap.

Who's that? Who's that with her? Eva asked. Mary Nell shrugged and led Eva back the way they had come, trying to get close enough to Grace to speak. It seemed to take a long time to get across the platform and as they came closer they noticed that the child, a girl, was rather big. Grace had both arms wrapped around her, holding her securely on her lap, and the girl's bare feet were flat on the wood floor of the platform, her legs stretching out and over Grace's skirts. She wore an odd-looking dress. It looked just like a big piece of cloth wrapped around her body several times.

What she got on? Mary Nell asked. *A windin' cloth?*

Eva shrugged, taking in the deep blue color of the girl's dress and noticing also the same color cloth wound several times around her head, so that no hair showed. Didn't look like no shroud, not that she'd ever seen one. Grace held the girl but kept her head turned away from her. The child sat perfectly still, a sad expression on her dark, dark face.

She sho is black, ain't she? Mary Nell commented, tugging on Eva's hand. *Come on, the train gon' leave. We got to say bye.*

But even as she said it, Eva saw Grace push the girl off her lap and stand. She strode toward the train, which stood huffing and puffing there beside the platform, and the girl followed, walking slowly, gliding really, but keeping up with Grace, who never even looked back to see if she was still there. The trunk they had been sitting on was gone. And just that quickly, the two of them were, too.

Mary Nell and Eva broke into a run, but the train was leaving and they could see Grace's face in a window and the face of the strange girl beside her. They still ran, though. Long after the train was gone they ran and the sounds of the station faded away and there they were, in the Johnson Creek woods.

The trees and plants cried out as they passed on the path where all their fears traveled.

14

June 1921

EVERYTHING BEGAN AND ENDED WITH DREAMS.

Mary Nell woke up and Lou was gone, probably feeding the animals. Good thing he was gone so she wouldn't have to explain this time why she was lying here in a sweat.

She had been having this dream for years, she and Eva. She knew Eva was waking up to it, too. The last time she'd had it had been back at the end of last year. That day, she recalled now, Grace had collapsed on Mama's front porch. Eva had given her Willow's hoodoo bag. She'd had the dream that night after all of those things had happened.

You didn't have to be asleep to be walking inside a nightmare. It was just another place to go, another world you had to live in. One foot in this one and one foot in that one, like strad-dling a barbed-wire fence that you couldn't quite make it over.

That first time, she and Eva had slept so deeply in their beds and that haze of fear had found them, so young and so unpre-pared to fight it. That had been a Sunday in June, a Second Sun-day like this one.

She threw back the bed covers, remembering that she had food to pack and her best dress to put on. She only had one best dress anyway, but extra care was to be taken today. Nearly every-body came to Second Sunday. Even the white folk showed up every once in awhile. She had to make sure Lou was looking halfway presentable. But mostly it was the food. She had time to make the icing for the cake, if she got hopping.

So she began the day with a vague feeling of unease. But she had gotten used to living with that feeling for most all her life now. An air of expectation. Feeling like something momentous, something life-changing, was going to happen at any time. Wait-ing years, for that moment, and still being unprepared when it came.

15

EVA HAD WALKED DOWN THERE a hundred times. She'd walked down there and stopped at the fearful place, letting it hit her in the chest before absorbing it and going on.

Today she tried to hurry past, not just because she was late, but because somewhere behind her something was pressing in, coming too close, breathing too strongly on the back of her neck. It was different; it made the air heavy and hard to move through.

It was because of the dream, because she had woken gasping for air, so that Grace, who was already up as usual, had given her a half-questioning frown. In the dream, she and Mary Nell were falling, hitting the mud and gravel path hard and fast, getting all tangled up together and feeling that weighty terror landing on top of them. And she opened her eyes, wide awake and trying to breathe.

It'd been hard to put it aside, harder than usual. Something pressed on her chest, compressing her lungs so that no air could get in. All through the morning she had moved slowly.

Now, trying to get to church, where Grace and Mama and Papa had already gone ahead, it was worse. The very air seemed to be holding her back. Swimming through molasses, that's what it was like. The beautiful white dress that her mother had made, that only a week ago had swirled like magic around her body as she turned and laughed, now tangled and bunched up between her legs, making her seemingly leaden steps even slower than she would have liked.

Especially when she began to run.

Eva started trotting first, right after she crossed the plank bridge. Her feet hit the board and the echoing sound of it made her jump and without knowing why she began to run.

In the back of her mind she chastised herself, because by running she might get dust on her dress if she wasn't careful. By running, she would ruin her hair; sweat would water those naps back to life. And now her breath came so hard, it was scraping the back of her throat raw.

But she couldn't stop. Even as her shoes crunched sand and gravel, she thought she heard another pair of feet on the path behind her. When she turned to look there was nothing but trees and sun and the muddy ground slashing through the woods.

Although she pumped her legs as hard as she could, she seemed to move slower instead of faster, and toward, rather than away from, the danger.

It was both behind and in front of her, as she rushed through the first and last cool air of the day, her dress beating against her legs. Behind her there was only the path and the trees waving their arms slowly, but something crowded from the sides and closed her in a box that she could not get out of.

Again, she looked back and saw no one. Then she looked ahead and there he was. Lou Henry stood on the path, smiling, his jaw tight as if he was trying not to grit his teeth.

"Eva, ya late for church, ain't ya?" he asked, as she stopped running so abruptly that she almost stumbled into a small tree beside the road.

His breath came just as hard as her own. Eva felt the thickness of the air just in front of her, emanating from where he stood.

"Yeah, I'm late, and you late, too," she said in a whisper. "Got to get on."

"Well, now." Lou took three steps closer. Eva found herself counting them, even as she took three steps back. "They prob'ly just now gettin' to the first one or two songs. You ain't got to hurry so. You plumb outta wind, girl. You don't wanna get to church sweatin' like that, do ya?"

"I best be gettin' on," Eva said firmly, closing her shaking fingers into fists.

"I'll walk with ya," said Lou, finally moving to the side.

The squeezing sensation had not gone; Eva felt it only getting worse as she walked slowly to where he was standing and he fell in step beside her. She still couldn't breathe right, it seemed. After a few steps, she stopped to put a hand to her chest.

"You all right?" Lou stopped, too, and took her arm, then slid a hand to her waist. Eva jerked away.

"Now, ain't no need to be like that, girl. I just thought you might be 'bout to fall out or somethin'."

He came up next to her again and slid his arm around her

small waist. "We's friends, right? I wouldn't want nothin' to happen to you."

Eva stood there gasping, trying to find the courage to look into his eyes and when she finally did, recoiling at the heat she saw there. It came from his body and was engulfing hers. So that's what it was. That's what the dreams had tried to tell her all this time. She had only thought of Mary Nell. She hadn't realized her own danger. She cursed herself for not listening to Willow. She had given Mary Nell the bag. For protection.

"No," she whispered, even as he slid his other arm around her.

"Oh, come on, now," he grinned, that smile she used to think was such a light. Now it burned her, inside and out. "Yes, we is. Friends.

"Come on. You gettin' grown. Gon' have lots of men friends 'sides me."

Lou dropped his eyes to her chest, which was moving up and down with her labored breathing. She felt naked. She folded one arm over her small breasts.

"Get away from me, Lou Henry Evans, I gots to get to church!" Eva tore her body away from his, but going only half a step before he was there behind her, wrapping his whole self around her and lifting her straight off the ground with one motion.

She screamed and he threw one hand up over her mouth, still strong enough to lift her with one arm. Lou carried her as easily as a sack of potatoes, walking quickly into the bushes beside the road.

Eva didn't know what stung worse: the hot tears seeping out of her tightly shut eyes and wetting his hands or the leaves and branches of bushes and small trees whipping her face and neck.

In her dreams of this moment, she had thought she was flying, skimming the top of the ground moved by some unseen force that surrounded her with deep, hot fear. She kicked her legs and flailed her arms, just as she had in the dream, trying to control her flight, trying to get away from the sting of the branches and out in the open, where she could lift herself above the treetops.

Her kicking foot caught Lou in the back and he cursed, but didn't stop until he reached a small clearing that was really part of a smaller path that led down to the big one.

"It's gon' be fine, you'll see," Lou said, smiling, even as he tried to lay her down on the ground. Eva immediately jumped up and ran. He leapt up after her, clipping her legs from behind and sending her sprawling. There she was, there she was with that fearsome weight on top of her, and not even Mary Nell here. In the dream, Mary Nell had been with her, they had borne that heavy fear together. But here she was alone, alone except for the kind of pain that cut the heart in half.

16

MARY NELL SHIVERED. SHE SCANNED THE crowd for her husband.

"You seen Lou?" she asked Grace, who sat beside her.

"Naw." Grace's own eyes swept the room. "And that Eva is in big trouble for being late."

Mary Nell went cold. She looked again and then closed her eyes, trying not to notice how heavy the air had become, so thick she couldn't draw it through her nostrils. She had to open her mouth to breathe. Then sounds began to knock against her eardrum. Grunting, as if from some confused animal, filled her ears, invaded her mind like fog. She felt it all down to the bone.

Mary Nell's eyes flew open again, darting around, searching every wooden corner of the church for Lou's face. He wasn't there, but she felt him, angry, hungry, heavy on her thighs as he pressed her into the ground. She absurdly worried about the leaves that were getting tangled in her hair. She felt like she was being torn in two, one part of her here in the pew and the other struggling on the ground, sure that Lou Henry was going to kill her. She kicked out at him, felt him wince, but nothing moved him off of her. Now he just put his hand around her throat. Why was he doing this to her? She couldn't see him and yet he held her there, in her seat, as the hymn rose out of the windows and over the trees. The song wound around and around the heads of the congregation and Lou's mutterings and grunts made a wall between Mary Nell and everybody else. She cried out, and another woman sitting a row back, taking Mary Nell's cry as a sign that the Holy Ghost was near, decided to punctuate the song with a "Thank you, Jesus!" Tears streamed down their faces, the Holy Ghost woman and Mary Nell.

Mary Nell looked at Grace, who was staring down at her sister's legs, kicking out and falling back against the pew with thud after thud. The rest of the church seemed too busy with song to notice.

What's wrong with you? Grace's lips mouthed. But Mary Nell just shook her head and tried to stifle the shriek that was rising in her throat. She closed her eyes again and glimpsed in her mind Lou's twisted face just before something tore at her—at her clothes and her body. Almost like he was here and some devil had him, making him hurt her this way.

She felt ripping flesh and blood seeping across her skin and she stood up suddenly and left the church. It took everything she had not to run.

Grace found her a few minutes later, sitting on the steps doubled over, moaning.

"Mary Nell. Mary Nell?" Grace sat beside her, putting an arm around her shoulders. "Honey? Is it you belly?"

Mary Nell just breathed hard and didn't speak. I have to find Eva, she thought, but it seemed impossible to move. Her shaking body wouldn't obey her. Eva. Something had happened to Eva.

And something had happened to Lou.

"Go on back," Mary Nell whispered to Grace.

"Sister . . ."

"Go on. Bad enough they be wonderin' why I'm out here, without them speculatin' on you, too."

"They know I'm tendin' to you . . ."

"Grace," Mary Nell bit out. "Please."

She was alone on the hard brick steps when Lou Henry came. She stood up to take him all in, the wrinkles in the trousers she'd ironed this morning. The mud on the knees, on his shirt, on his boots. His face gleaming with sweat and evil.

He ran his hand over his shirt again and again under his suspenders. The dirt and wrinkles didn't disappear.

"Damn cow," he muttered as he approached. "I had a time keeping hold of her. Got out just as I was gettin' ready to come."

"I thought you was just gon' milk her," Mary Nell said quietly, wiping a hand across her wet cheek as quickly as she could. "I don't know why you waited till you had your good clothes on."

"I left the gate open, too. Thought I had her. And then she gon' try to run. Stubborn old girl. Took me awhile to get her. I suppose it ain't the first time I been late." He grinned almost sheepishly and Mary Nell felt her heart tighten into a hard knot.

"What you doin' out here? Waitin' for me?" He climbed the steps and stood beside her, taking her hand and kissing her lightly on the cheek. His fingers, his lips were hot. There was dirt on his hands; there was blood on his cheek. She put a finger to his face and traced the red line of the scratch.

"I didn't feel good," she said, taking her hand away and staring at the smear of blood. Lou looked at it, too, and then looked away over her head. "You see Eva on the way? Seem like she late, too."

"Naw," he said, giving her arm a little tug, then letting go when she stiffened. "I ain't seen her. Let's go in, huh? I'm sorry I'm late. Don't be mad."

The song coming through the cracks in the door rose to a high pitch and then dropped down, down low into a moaning hum. The collection had been taken and the prayer was about to start. Lou Henry got behind Mary Nell and put a hand in the small of her back, pushing her and then nearly shoving her to the door when she didn't move right away. She looked back over her shoulder at him, tears in her eyes. She looked again at his cheek and he stared back at her, his smile hard. He wiped the back of his hand over the scratch, brushed again at the mud on his pants, and pushed her forward.

Hardly anybody looked up when they came in. All eyes were closed except those of the children as Deacon Porter knelt beside the little table that held the collection basket. The hand he had placed on the table shook and a few coins in the basket made a pitiful kind of music to go along with the ocean of voices humming and the fervent prayer that poured from his lips.

"Oh gracious heav'ly father we ask that you look down 'pon us in this hour and bless us and bless this humble offerin' . . ."

Mary Nell turned away from Lou and slipped back into her seat beside Grace, who had her head bowed but her eyes open and was peeking at Mary Nell from under her eyelashes.

Mary Nell couldn't let anyone see her distress. She bent her head quickly, ignoring the prayer, trying to put names to the feelings that were assailing her mind and body. Her mind groped for Eva and found pain built up like a fence holding her inside of it. She was like an animal in a cage, being prodded at from outside, and inside trying to keep her heart from bursting and killing her right there. For when she closed her eyes, there was Eva lying in the dirt, her dress torn almost clean away. Her tears soaking the fallen leaves.

She looked across at Lou and heard his whisper. *"Bout time you was a woman, ain't it? You walkin' 'round here with all the right parts. Walkin' 'round here like you know somethin'. And them boys lookin' at you. You like them lookin' but they young, they don't know what to do with you yet. I knows though. I knows what to do . . . You gon' like it fine, you'll see . . . what you gon' cry and holler for?"*

Mary Nell heard the words spinning around and around Eva's head. She looked across the room to where he sat, his head bowed. She thought about last night, when he had laughingly held her in his arms and played with her, teased her, before lifting her nightgown and riding her fast and fierce.

In the dream they had both been there. The fearful thing had been behind them and before them, but had never showed its face.

So maybe, Mary Nell thought, as the prayer ended and the congregation lifted their heads as one body and the moaning erupted again into a song, maybe Eva lying there on the path and Lou Henry with the dirty clothes and hands and the bloody cheek had nothing to do with the dream. Maybe Eva had done something or said something. And Lou was a man. Girls sometimes teased men with their newborn womanliness, their rising breasts or their just-discovered sashaying walk. Mary Nell had seen that walk, had seen Eddie Adam and Son sighing behind Eva's back.

You like them lookin'.

Mary Nell lifted her head, too, and there were tears clinging to her lashes. Lou had been going to church. He had been staying with her and not going out running 'round. He had settled down. Till now. Till now.

There was Eva moaning and hurt in the woods and there was Lou sitting across from her in the deacons' section, where he had just earned a place. After church, all the men would walk outside and smoke and talk while the women fixed the dinners and Lou would be there and the old men of Johnson Creek would pat him on the back. And she would stand with the women and their boxes.

Yes, Lou's got a good crop coming up this year, she'd say. *He takes good care of me. He's a good man. Marriage sho does settle a high-spirited man down,* someone would say to her. *But then it takes a good woman like you, Mary Nell, to rein in a wild one like Lou Evans. And look at him now. On the deacon board and everything.*

And the two of them would go home together to their own house and nobody would be able to say that they weren't anything other than good, respectable folk. Nobody would be able to say anything else, Mary Nell thought, because whatever happened back there in the woods would stay there. And Eva would pick herself up and clean herself off and Mary Nell would talk to Lou Henry and that would be that.

So she closed her ears to Eva's moans echoing in her head and to the stabbing pains that she knew were not her own. She felt

Eva's confusion and disorientation and struggled not to let it over-whelm her. She had to think about this. She had to get straight in her head what to do. If she rushed out of the church to her sister's side, everyone would know something was wrong. They had seen Lou come in late. But if she didn't get to Eva first and talk to her, if Mama and Papa found her, there would be no chance. There would be no chance. She had to talk to Eva first.

So Mary Nell sat back tensely in her pew and made her decision. Made her mistake.

17

SHE DIDN'T MOVE. SHE WASN'T SURE she could, that she still lived. But the trees were the same, after he'd gone. And lying here, among the mud and leaves, she looked right up to the sky and felt her life leaving her, leaving behind battered flesh that somehow still breathed in a raspy whisper.

Eva. Eva! You hear me?

God didn't have a voice like that, not that frightened, shaky voice that she heard now close to her ear. So she must still be alive, and Mary Nell must be there.

But Mary Nell was speaking to her as if she was some *thing*, some disobedient dog. Not her sister. Not her little sister with the gift to share. No, there was a hissing in her ear, the slight wind made by Mary Nell's anger and hot fear touching her cheek.

Listen to me. Listen now.

And there was Mary Nell lifting her up by the shoulders, and Eva's view of the sky shifted, slanted, but she tried to keep her eyes open.

Oh, my Lord. My Lord.

Mary Nell's hands tried to smooth down the dress, touched the inside of Eva's thigh and Eva let out a cry of pain.

Lord, no. It's true. It's true. Why'd it have to . . . ? I couldn't have helped you, Eva. You shouldn't have . . . He a man. A certain kind. He can't help that. Some mens can't help that. But you know'd that, of course you know'd what kind of man he is. Ev'rybody do. He done got better, so much better. But thangs is a temptation to him, you know. You shoulda know'd that, but you had to walk that way and be all under his nose. He liked you, his new little sister. But you got to be careful 'round a man like that. Ain't you got no sense? Lord, Lord. What I'm gon' do? Papa—Papa will kill him. Shoot him dead. Then what I got? I ain't got nothing. I already got nothing. Then I'll have the bottom of nothing.

Eva's shoulders were being lifted off the ground. She winced as Mary Nell pulled her into a sitting position.

My husband! You did that with my husband!

Eva could see Mary Nell's face now, but she had no words for the expression there, twisted into something between terror and anger. But no love. Eva saw no love there. Something that had been available to her, always, since the day she was born, was gone suddenly. One day there, the next day gone. The connection between them only served as a conduit for pain, going from Eva's body to Mary Nell, who gave it back to her as anger.

Listen. Listen. You gotta stay quiet, Eva. What you gon' say anyway? You know what they's gon' call you when they find out you did that with your own sister's husband? On the way to church? Lord . . . on the way to church! You can't say he made you. You can't say that. Papa will kill him. You don't want that to happen, do you? Make me a widow.

Eva felt herself being shaken. She moaned, unable to form any words. She couldn't move. Mary Nell's strangled whisper seemed to be coming from somewhere inside her and for the first time in her life, she cursed their gift, their special, silent language. Shame covered her like a shroud as her sister whispered the words: harlot, trash and no better than trash. What had she done? What could she have done to be given such pain to bear? She had fought so hard, and it didn't matter. She had tried to stop him, but it didn't count. In the end, it didn't count.

Her sister's voice had taken on a sing-song quality and she felt herself being dragged up from the ground, an arm around her waist keeping her from falling down again immediately. Eva realized her dress was torn down the front, from neck to knee, and she put up a hand to hold the pieces together over her small tits. Mary Nell walked her through the mud, her lips against her ear.

She asked for it. She shouldn't have shown herself to Lou. She shouldn't have bent over in front of him. Or passed so close when she walked by. And the way she walked . . . what did she expect from a man, a robust man, like Lou Evans? She was old enough to know now about these things. She couldn't tell anyone. Then they would all know what she was.

They held on to each other, and Mary Nell whispered to her, even as the sound of Eva's name rang through the trees. Eva grasped at her sister, seeking comfort, but there was only the rigidity in Mary Nell's embrace and the insistent words in her ear.

They called her, Mama and Papa, Grace and Son and Eddie Adam. But she didn't respond. Mary Nell's voice was hypnotic. Eva's feet didn't seem to be really touching the ground, although they moved away from that startling place where everything had changed.

Mary Nell urged her on. *They'll be coming. They'll be coming 'long here any time.*

She turned off the road, and dragged Eva with her. Eva closed her eyes. Branches and bushes whipped her relentlessly, stinging her skin in the few nonbruised places she had left. She was bad, they seemed to say, echoing Mary Nell's voice in her ear. They beat her without ceasing.

When we get there don't you say nothing. Let me talk and you just nod your head. Say yes to what I say, you hear? You missed church because you stopped to watch them heathen men play baseball. Everybody know how crazy you is 'bout some baseball. You just stopped for a minute. But then you know'd you was late so you ran on, but you fell and tore your dress. And you couldn't come to church anniversary like that, could you? Could you? Yes, that's what happened. And when they get home, we'll already be there and you'll already be wearing something else and I'll be bundling up your church dress to fix for you. Nobody gotta see it's tore up. I'll just ball it up . . . And then you all can go on back to the church and eat. And you don't even have to say nothing. NOTHING.

Eva opened her eyes. She saw the back of the house as they emerged from the woods. She let Mary Nell take her in. She let Mary Nell's cold hands undress her and clean off the dirt and blood. Wasn't nothing else to do now, was there? Mary Nell was right. Folk would call her some of everything. Even though it was Lou. Because you know he was a church man now and had a wife and wasn't doing all that running around like before. No, that Eva gal was over there all the time at her sister's. Right under his nose. Got the smell of new woman all over her. Done got womanish and didn't know what to do with it. That's what they'd say. The Etta Maes and Janies and all the rest of them women. Eva had heard them so many times before, berating some woman who may or may not have done the things of which she was accused. But after they were through, did it matter? After they were through, always and forever a hussy.

Mary Nell threw a dress at her. Eva didn't notice which one, she just put it on. The dress covered all her sore places except one around her throat, under her chin. She felt a bruise coming there. She closed her eyes, feeling her windpipe tighten as he squeezed and squeezed.

Button up! Mary Nell was looking out the window of the bedroom they used to share. This was the room they dreamed in together. But now Mary Nell might as well have been on the other side of the world.

They coming.

Eva could heard their voices. Papa's above everyone else's.

"Well this the only place left she could be. I'm gon' get that gal for keeping me from my dinner." Eva heard fear underneath his annoyed snorts.

"I don't understand," Grace said. "She was up and washed when we left. All she had to do was get dressed. Comb her hair."

"Eva!" Frank called, stomping on the porch and rattling the screen door as he opened it. Mary Nell glanced at Eva lying on the bed, motioning her to sit up. Eva didn't move, and Mary Nell frowned at her before stepping through the doorway to greet their father.

"She here, Papa. Missed all of church, I reckon."

"Sho nuff did!" He poked his head through and glared slightly at Eva half-lying on the bed. "What's wrong with you, gal? You sick? Why you didn't say nothin'?"

Eva tried to get some words up out of her throat but nothing came to her.

"I think it just came up on her, Papa," Mary Nell said, quickly tossing the baseball story away as she glanced as Eva's dazed expression and shaky hands. "She was on her way, she told me, but she felt light in the head and fell down. Messed up her dress." Mary Nell lifted the jumble of white fabric that she held in her arms. "I'm gon' fix her dress for her."

Frank's frown faded, then disappeared, and he came in to sit on the bed. "Aw, baby girl, I'm sorry. Why you didn't say?"

Grace and Joy had come in and Joy came and bent over Eva, pressing her palms against Eva's two cheeks. She examined the scratches on her face and hands and arms, shaking her head.

"Put that dress down, Mary Nell," Joy said, not taking her eyes off Eva. "I'll see to it later."

"Nah, Mama, it's got a tear in it. Don't you worry about it none. I'll fix it for her." Mary Nell balled the dress up even more.

"I didn't want to come to church," Eva whispered. That was true.

"What you say?" Joy leaned closer.

"I didn't want to come like that," Eva said, putting her hand on her mother's arm and looking at her. Grace stepped all the way into the room and stood looking down at Eva.

"Well, that's all right, baby," Joy said. "Nah, course you couldn't come with your dress all like that. It was a short service anyways."

Papa patted Eva's arm and stood up. "Well what we gon' do? Go back to church for dinner? We left Lou Henry with the food and I don't know if I trust that boy." He laughed. Eva felt a shuddering pain go through her. She saw Lou's face again, above her, moving into and out of her line of vision with every hard assault on her body. She felt as if she was bleeding again and dared not move in case there was a stain on the bedcovers and her mother saw it. She could always say it was her time of the month, but Eva wasn't sure she could make the lie come out of her mouth.

Her father had straightened up, stretching, the mystery of the missing daughter solved. Eva looked up at him. She could tell Papa and he would fix it. Papa would take his shotgun off the wall and she would never have to see Lou again.

But Mary Nell's eyes burned a hole in her from across the small room. Mary Nell clutched the dress, folding it and refolding it so that the blood that stood out on the white linen was well hidden. Mary Nell, who used to share her dreams right here in this same bed. And if she told and Lou died, Mary Nell, her best friend, her sister, the other half of her, would never speak to her again. She would cut Eva in half with her anger. Cut them both in half and leave them bleeding and wandering inside dreams that meant nothing.

Eva swallowed hard. Grace stood beside the bed, a hand stroking Eva's hair, but her head turned so that she watched Mary Nell wrestling with the folds of fabric. She watched Mary Nell watching Eva.

"Oh, I'll go get Lou," Mary Nell said softly, smiling, never taking her hard eyes off Eva. She didn't really look like Mary Nell anymore. Grace stared at her. "We can all eat here." Mary Nell tucked the dress under her arm and went over to the bed, bending down to Eva. "You feel better, sister," she said, leaning in a little closer to murmur something in Eva's ear.

Hussy.

$\approx$18$\approx$

July

MOST OF MARY NELL'S DREAMS WERE just sounds now. Bits of conversation and song, just words flying around and around inside of her. Lou Henry had been talking to her in a dream and it was only after she'd sat up in bed that she realized that he wasn't there beside her. It wasn't even night. She had come from work and laid down for a moment and his voice had begun in her ear.

"Now I don't know why you wanna make me hurt you like that. You don't know how good it could be. You done already felt that, huh? You was fightin' but I knows you felt it . . ."

And so on, his hand—Mary Nell knew those hands, calloused and long-fingered—closing around her throat. No, Eva's throat. Eva's throat.

How good it could be, he had said.

Hands that had held and caressed her, that had tucked her inside his warm circle. Hands clamping down, again, cutting off her breath so that she couldn't even scream. And his voice, that had often sung her to sleep, now hissed and grunted, laughed at her sobbing. Only Eva cried like that.

And the crying rang in Mary Nell's ears as she got up and began to walk in a circle around the room, stumbling sleepily. She pictured Eva, not the girl who'd recently become a silent stranger, but the real Eva, life-filled and shining with light, playing Saturday afternoon games with the boys, with her dark mass of hair flying and her dress wrapping around her long legs.

Mary Nell stared out of the window. The woods seemed too close. Most houses in Johnson Creek were like this: little islands among the trees where they all scraped at the dirt, annoying it until it gave them something, a flower, a patch of greens, some cotton or sorghum or corn or peanuts. She had a yard with roses growing in rusty-bottom tin tubs by the porch, bursts of color that relieved the sandy red of the dirt yard, where not a bit of grass grew, she was proud to say. Some of those cuttings she'd gotten from the Wards, when the garden man pruned their old bushes. Some of them she'd gotten from Mama, who'd gotten them from somebody else—maybe Papa's mama. They were a wedding gift, those bare little stems with the promise of velvet color locked inside and Mary Nell had thought of them as beauty waiting for the right soil to grow, the right amount of love and rain and light.

It had taken awhile for them to root, and a couple of years for them to bloom, but there they were, lush and full, completing their mission on earth by being abundantly themselves, those flowers. But marriages took longer to root and grow, she thought. And something—someone—was already cutting it off, strangling and smothering it.

Just standing beside Lou Henry on any given day at any given time, Mary Nell felt his restless heat. That was the way he'd been when they first met, and she'd been so proud of herself for convincing him to wait until it was right and proper, until they had said their "I-dos" and God had smiled on their union. He had tried all of his usual methods on her, but she was going to be a proper woman even if she didn't exactly end up married to a proper man. And until now, until Second Sunday, everything had been right, everything except her childlessness. But she was sure God had an answer for that as well.

And he'd been fine! He didn't even keep his old friends; they had all drifted away, going to Montgomery or Troy or Columbus or wherever they went to do their dirty living. And he stayed with her, went to church on Sundays, worked and sweated every day in between, and took whatever sexual hunger he had and poured it into her and no one else. No one else.

So what was Eva doing? When and how did it happen that her sister had decided to do this? Because—Mary Nell knew—a woman could do things with her body and be unaware. In some part of the mind, some deep cavern of careless thought, Eva must have wanted him. So she had moved a certain way when he was around, fixed her mouth a certain way. Of course Mary Nell had missed it; she had no reason to suspect. She had only been aware of the growing fear. She and Eva had talked about it many times, and about how Eva was sure Lou Henry was going to hurt Mary Nell.

She went to the chifforobe and opened it. In a drawer, under the little pile of stockings, was the bag Willow had made. Mary

Nell took it out and turned it over in her hand. Eva had said Lou Henry would hurt her. Eva had given her the bag. She had known that she would do this. And why would Mary Nell ever suspect that Eva—little more than a child—would bring back that wild rawness into her husband's body? Eva was becoming the woman they all became. The hips change, and they have to shift their weight when they walk. Just can't carry hips like that in a straight line.

Eva had been playing with him maybe. Trying out her new womanliness on someone she thought was safe.

Mary Nell couldn't say she had felt nothing, no clue. But who knew what those were clues to? Like that day she'd been making that cake and sent Eva out to the barn. She had felt something then. Just the grip of sudden emotion, a fear squeezed her heart and startled her into tipping over her mixing bowl. And maybe what she thought was fear coming from Eva was excitement that Lou had touched her and spoken to her the way that men speak to women.

Her own sister had wanted her husband, and now she had had him. Because he was aching for Eva the way he used to ache for Mary Nell. Maybe even now, he was thinking of ways to leave and run off with Eva. Mary Nell tried to peer into the future, needing her prophetic dreams and visions, but without Eva they failed her; she couldn't see what Lou Henry would do. She could only imagine being alone here, without children or husband, and there would be no Eva, the sharer of dreams. She would just be something for folk to pity.

She couldn't let that happen.

19

EVERY NIGHT, EVA'S BREATH LEFT her body. Her dream ended before her next inhalation. There would be none. He was going to kill her. She knew the feel of his hands around her throat. Really he only needed to finish her, since she was half dead already.

SUMMER'S FIRST PEAS FELL IN THE earthenware bowl. Joy talked on and on, rocking and shelling, splitting the hulls with her strong fingers.

Grace had barely started shelling and now her hands lay still in her bowl, wrists resting on the edge, unshelled pods clutched in her fists. She silently prayed, giving thanks to God for dreamless nights and quiet days.

Though there was one bit of quiet that was disturbing at the same time.

She looked at Eva, who hunched over her bowl, unsmiling and with her hands carelessly in motion. The bowl was almost full, but she continued to rip the peas out of their little wombs.

"Baby doll," Grace said, putting her own bowl down on the porch boards. "You might need to empty that bowl."

Eva looked up at her sister sleepy-eyed. Grace recognized her expression, one of two that Eva had continuously worn since her bout of sickness a few weeks ago on Second Sunday. The other expression was terror.

Obviously, Eva had not recovered. She'd barely left the house. This morning, Grace had seen her slip behind the barn, still carrying the pan of feed she was using to feed the chickens. The hens scrambled after her and Grace, too, had followed at a distance, rounding the north wall of the barn in time to see Eva crouching behind some bushes, vomiting, the chickens clucking all around her.

The peas in Eva's bowl spilled over the rim and pitter-pattered on the porch.

"Watch yourself, girl," Joy said sharply, but her glance at Eva was puzzled, as it always was these days. Grace rose from her chair and took the bowl out of Eva's lap, emptying it in a larger bowl before giving it back.

"Really, you don't need to do no more," Joy said. Eva nodded, getting up and slipping inside the house. The door barely moved as she went through.

Joy stared after her, her hands still for the moment.

"What's wrong with her, Mama?" Grace asked. "You seen her these past few weeks? Her and Mary Nell both goin' 'round like shadows."

"I don't know. Still not feelin' good, I reckon. I don't know 'bout Mary Nell, either. Them girls done barely seen each other in the past few weeks. I guess Mary Nell being married do keep her busy. Eva must be lonely without her. She been sick since June . . ." Joy paused, looking down at her hands, falling silent.

"Mama?" Grace asked. But she knew what her mother was

thinking. She had thought so herself this morning as she watched Eva hunched over, her face nearly touching the ground. Eva was old enough and she tried to remember if something had changed about the way she was with Eddie Adam or Son Jackson. Those two were the only ones it could be. But she couldn't recall anything different in their attitudes toward Eva, except now and then they asked about her, because she barely left the yard these days.

If it was true, Mama and Papa would have a fit. And she would, too, she guessed. Eva wasn't no way near ready for that. She looked over at Joy, who was shaking her head and fingering the peas.

"Maybe . . . she gon' have a baby," Joy said, sighing. Sweat trickled from under the red rag she had tied haphazardly around her thick hair. A drop slipped down her forehead and dripped off the end of her nose. "But ain't no need to mention it to yo' Papa 'til I know for sho." She poured her peas into the big bowl. Grace added hers.

"He got plenty to worry about," Joy said. "Plenty." And she took the peas into the house.

Grace got up for the broom that leaned in the corner. She absently swept pea hulls into a pile. This was normal; she wanted normal. Even Eva being pregnant—maybe—that was real and solid and the way the world worked. But not the visitations of her dead grandmother. She couldn't accept that that was going to be her life, that until she died she would be in the clutches of Ayo's sad, blood-filled memories.

But maybe not, she thought as she stopped to pick up a heap of hulls with both hands and throw them in a crocker sack for the hogs' supper. She'd been busy lately helping her mama. Eva had become so useless. Grace hadn't even had much time to think about anything but work. If I keep my mind busy and make myself so tired that I sleep hard, she thought, she'll stay away. I can make her leave my mind.

She picked up the sack and turned around, gasping because George was there, putting his foot on the first step.

"Smile!" he said cheerfully, laughing at her surprise. Her heart contracted, almost painfully. Would there ever be a time when seeing him didn't make her feel this strange, nervous joy. She felt a smile coming, but she tried to make her face stern.

"What you mean sneakin' up like some kind of thief? If I had had a shotgun by me, you'd be dead by now, dead befo' I could even see it was you. I woulda shot first and asked later."

"I don't believe that. Something would have stopped you. Something would have told you it was me." George stopped at the bottom step. "You woulda seen me smilin' at you, just before you pulled the trigger. Just a hair before, and you woulda stopped."

"Don't count on me that way," Grace said, coming down the steps, tugging the sack. "I don't know who myself is sometimes. Bad or good."

"Well, I know who you is, sweet girl." He took the sack from her.

She smiled, reluctantly at first, then she felt it spreading all over her face. She stepped down and gestured for him to follow her. He came behind with the sack.

"Thought you might like to go on down with me to the creek," he said.

Grace stopped at the hog pen and took the sack from him, throwing the hulls at the feet of the happily grunting animals.

"It's late, and I still got things to do," she said. "I can't leave her with all those peas to cook and put up. And how is it that you so idle on a day that's not Sunday, George Lancaster?"

"I was up early, buildin' a new coop. Can't a man take a rest? Come talk with me, just for a little while."

Grace hung the sack on the fence and stood there brushing off the remaining peas and hulls that still clung to her dress while she thought. She wished she didn't look so tired. She wished she didn't have those little circles of sweat under her arms and moisture clinging to her forehead at the edges of her hair. She swept a hand casually over her face, fighting the dampness.

She wondered why George kept coming back, why he kept sniffing around and around her, even in those moments when she was practically screaming at him to leave her alone. The last time she had done that they had been sitting on the porch and she had been holding her head in both hands, trying to keep from falling apart. She had felt then as if Ayo was sitting there with them, her heavy sadness thickening the air. Grace almost physically put up her hands to try to fight through it, and ended up just crying and screaming at George as he again pressed her about marriage.

"You don't know! You would never stay! You would never stay!" she had yelled, doubling over in the chair as George sat there bewildered.

"I'm not goin' to go anywhere," he said. And he sat there as if to demonstrate the truth of his words.

"You might as well go on," she said, knowing that he wouldn't. She rocked back and forth with her head in her hands as George sat beside her not touching her at all. She said again, "You should go." She didn't want him to. She wanted him to wait until she was rid of this thing. But she couldn't ask him to, knowing she might never be free.

That had been a little more than a month ago, and still he came often. She was starting to feel better. She felt more like herself when she was with George than at any other time. Between that and her work at home, Bessie's voice had grown dim. And to her relief he hadn't mentioned marriage for a while.

"Sure you don't want to go down there with me?" George asked now as he leaned over to watch the hogs eating and rooting around in the dirt.

She turned and headed back to the house, but he stayed where he was. Her mother was at the door.

"When George get here?" she asked, smiling slightly.

"Not long ago. Wants to go down to the creek. I told him I couldn't."

George came over, waving at Joy.

"Go on," she said as he came up. "Better for you both if you go on. Mr. Mobley don't like it so much you hangin' around here, George. Nothin' personal to you. He just like to watch over his girls."

"Yes'm," George said, putting out a hand to take Grace's arm as she came down the stairs and quickly withdrawing it when Joy lifted an eyebrow.

"Just get back befo' dark, y'all hear me? Way befo'!"

"Yes'm."

They just walked. George led her out back of the house and down the Indian Road toward the creek. He was one of the few people who could keep up with Grace when she walked. She never strolled. She liked feeling a little bit of breeze when she moved.

For a good ten minutes, they went on along without speaking, without touching.

She wanted to put her hand on his arm, but couldn't seem to make her muscles move.

If them dreams and ghosts is truly gone, she thought, I could. I could just reach over right now and just touch his arm or his fingers. Maybe even hold his hand. If they gone, I can smile at him and walk a little closer, a little farther. I can touch him, I can taste him.

Grace peeked sideways at George and met his soft, brown eyes, looking right at her, like he was expecting something.

"What you lookin' at, George Lancaster?" she half growled at him, her voice low and not a little frightened.

"Heaven, I guess," he said seriously. The playful smile she was expecting never appeared. After a long moment, with the sound of their feet hitting the ground magnified by the still, hot air, she looked away up the road in the direction they were heading and then slipped her hand into his, curling her long, slim fingers around his rough palm. His hand bore the imprint of soil and wood and work. It felt like it had been buried an eternity in the earth and he had been digging to get out, sifting ancient dirt through ancient fingers.

They came to the plank bridge, but George stopped before they crossed, tugging her down the bank beside the path, down to where a tumble of rocks made a hard path of their own, down to where the water emerged from under the bridge. Here Johnson Creek was small enough to leap over, and that's what George did, keeping Grace's hand and walking along the other side of the water. With their arms stretched out, their fingers barely kept a hold on each other.

Grace laughed. "What you doin', silly? Where we goin' anyway? You know I can't stay out here long."

"You know where we goin'," George smiled.

She looked down, her lips curling. She could see the place in her head, where the stream widened. The streambed was deep there, and for a little distance it divided into two small rivulets with a gravelly, sandy island in the middle. There was an old building near the bank, a tumbledown log place. It was on Johnson's land, part of his timber tract, but she didn't know who had lived there. It was old enough to be a leftover from slavery days, but it was far away from where the old quarters used to be.

They had all played there as little children. It was a favorite wading spot—too shallow for fishing, but perfect for splashing and cooling your feet in summer. You just had to watch for water moccasins, especially in spring. Grace scanned the stream and the bank for snakes, even as she clutched George's fingers across the little stream.

"I gotta ask you somethin' . . ." George said.

"Again?" she said half-mockingly. She looked at him, but he wasn't smiling. They were coming to the place where the stream divided.

". . . and you gotta promise you gon' listen and not fuss, and talk and clap your hands on your ears." George stepped down from the bank and onto the little sandy island, still holding her hand. "Don't shut your ears, Grace."

Grace still stood on the opposite bank. He enclosed both her hands, making them disappear inside his, and he stood with the water flowing around his feet. Grace looked down into his uplifted eyes. He had never before looked so much like a man to her. His eyes said everything. They were serious eyes, but they shone with fearless, joyful light. Like he had the sun inside him, fierce and warm, harsh and life-giving.

George slid his fingers down her wrists. She stifled a wince as he touched the sensitive skin there, but kept smiling at him. Already, the pain was fading as their arms formed a bridge across the water. Behind her, the glassless windows of the old cabin looked out from the darkness within its walls. For a moment there was only the sound of the water skipping over sand and rocks.

"I know'd I done—I have—asked you befo' to be my wife."

Grace opened her mouth, and George shook his head at her.

"See, Grace, we been goin' 'long side by side all our days. Like God done matched us up long ago. Maybe that's why you scairt of it. I know. I know it seem to be too good to be the right thing. But you know we gon' end up there, we gon' end up together."

Grace took a deep breath. He tightened his fingers around hers. She smiled a little at his emotional discomfort.

"So," he said. "Marry me. God done already said yes."

She fought with herself as she looked up at the sky, searching for the absolute right thing to do. She strained to hear an answer to the many questions she had. She strained even to hear Bessie's whisper, because that would be the sign that she should let him go.

All she heard was the water and her own heart beating and George's anxious breathing. Looking into his shining eyes, all she wanted to do was to walk into his arms and never leave.

So she went with that.

21

August

On Sundays Eva rose before everyone else and made breakfast. Joy and Frank, weary from a week's worth of bending and unbending over work, were happy to come to a table already blessed with food. It was the only time Eva showed signs of being a human being again. They wanted to encourage that.

She made biscuits and fried fatback, grits and coffee. She laid out the butter and plum jelly. But she never sat down to eat. As soon as they came to the table, she left the room to get ready for church.

Again on this Sunday, as he had every Sunday for two months, her father asked, "Ain't you gon' have a sit, baby?" He pulled out his chair and glanced at the back of her neck. She stood near the doorway with her head down, taking off her apron. "No, suh," she said, like always, and slipped through the doorway like a ghost.

"Leave her alone, Papa," Grace said softly.

In their room, Eva carefully laid her second-best dress on the bed. The last time she had seen her best one, it was being compressed into a bloody ball under Mary Nell's nervous fingers. It disappeared when Mary Nell did; Eva had hardly seen her since that day except in church, where she sat in a corner watching Eva mournfully. She didn't sing. She didn't pray. She watched Eva and she watched the door. Lou Henry had stopped coming to church.

That didn't mean that he was gone. Eva felt him waiting. His waiting made the air all around the fields and woods suffocating to Eva. She smelled his waiting, his watching from places she couldn't peer into. He was going to kill her. She could feel it and her feelings were rarely wrong. In dreams she heard it coming there somewhere in the bottom of her mind, the echo of nothingness that she would become, after he saw her again. She had asked God to forgive her and He sent fear-heavy dreams.

She tried to prepare herself. If she was ready, it would be less painful, maybe, when Lou finally took her away from life.

Eva began putting on her clothes. She almost didn't want to wait. Waiting for death was a hard thing. But she didn't want it to be today. That was why she had made sure to get up in time, so she wouldn't be here alone, so she wouldn't walk down the Indian Road alone. She was never late anymore.

Joy and Frank invited Mary Nell to dinner after church, and she came. They had asked her a lot since Lou Henry stopped coming to services. But this was the first time she had accepted. She walked back home with them, talking quietly to Grace, while Eva drifted along just behind, alongside their mother. Joy slipped an arm around Eva's waist.

"New dress?" Grace was saying. "Yeah, but I ain't had no money for cloth. Sho would like somethin' like that dress I saw in McCall's."

"Hard to believe you finally told that man yes," Mary Nell said.

"Um-humm," Joy murmured from behind their backs, and Grace laughed.

"Mama and Papa been waitin' years to get me off their hands, ain't that right Papa?"

"I just don't know why you had to go and pain that man so," he said, shaking his head, smiling. "George one patient fella. I know'd I couldn't a waited long as he did . . ."

"Yeah?" Joy sniffed. "Seems like you took your time when it came to me."

"Had to! Miz Bessie tried her best to drive me away. When I come to see you, she would watch us from the porch or stomp around the yard pokin' at the ground with that long walkin' stick of hers mumblin' in that strange voice." He stopped in the road and stamped his feet in imitation of his late mother-in-law, eliciting laughter from Mary Nell.

"Don't you be mockin' my mama!" Joy said, stopping, too, and putting her hands on her hips, her eyes glinting with barely concealed laughter.

"Then one day, I come over to see your mama," Frank said to Grace. "And when Miz Bessie saw me, she just looked at me for a long time, and then without sayin' nothin', she just marched off into the woods. Gone 'bout two hours. We was 'bout to go look for her when she come back just as calm as you please. Then she just nodded her head at me and smiled and after that every-thang was all right."

"Where she go off to? She did some hoodoo?" Mary Nell asked.

"Girl! It's the Lord's day!" Joy snapped.

Grace stared off into the trees, completely still except for a nervous tapping of her left foot. Eva moved closer into the circle of Joy's arms.

"Don't know," Frank said. "Just when she came back up to the house, she smiled at me and patted my arm as she passed by. And that was that. We was all right from then on."

"I didn't understand half the things Mama did," Joy sighed. "Come on, now, we got to eat."

They walked the Indian Road from the church to the house. Mary Nell glanced often at Eva, who stared back. The heavy fear that had once lived on this path was gone, but still they were uneasy. Eva thought she knew why. She waited for death.

22

Lou Henry remembered a time when he had tried not to let Eva even cross his mind. And when she did, he could never put his finger on why. But soon she was there all the time, a small, persistent little problem.

One day he had looked across the cotton rows of Frank Mobley's fields and watched her pour a dipperful of water over her head. She had shaken the water out of her eyes and laughed. It was at that moment he had felt the stirring in his groin.

He carried that picture of her in his head. He preferred it to the look on her face as he had pulled away the skirts and taken her there in the road. He wanted the laughing Eva. Not the dead-faced girl who now looked at him from the doorway of his barn.

Lou Henry had looked up and she had simply been there. For a moment he even convinced himself that she had come to him.

Leaning against the side of a stall, he imagined he saw something in her downcast eyes, shy longing maybe. Even though she mumbled Mary Nell's name, asking for her, he had gone to her, put his arm around her, told her not to be afraid of him.

She tried to wiggle away, crying, and he loved the way it felt to have her straining there in his arms. He loved the feel of her, slender and small, with skin like silk. The more she struggled the tighter he held on.

And once again she was beneath him, his hips fitting into the hollow of her young bones, his chest pressed down on hers so that the thumping of her heart hit him squarely in the ribs. He closed his eyes, wishing he had the time, the luxury of sinking into that open space. But—he opened his eyes again, looking at Eva's lids fluttering above the rough hand he had clamped over her mouth. He didn't have time, he didn't have time to coax the rigidness of her fear into something warm and welcoming. He didn't have time to show her. Someone might come, Eva might scream, the dark, dim uncertainty of his mind might overwhelm the insistence of his body. He had to get on with it, because already it was too late.

Her body was wooden, her eyes closed. Her lips trembled beneath his hand.

"All right, now, girl," Lou Henry said, using his free hand to move the folds of cloth around her legs. "Just take it easy, now." He felt her bloomers and slipped a hand under them to pull them down, fast, rough, tearing the string around the waistband. For a few moments he saw in his mind himself and Mary Nell, rolling over and over in bed together until they almost fell out. Him laughing, his hand skimming over all the soft parts of her. Rolling over and over until she was breathlessly beneath him. He tried to remember what their love had felt like. He was sure he had loved Mary Nell. But something, a feverish kind of longing that he thought Mary Nell had banished from his life forever, had seized him once more in the form of this girl beneath him now.

He looked down at Eva, rigid under his body, and took his hand away from her mouth. She didn't scream, and he smiled. Maybe she was ready for him after all, even though she struggled last time—the first time.

His dick felt like it was going to make a hole in his trousers. His hand fumbled beneath her underpants; he rubbed a finger over the downy hair over her pubic bone. He tried to slip a hand between her legs but they were clamped together.

"Open your legs," he whispered. "It ain't gon' hurt this time, Eva . . . The first time always hurt the woman, but this time . . ."

She didn't move. He had imagined things differently. But he didn't have time. Someone might come. Mary Nell had said she was stopping at the Rogers' after work, but suppose she didn't?

"Open 'em!" The words spewed out from between his gritted teeth. He slapped her across the cheek, but she didn't open her eyes. A tear slipped from under her eyelashes.

Lou Henry moved down her body and grabbed an ankle in each hand, prying the legs apart. Eva sat up then, and he immediately scooted his body up again, placing both his legs between hers and putting a hand around her throat. She fell back into the dirt that covered his barn floor, whimpering now. With his other hand he opened his pants as quickly as he could, taking out that thick bit of flesh and giving it one, two strokes, anticipating the moment it would be inside that tight warmth. Then he leaned over her, moving her underwear down her thighs and forcing her legs open wider, his fingers still encircling her neck.

Lou rubbed the head of his dick between her legs, feeling for the opening. Eva opened her eyes and looked straight at him. Or rather, she looked straight through him, the tears drying on her cheek. She didn't whimper anymore. She didn't make a sound. She seemed to not even see him.

He jerked his hand back from her throat and sat back quickly on his heels. Eva's eyes stared straight up, obviously not seeing anything. She looked dead, and he felt the giant hand of God squeeze his heart, because he realized he had just had his fingers around her very slender neck. The bruises there were being born as little red marks in the shape of his hand.

But after a moment he saw her chest move slightly and she blinked, but still lay there with her legs open in the position he'd placed them in. And with one movement he decided, sliding again between her legs and into her, pumping hard and fast. He closed his eyes against Eva's blank stare, and an intense wave of feeling washed over him, crawling up over his striving flesh and into the belly of his soul.

This is somethin', he thought, she ain't even moving, but this sho' is somethin'! The moment deceived him, because it was all emotion, all feeling and for a tiny bit of eternity, all pleasure. He began to sink into physical joy, but the sensation turned itself inside out and he found himself shaking with something other than pleasure. Was it the hand of God again, this time clamping down on his penis, cutting off his blood and his breath? He gasped for air and when he opened his eyes, he saw again the now-darkening marks on Eva's neck, as her head lolled like a worn-out doll's. He had his hands underneath her behind, but quickly put them to his own throat. The air had left his lungs and there was no way to get any more. Still, he continued to move inside her, because stopping seemed impossible. And going on seemed impossible. His whole body was alive with a fear that had cut him off from the world.

Eva lured him here, used something on him. His heart burned with terror even as his body jerked and he spilled himself inside her.

"Oh, God . . ." Lou pulled out of her body, rolling over and over on the hay, breathing as hard and fast as his lungs would let him.

He didn't know how long he lay there, heavy in heart and body. When he looked up, finally, Eva was gone.

He knew then that God remembered his name.

23

THE PORCH WAS BARELY COOLER THAN the sunny yard, but that was where the Mobley women sat, where they always sat, their hands full of something that must be done, must be sewn, beaten, shelled, crocheted, cleaned, knitted.

Mary Nell looked at her mother's hands and how the fingers had become knotted at the joints. Joy grasped folds of cloth in one hand and a needle in the other as she frowned over the patches in her husband's work shirt. In another year before this one, another year when Mary Nell had stood at her mother's knee watching such a task, the needle hand would have whipped through, it would have danced in and out of the cloth. Today it slowly tugged through and Joy sighed and puckered her brow.

"I ain't stayin' long, Mama," Mary Nell said. "Got too much to do today."

Joy nodded without lifting her head. "I know that. But you ain't never been so busy before you couldn't come to see me. Lately you been that busy."

Mary Nell silently looked down at her lap, but also tilted her head slightly toward the house, listening for any sign or any feeling of Eva.

"She ain't here," Joy said.

"What?"

"Humph." Joy lifted the fabric to her mouth and bit through the thread. "I don't know what it's about, but y'all mad about somethin'. Well," she paused and looked over at Mary Nell, "*you* is, anyway." There was a question mark at the end of Joy's voice that Mary Nell ignored.

"Where she at, then?" Mary Nell asked.

Joy shrugged, but Mary Nell could see that she was worried. "She left the house this mornin'. I was 'bout to try and go look for her myself when you came. That girl ain't really with us these days. I need to keep a close eye."

"What you mean, Mama?"

"Girl, don't you sit there and play like you don't know nothin' about Eva! You the only one that do know, I reckon. You don't want to be 'round her, but at the same time it's like you watchin' her. Like a hawk. What's the problem with you two?"

"Nothin' Mama."

"Somethin'."

Mary Nell couldn't think of a thing to say that would satisfy her mother. She thought of the last time she had seen Eva, two or three weeks ago. Mary Nell had been coming home from the Rogers' house and as she turned a bend in the road, she saw Eva far ahead, walking unsteadily. Mary Nell instinctively began walking faster to catch up with her. Eva swayed from side to side like a drunk and then she had stumbled and fell to her knees. Mary Nell broke into a trot, but stopped dead when Eva turned around to look back at her.

There seemed to be nothing left of her sister in that gaze. Mary Nell almost wished for the fear to come back and embrace them both. Anything else but this nothingness.

"Oh . . ." Mary Nell whispered, finding that her knees were buckling as well, and in a moment the rocks in the road were digging into her through her dress. The croaker sack she was carrying slipped down off her shoulder. Even as she hit the ground, she saw Eva struggling to her feet. She kept her gaze on Mary Nell for a moment and Mary Nell felt a deep ache enter her body from somewhere beyond her sister's stare. The void behind Eva's eyes reached across the red dirt and gravel of the road to her and swallowed up all the sound. The birds were silent. Mary Nell felt herself crying in that terrifying silence. How could Eva stand it? But she could, Mary Nell knew, because she didn't feel it. Maybe the evil thing that Eva had done had eaten her heart right out. Oh, yes, Mary Nell thought, in that moment it seemed as if God had died.

Mary Nell had closed her eyes to shut out her sister's face. In an instant her head exploded with sound, but not the birds or the breeze of a summer day. Instead it was heavy breathing, whispered threats, a body thrashing, the sounds of subdued terror and helplessness. "Not again, not again," she whispered. "Not Second Sunday again." A voice. Lou Henry's. *The first time it always hurt the woman. That's what I'm told. But this time . . .*

"Again . . ." Mary Nell sobbed. So Second Sunday wasn't the only time.

Oh, God. Lou's fearful whisper sent an echo through her

mind. And then again there was that emptiness, that void that had come to live behind her sister's face.

She opened her eyes. Eva wasn't there. She hadn't seen her since, and when she came home that day she had found Lou Henry sitting on the back steps, his head down, his hands hanging loose between his legs, that same deadness in his stare. She had gone past him without speaking, telling herself that she was glad. What they had done had eaten them up, taken away their joy, she thought. That was how it should be.

"I'll go look for Eva," she said now to Joy, pushing back the chair she was perched on.

Joy looked up in surprise. "I thought you had things to do, huh?"

"I'll go look for her," Mary Nell said again, starting off down the steps. She knew where Eva was.

Eva was on her knees. The day was calm, still, hot. No wind or breeze moved the trees. Her eyes looked out on a quiet day.

Yet she felt air moving quickly over her skin; her cheeks stung from the little bits of dirt and leaves and flying invisible pebbles. They came at her out of the calm, through some inner doorway that she had inadvertently opened. For weeks she had tried to be still, but all the while, the storm whipped endlessly inside her. She was tired of such happenings and the confusion that came with them.

She had left Lou Henry's barn alive. Violated, shaky, reeling, but alive. Most of all, she had been released from her fear of him. As he had driven himself into her, down again in the dirt, Eva had asked for a swift delivery from pain. She closed her eyes and saw in the darkness a small, glowing light. Even as Lou Henry sweated on top of her, his fingers creeping up around her throat, she had gazed at the light. It grew in front of her, blue and pulsating; her vision was filled with this incredible orb. The light surged up from her belly and through her whole body and when she opened her eyes, she no longer saw Lou Henry, or felt him. Just as she had asked, there was no pain, her body was numb. Death, she thought, was nothing to fear. For a long time, she existed only in the presence of this comforting energy. Eva couldn't have been more surprised when, as the light receded into the distance, she found herself back in the barn and Lou Henry huddled in the straw, mumbling to himself.

After that, she had found some rest from fear. But that journey to the other world, for Eva was convinced that that was where the light had taken her, had surely turned her into some kind of ghost. She sunk back on her heels and touched her fingers to the bruises on her throat. She knew now how ghosts felt, dead but not free, silently angry at the living. That's why Grace had to speak with the spirits, why she and Mary Nell had to see the things they saw. And like the spirits, Eva was unable to banish emotion from a body that no longer belonged to this world.

Her fear now was not of Lou Henry, but of Mary Nell, who even now she felt coming toward her, driving her own anger in front of her.

Eva sat back on the grass and gazed deep into the running water of the creek, her back to the tumbledown cabin that got closer to the water every year as the ground on the bank fell away under the relentlessness of rain and wind. "I'm a ghost," she whispered. "I don't need to be here eating up food from everybody else."

She felt the wind pick up, but the trees were still and the surface of the creek moved in its regular pattern. The storm rose from inside her body, darkening her vision.

Eva just watched. Experience had taught her that there was no running from God's gifts, whether you wanted them or not. She had the kind that came and knocked you down, right upside the head, and didn't let you run away.

As the first few drops of cold rain fell on her face, she saw the trees finally being flung about by the wind. There was always a storm, it seemed, going on somewhere. The water in the creek grew dark now and churned over the sand and rocks in angry swirls. The sky was purple.

She saw a woman struggling through the wind toward her, her head down and her dress flying in all directions. It had to be Mary Nell; she was the only other person who visited this world of theirs. Eva waited for her and clasped her arms tightly around her knees, drawing them to her chest. The rain fell thickly now and wet her skin and clothes. But she made no move toward the shelter of the cabin. It wasn't real rain; it came from one of the in-between places that only she and Mary Nell seemed to be able to step into. And maybe Grace. No, Eva thought. Grace had a place of her own.

Is it yours? Mary Nell asked, and Eva looked up at her older sister. Mary Nell stood in front of her, her wet hair whipping around her neck.

Yes, Eva said, still clasping her knees to her chest—her knees and something else. She closed her arms around soft warmth and looked down at the naked child on her lap, cradled in the V made by her bent knees. Eva was naked as well, completely exposed to Mary Nell's heated glare. *How did that happen,* Eva wondered, even as the baby boy reached for her tit. *It is mine. He's mine.*

Mary Nell screamed then, a heartbreaking sound, and Eva fell back. The baby tumbled from her arms. The day had gotten very dark, but there were flashes of light, like soft lightning, and Eva saw Mary Nell walking away.

She blinked in surprise and opened her eyes to the sun, and the still trees and Mary Nell staring down at her calmly.

"You havin' a baby," Mary Nell said blandly, as Eva tried to reorient herself to the world of the living. She looked down at her body, clothed and dry. There was no child. She sighed. She could live a lifetime without another vision.

"It's gone," Mary Nell said, "but I saw you with the child. You shook you ass at my husband and lay down with him. He gave you that child that should be mine." Her voice was a breath of winter, a cold, honed blade. Mary Nell stopped, seemingly surprised at her own words. She clamped a hand over her mouth, but the sob escaped from the bottom of her throat anyway.

"I'm not havin' a baby," Eva said. She involuntarily placed a hand over her bellybutton and felt her own lie.

"Ain't no use lyin'. That's what the vision meant." Mary Nell was silent for a few moments, as if waiting for Eva to say something, which she didn't. She didn't know what to say.

"We'll all know soon enough," Mary Nell said finally, going to sit down a short distance away, her back to the water. "And when Papa comes at you screamin' and yellin' and wantin' to know all about it, you ain't gon' say nothing. Let him think Son or Eddie Adam did it. I don't care. He can kill 'em, I don't care. You ain't gon' say nothin'. If you do everybody gon' know what kind of woman you is. And I ain't gon' have folk laughin' and pointin' at me. Pityin' *me*."

What kind of woman? Eva thought. Is I a woman? I don't

know. She curled her legs under her body, covering everything with her skirt. She tried to draw herself up into a little ball, but Mary Nell's anger pecked at her like a hungry yard hen. Even when she glanced up from her misery and saw that her sister was no longer there.

GRACE MOVED THE QUILT OVER THE bedroom doorway aside, came into the room and nodded at her mother before dropping her head and looking at the floor.

Joy sighed and reached across the table to put a hand on her husband's arm, which had become a hard bit of tensed flesh under her fingers.

"Eva?" he whispered. "Who she been with?"

"She won't say nothin' 'bout him," Grace said.

"That's all right. Can't be nobody but one of them two. That Eddie Adam. Son Jackson. One of 'em. Should have known she was gettin' too big to be playin' with them like she was still a chile." Frank's voice was low, but he thumped his hard-worked palm on the table, rattling the bowl of okra Joy had just cut.

Frank sent Grace to get Mary Nell. They were going to have

to talk about this, he said, all of them together, to see what must be done. And Mary Nell and Eva were so close, he said, Mary Nell would know who the boy was that had done this to his baby girl.

Grace began to wonder about that as the toe of her worn boots kicked up the dust in front of her going down the road. Mary Nell and Eva hadn't talked in months, not really. There was no talk about visions or seeing or anything. She had wanted to ask them about her own dreams, but the two of them were so distant, with her as well as with each other, that every time she had thought to open her mouth and try and explain about the things she saw and the voices that spoke to her out of nothingness, she had encountered Eva's dead stare and Mary Nell's barely concealed hostility. They hardly seemed like the two laughing girls she knew.

Help me. Mama, where are you?

Grace stopped, closing her eyes. Damn. The last thing she needed today was trouble of her own. She started walking, hurrying for a few more steps until she felt the sights and sounds welling up, creeping up from under the surface of her being. She stopped walking again, waiting for it.

What was it to be this time? A sweet, female voice singing strangely? The noise of a crowded marketplace? Dark, dark faces against bright clothes, laughing, calling out, weeping, despairing?

There was no way she can stop traveling on this road, the road that led to every place in her small world, to the church and out to the main road that went past the store, the post office, the cotton gin. But this road was also haunted, at least for her, and often when she walked it, as it brushed the edges of her grandmother's abandoned yard, Grace found herself listening to the sounds of a distant life, interspersed with moments of startling clarity. It all came from deep inside her own being.

Often as she walked, she pressed a fist to her chest, trying to hold it at bay, but at the same time leaning forward in an attempt to pierce the gray veil that kept her from understanding everything. If only she could get close enough she'd understand everything. But would that understanding free her, or kill her?

Her hands were balled up now and pressed against her breastbone. The voices were very faint, but underneath her hands fear assaulted her heart and weakened her knees. She could almost see the very thing that she was feeling. There it was all round and red and hot, spreading from her chest through her long legs.

From inside that fear came the sounds of a child crying and the *clank clank clank* of metal on metal. Heavy metal. A strange, incessant roaring sound.

Now, the smells. She had never had to deal with smells during one of these things before and they came at her all at once. Human sweat, surely. But there was something else, something light, but overpowering all at the same time. Something she'd never smelled before, yet which tugged at something down, down deep.

Grace opened her eyes almost instinctively. It was gray. Yes, there were those shadows that had become so familiarly frightening. She leaned forward, hands still pressed to her chest. She noticed then that she was sitting down, and she could sense someone beside her, a man whose sweaty scent washed over her and mingled with her own dank terror. The other scent was a mystery.

She leaned a little more, her head feeling achy, her eyesight blurred. Mama, she thought desperately, where are you? Help me. Grace tried to picture her mother, there back at the house, her fingers twisting and turning the knife that sliced the okra pods for their dinner. But she couldn't close her eyes to the grayness in front of her and it was that that filled her sight and mind. Her head pounded, she tried to feel the ground near her feet. Damp, sandy. Then there were her bare toes, her arms weighed down with some dragging thing that *clank clanked*.

Grace started to cry. Mama, help me.

"I'm right here," a voice answered. "I'll help you, chile. Don't worry, I'll do my best for you."

Grace closed her eyes in relief as a warm hand stroked her forehead and fingers laced through her hair, rubbing the scalp. She leaned forward this time into a pair of rock-hard arms, arms that had grown like steel from stirring and stirring wash pots filled with the dirt of white people's laziness.

"I'll do what I can," Willow said in a voice more soft than Grace had ever heard her use before. And there they were together, the two of them half sitting, half sprawling, when Grace again opened her lids to the world she knew.

Taking a deep, shaky breath, Grace said, "Is it gone?"

"What, chile? Is what gone?"

"The fog." Grace tried to untangle herself from Willow's arms and stand up, but the old woman held on tight.

"Look and see. Ain't no fog. 'Cept in your mind. What was you seein', chile? What was you seein'?"

Grace just shook her head and finally struggled to her feet, looking down at Willow sitting there in the middle of the road with her intense, eager face turned up.

"I gotta go," Grace said, slowly. "I gotta go somewhere."

"Where's that?" Willow asked, holding out her arms to Grace for help in getting up from the ground. Grace linked wrists with her and pulled her up.

Grace thought for a moment. She couldn't remember. She looked back down the road toward her house, from the direction she had come.

"Mary Nell," she said, still speaking slowly and deliberately. "I'm goin' to Mary Nell's house. 'Scuse me, Miz Willow." Grace tried to brush past, but the older woman grabbed her upper arm, holding her there in an iron grip.

"If I'd a known 'bout you, we could have worked on it," she said softly, as Grace looked at the ground. "Still can. Your mama and papa don't have to know."

"Worked on what?" Grace said, biting her lower lip. Wasn't no way she was going to allow this—this whatever it was to become the preoccupation of the local root doctor. She'd never get any peace from Willow—or from Ayo.

Willow frowned in annoyance, dropping Grace's arm.

"It don't always have to be that way. It don't always have to be bad. I meant it when I said I'd help you, if I could. I owe it to your grandmama who was my true friend and teacher my whole life to help y'all. But y'all gotta let me. No good can come of forcin'. No good can come of pretendin' it ain't there."

"I gotta go talk to Mary Nell," Grace said, turning her back.

"A thang like that ain't gon' just get up and walk off from you, even if you try to walk off from it! You gals better learn!" Willow yelled, as Grace walked around a twist of the road and was alone again. There were more things, more important things, to think about right now than her own haunted heart.

She moved on, though now and then, the road was obscured by mournful fog.

FRANK'S FEET WOULDN'T STOP MOVING across the floor. He became irritated by the scrape of his tattered-soled shoes on the wood, by the creaking of the floorboards every time he moved over the place just to the right of the table. But he couldn't stop.

Joy stroked Eva's hand as she talked, the big blue bowl in front of her. Frank stopped for a moment to look at the glistening okra rounds heaped in the bowl, and then began walking again so his eyes wouldn't move upward to Eva's face.

Not more than five minutes before he had almost hit her, his upraised hand arrested in its movement by the sight of her, limp and lost, so unlike his smiling child, that he wanted her to go, to leave them to mourn. His hand had stayed up there above his shoulder for the longest time, until he'd heard the door open and there was Grace, Mary Nell and Lou Henry coming through.

He heard one of them gasp—Mary Nell maybe. And then Eva's eyes had lifted and met his and the half-deadness on her face had frightened him into inaction. His arm came down and he began to walk back and forth across the floor at a fevered pace. Mary Nell and Lou Henry took the two rocking chairs in the corner and soon their creaking added to the tense rhythm.

"There really ain't no need for nobody to know," Joy said calmly. She stroked and stroked, and Eva's hand reddened.

"No need . . . ! Ma! How you gon' hide a thing like that?" Grace said, coming and sitting down across the table from Eva, frowning at her in concern. "Little as she is, everybody gon' know soon. How you gon' keep a thing like that from being talked about?"

"She can go 'way."

"Where?"

"To be with family. Sure. Brother's wife, Pearl, in Tuskegee. Really there ain't nobody else got to know 'cept your Aunt Pearl since Sam done gone on, rest his soul. His chillun is all away from there. She can take Eva till the baby's born and she won't tell nobody."

"And then what?" Mary Nell said quietly from the other side of the room. Eva's head jerked a little at the sound of her sister's voice, and Frank saw that though she turned in Mary Nell's direction they didn't look at each other.

"You know, don't you?" he said suddenly, stopping his trek right in front of Mary Nell.

"What you talkin' about?" Lou Henry asked before Mary Nell could respond, stopping his nervous rocking and leaning forward, his chin jutted out and his hands gripping the arms of the chair. "Know what? What you think she know?"

"And you, too." Frank turned and faced Lou Henry. "Both of you know who it is, don't you?"

"Papa . . ." Mary Nell said in what seemed to Frank to be a warning tone.

"You know who done this to her! You and Eva, y'all know everythang 'bout everythang, don't you? Least that's what you want to make us believe all this time, all these years. If anybody knows, Mary Nell, who done treated my daughter this way, dirt-ied her . . ." Frank felt the weeping coming up on him. The tears were in his chest and then his throat. He beat them back with anger. "You do."

Mary Nell just shook her head. Lou Henry leaned back in his seat, still gripping the chair arms.

Frank glared at Mary Nell and she pressed her back into the wood slats of the chair. Then he resumed his walk, coming to stand at the head of the table.

"I'm gon' talk to them boys," he ground out between his teeth. "Son Jackson and that Davidson boy."

"No you ain't," Joy said. "No point in tryin' to keep it quiet then."

The tears leapt from his throat to the backs of his eyeballs and he roared. "What you mean I ain't?! Look what they done, Joy. Our girls is . . ." He swallowed hard, letting the tears come but still managing to keep the sob that was rising from escaping his lips ". . . was well thought of, despite all that strange mess . . . ! Our girls is respectable, huh? Everythang you wanted. We done had a hard row to hoe, but we is respectable people. We ain't run-nin' around out there doin' any ole thang and sayin' it's right when it's wrong. And they done ruined it! One of them boys . . . and worse than all of that, worse than all of that, they done hurt her.

Joy . . ." he sobbed. "They done hurt our little girl. Look at her. Can't you see?"

"Papa," Grace said, standing and going to his side. She put her hand on his. "Don't."

"They done hurt her . . ."

"But we gon' take care of her, you'll see. She gon' be fine."

Frank felt his knees go out from under him and he let Grace sit him down in a chair. All these years of sweat and work and scraping, all these years of holding on by the fingernails sometimes to what was theirs and he had never felt so helpless, so tired. He hadn't protected her, hadn't known she needed protecting.

He put his forehead on the kitchen table, so that the women wouldn't see his tears. Two hands stroked his head: Grace on his right, and on his left, Eva. He recognized her slender, small fingers. She gon' be tall and slim like Grace, he thought, when she grows up.

"And then what?" Lou Henry asked impatiently. "After the baby done come?"

Frank felt Eva's fingers tighten, gripping his hair and he raised his head slightly to look at her taut face. Did she want the baby? What else was there to do anyhow?

"I wanna ask Pearl about it," Joy said softly, cautiously. She continued to stroke Eva's hand. "Before we decide anythang. And I wanna ask God about it."

"You ain't gon' go and tell that preacher," Frank snapped, his head coming up off the table like a bullet. "Then won't be no use in tryin' to keep nothin' to ourselves."

"Papa, how you gon' keep it anyway?" Grace shook her head. "Even if she do go and have the baby at Aunt Pearl's house what gon' happen then? She gon' come back here with a baby all of a sudden? She gon' stay up there in Tuskegee? We might as well get ready for the storm, 'cause it's gon' get known."

"I gotta see what Pearl thinks," Joy said again. "Maybe . . ."

"Maybe what, Mama?" Mary Nell asked tensely. "What you thinkin'?"

"We'll talk about it later," Joy said, visibly straightening. She patted Eva's hand once more and stood up. "I gotta get on with supper. Mary Nell, Henry, y'all staying ain't ya?"

"Nah, Mama, I got somethin' already started back at the house. We ain't gon' talk about this no more?"

"Not today," Joy said, picking up the bowl of okra.

"Papa?" Mary Nell stood up and cautiously approached the table, where Frank sat rigid with a kind of grief he couldn't describe. Eva's hand stroked the back of his neck.

He looked again at Mary Nell.

"You know," he whispered. "You know who done this. I can see that you do."

"No, Papa . . ."

"You know," Frank said again, and put his head back down on the kitchen table so he could let the tears flow without shame.

EDDIE ADAM'S WHOLE BODY SHOOK. Eva saw it tremble. Son Jackson stood, farther off, kicking at the creek bank in his high leather boots. His face told her that he hated her; she knew he would. Maybe she shouldn't have said anything, just lied about why she was going to Tuskegee. But she couldn't take any of it back now. And there was more to come because she could see the inevitable question forming on Eddie Adam's lips.

"So who's that baby you gon' have?"

Eva looked down at her hands in her lap as she clutched at the white linen of her apron. She had waited until Sunday, when she was looking her best, to tell them about the baby. About everything. She didn't want to be looking broken-down, tired and crazy-eyed. She needed the strength of God, or whatever was passing for God during these hard days, to find the words.

Her dress smelled of lavender water. Her hair was piled up on her head for the first time in her life. Mama had seen to it.

When she approached them both after service, she saw by their shuffling stance that there was much they already knew. Her father had gone to their houses with his anger running in front of him, and they knew. Soon everybody would know some version of the story, she suspected, no matter what her folks decided to do.

She saw the questions on the boys' lips, the pain of betrayal in their furtive glances. Who. Why. She couldn't let either of them think it was the other one.

Here, with the creek drifting by, tamed into a listless tumble by a dry summer, Eddie Adam's question hung in the hot air just above their heads.

"It was Second Sunday it happened. Of all days for somethin' that evil to grab me," she said, her voice barely audible. Eddie Adam lifted his eyes at the word "evil" and Son's head turned slightly toward her although he continued to stare straight ahead.

"I was late. Y'all remember? Everybody else done gone on and I'm comin' up the path, the back road . . . and that's when he done it . . ."

"Who, dammit? Who'd you do it with?" Son burst out, hatred flaring in his eyes as he turned his heated gaze on her.

"I couldn't . . ." Eva tried to keep her voice even and calm; she didn't know why appearing calm was so important. But it was a vain attempt. The words she spoke seemed to break into a dozen little pieces long before they left her lips, each one nicking the inside of her throat. "I cou-ld-n't . . ."

Eddie Adam stared at her and the more he looked the harder it became to say the words, to even breathe them.

"You couldn't what, Eva?" he asked softly, his eyes wide and probing.

She locked onto his gaze and took a deep breath. "I cou-ld-n't st-op him . . ." Eva pressed her lids tightly closed. ". . . st-op him. On me . . ." She could hear Eddie Adam breathing harder and opened her eyes again to find that he had crept nearer.

"Who?" His lips barely moved. "Who was it?"

"It was . . . Lou Hen-ry. He . . . he . . ." She shook her head and stopped trying to talk. She knew by Eddie Adam's expression that she didn't need to say more. It was a relief not to have to say more. She dropped her head, resting her forehead on the tops of her knees.

She felt his fingers, tentative at first, and then sure, touching her hair and cupping the curve of her skull. A kind of gentle warmth pierced the deadening sorrow that had gripped her from the moment Lou Henry Evans dragged her down in the dust. Relief surged through her; her cheeks were wet with it. She relaxed as she turned her head to one side, letting Eddie Adam's fingers slip across her damp face. He didn't hate her. He couldn't touch her like that and hate her.

But she heard the distinct sound of grass slapping against leather as Son Jackson strode away from them through the field.

"Son—" she whispered.

"Don't worry about him," Eddie Adam said. "Don't worry. Please. And don't go away. Why do you have to go away?"

"I have to. I have to."

HE COULD STILL PICTURE THE FUTURE he had laid out in his head, plank by plank. He knew, for a fact, that Eva would have married him. If he closed his eyes, he saw Eva standing at a distance on the porch of the new house he would build. It was evening. He was coming home. And her dear, dear face got bigger and bigger as he came close, until his vision was filled with nothing else.

By the time Son Jackson stopped stomping, stopped moving, Eva and Eddie Adam were nowhere near. Eva opened her mouth and said those things and he couldn't stand to hear it. So he had just left them sitting there on the grass. How quietly she had said those things. Like it was nothing at all to lay down with her own sister's husband.

Now he saw that he stood in front of his mother's house. He

went in and sat down. He sat for two days with his elbow on the kitchen table and his forehead pressed into the palm of his hand.

She came in and out, putting food in front of him or a cup of coffee. At night she threw a quilt around his shoulders, even though it was too hot for such.

"I knows what this is all about," she said on Sunday night. "That girl. If you done somethin' to her, I'll whup you."

Late Monday morning when it became clear he wasn't going to move, she put a cup of coffee in front of him and cursed at him for not feeding the chickens. By that night, she was so exhausted from doing all the chores, that she just walked by and glared at him, ate her dinner and left him there in the dark.

Tuesday night she said, as she sat across the table trying to sew by the light of the lamp, "What you think you gon' do? It's done now, boy. She gon' have that baby. Well, I guess she is . . ."

"Why him?" Son Jackson asked suddenly, startling her, although he wasn't really needing her to answer. He asked the question of some other person, God maybe, or whoever it was that arranged the bits and pieces of life in what seemed to him to be a slapdash way.

"Who?" His mama put down her needle and leaned forward. "Why who? Who you talkin' 'bout?"

He lifted his head from his palm and wondered what day it was. His mother's eyes across the table were hot with curiosity.

"I was right there," he whispered. "I was gon' give her every-thang."

"And where was you gon' get it?" His mother laughed, her hand moving the needle quickly in and out of the fabric that she held in her hands.

"Why him?" he asked again.

"Ain't no way to know why a woman might take to one and not the other. That Eddie Adam a cute little thing."

He parted his lips; they formed around Lou Henry's name, but he never uttered it. He never corrected her. Let her think it was Eddie Adam that did it; he didn't care one way or the other. Not that he cared anymore about Eva neither. Not now. He just didn't want to hear his mother crow if she heard Eva had accused her sister's husband. His mother didn't much care for Eva's people.

"She ain't no woman," he said.

"She is now," his mother answered, her needle flashing in the dim lamplight.

"She said he made her do it."

"Who? That chile?" She laughed again. "Uh-uh. She and he just did what folk do. Ain't none of y'all chilluns no more."

Son jumped up from the table. He thought about the time he saw Eva and Lou Henry dancing at the wedding, Eva swinging around and around in that breezy dress and Lou laughing.

"You think she wanted him for to do that? Eva?" he asked, almost choking on the words.

"I'm sure I don't know. Who knows? Some gals get awful loose when they get round that age. Just 'bout lose they minds, some of 'em. Maybe she say he forced her 'cause she didn't want nobody to know she loose like that. 'Specially with that high and mighty family of her'n. They 'bout to die over this, I reckon." She laughed again, softly, and shook her head. "Ain't nobody gon' let her in no school with a baby, let alone teach in one. Ooh, I bet Joy 'bout to fall down and die over this."

"I gotta know."

"Know what? What mo' you wanna know 'bout it? What difference do it make now anyhow? You gon' marry a girl that got somebody else's baby? I mean you could if you want, I ain't gon' stop you. But is that what you want, lookin' at that chile for the rest of your life and knowin' it ain't yours and knowin' that maybe she like Eddie Adam and still like him and no tellin' what they doin' when you ain't lookin'? Naw, I can't see you doin' that. How come they ain't gon' get married anyway?"

"I gotta know if what she say is true."

"Ain't no way to know."

"I gotta know."

"Then Lord help you, son," his mother said, bending her head again to her work.

MARY NELL WONDERED IF THIS WAS what Lou Henry wanted, for her to hear this conversation.

Son Jackson's straight-leg stride up to their house told her that something was about to happen. He had barely glanced at her when he came to the door and when he and her husband had gone out onto the porch and Son had suggested a trip to the barn, Lou Henry had said, no, right here was just fine. And Lou must have known what Son wanted to ask about and he must have known she would hear everything they said as she stood there sweeping the floor of their bedroom, hear all their words echo throughout the little house. He wasn't just talking about all that to cool Son Jackson's heated stares; he was talking to her about it. For the first time. And she leaned on her broom and stood near the open window.

"I'm just gon' ask you straight out, Mister Evans. I knows I'm just a boy to you, just a chile." Mary Nell saw Son drawing up his long, awkward body as tall as possible as he said this.

"Go on, then," Lou Henry said. He stood at the top of the steps with his back to both Son and the house and leaned against the support post.

"It's Eva. She say she gon' . . . have a chile. And she say she gon' have a chile 'cause of you. And I got to know if that's true." Son let out a sigh at the end of this speech. Mary Nell thought maybe it was more words than she had ever heard him speak at once.

"I'm married," Lou said, quietly. His body was very relaxed; he expressed no surprise at Son's questions. "What you tryin' to say?"

"It ain't what I say, Mister Evans. It what she say. And I gots to ask you if that is true."

"Nah, boy! What I want with that girl? Just 'cause she come 'round here all the time shakin' her rump at me don't mean I'm gon' run after her." Lou Henry laughed. He caught Mary Nell's eye through the bedroom window. "Yeah, she come 'round all the time, at least she used to. But I'm a married man and I tole her she ought to be shame, comin' up to her sister's husband like that. So I guess if she tell you it was me, she just wishin'!"

Son didn't say anything else for a moment. He just stood there with his arms straight down beside his body, a hat in one hand and the other hand clenched tight. When Mary Nell saw Son's face, she knew Lou Henry was in danger from this boy. He looked at the back of Lou Henry's head for a moment and then moved down the steps and around the older man, so that he stood right in front of him. She dropped the broom with a clatter and Lou

Henry turned his head slightly in her direction, but Son didn't move a muscle as he asked his question again.

"Did you lay down with her? Did you . . . force her like she said?"

"Boy, you better get away from outta my face!" Lou Henry's tone had taken on a kind of tense nervousness. The laughter had left his voice. "I done tole you. That girl done got you thinkin' crazy. She came at me, you hear?"

"But did you . . ."

"I ain't got time for this!" Lou Henry met Mary Nell's eyes again for just a moment where she stood at the window, before striding over and opening the door. She heard him stomping all the way through the house and out the back.

Mary Nell swallowed hard, picking up the broom again. She swirled the dust around with it, watching the sun illuminate the dancing dirt. She willed her heartbeat to slow down. She watched the dust instead of the picture show in her brain of Eva and Lou Henry, maybe in this very room, in that bed that she had just swept under on those sheets she had washed.

Maybe Second Sunday wasn't the first time. She knew it hadn't been the last. Eva would have come when Mary Nell was gone somewhere and she would have maybe asked Lou Henry where Mary Nell was even as she pressed herself against him. And he, dirty dog, he would have laid her there and spread her legs and drove his body into hers while she gasped and whispered moans to him. Her little sister. She thought about their once-shared dreams and felt empty.

She couldn't stay in the bedroom. She flung the broom down and left, glancing out the window as she walked. Son Jackson sat on the front steps.

He was still there an hour later, his head bent. Mary Nell came out on the porch and looked down at the soft, smooth, almost baby skin at the back of his neck and the glint of tears on the bit of cheek that was visible to her.

"Go on home, now," she said, her voice already pleading before she could even get the words out. "Eva done made her mistake and she the one that gotta pay for it. Not you. Not me. You go on home, fo' yo' mama get worried."

She went back in the house to start dinner, wondering what she was to do about Lou Henry. When she looked out at the front again, she saw stumbling footprints in the dust of her neatly swept yard, as if the poor boy had lost his balance.

29

WITH HIS LEGS INVISIBLE BEHIND THE almost waist-high cotton plants, Frank seemed to glide over the rows, his torso turning this way and that way. Grace watched as the leaves, a thousand long, green hands, caressed him.

When he was upset or bothered, her father did one of three things. This was one. He walked in the fields. He looked at what grew there and if nothing was growing there at the time, he looked at the bare ground. If that didn't satisfy him, he took down his shotgun, called his speckled-coated bird dogs and disappeared into the woods. Sometimes he came back with something for the pot. Rabbit or coon, quail or squirrel. If that didn't do it, he went out to the barn and picked up his favorite pole and put on a certain pair of mud-encrusted boots and they knew he was going down to the creek to fish. Often he stayed there until the stars appeared.

He had been walking a lot since Eva's news. Grace had never seen him walk so much. Otherwise he might have killed somebody. She saw her mother start every time he took down that gun these days and he had to say, "Goin' huntin'." And still Grace wasn't sure her mother was convinced he wasn't hunting boys. He said it's one of them. One of the two. Son or Eddie Adam.

Grace leaned a little further over the windowsill.

Frank had stomped out to the far end of the field, his ruddy skin gleaming in the sun, until he came to the edge where the cotton rows gave way to pine. She knew he wasn't looking for boll weevils in the crop; he slipped underneath the pine boughs and she couldn't see him anymore.

"Why don't you just tell them who it was fo' sho?" she asked quietly, still straining her eyes to see her father moving through the trees. "You 'bout to drive Papa mad and peoples do awful things when they go wrong in the head." She turned around. Eva didn't seem to be listening. Eva was looking at Mary Nell, who sat cross-legged on the bed with her. Grace thought she saw Mary Nell's lips moving for a moment. But no, they weren't. She was just sitting there, seemingly undisturbed by either Grace's question or Eva's silence.

"Leave her alone," Mary Nell said. "Her keepin' quiet is 'bout the only thing that's saving them boys."

"Well," Grace said. "I guess you right 'bout that. He's mighty troubled. I ain't never seen Papa walk about so."

"Sometime it ain't good to be talkin' 'bout everythang."

Grace laughed. "What? We talkin' 'bout Eva, ain't we? Who used to open her mouth about every little thing that went through her mind? Y'all and them visions. Ghosts and blood . . ."

Grace's voice faded. A small whisper from deep inside her killed her smile. The voice gave her no words, just a fearful murmur.

No, she remembered. It wasn't good to tell everything. Her sisters' faces told her they were haunted, just as she was, though by what she couldn't fathom. Maybe by other people's nightmares. She was grateful for that at least, that she didn't have their gift for looking into the future and seeing horrors to come. She only had her own very private pit of confusion. Very narrow and dark, with the sides so close they scraped her shoulders as she turned around inside of it. And if her two little sisters saw anything about her future, they weren't telling her. They seemed to have lost the desire to speak of such things. Or maybe lost the gift altogether.

They sat together without touching, these two who had once practically lived in each other's pockets.

"Well, whoever it is, he should be askin' you to get married," Grace said now. Mary Nell looked startled. Eva didn't answer. Grace sighed and shrugged. Eva had made up her mind not to tell, so they might as well learn to live with it, she supposed.

Eva woke up chewing on the pillow, the pillowcase soaked with spit. She lay there dazed. Daytime was hard, with Papa scowling and Mama tiptoeing around him. With Mary Nell's absences and silences. With Grace growing more haggard by the day. And Eva, having become her own jailer, reluctant to venture beyond the front yard.

But nighttime was worse. When she could no longer avoid sleep, Mary Nell came and talked to her in her dreams. She came and covered Eva with her anger. Eva was the root of all her problems. Her problems with Lou, her childlessness, her struggle to lead a Godfearing, moral life.

Every night, in her dreams, Eva sat with Mary Nell on the grass beside Johnson Creek, the old slave cabin behind them, the woods marching close to the shore.

Who'd a guessed? Mary Nell would say. *You always was so sweet, weren't you? Who'd a known the devil was livin' in that lil' body of yours?*

Sometimes, Lou Henry hung around on the edge of things, listening, nodding the way the deacons in church did when the preacher pressed home some moral truth. Sometimes Son Jackson or Eddie Adam. Often it would be the three of them—Grace, Mary Nell, Eva—sitting together. And Grace would speak in tongues and change shapes. Mary Nell ignored Grace and Eva had no words to comfort her. Her tongue always seemed to rot in her mouth. She always had a strong urge to jump up and run into the trees to escape. But she couldn't move.

Or sometimes Mary Nell sat across from Eva on the grass crying, her arms cradled as if holding a baby that wasn't there and Eva felt empty and sad beyond measure as she watched. And nothing was said in those dreams. Grace would be there, but on the bridge or the opposite bank, and always moving away, her body tense as if she was trying to decide whether to run.

Eva and her mother walked into the house at the same time, Eva coming in the back after hanging up wet clothes, and Joy moving slowly through the front door, holding an envelope in one hand and a letter in the other. She sat down at the kitchen table without taking off her hat, her head bent over the words on the paper, the sweat gleaming on the back of her neck. Her lips moved painfully slow and silently. Eva thought about her dream last night when she sat across from Mary Nell on the grass with her own mouth moving and nothing coming out.

"Well, she say it's fine if you come," Joy said, letting the letter fall on the table and lifting one hand to whip off the straw hat. "Pearl say it's fine. She may even know somebody for the chile."

Eva put down the clothes basket beside the back door.

"You know, somebody to take the chile in," Joy continued, looking down at the table. "That's what the best thing is, ain't it?"

Eva hadn't thought about it. Her mind and soul were filled with Mary Nell's venomous hiss. She was afraid to sleep or even close her eyes. With the baby gone, maybe she wouldn't have to endure it.

"I want to go right now," Eva said clearly. Joy's head swung up jerkily to look at Eva.

"You ain't gotta do that, baby," she said. "I believe we got quite some time before . . ."

"I want to leave. Can Aunt Pearl take me now?"

"I'm sho she will," Joy whispered. "I gotta write her back though and say when you'll be coming."

Eva nodded slowly. "Yes," she said. "Write her back."

More than two weeks passed before another letter arrived from Tuskegee, two weeks of cruel dreams and the growing thought that maybe Eva wouldn't have to go to Aunt Pearl's at all.

"I can't believe you came here," Willow said as she scooped some sweet-smelling salve into a glass jar. She put the jar down in front of her and opened a drawer full of canning lids.

"I couldn't have you coming to my back door now, could I?" her customer answered.

Willow smiled and the woman shifted from one foot to the other and continually lifted her shoes to examine the soles. They stood in Willow's kitchen, not looking at each other.

"Now Miz Ward, if there's one thing I know, it's how to be quiet. Come and go without nobody seein' me."

"Well . . . I know, Willow." Mrs. Ward's shoulders relaxed from their hunched-up position and she let out a sigh. "It's not like I'm coming down here to get one of your love potions or something." She gave a thin, little laugh that did nothing to animate her face. "It's just something for my husband's sore shoulders. Yours is better than store-bought."

"Fresher," Willow said, nodding.

"It's just that a lot of people might not understand about me coming down here. I tried to send Mary Nell last night, but she said she had to get home. She just about snapped at me. I was so surprised, I let her leave without another word."

"Did she, now?" Willow paused, wondering, trying to think of the last time she'd seen Mary Nell. A good while. Yes, it had been a good while. Hadn't seen her or Eva either. Not since news of the baby.

"Now normally I wouldn't let that kind of thing pass, but . . ." Mrs. Ward smoothed a stray gray-blonde hair back under her hat. "I was just so surprised and then she swooped out the door . . ."

"Maybe she ain't feelin' well," Willow offered.

"Well, I hope she's all right. I've got to go to Montgomery tomorrow and I simply can't take the children. So she'd better be all right."

Willow turned away to find a bag for Mrs. Ward's jar, swiveling her head quickly to hide her grimace. She thought maybe next time this white woman came to her for something, she would be out of whatever it was. But then again, she could charge her double what colored folk paid.

"There . . . you just rub this into the shoulders good and hard till your hands is hot," Willow said, handing Mrs. Ward a small flour sack with the jar inside. "Every night. Twice the day, if you can."

"Fine." Mrs. Ward opened her little purse and placed a stack of coins on the table between them. "Next time I'll be sure to send Mary Nell."

"You do that," Willow said, opening the front door and almost jumping out of her skin to see Eva standing there, Eva whom she was just thinking about not five minutes before.

Eva shrunk away a little, standing quickly aside when she saw Mrs. Ward.

"You're Mary Nell's sister, aren't you?" Mrs. Ward asked.

"Yes, ma'am," Eva said, her eyes on the floor.

"Tell me, is she feeling all right? Has she been ill?"

"I don't know, ma'am."

Mrs. Ward let out a huge put-upon sigh. "You tell her I can't possibly be without her tomorrow." She stepped gingerly down the front steps. "Thank you, Willow!"

Willow nodded and waved with one hand and then clasped Eva's arm with the other, pulling her gently forward into the house.

"I thought you might come some time or the other," she said. "You or Mary Nell or both y'all."

Eva wasn't saying anything. The sound of her breathing filled the tiny kitchen. Dusk was coming and the crickets were starting up and those were the only things Willow could hear, that insect chirping and the rasp of air going in and out of the girl's lungs.

Willow put more wood in the stove and made sure there was

water in her kettle. She scanned the shelf above the stove for a certain jar holding a certain blend of leaves. Then she pulled a chair out for Eva and sat across from her.

Eddie Adam appeared at the back door, his eyes widening as he saw Eva sitting there. He took a step inside the door, and then one back when he met Willow's eyes.

"Where your brother at?" she asked him quietly. He shrugged. "Y'all go find somethin' to do for a while," Willow said. Eddie Adam tried to catch Eva's eye but she was looking down at her hands on the tabletop. Willow frowned at him and he scurried away.

Again, just silence and then the sound of water gathering heat in the kettle.

"It weren't him," Eva said, lifting her chin a moment to let her eyes dart toward the doorway where Eddie Adam had just been standing.

"I know that," Willow said.

"I mean, Papa came over here and probably scared all y'all, but I just want you to know Eddie Adam ain't done nothin'." Eva stared at the back door.

"I know, chile." Willow got up and found a tin cup. She emptied a few dried leaves into it from the jar on the shelf.

"He would never do this to me," Eva said.

"I know'd who done it."

Willow could feel the girl's eyes on her, even as she stood at the stove, her back to the table. She touched a finger quickly to the side of the kettle, which was only just warm.

"I shoulda listened to you, I guess. I shoulda forgot 'bout what everybody said 'bout you and the hoodoo." Eva's voice softened to just a wisp of sound. "But maybe you can help me now."

"I can't do nothin' now but advise you. You take that baby God done gave you and love it. Find peace with that. That's all you can do. You young. What is you now? Thirteen?" Willow paused, murmuring to herself. "Seem like I done just drew you out the womb, and here you are . . . Anyways," she said louder, "you got a lot of years to go, and you gon' be just fine."

"You've helped people befo'," Eva continued, as if she hadn't heard what Willow said. "I know you have."

The old woman sighed. She stirred the dry leaves with her finger. They were just something to calm the rapid hammering of the girl's heart, a sound that Willow thought she could almost hear in this dead-still room. She didn't have the cure the girl was looking for, the leaves that you brewed to poison the womb. She never kept those.

"I heard my mama say one time that you didn't do it no mo' since that time that girl died, but you still know how, don't you? Don't make it so strong this time, and I'm sho I'll be all right." Eva's voice was starting to break in half.

Willow closed her eyes. That evil story would never die, that story of how she'd killed someone. No matter how many times she said it was untrue, it was still hanging around on the edges of people's conversations. After all this time. Because everybody knew the girl had come to her looking for a way out. Clara. Sweet, that child. Just about the same age as Eva was now.

"I can pay . . . well, I don't know how much you want," Eva said. "But I have some . . ." And then came the sound of cloth rustling and the dull clunk of two, three . . . four coins against the old wood table.

Clara had come to the back door that day. It was cold in a

way that only happened in spring, and the girl had stood shivering in the rain. She had no money and she didn't believe Willow when she said she didn't do that kind of thing. Everybody knew root doctors did that, Clara said. It's 'cause I can't pay. Willow remembered her bitter expression as she slipped and slid out of the muddy yard.

"I know it ain't enough, but I can give you some more by and by, Miz Willow. I promise." Eva had soft tears in her voice now. Willow again felt the side of the kettle and decided that it was warm enough. She poured water over the leaves in the cup and reached over to the shelf for the syrup can, feeling the heat from the stove warming her belly.

"I'm outta real sugar," Willow said.

"Miz Willow?"

Hours after Clara left someone came pounding on the door. The rain had not stopped. Willow had pulled on her oilskin and hat and followed a frightened boy-child through the wet woods to where his sister lay in a blood-soaked bed.

The short, whispered lie that came with the dawn of the next day was that Willow had given Clara something and then she died. Somehow no one mentioned the fire poker that the girl had used. Like them stories you used to hear about soldiers falling on their own spears. The compresses Willow used to try to stop the river of blood came hours too late. And the girl's mama stood there, her face hard as rock. Wasn't our fault, she said. That's what she kept saying even as Willow cleaned the blood away, wrapped two dead children in clean sheets.

They were all dead now. All of them in that room, except Willow. But the story of how she'd killed Clara with one touch of her hand was very much alive.

She stirred the leaves in the cup. Then she turned from the stove and set the cup down in front of a trembling Eva.

"Is that it?" Eva whispered, her hand folding and unfolding the white handkerchief she had knotted around her money. The four coins on the table shimmered in the light of the dying day.

"It's just tea, chile. Like I said, I can't help you with what you want. But if you want some peace, if you want to feel clean again, that I can help you do."

Eva stared at the cup of tea. Willow heard a noise and turned her head slightly to see the boys hanging just outside the back door. She leaned forward and took the girl's limp hand.

"All I'm sayin' is, you got to get clean on the inside, whatever else you do or whatever tribulation come down on you. If you healed inside then they can't hurt you no mo'. I can help you with that. But that baby you carryin' 'round with you is here to stay."

The fingers underneath Willow's rough palm curled into a little ball and she could see Eva fighting the urge to cry.

"You hear me girl?" Willow jiggled Eva's hand a little, frustrated. "You can get through this storm. Let me help you."

Eva shook her head, standing up suddenly and knocking her chair over with a clatter. She leaned over and scraped the coins off the table and began fumbling with her handkerchief, finally getting them tied back inside.

"This what you do, Eva," Willow said, standing up, too, sensing that she had already lost this one, but not willing to just let her go out into the encroaching night alone and hopeless. "Next time you see the sky cloudin' up like it gon' storm, like a tornado comin' or somethin', you come right over here. The very next time, you hear?"

She couldn't tell if Eva was listening to her or not. The girl was turning in every direction as she stuffed the handkerchief back down in the front of her dress.

But then she said, "Too late now, Miz Willow. Some kinds of dirt don't never come off."

Willow closed her eyes, shaking her head and dropping her chin. She heard the front screen door squeak closed.

"I thought she wasn't gon' never leave, Grandmama," Clay said in an annoyed voice. "When we gon' eat?"

But she stood there a long time, trying to think of something to do. After what seemed like a long time she felt a hand on her arm. Eddie Adam stood beside her looking sorrowful, looking like a child without a mother, which was what he was, really. All his bruised feelings were there in his face, all of his love for Eva and his complete confusion about what he was to her now.

"She a good chile," Willow said. "A good chile havin' a bad time. That's all."

Eddie Adam nodded. Clay sat at the table sniffing at the abandoned cup of tea.

"In a minute, boy!" she said to him. "You ate this mornin'. It ain't like you gon' die!"

30

November 1921

MARY NELL SLEPT AS FAR AWAY from Lou Henry as possible. She felt his heaviness in the bed, even as she dug deep into her dream, sitting there at the table with Willow and Eva, the cup of tea cooling and Eva's stack of coins gleaming against the rough wood. She saw Eva tie the coins into her handkerchief, and then the two of them were together again on the grass bank by the creek and Eva was crying, looking down at her empty arms. Mary Nell's breath became a wind that reached all the way into the highest pine branches; the crowns of the trees whipped around on fragile bark-covered necks and a storm cloud rose up behind them. It looked like a tornado and Mary Nell watched the tops of the trees snap off and splinter as they hit the ground.

But there was no sound. There was never any sound, except the sound of breathing, hers loud and windy and Eva's broken by heavy grief.

So you gon' be goin' to Tuskegee for sho, Mary Nell tried to say. *To Aunt Pearl.* She couldn't hear her own words. She tried to inch a little closer to Eva, who sat with her head bent, but her body didn't move, either. She had only her thoughts and Eva's. She felt a moment of tension in her sister's body and then a release, an acknowledgment of the inevitable. She was going to Tuskegee and coming back with empty arms.

The dream exhausted her. When Lou Henry got up to go out in the morning, she didn't move from the bed. She felt him looking at her and she kept her eyes closed and her head turned to the wall. He dragged his feet as he left, pausing briefly beside the cold stove. In better days, Mary Nell would already be up and in there, making sure he had something in him for the long day. But today he left empty.

That's all right, Mary Nell thought. Won't hurt him to be hungry for a minute. Hunger might be good for him. Get some God in him. Didn't Jesus fast for forty days, the preacher said, and the devil came and Jesus was able to turn away from evil?

The devil had been having a good time in Johnson Creek lately, she thought. Never thought he'd get Eva, as much as she seemed to love the Lord. Of course Eva was never as watchful as Mary Nell about these things. If it had been left up to that girl, Willow would have taken them off and made witches out of them long ago. Eva never really understood that was against Jesus. So maybe she'd had the devil in her all this time, just lying around inside of her, waiting to come out.

Mary Nell would make sure Eva understood what she'd done.

Destroyed a good-man-in-the-making. Did she know that? Surely she knew that's what she'd done.

The next day, she went to help Eva pack.

"What you go bother Willow for? I know you went over there." Mary Nell stood for a moment holding Eva's good nightgown, the one she had given her last year that was already too short. She ran a finger over the crocheted lace edging, remembering sitting in her chair night after night with the thread flashing in and out of her hook. And then having to unravel it when it wasn't right. Which was often. She hated to crochet. But that's what ladies did, of course. They did needlework of all kinds, made quilts and embroidered and such. Her mother was fair with a needle, and Grace and Eva were good at it. They could talk and work at the same time. They would sit there on the front porch with their baskets of cloth and thread at their feet and rock back and forth with the needles shimmering in the sunlight. The white ladies who sat in Mrs. Ward's parlor would sometimes sew and drink honey-scented tea from thin, white cups ringed with delicate flowers. Mrs. Ward just did it for show. Half the stuff she owned with lace or embroidery on it had been handed down to her or it had been made by some colored woman somewhere. Mary Nell hated that kind of work. Eva was the only person she had ever made anything for just because she wanted to.

Mary Nell folded the nightgown into a small square and put it at the bottom of the small trunk that Eva was taking.

"I know Willow didn't give you nothin'."

"No," Eva said.

Mary Nell tried to imagine what that would have been like, a child not yet formed coming out and dying. She went over to Eva and put her hand against the belly. Her sister's flesh seemed to shrink away. Mary Nell felt nothing else except the thin cotton of Eva's blouse and her rigid muscles underneath. Mary Nell untucked Eva's blouse from her skirt waistband, which she inched down a bit, and pressed her fingers, just the index and middle fingers, against the warm skin just under the navel. Eva stood mutely watching. Mary Nell waited for movement that never came. But when she closed her eyes she saw a shape form against the black backdrop of her inner eyelids, something small and floating. Eva brushed the hand away with a soft, choked cry and Mary Nell stood with her fingers cupped and her eyes closed.

She didn't know how long she stood there trying to catch that floating figure, but she couldn't. When she opened her eyes again, Eva had tucked her blouse back in and was moving to close the suitcase.

"There you were—running to Willow, hopin' to get rid of it, kill it," Mary Nell said quietly. "And here I am with this barren belly, praying every day of my natural, Christian life for what you got by sinnin'." She turned her head and her whole body away from Eva, although she didn't know why she bothered. It wasn't as if she could hide her sad anger. Not from Eva, of all people. And she didn't want to anyway. "God got strange ways sometime. Nothin' a humble person can understand."

She heard Eva sigh, she heard the deep mourning in it. She knew that saying those hurtful things to Eva wouldn't make anything better, because her anger was a part of everything they felt, it mingled with Eva's fear and Eva's self-loathing. The force of betrayal had pushed her and Eva into some other realm, where they only existed to make pain and grow pain. She didn't know how to stop it, to step out and live in the world again.

But she knew that she deserved something out of all this. She had been good and done everything right. She had put everything in place, everything needed to be decent and respectable. In Johnson Creek, there was just as much sorrow as love floating around and you had to build yourself a safe place— in your mind and heart as well as on your own piece of ground if you could. You had to work hard to be happy and decent, because the world worked just as hard to keep you down in the dirt.

She deserved something better than this, her sister, the person she loved best, walking around carrying her husband's baby.

"I'm sorry," Eva said.

"You oughta be," Mary Nell said.

When they came out of the bedroom after packing, they found Joy at the stove stirring a pot and Frank nowhere to be found.

"He went up to the store to fetch some ice," Joy said. "All of a sudden, he wanted ice cream. He say he got to send his baby girl off with somethin' sweet on her lips. I gotta make this custard real quick."

But by the time the sun had set, the ice cream remained mostly uneaten. Mary Nell had gone home and the rest of them sat on the back porch with their bowls in their hands. Eva held hers between her knees, cradled in the folds of her dress. The syrup bucket, half full of melted ice cream custard, floated serenely in a tub of salty water. Papa had turned the bucket himself. Usually they all took turns turning, but he had pushed them away this time, spinning the bucket in the tub of ice without stopping to rest. Mary Nell had left before it was done.

Somehow, now, with the evening coming up fast and the morning coming up just that much faster after that, all Eva could think about was getting on that train and going off and how the next time she saw them all, maybe she would have had the baby. What would she do then? Nobody had talked about what she would do then. Frank had nothing much to say lately and her mother seemed always to be immersed in thought. Eva could almost see Joy's mind working things out, planning what to say to people when Eva came home, whether she came home with that baby or not. And however badly things were between her and Mary Nell now, the baby in her arms would make them all the more worse.

She tried to picture the baby sucking on her breast, but she couldn't. Ahead of her, the emptiness that she had already become too accustomed to just grew.

She tried to remember what she was before. She closed her eyes and tried to picture herself on the baseball field, running, running, running around the bases. She tried to see herself sitting in the dying light after supper, leaning her head against her mother's knee as she told her about the day. She tried to remember the feeling of a fishing pole in her hands and only succeeded in letting go of the bowl, sending it crashing to the porch, sticky liquid ice cream splattering everywhere.

"All right," her father said, as she opened her eyes. "That's all right."

She looked at him, crying. She thought, as he looked back, that he was crying too. But there wasn't time to tell, because he was the one who got up and picked up the bowl and took it inside. He came back with a dish rag and wiped her sticky hands, dabbed at the ice cream on her dress. Not once did he look up at her, so she couldn't tell if he was crying or not.

"That's all right," he said again.

It was Frank who drove her to Union Springs and sat on the platform with her waiting for the train to Montgomery. It was late.

"Hope it don't get all backed up. Your auntie will be waitin'." He sat down on a bench nearby, and Eva sat down next to him. He took a red tin of tobacco out of his shirt pocket and a packet of the thin papers he used to roll cigarettes. He finished four before the train came, never saying anything, not looking at Eva, just pinching the tobacco into the paper and rolling, rolling, rolling, licking it at the appropriate moments to make the paper stick together.

But after watching her mount the metal steps to the car, he handed her the small sack her mother had packed with food and he tried to smile a little.

She smiled back. Someone else was on the steps behind her, trying to get on, so she gave her father a little wave and turned away.

"You take the Chehaw train after Montgomery, remember?!" Frank called and she nodded at him out of the window. The car was packed and some people sat on the floor. After a sluggish start, the train moved quickly away from the station. Her father stood on the platform and she watched until he was gone. Rather, until she was gone.

Gone off to become somebody's mother.

31

March 1922

FOUR MONTHS AFTER EVA LEFT, an envelope with money and a note addressed to Grace arrived in Johnson Creek: "Come, you are needed."

Aunt Pearl didn't say more, but they all assumed Eva's time was near. Mary Nell watched Grace pack, just as she had watched Eva.

"Shoulda sent for us both, I think," said Grace, glancing at Mary Nell. "But y'all still mad I guess."

Mary Nell had already decided to go. She had told no one except the Wards, and only because they were going to have to look after their own children for a while.

Grace had been gone two days when Mary Nell fished money out of the coffee can under the bed and stuffed as many things as she could into a cotton sack. She ironed her Sunday dress and wore it with her best shoes. She made sure her gloves were clean and her hat free of dust. She left a note for Lou Henry to find when he came home from wherever he went to these days.

Then she waited on her porch for Willie Lane to pass by on his way to Union Springs like he did every Thursday, and asked for a ride. She wasn't sure exactly why she had to be there when Eva had the baby, she just knew she couldn't stay away.

Aunt Pearl didn't seem surprised to see Mary Nell standing at her front door in Tuskegee. Mary Nell barely said hello and brushed past her into the house, hauling her sack behind her.

She didn't ask about Eva. Mary Nell knew her time was close, maybe even tonight. In the front of the narrow hall, she took off her hat as a door opened near the other end. Grace came out and stood with a hand braced on either side of the wall. From her cold glare, Mary Nell knew Eva had been talking, spreading shame.

Aunt Pearl closed the front door and came toward Mary Nell, smiling. The smile stayed on her face even as the silence in the house stretched before them.

"Don't you got a husband to look after?" Grace said, biting the words out through clenched teeth.

"Eva's my sister, too," said Mary Nell quickly. She tugged off the gloves. "She might need me."

"You know'd I was here with her," Grace said. "Me and Aunt Pearl, too. You just makin' things crowded."

"You don't expect me to go back now, do ya? I spent a lot of money on that train ticket so I could be here."

"What did Mama say?"

"She don't know."

Grace's face twisted in a grimace. "Now you know you can't

just go off somewhere and not tell nobody. She gon' make herself sick worryin' 'bout you and Eva, too."

"Had to come," Mary Nell said, "while I still had the backbone for it."

Grace put her hands on her hips. "Now what you got to be afraid of?"

Aunt Pearl just looked from one to the other. Eva let out a whimper from behind one of the closed doors. Then she cried out and Grace turned to go into the bedroom.

"Just in time, I see," she said, as she pushed open the door. "Why you here, Mary Nell?"

Mary Nell pressed her palms on her cheeks and, ignoring the question, asked Aunt Pearl where she might sleep.

"I'm out of beds; you can sleep with me," Aunt Pearl said, turning and slowly gliding down the hall and opening the door immediately to the left. Without another look at Grace, Mary Nell grabbed the limp neck of the sack and followed her.

If Aunt Pearl thought it was strange that Mary Nell had come all this way and made all that fuss and then not lifted a finger to help, she said nothing about it.

Mary Nell listened to Eva whimpering in the next room while she got ready for bed.

She opened up the sack and took out the nightgown. Carrying the water pitcher to the kitchen, telling herself she didn't really hear the sounds going on in Eva's room and that it was not time to go in yet, she pumped her own water at the kitchen sink and brought it back to the bedroom. She washed her face and feet and slipped on the gown. She said a prayer. She put it in the Lord's hands.

God does work in mysterious ways, Mary Nell thought, as

she knelt by the bed. The mind of God was not for the understanding of men. She prayed that she would know what was
right, what to do to make her pain go away. She had to be able
to look at Eva and not feel pain.

When the noises in the other bedroom stopped, she dug
down in her bag and pulled out the small quilt she had brought
with her and went down the hall.

"Mary Nell . . ." Grace said, when she came into the room.
Mary Nell ignored her and Aunt Pearl and paused to glance at
Eva's sweaty face before coming to stand at the bedside.

"It's a boy ain't it?" she said, and not waiting for an answer,
swept back the little blanket he was wrapped in. Then she lifted
him out, leaving the blanket behind, leaving Eva's arms reaching
into the hot air grasping at nothing. Grace stood up abruptly,
looking at Mary Nell standing there with the baby's legs dangling. But before she could move, Mary Nell was talking softly
to the little boy, wrapping him in a blue-patterned quilt, laughing
gently.

"Didn't I ask the Lord for a chile?" Mary Nell said quietly
and Grace whispered, "No . . . Mary Nell . . ." Aunt Pearl was
rooted to her spot, her eyes wide.

Oh, yes, Mary Nell thought. Here was a child, right in her
arms, still wrinkled by the womb, eyes still closed to the world.
The Lord had provided a child whose veins would surge with the
blood of her family and the blood of her husband. Through the
body of the one who had been the other half of herself, God had
spoken and in such a clear voice that there could be no mistake.

She spun around the room with the baby in her arms, and he
began to cry. When she turned back to Eva, her eyes sparkled.

"God is wise," she said as she laid him in her little sister's arms. Grace let out a sigh, letting her shoulders sag. Aunt Pearl sat down, fanning herself with the hem of her apron.

Mary Nell sat on the edge of the bed, watching the child nudge Eva's nipple. Eva and Lou Henry had been God's instruments. God had known about the sins to come, the treachery lying deep in their hearts, and had used that to bring Mary Nell something good.

32

EVA WOKE UP—SUDDENLY, FEARFULLY.

The soft, baby breaths that had brushed coolly against the skin covering her collarbone had stopped.

The child had claimed the space under her chin immediately after birth. He had settled in there, sighing and gurgling and Eva had been ashamed that she loved him. She wanted him gone, but here he was with his little fist balled up against her breast and his face with its compacted features pressed against her. He had opened his otherworldly eyes and looked at her without seeing, blinking in the dimness, and she knew it immediately, intimately, this odd mingling of love and loathing. He was the most important event in her life, and he had stolen her life away.

But now she no longer felt that small, warm weight on her

chest. She placed her hand there and her fingers closed around the front of her nightgown.

She thought for a moment that she was inside one of her dreams. Just for a moment she thought that. But the feeling quickly left her. She sat up in bed. *The baby gone.* That silent sentence flew around her brain like a caged bird. *The baby gone. The baby gone.*

And the words were no longer silent. She repeated them aloud as her feet touched the floor beside the bed. "The baby gone. Mary Nell and the baby gone."

Every time she repeated it, she felt them, moving away from her, faint presences amid all the other presences out there. They were far away now. Mary Nell was trying to quiet the little boy. Eva felt their distress. Mary Nell, unfocused, worried, was holding the child in the most tender way, but Eva's son was hungry. He'd only had a taste of the titty. He was disturbed not to be lying on the warmth of his mother, speaking to her through her skin.

His small, helpless fear made Eva gasp a little, the air escaping her throat almost coming out like a sob. She stood up, her toes gripping the floorboards. She knew what he was feeling. And he was moving away from her.

"The baby gone . . ." she said aloud. "The baby gone!" The last came out as a scream at the end, a shriek. Then one long shriek came out of her. She couldn't stop. She held on to the cold iron of the bedstead with one hand and closed her eyes against the tears and let out a long, wailing sound. That's how Grace found her when she rushed in.

Eva closed her mouth. She met Grace's concern with silence. She felt that her eyes would pop out of her head with the strain of looking ahead of her into the darkness. Once, when Mary Nell was still her sister, things to come had shown themselves to her without any effort. Now she would give anything to see where they were, where they were going.

"Eva," Grace whispered, staring first at the empty bed and then at her sister's features, shocked into some strange color between brown and gray. She dared not touch her. "Where the baby? Eva . . . the baby?"

"They gone," Eva said softly, and she let out a breath, her features relaxing. She smiled slightly. Mary Nell would take care of him. She loved children. No one at home would know what had happened. And maybe one day, when they were both forgiving and forgiven, she would see him again.

"God is wise," she said to Grace, who took another look at Eva's strange expression before bolting out of the room, calling for Aunt Pearl.

They waited a week while Aunt Pearl wrung her hands and Eva recovered her strength and energy. She went about the house straightening and cleaning, cooking their dinner, as serious as a preacher but with purpose in her step. Grace detected no sadness from her little sister and no joy either. She seemed as if she felt nothing. She fell asleep every night as soon as the light went out, while Grace turned over and over in bed, wondering what was bedeviling them all. Mary Nell had lost her senses and Eva was not Eva, but some busy-bee shadow that flew around the house swirling the dust and making no noise.

Often while they were still at Aunt Pearl's and later after they returned to Johnson Creek, Grace got up at night and went to sit on the end of Eva's bed watching her breathe. Her sleep looked like the edge of death. Grace was used to Eva always being restless in her sleep, turning, muttering, sometimes crying out. But this new Eva just slept, expressionless, her mouth slightly open.

She thought about the day they had all sat in Papa and Mama's house talking about what to do. All of them. Mary Nell and Lou Henry, too. Papa pacing and looking as if he was about to fall out. Mary Nell, sitting there, saying "what we gon' do after the baby come?" or some such question. Right then she was probably deciding what to do. And them not knowing anything about it. Lou Henry right beside her, acting like it was some great tragedy to him. Grace would look down at Eva's soft face and wonder how they could do that to a child.

A few times, at breakfast, Grace asked Eva about her dreams. But Eva would only shrug. "I don't remember having any," she'd say, unconcerned.

A week after Mary Nell disappeared, Grace wrote a letter to Papa and gladly accepted the money Aunt Pearl gave her. She bought two tickets and waited until Papa wrote back. Union Springs, 3 P.M. He'd be there. He had to be there anyway. He didn't ask about the baby.

They sat like rag dolls on the train from Chehaw to Montgomery, from Montgomery to Union Springs.

"She gon' be there with the baby when we get back," Grace said as they watched the porter take their bags out of the colored car. She scanned the train platform for their father.

"No, she ain't," Eva said clearly, sitting down on top of the trunk. She adjusted her limp hat and fiddled with her gloves. She fixed her features into a benign mask.

"Where else would she be?" Grace wanted to know. "Can you imagine Mary Nell out there by herself? With a child? Uh-uh."

"She ain't in Johnson Creek," Eva said, standing up as she saw Frank Mobley on the far end of the platform. She waved to him and he acknowledged them by moving in their direction.

"We'll see if Papa say anything about Mary Nell," Grace said.

He didn't smile as he came up to them. He gave them each a small embrace. He was dressed immaculately, as was his custom. Frank dressed well, even when he was going out to the fields to work. He might be wearing his most threadbare pants and shirt, but they were well taken care of by their mother. He had more clothes than any of them—shirts for work, for the fields, for church and for going to town. A good supply of hats. Today he was wearing his second-best hat, pulled down so far over his eyes that they couldn't really see his expression. Except that he wasn't smiling.

"This yours?" he asked, gesturing toward the trunk, and directing his question at Grace.

"And this," she said, holding up Joy's old carpet bag, which she had hastily packed when she decided to come and take care of Eva.

"All right then," he said bending down and maneuvering the trunk onto his shoulders. "I brung the wagon."

It was two hours from Union Springs to Johnson Creek behind Frank's plow mule Jilly. Jilly took her time with everything. Frank slapped her broad rump several times with the reins, and waited until Jilly took those first few reluctant steps toward home before quietly saying, "I didn't want to tell ya'll this in the letter, but . . . Mary Nell done gone off."

Jilly clip-clopped her way down the street. Grace, sitting on the front seat beside him, looked back over her shoulder at Eva, who sat on blankets in the bed of the wagon leaning against the trunk with her knees drawn up to her chest.

Grace sucked in a breath, trying to form the right words to tell him about Mary Nell taking the baby. All the pictures she ever had in her heart and mind of her father and Mary Nell together came to her. Loving, laughing pictures, all of them.

She glanced to her left. His expression was so grim that she let out the air in her lungs, exhaling softly, saying nothing.

"Awhile after you left for 'Skegee, Grace, she took off, too. Don't know where she went to. She didn't say. Nothing to nobody. Left Lou a note saying she'd be back, but ain't nobody seen her. Your mama is grievin' hard."

"Papa . . . I'm sorry." Grace decided at that moment that she would talk to her mother first about Mary Nell. She didn't want to upset Frank while he was driving the wagon.

"People been askin' us a lot of questions. We told everybody that all three of y'all was off visitin' Pearl in Tuskegee."

"That was probably the best . . ."

"She took my baby," Eva said clearly.

Frank's hands on the reins jerked and Jilly snorted and swung her long head around to look at him. When Grace looked back, she thought she almost saw a strange smile on Eva's face. But it disappeared quickly.

"You better give me more than that, gal. You better say what you talkin' about," he said, his voice tumbling awkwardly over the gravel in his throat.

"She came to Tuskegee, to Aunt Pearl's. She stole my son. She gone. She moving away fast."

He jerked back on the reins, and although Jilly protested the abrupt change of intention, she stopped, right there in the middle of the road. They sat there for a while, Frank looking out at some point between Jilly's ears, Grace gripping the rough-wood edge of the wagon seat, and Eva, in the back, folding and unfolding her legs, smoothing her skirt, then gathering it up in bunches in her hands.

Grace felt a faint, but growing roar coming from somewhere. At first, she thought, it was coming from inside her own head. But she saw Jilly's ears point straight up and then lay back, and she realized the sound was approaching from behind. And then a honking added itself to the noise.

An automobile, black and shiny with two young white men in the front, pulled up alongside the wagon. Grace caught the movement of hair and scarves being beaten by a wind that wasn't wind, just the frenzied movement of air created by the ferociousness of that machine. The men in the front seat never looked their way. They moved on past, around and in front and then gone, all the time making such an unnatural noise that Jilly stepped nervously from side to side, almost turning perpendicular to the wagon and causing it to jerk toward the edge of the road.

"Whoa," Frank said, tugging on the reins and Jilly's head. She straightened herself and seemed disinclined to move for a while. Then she found something tasty on the side of the road.

Frank didn't seem ready to get going again anyway. He sat for a few long moments, staring at the space between the mule's ears, caressing the soft leather of the reins in the palm of one hand. The cloud of dust had swallowed the car as it left them, and he seemed to be looking after it. But Grace could see that he was really looking at nothing. The reins lay limp in his hands.

After a long while, during which Grace couldn't let go of the wagon seat, even though her fingers were starting to cramp up, he turned his head ever so slightly in their direction as if he was straining to catch something just out of earshot instead of preparing to speak.

"How she gon' do a thing like that?" he murmured. "How she gon' do a thing like that?"

Then he said nothing else for a moment and Grace whispered into the void. "She sad, Papa. I can't tell you why. But she ain't thinkin' right. That's why."

"Y'all ain't tellin' all," he said. "I know it, but I ain't gon' mind that right now. I got to think of what to tell your mama."

"Let's go home," Eva said quietly. "I want to see Mama."

Her father pulled his hat off and rubbed his eyes. For the first time that she could remember, he looked old to Grace. The dark red skin seemed to be stretched just a bit too tightly over his bones. The flecks of gray in his thick black hair, kept so carefully cropped, had multiplied without her really noticing. Grace thought that maybe she hadn't looked at him really hard in a long time. He was tired, she could see that. He had told her once that he kept his hair very short and his hats always on his head so that he wouldn't startle white folks with his Indianess. To the black people he had lived among all his life, his Indianess was a wonder, something natural and beautiful in the world. His presence gave them permission to be here on this land, living with the ghosts of red and black alike. But to whites he was an Indian nigger, an affront on two counts.

"Yes, Papa," said Grace. "Let's go. We don't want to be caught in the dark, do we?"

"No," he said, placing the hat firmly back on his head and pulling it low before slapping Jilly's backside once more. "We don't want to be caught in the dark. You are right, my daughter."

33

November 1922

EDDIE ADAM'S FAVORITE FACE was the one Eva wore in the mornings, just after she'd splashed the cool water over her cheeks. He'd watch her from the bed.

He fell asleep every night under her dispassionate stare. He could never wake before she did. He wasn't sure she slept at all. He'd close his eyes as she knelt beside the bed at night, falling off as her lips moved over the prayer. It was always the same prayer. He'd watched her mouth so much, he knew she was whispering the same words every night. But he didn't know what they were. He didn't know what she was asking for, or he sure as hell would try to get it for her.

He always woke to the sound of splashing water. His "Good

morning" would make her turn to him, and, for a few moments with the droplets hanging on her eyelashes and the dampness clinging to her cheeks and all the hardness swept away, the old Eva, the girl he'd known all his life, would look out of his wife's eyes.

Then, she'd say good morning, too, and she'd very slowly wipe the moisture from her face with the frayed white wash rag, reminding her features, her eyes, nose, cheeks, mouth, that they were unhappy.

She didn't seem to care if he watched her washing herself. After her face was done, she'd slip the top of her nightgown down over her shoulders and work on her body with the rag and a lump of soap. He would lay like a stone man in the bed as Eva soaped herself—her breasts and underarms and upper back. Then she'd lift the gown, sliding it over her slightly rounded belly, and squat a little so that she could draw the washrag gently between her legs. And he would lie there, not daring to move, because she might stop. He just lay there with the tears pricking the backs of his eyeballs. He'd think about the child she now carried—their child, trying not to hate it, because it was when the child came that Eva had turned away from him.

She was quick, thorough. Her wash-up never took more than a few minutes, then she was tossing the water out of the window and pouring a fresh bowl for him.

No one danced at their wedding. Eddie Adam and Willow and Clay had gone together to the Mobleys' house and arrived just as Grace was placing May Day flowers in Eva's hair. The Rev. Jenkins talked quietly with Frank and Joy at the kitchen table, but as soon as the Davidsons got there, they stood. The seven people there in that room seemed to hesitate, all of them. But then Eva slipped her hand inside his and took two steps forward. Before Eddie Adam could take one good breath, it was all over.

Eva kept her hand in his, smiling slightly as if she were really happy, when he knew she didn't feel happy exactly. Maybe what she felt was safe. Safety and love, Eddie Adam thought. Ain't no difference.

Eddie Adam owned up to the fact that it didn't take much to convince him that Eva should be his wife. Even on that day when she told him why she was going to Tuskegee, he was already thinking about what to do. He had cried inside for her, but he was mad at her, too. Why had she let that happen? Everything could have been so nice. Even if she hadn't married him and married somebody else, Son Jackson or somebody else, she could have been happy. Instead it was like she was already dead. Thirteen years old and already dead.

That day after Eva had told him about Lou Henry, Eddie Adam had wandered home. His grandmother was sitting at the kitchen table and he went right over and sat on the floor at her feet and put his head in her lap. He didn't know why he did that. He just needed something solid.

"Just 'cause some fool got a hold of her, don't make her dirty," Willow said. "Don't make you wrong for lovin' her just as much as you always did. You love her, my baby?"

"Yes, Grammy, I do."

"Then do what love asks and put yourself between her and that evil."

"Don't know if I can . . . I ain't no man. She ain't a woman . . ."

"Well, she ain't no girl no more, I reckon. She should have had more time to be a chile, but sometimes it just don't work out that way. People won't let it. And God—I love the Lord—but God got some funny ways. So Eva is a woman now, I guess. Been forced into it. But she a virtuous woman. And you a man, now, I reckon. You the man gon' marry her."

It wasn't a question, but he answered her anyway. "Yes, ma'am."

"Adam and Eva. That sound 'bout right to me. But it sho ain't no paradise y'all livin' in. The serpent done already come."

He had missed Eva during those months. And he missed Son Jackson, who had been his friend until Eva told on Lou Henry.

He never again saw Lou Henry and Mary Nell touch each other, even in the most casual way. They sat in church on opposite sides. Soon Lou Henry stopped coming at all. Eddie Adam tried to watch and see whether he betrayed any guilt or concern about what had happened to Eva, but there was nothing. He acted the same, as far as Eddie Adam could see, except that he never spoke to his wife. He ignored her and she came and went without him. That alone convinced Eddie Adam that *something* had happened.

About a month after Eva had gone, Eddie Adam saw Lou Henry down by the creek in a spot that was popular for fishing. As a matter of fact, Eddie Adam had his hook in the water when he saw Lou Henry approaching, clutching a bait bucket in one hand and a cane pole in the other. He had been walking fast, but he stopped short when he saw Eddie Adam sitting there. He just stood in one spot for a long moment, and Eddie Adam made himself stare right at Henry's face, wanting to see once and for all what kind of man this was. And he saw something—discomfort, or maybe sullenness—Eddie Adam didn't know. Whatever emotion Lou Henry was feeling merely brushed his features, and Eddie Adam saw in that moment some secret pain. Lou Henry didn't say a word, but there was an unsteadiness in his stance; he didn't meet Eddie Adam's stare. He looked off at a point just above Eddie Adam's head and to the left. And then it—that wisp of emotion—drifted away, like smoke on a breezy day. Lou Henry's face reacquired its customary expression of bored annoyance. He squared his shoulders. He turned around and walked away, swinging the bucket.

Eddie Adam didn't have a name for whatever it was he saw on Lou Henry's face, but he knew for certain at that moment, as he sat there with his cork bobbing up and down in the creek's current, that he had done that thing to Eva, just like she said.

Everybody was talking about the Mobley girls. Nothing could stay hidden here, and that little bit of the south Alabama woods buzzed with news of Eva's pregnancy. Her absence, instead of preventing talk, had merely increased it. Son Jackson's mama had plenty to say about Mr. Mobley coming over to her house—"stompin' up on my porch like a mule"—and quickly assured her friends that her boy Isaiah didn't have nothing to do with nothing.

"Must be true—she ain't here, is she? They had to send her 'way befo' she start to get big in the belly," Mrs. Jackson had said just this past week at the quilting. And Eddie Adam had tried to imagine Eva becoming round, with the child wiggling inside her.

Then when Grace had gone, followed by Mary Nell, there was no end to the talking.

Lou Henry didn't seem to mind that Mary Nell had left; he certainly didn't seem sad. Eddie Adam thought even that he walked with a little extra lift in his step.

Eddie Adam watched him all the time. He wanted him to know that he knew what he had done to Eva. Eddie Adam could tell he had been making Lou Henry uneasy; the older man had proven it there by the creek, when he turned around and left that strange silence in the space between them.

But after Eva came back, he didn't have time to think about Lou Henry as much.

The first night after their wedding, his grandmother and brother had left him and Eva alone in the house. And Eddie Adam had sat on the bed with Eva for a long time just holding her hand, not quite knowing what to do.

But she had said, "It's all right," and slipped an arm around his waist. Still they had just lain there in the bed together all night, without even taking their clothes off, and talking about all the things they used to do together. And in the morning Eva had gotten up and tried to make him some breakfast. But he had to come and light the stove for her and then he stayed in the kitchen with her while she burned biscuits. He didn't care. At that moment he could pretend that everything was going to be fine, that they were in their own house with all kinds of possibilities within reach. He had told her about wanting to own a sawmill and about trying to convince his brother that it was a good idea. And she had sat at the table and nodded at everything.

It took him four days to make love with her. Willow and Clay came back and still they fell asleep every night almost fully dressed. He'd never touched a girl that way before and he couldn't think what to do. He had to be sure he was something other than what Lou Henry was. He wanted to know how to erase that from her memory and from her body.

On the fifth night, she again said, "It's all right. It's all right, Eddie Adam."

He kissed the side of her neck. And then she stood up and took off her clothes, every single stitch, and he did the same because she had.

The first time he laid down with her and pulled the covers over them, he simply fell into the softness of her body. Eddie Adam touched everything. He combed his fingers through her hair and kissed her ears. He pulled the covers back and looked at her breasts, still disproportionately plump from having the baby. When he touched her nipples, little droplets of milk appeared. Instinctively, he bent down to lick it away, and she started to cry. He drew back as if scorched.

"No, no," Eva said, guiding his head back to her breasts. "You have to . . . you have to . . . I can't stand it if you stop."

"Eva?"

She was sobbing now, curving her arms around him so that he breathed her in. He felt drunk. "You feel good," she said. "How come you feel so good?"

He suckled her nipples, tasting the thin, sweet baby's milk. When he slipped his hand over her thigh and between her legs, she stiffened, so he stopped, stroking her back and buttocks with easy strokes. He marveled at the feel of her skin and the moist heat coming from between her legs. Her voice pleaded softly, but her legs and arms were heavy and tense.

"If you do it, he won't be there anymore," she whispered.

Eddie Adam lifted his head from her chest. Her eyes were closed and moisture peeped from under her eyelids. He didn't know what to do and his dick felt like it was going to leap away from his body. He breathed harder. Trying to slow it down didn't help. It just started to come faster and faster through his lips.

He took a deep breath and drew Eva to him as close as he could. He imagined the two of them going through life this way, fastened to each other, their hearts beating like crazy. "Just hold on to me, sweetheart," he whispered. "We ain't gon' let him win."

She sobbed. But slowly he felt her arms come up and around him and she was pressing herself hard into him, as if trying, like he was, to make the two of them one person. One person who was strong enough.

He drew back a little and took her hand, stroking the palm for a moment before guiding it down over the quivering flesh of his stomach and pausing for a moment at the crisp tangle of pubic hair.

"Whatever you want, Eva," he said, taking his hand away. "You got it."

She didn't look at him as she slipped her hand around his penis, closing her fingers around him. Already hard, his dick seemed to blossom into her hand. She stroked it tentatively. Eddie Adam's groans came tumbling out and he flopped on his back, taking her with him, because he still had one arm wrapped around her. He lifted his lips to her breasts, again tasting the sweetness of her. But as he began to probe between her legs with his hard flesh, she tumbled off him, this time pulling him, spreading her thighs as he landed between them. And he no longer was afraid. He no longer was ignorant. It was as if the two of them had never been children.

Her body from foot to head was reaching upward and outward to him as he slid into her.

It was simply another embrace. Warm and sweet. He felt so happy that his body knew what to do. He had often heard the older men talk about riding women, and he did feel as if they were going somewhere. He quickened his pace, throwing his dick forward into her. He put his hands underneath her thighs to spread them wider, and she began to move with him, as if just understanding that she didn't have to simply lie there. She could go with him.

She moved her hips up to meet him. Her soft moaning made him hungrier; he had never felt so much hunger. He was touching something that reverberated throughout his body, throughout his whole being. And then it felt as if he burst open. An intense wave of pleasure threw him forward over Eva's still moving body. He felt half-dead. He had been moving like lightning only a moment before and now he couldn't lift his head from her shoulder.

Eddie Adam kissed her and kissed her, sighing against her skin, a delightful drowsiness settling over him. Eddie Adam was in some kind of heaven, and he was young enough and ignorant enough to think that it would always be so.

He dipped his hands in the water Eva had poured for him. She and Willow moved together in the other room. Clay was already up, chattering, grumbling about breakfast.

When Willow had told him Eva was going to have another baby, he had been scared and happy. Mary Nell had not come back to Johnson Creek. They didn't know where she and Eva's boy were. Eva might never see that child again. Sometimes she sat in the chair in their room, looking out of the window and rocking, and he thought that maybe then she was missing the baby.

Another child. Another child might be the something that

would put away some of Eva's sadness. At least it would give her
something else to think about.

But as soon as it became clear that she was pregnant again,
Eva broke down and cried. She sat in the chair, rocking and
crying, and nothing any of them could say helped. Grace and
Mrs. Mobley came over and sat with her for hours, none of them
saying much that he could hear. He stayed in the other room out
of the way, afraid to do anything, afraid not to. He just stayed
close by, because maybe Eva would need him. When the other
two women left, Grace had smiled at him encouragingly and her
mother had patted his arm. Willow took Eva some tea.

In the late afternoon, he went in the room finally and looked
down at her while she slept. The half-cup of tea sat on the floor
by the bed. He watched the golden light move across her face.

She was different when she woke up from that nap. There
was no more lovemaking. She still cooked for him and made sure
his clothes were nice. She rubbed Willow's liniment into his tired
muscles when he came home at night from the sawmill where he
worked now. She smiled softly when he told his little jokes. She
was polite in every way. But when he turned to her in bed at night,
she made sure her face was always turned away, looking at the
wall or out of the window just above it. She would let him lie
against her body. She rocked him like a baby, but she no longer
allowed him between her knees.

He dreamed of the days after their wedding, when he would
bury his nose in the little folds at the tops of her thighs and get
drunk with the scent.

The smell of her was still there in some dark, hidden place in
his head and when he watched her wash in the mornings it would
come rushing back. His head would ache, his hands would fly.

He found out quickly that he was no longer a boy. He had lain between her legs and become a man.

He could seek his release with his own hands between his legs or he could seek it underneath a skirt. But he would never become like him—like Lou Henry. And Eddie Adam's hand would slide down his body. He always waited until Eva left the room to relieve himself. He always cried as he came, and afterward as he washed his sticky fingers in the bowl of fresh water she had poured for him.

Check Out Receipt

Cita Dennis Hubbell Branch
504-596-3113
http://nolalibrary.org

Monday, January 28, 2019 5:00:40 PM

Item: R0030594416
Title: A Sunday in June : a novel
Call no.: PERRY
Due: 02/13/2019

Item: R0013984726
Title: Clifford's family
Call no.: E BRIDWELL
Due: 02/13/2019

Total items: 2

For renewals, call Telemessaging at
(504)596-2693

Thank You for Your Patronage!

34

WHEN THE DOOR TO AYO'S HOUSE SHUT, the world faded into nothing but soft light and twirling dust. Grace sat on the old trunk, her head cocked as if listening for something. Eva stood with her feet firmly planted on the floorboards so that a finger of sunlight stroked her shoes, warmed her toes.

"She here, ain't she?" Eva said.

"I don't know. Don't you know?" Grace answered. "I used to think so. Thought I saw some ghosts walk right in here one time."

She leaned her cheek against her palm. Eva couldn't take her eyes off her. It was easy to see the many, many colors surrounding Grace. They illuminated the dust that had risen as soon as the two of them stepped in the house not more than five minutes ago. The particles of dirt had become tiny, shimmering jewels. Blue, green and gold.

"Grace," Eva said softly.

"What?" Grace looked up and Eva took a step backward, because her sister's face wasn't the same as it had been a moment before. It was Grace, but it was not.

"What? What?" Grace said loudly, standing up, seeing the gentle surprise painted on Eva's features.

"She is here," Eva said. "Grandmama."

"Where?" Grace whispered her question. Eva shook her head and smiled slightly. It was even more evident when she stood up. Eva pointed at Grace.

"There," she said.

Grace stared out. Then she smiled, too.

"You really can see?"

"Not that clearly. It's like I'm looking through you to someone else standing in the same spot. I can't explain it better'n that."

Grace sat back down.

"Where you think they are now, Grace?" Eva asked softly.

Grace shrugged. "She done gone off crazy, that girl."

"You think Ayo knows?"

"You know, Eva. If you weren't hurtin' so much, you'd know where they were."

Eva shook her head. "I ain't never known nothin' for sure without Mary Nell being with me. Ain't that something? I know I don't have no right to ask God for nothin', Grace, but I sho would like to know where they are."

"You got every right," Grace said, standing up again and taking one big step over to where Eva was standing. She took the younger girl by the shoulders.

"Wasn't none of this your fault, Eva. You hear?"

Eva didn't have an answer for that. How could it not be her fault when she was in the middle of everything? She looked up at Grace.

"She gone," she said.

"Well, I know—"

"No, I mean Ayo. I guess it was her I saw. It's just you now."

"Did you hear me? It ain't your fault that Mary Nell married crazy and then let it rub off on her." Grace squeezed her shoulders and then let go, turning briskly back to the trunk. "Let's get on with what we came for, huh?" She lifted the trunk lid.

"Now you gon' have to wash these. They been in here since the beginning of creation, I 'spect. You ain't had time to make things of your own, but that don't mean you can't have good things for you and Eddie Adam and the baby." She began pulling out various pieces of cloth. "Mostly quilts, but they'll get you goin'. We can make you some other things as time goes on. After you got married, I remembered that these were here. Oh, these are good!"

She pulled out three or four fairly heavy quilts. They were alive with color, softly fading hues of once vibrant greens, golds, reds and blues.

"Funny," said Grace. "I thought the colors were louder. Almost like new."

"You think Eddie Adam will like these?"

Grace turned to stare at her little sister, one hand deep down in the trunk. Then she snorted with laughter.

"It don't matter! At this point, whatever make you happy, make him happy, too. He'll do anything for you right now."

"Even . . . love me, you think?"

"Don't start talkin' like that again."

"He does love me, Grace. He loves me so hard. And I ain't got nothin' for him. Got took away, what I had . . ."

"He loves you. That's all that matters. That's all that'll get you through. Here." She held out a folded quilt and Eva took it, cradling it in the crook of her arm.

"When he asked me to marry, it wasn't like love. It was like he wanted to borrow something from me. 'Would you mind very much being my wife?' he said. We was sitting there at his grand-mama's table. She had sent word, that same day I got home, and I came and sat there. He didn't even hold my hand. But when I looked at him, Grace, I knew he wanted to help me. And I was tired. So I said yes. But I don't know now. I can't love him. Can't love nobody."

"What about that chile you carryin'?"

"Don't know. When I think about him, I get so scairt I can't breathe. I don't want him to come."

Grace straightened, coming up with two more quilts and a sack of fabric. She shut the trunk lid with her foot. "That chile is your gift for everythang that done happened. And Eddie Adam, he a gift, too. Don't be dumb. Love can turn to hate faster than you know. Say yes to it, to all of it, so you can start to forget."

"I ain't gon' never forget. Ain't that much love."

"Well, so you can start to live, then." Grace put the quilts she had down on the lid of the trunk and opened the sack, pulling out cloth scraps—pieces of old shirts, children's worn out Sunday clothes, white ladies' tea dresses and men's wool britches. She paused to finger a small bit of blue cloth, murmuring to herself, but when Eva failed to respond, she turned and stood there look-ing at her with the piece of blue cloth clutched in one fist.

"I'm gon' try. I'm gon' try," said Eva. She smiled a little, because

Grace was looking at her as if willing her to be happy. *Be happy, baby doll. Be happy.* And she wanted to be. But what she wanted and what she felt had nothing to do with each other.

Eddie Adam was a gift. In marrying him, she had only thought to hide from the life she'd had before. The life of a little girl, with dreams that turned out to be too big for the world she lived in. She had been walking around and about these backwoods roads as if she owned the dirt they were made out of. She had dared to think that her world would somehow be bigger than her mother's and father's, that it would stretch beyond Johnson Creek. Where, she didn't know. But she had always assumed. And it turned out to be unsafe out there, even in the places she'd known all her life. Things could be taken away before you even knew what they were worth. People could just disappear. Not other people's people. Your people.

God slapped me right down, she thought.

So there had been Eddie Adam, sitting at his grandmother's table, his head down, his body rigid with hope and fear. The fact that he'd believed her and tried to comfort her that day, the day she told him and Son about the rape, that'd been enough for her. She looked in his eyes and knew who he was and that had been enough. She had married him and waited for the day when he'd erase Lou Henry forever. Somehow it would be made right. One day soon they'd be lying together in that big iron bed and Eddie Adam would kiss her and slip into her and Second Sunday would fall away like it never happened. Eddie Adam forgave her. He forgave her with kisses.

After all that had happened, he loved her anyway. He loved a girl who had shamed herself and her family. He cried with joy and wonder every time he moved inside of her.

Eva didn't wonder why. It didn't matter why. She would wait all day for him, wanting to be touched. And when the night came, she would try to stay with him, wherever he was going when he rode her so hard. She didn't find it hard to match his energy. She would drive herself into him, waiting for that moment of exciting release that never seemed to come. Eddie Adam would groan and contort his face and body into all kinds of new expressions, while she waited. And every time, he would fall asleep with his arm curled around her waist, while she wondered what it was she was waiting for.

He was beautiful to hold, Eddie Adam was. Then he would move inside of her, and nothing would happen. Just for a moment, she would feel something struggling to break the surface and nothing would happen. Whatever Lou Henry took from her, she could never get back. She would never make Eddie Adam happy this way. Better just to not disappoint him anymore. She would have to close her ears to his heavy breathing, because if she let her mind get away from her, there was Lou Henry again, there on top of her, spitting his evil into her face and wanting her to thank him for it. But Eddie Adam was Eddie Adam. He tried. She was just not good enough for him.

"Eddie Adam gon' like that," Eva said, pointing to the quilt that Grace had just thrown over her forearm. "He like greens and blues. Sky and trees."

"Good. I'm glad we came here then. Mama said it's all right, you can have these."

Eva took the pile of cloth. Grace still clutched that torn piece of blue fabric in one hand.

"What you gon' do with that?" Eva asked.

"I might do a little sewing of my own. Ain't never started my own quilt. Always just helped Mama on hers. And I got a basket of scraps so big I could make ten quilts. I think this belonged to Grandmama and I thought I'd put it in there."

Eva nodded. "Looks old."

Grace uncrumpled it and stretched it gently between her two hands. She held it up to the light coming in through the window. There were faint designs on the cloth, swirls and loops in a fainter blue.

"It don't look like no cloth I ever seen before," Grace murmured. "It's got to be old. As old as Old Bessie was, I reckon."

She folded the cloth into a small square and tucked it in the pocket of her apron.

When Willow saw the two of them struggling toward her house under the weight of the quilts, she quickly went to meet them, smiling as she gathered up a quilt from Eva and one from Grace.

"Bessie's," she said softly, turning to lead the way over the dry pine needles that lay on the path from the road to her house. "I'd know them anywhere, anytime. Lord, I wish I could sew like her!"

"What about this, Miz Willow?" Grace asked, pulling the little square of blue cloth out of her pocket. They were stepping around the side of the house now and up onto the porch. Willow plopped the quilts down into a rocking chair and Eva piled the two she was carrying right on top.

When she saw what Grace was holding she let out a heavy sigh. She put a hand to her chest, over her heart. She felt a heavy weight there and a twinge of sorrow that made its way up to her throat and behind her eyes.

"That there Bessie's, too." She put out a hand and Grace placed the blue cloth in it. "She was always talking about using it in somethin'."

Willow sat down abruptly on the back porch's top step, suddenly dropping her head in her hands and pressing the cloth to her forehead. She remembered another day, long before now, when she and Bessie had sat together at a place not far from here and Bessie had told her about being taken away from her home.

"All I had was what I was wearin'. Nothin' special about it you know." Bessie had looked off over Willow's head, her black skin shiny with the sweat of a late summer's labor. "Ordinary clothes for us. But we didn't wear no rags ever." Bessie had looked down disdainfully at the frayed dress she was wearing. "And my head was wrapped with the most beautiful cloth, just like my mother's." She demonstrated this by gesturing around her head several times. "But they took me and snatched at me and tore my clothes, until I was wearing a rag. And when I came here and they put me in these kinds of things"—she dismissed what she was wearing with a sweep of her hand—"I secretly kept a piece back. It was the only thing I had left of my mother. I'm gon' put it in a quilt and put the quilt on my bed and lay under it, so I'll always have her with me."

Willow remembered just staring down at the blue cloth in Bessie's hand, not quite believing that something from over there had come to be over here. Bessie was silent for a moment, then she said, "Could be somebody of yourn from long back—a great-grandmama—wore something like that 'round they body." She stared intensely, longingly into Willow's face. "Yes, you have the look like my people. That is why we sisters."

Willow had almost forgotten about that conversation, but

she had never forgotten Bessie's love. The one person in the world who had really understood her, and she had to come all the way over the water to do it.

"She told me 'bout the day she was took away," Willow said now to Bessie's two granddaughters, who had come to sit on the steps with her. She smiled at how comfortable they seemed with her after Eva's marriage. Only last year, they'd both been afraid to come near her or her house.

"Bessie say she only had the clothes on her back when that man snatched her, and through everything she kept this . . . Only thing left of her real clothes, of her mother, of Afraca . . ." Willow held the cloth against her cheek for a moment before handing it back to Grace. She leaned back abruptly when she saw the girl's expression.

Grace looked stricken, on the verge of tears. She began folding the cloth again with fingers that trembled.

"Baby, what is it?" Willow asked.

Grace just shook her head, her bottom lip trembling like a newborn baby's. Eva slipped a hand inside hers and with the other wiped a tear that had just slipped down Grace's cheek.

"Just a minute, just take a minute," she murmured, rhythmically squeezing and releasing Grace's hand.

Willow didn't quite know what to make of this. What was wrong with the girl? No wonder the two of them were no longer frightened of her. They were a world and a power unto themselves. Lord knew what kind of spirit would be moving if the other one, Mary Nell, was here, too.

"Sorry," Grace said to Willow after a moment. She smiled wanly and again tucked the cloth into her apron pocket. "I just remembered . . ."

"What, child?"

Again, Grace just shook her head. She looked at Willow, and for a moment Willow saw something of her friend in the girl's melancholy smile. Grace stood up to go.

"If you need any more things, Eva, you let me know. Though I know Miz Willow here"—again she smiled at Willow—"is takin' care of you." Eva kissed her cheek and began lugging the quilts into the house.

But Willow watched Grace leave, standing staring into the trees long after the girl's tall body had disappeared from view.

35

A Sunday. Mary Nell didn't have to work. She lay on the bed and told Jimmie Bible stories. She had no idea whether he understood her or not. But he looked at her and smiled that baby smile, with his tiny teeth all in a row, and when he did, it was heaven to be in this bare room in this town where a year ago no one there had known she existed.

Mamie Taylor's had better beds, no doubt about that. And Mamie didn't complain if the baby cried. No one here knocked on your door and screamed at you to "shut that chile up or I'm comin' in there to do it for ya!" And Mamie at least gave you one good meal a day for your money. And she was careful about who lived here. No men. No whores. And always somebody to watch the baby.

She was in the middle of Noah's flood, but Jimmie wasn't interested anymore. He pulled the blanket over his head and played underneath for a while, then he slid down off the bed and toddled around the room, falling and getting up and falling again. Every time his bottom hit the floor he laughed out loud.

On the days she came home from Mrs. Steepe's she was always so tired, that she would just feed Jimmie and fall into bed and sleep hard. Sometimes she would get sleepy at work and fall into a nap right there at the kitchen table or on one of the beds upstairs as she was taking the sheets off the mattresses. She didn't like the naps, not only because she knew Mrs. Steepe would be upset to find her sleeping during working hours, but because she always dreamed during naps. She didn't dream at night anymore. But if she let herself slip into a quick sleep as she sat among the soft towels and sheets on the floor of the laundry room, or as the afternoon sun streamed into the kitchen after she'd put the potatoes on to boil, she dreamed. She always dreamed of home and Eva and Grace. She walked with them still in those dreams, although she didn't know if they were visions of things that were or things to come or things that might be. She always woke up with a knot in her throat.

Luckily, Mrs. Steepe hadn't caught her. She seemed nice enough, but Mary Nell didn't want to test her.

Mrs. Steepe was a big-busted widow with frizzy red hair who lived alone in what seemed to be the biggest damn house in Birmingham. She entertained a lot, and insisted on the house being perfect at all times, just in case she had the notion to throw a party.

"Once a month, I'll need you to do the downstairs floors and sometimes I might want you for when I have company," she had said on that first day. They had been standing in the front hall with Jimmie on the floor between them, sweeping his plump hands back and forth over the polished wood.

"What's his name?" Mrs. Steepe asked, bending for a closer look.

"Jimmie, ma'am," said Mary Nell. "James."

"Oh, he's a pretty little one, isn't he?"

"Thank you, ma'am. Would it be all right if I bring him with me sometime? He don't make much noise and I'll keep him with me so he don't get into nothin'."

Mrs. Steepe straightened. "Well . . . sometimes will be all right, I suppose. As long as he's quiet. But if he's getting in the way, you'll have to make other arrangements."

"Yes, ma'am."

Sometimes when she was down on her knees on that very floor, she tried to remember the little girl who wanted to go to school and be a nurse. Always, always a moment came back to her, one in which she had been completely happy. Like the day Lou Henry had asked her to get married. No, he had said, he had no problem with her going on with school if she could. They'd find money to do it. He'd be so proud of her being a nurse with a uniform and everything. He was sure Joy and Frank would help with any children they might have.

But after they got married, every time she brought it up, he had said they would do it next year, or later, or sometime. If only she had known that it was just the beginning of his betrayal. But for a long time she still hoped for that education, just like she hoped for a child.

She looked drowsily over at Jimmie, who was trying to turn the doorknob. She was relieved to be working at Mrs. Steepe's. It was hard finding work with a baby on your hip, and the girls at the boarding house weren't always available to look after him.

"If we was at home you could be with me all the time," she whispered to Jimmie.

But even as she said that she wasn't sure. She didn't know what would happen if she went back. She tried to picture herself there, walking up to her parents' house. She could picture them all on the front porch waiting for her—Mama, Papa, Grace—and Eva. Of course, Eva.

She turned over in bed, feeling herself drifting. If she went, maybe she would lose him. She tried to imagine talking to Eva again and she always felt empty after these imaginary conversations. She would grope around for her sister, but there was nothing there.

So that part of them was gone. It was a hollow feeling. But then Jimmie toddled back across the room and stood by the edge of the bed making faces at her and she smiled.

36

GRACE UNTIED THE CORNER of her handkerchief and looked again at the five pennies as if staring at them would somehow make them multiply. She was sure there wasn't any kind of help she could get for just five cents, and if George found out she had taken any of their money through the woods to Willow's house, she would have to do some fast talking.

She had listened to him, finally, whispering in her ear.

"I don't care what it is, Grace, I'm gonna marry you. Whatever it is that's botherin' you, it don't matter to me, you hear?"

Grace could almost see her mother visibly let out a relieved sigh that day the preacher had pronounced them man and wife there at the front of the church. It wouldn't have done for her eldest to be unwed, when the two younger ones already had husbands. Eva had been there, standing beside her as matron of honor. She pushed the thought of Mary Nell far, far away.

And now, less than a month later, here she was, her head pounding with the constant clamor of distant voices, voices she had hoped would disappear underneath the force of her husband's love.

She saw Eva come out front, carrying a bucket, her big belly slowing her down considerably. Grace broke into a trot.

"Wait, now," she said, coming up and stopping the other girl in her tracks. "If you going to the well, I'll do that. Look like you 'bout to drop that baby right now."

Eva smiled, handing over the bucket. "I wish I would. Willow say I got another few weeks yet." She fell into step beside Grace. "You think 'bout what I said?"

"Yeah." Grace stopped and leaned over the edge of the well, tightening the knot that fastened the bucket handle to the rope. She dropped the bucket down the hole and couldn't resist leaning over to watch it fall. Cold water glimmered far below. Her head was hurting something fierce and the whisperings in the back of her brain rose up into a small roar.

"Grace!"

She felt Eva's hand slip inside the waistband of her skirt and she straightened, pulling on the rope and bringing the bucket with her. The voices crept back down underneath her own thoughts.

"Yeah," Grace said, letting out a deep breath as she grasped the bucket handle. It was heavy and she lifted it onto her head. "I thought about what you said. Maybe Willow is the only help I got left. What choice I got anyway? You sure she won't tell George?"

"Not if you don't want her to. That woman's carrying the

secrets of everybody in Johnson Creek. I 'spose she's used to hangin' on to them by now."

"But Eddie Adam . . . ?"

"He ain't here." Eva took Grace's arm. "Come on. She's 'round the back, washing."

"I wish you . . ."

"Can't. Can't see much. You know since me and Mary Nell . . . All that glorious stuff, all them wonderful pictures of future times, they gone, Grace. Just muddy water now when I dream at night. Like lookin' at the bottom of a pond full of muddy water." Eva wiped a hand over her eyes. "I wish I could help you."

Grace slipped an arm around Eva's back. "It's all right, baby doll. You always some good to me."

Eva nodded, walking off around the house to where Willow was working.

Grace didn't understand how a woman could look like that while standing over a hot wash pot. But there was Willow, her back straight as a rod, a red apron covering the front of her muslin dress. She was sweating and straining, but the red, worn-out head-rag she wore could have been a crown.

Eva poured the bucket of water into a large tin tub nearby and left, lumbering up the back stairs with a solemn look over her shoulder at Grace. Willow didn't seem to see Grace. She swirled the water with a large stick and then began dropping white sheets in one by one.

"Willow?"

"Come back." Willow spoke without turning her head.

"Ma'am?"

"Eva said you might want some help. But I didn't think you would come so soon. Come back. My mind somewhere else now."

"But you don't even know what . . ."

"Don't matter. If I'm gon' help you atall, I got to give my whole mind to it. Busy at the moment."

"But," Grace took a step—then two—closer. "My husband . . . I might not be able to come later on."

Willow dropped the last bed sheet into the boiling water. "Come on and tell me, then," she said, still stirring. Grace sighed with relief. She couldn't imagine trying to come up with a story that would explain to George why she was away so much in one day. He, who knew her so well in some ways, would surely know she wasn't telling the whole truth.

Willow gestured to an overturned bucket and Grace squatted down to settle on the unsteady perch. Willow leaned her stick against the tree and came to sit on the ground across from Grace.

"It's them dreams, ain't it?" she asked.

"I think I'm losin' my mind," Grace said.

"Not hardly."

Willow didn't say anything else for a while. The two of them sat across from each other, and Willow got up every once in awhile to check on her clothes. The pot bubbled and Willow's stir stick made a dull thud as it occasionally hit the inside of the iron pot. Then she'd come back and sit again and she seemed satisfied with that.

"I was twelve or thirteen, I think, when it started," Grace said finally.

"That long ago?"

Grace nodded. "A long time to live with a ghost," she said.

"You been hearin' voices all this time?"

"It started out with just dreams. These days, I get it all," Grace said. "The voices, the visions, the dreams. Sometimes I walk out my front door and into whole 'nother place, Willow. One day I ain't gonna be able to get back."

Willow grunted, and then nodded to signal that Grace was to continue.

"I know they be dead people. I know that," Grace said.

"Tell me what the people look like."

"A lot of times I see two people, a woman and a girl. Wearing clothes wrapped 'round 'em, all around they bodies, but they shoulders and arms bare. And they heads be wrapped up in the same cloth. They carrying something, baskets, on they heads, like carrying a laundry basket. But I can't see what's in them. And they just walkin' down the road." Grace let out a long breath after this description. She hadn't realized she'd been holding her breath. Once she had started it wasn't hard to say it all.

"Wait, chile!" Willow jumped up from her perch and went over to take the sheets out. She lifted them into the tin tub. Then she came and sat down again.

"Now," she said. "They African people you see. They must be your peoples. Bessie tryin' to tell you somethin', I suppose. Maybe she just want to be with you."

"I don't want her to, Miz Willow. I want it to stop. That's why I came. I got a husband now, I can't be goin' 'round in a fog, listenin' to people what ain't there. What you think she want?"

"I can't say, chile. You have to listen to her in order to find out. Really listen and open yo'self up. And you say you don't want to do that."

"If I listen, I lose myself, Miz Willow. I get lost in there with all them voices and visions. If I pay attention to her, there won't be any of me left. I know it. You can give me somethin' or tell me somethin' to say to her to make her go away. Can't you?"

Willow shook her head. "I wouldn't know what to do unless we could find out what was makin' her come back. Bessie a strong spirit, in life and in death. She ain't gon' stop doin' what she doin' just 'cause I say so."

"What do I do, then?"

"Set some time aside to listen to her. Next time she speaks, if you can, just stop what you doin' and sit down and let her come and see what's what."

"Oh, no, Miz Willow. I don't want to . . ."

"That's the only answer I can give you right now. Unless you know what she come back for you won't know how to send her on her way."

There was the quiet crackling of dry pine needles from behind Grace and she turned to see Eva approaching. While she slowly walked to where they were, Grace thought about what Willow said. She couldn't do that, could she? Just let some spirit come and take over? What if what Grandmama Bessie wanted was to make her crazy? Who knows what kind of intentions people had when they died and went over? If she was a good spirit, she'd be happy in heaven and wouldn't be bothering anybody.

If I just do nothin', Grandmama may take my mind, and I may never get back, she thought. Then what? George would have to put me into one of them places. Them crazy houses. I'd likely never see the light of day.

"What we gon' have for supper, Miz Willow?" Eva was asking. She leaned on Grace's shoulder for support.

The old woman stood up again slowly. "Didn't I tell you to just call me Willow? Willow is enough."

"Ain't respectful."

"It is if I tell you it's fine to call me that. You can go in and mix up some cornbread. We'll find somethin' to go with it." She began to amble off toward the back porch. "I's got to get the wringer," she said.

"So," Eva said. "Willow help you?"

"Nah. Well . . . she give me somethin' else to think about, I reckon." Grace rubbed her hand back and forth over her forehead, trying to discourage the headache. "Somethin' to try. But I don't know if I'm gon' do it."

"Why not? It's somethin' to try," Eva said. "Is it root work?"

"Nah."

Eva laughed. "For a woman with the reputation she got, Willow don't seem to do much castin' of spells or nothin'. I mean, I watch her, 'specially when folk come to see her. She mostly give them medicine—teas and such—for they aches and pains and colds. And she talks a *whole* lot. And of course she does help with the babies. But I certainly ain't never seen her mumblin' no spells. Just sayin' her prayers like regular folk."

Grace sighed. "I think that what I got, she can't cure."

Willow was making her way back across the yard with the clothes wringer.

"I guess Eddie Adam and Clay be home soon; I better get on that cornbread," said Eva, struggling to stand.

"He like it over there at the sawmill?" Grace asked.

"Well, I 'pose. He say he just want to stay long enough to learn the business so he and Clay can have they own mill."

Grace shook her head, laughing. "They just little boys, Eva. You all just chilluns. What make him think he gon' have a sawmill? White folk 'round here ain't gon' let no little nigger boys own nothin' like that. Where they gon' get the money?"

Eva shrugged. "He say he will. Why not believe him?"

"He will," said Willow. She set up the wringer and began maneuvering the first clean sheet out of the rinse water. Grace jumped up to help her.

"Thank you, baby," Willow said. Grace turned the crank of the wringer as Willow fed the corner of the sheet between the rollers. "Now. You think about what I said. Maybe you should talk to young George about it."

"No! No, I ain't gon' never tell George." Grace shook her head emphatically.

"You think he won't understand?"

Grace nodded.

"Well, you know him better than me," Willow said. She stood so that she could catch the wrung-out sheet with one hand while still feeding the soggy end with the other. "But you gon' have to do what I said about listenin' if you gon' ever have any kind of peace from your grandmother. I tell you, chile, she was a strong person. Strong and big-hearted. If she came back to tell me anythang, I sure as hell would listen."

But the thought of opening that door, and allowing Bessie to come in made Grace shiver. What might come behind her? Grace wondered. Maybe what Mama said about visions and such was true. The devil was in that kind of thing maybe.

She better keep the door shut.

37

May 1923

FOR THE FIRST TIME SINCE HE was a small boy, Eddie Adam wished he could talk to his father. Not a chance of that, since he was long dead and buried. He didn't think about his mother so much, which was strange, since she was still alive out there, somewhere.

But as he listened to Eva's low moans from the next room, and watched his grandmother and Grace and Mrs. Mobley hurry back and forth, he wished he had a man here to wait with him. He knew Mr. Mobley had gone out hunting and wasn't home. He walked back and forth, trembling at the thought of being someone's father. When he married Eva, he had only thought of helping someone he loved. He hadn't thought much about children, and he certainly wasn't ready for one so soon.

Eva was crying, not loudly, but deeply. He could hear that. His heart contracted into a tight knot, because he knew women sometimes died trying to have babies. Grammy know what to do, he reassured himself. But he couldn't sit still, all the same.

There was a hard knock on the door and Frank Mobley came through it the very next moment. There was Son Jackson behind his right shoulder, looking wildly about. They were both covered in mud.

"Well," Mr. Mobley said, loudly. "What's the news? I seen the note on the door. Where's my little girl?"

"Papa!" Eva cried out. And Mr. Mobley started for the door between the two rooms.

"Frank!" Joy Mobley stepped through, closing it behind her. "Don't you come in here! This women's business."

He frowned and sputtered a little, as if he were about to let loose a long stream of words, but in the end he said nothing. He went and sat at the table, where Son Jackson had now parked himself. They both seemed dripping with mud and vegetation hanging all about their clothing. Son cradled his shotgun in his lap and Mr. Mobley leaned his against the wall. Son had said nothing since coming in and now he looked quickly at Eddie Adam and then quickly away again, as if embarrassed to be there. Yet he didn't make a move to leave.

So now there were three men—or one man and two boys—in the room and Eddie Adam felt no better than before. The silence between them was as heavy as Eva's moans. Every time she let one loose, Son would put his forehead in his hands.

The afternoon slid into evening. Now accompanying the

sounds from the other room was the noise of their stomachs growling. But nobody moved.

Just as the last light of the sun was visible over the horizon, Grace came out, wiping her hands and smiling and saying to Eddie Adam, "A girl, little Papa."

Eddie Adam stood up, now knowing what to do. Frank began laughing. "Of course, a girl! Of course!"

Son mumbled something that sounded to Eddie Adam like "congratulations," although he couldn't be quite sure, and stood up to shake his hand. He then slipped out the door with his gun. Eddie Adam still couldn't figure out why he had even stayed.

But he didn't dwell on it too long, because now the child was crying and he stepped closer to the door.

"Just a minute, now!" he heard his grandmother Willow say. "We's got to clean 'er up for you."

But he didn't stop. He kept going until he was standing in the doorway, kept going until he was by the bed and looking down at the tiny wrinkled face of his daughter. Eva was holding her loosely in one arm, while Willow stroked the baby gently with a clean washrag that she dipped now and then in a basin of water. Joy Mobley, on the opposite side of the bed, stroked Eva's hair.

Eddie Adam sat on the edge of the bed and took Eva's hand. She turned to look at him and smiled faintly and he thought maybe it would all come out all right. Then he touched the baby girl's cheek tentatively with his forefinger. She stopped crying, looking puzzled. And as he leaned forward, she seemed to look at him, she seemed to recognize him.

And he thought maybe it would come out all right.

38

MARY NELL THOUGHT SHE WOULD lose her mind. The baby was crying and crying and crying. She sat on the edge of the bed and stroked his cheek, singing, and talking softly.

But the crying wouldn't stop. She didn't know what to do.

Finally, she pulled the bedcovers back to lift him onto her lap. But she was surprised to find that he was so tiny.

"Jimmie," she said faintly. And it wasn't him. It was a newborn. A little girl, barely out of the womb who stared at Mary Nell with annoyance and then began to cry. "Jimmie!"

As she said his name a second time, she realized that she was dreaming. A waking dream, like she'd had many times before. But seldom were her dreams this clear anymore. It had been a couple of years since they'd been that vivid, the edges that sharp.

She continued to hold the baby. And looking down at the bed, she saw Eva lying there, sweat anointing her forehead. Mama was there. Willow was there. Eva was holding out her arms for the just-born girl. And Mary Nell put the child on her sister's chest. A child. Another child! A different child . . .

Mary Nell shook her head, trying to clear it, trying to shake the image. But for the next few seconds she was trapped by the picture, the two women and Eva in the bed with the baby. And then it began to fade slowly and she was again there in her room. Jimmie was sleeping quietly in the bed. He hadn't been crying at all.

So Eva has another baby. A little girl. Something bitter rose up in the back of her throat when she thought of Eva and Lou Henry together. She didn't understand how Mama could stand it, her baby daughter being something like that.

Mary Nell stood up and paced around the small perimeter of the room. She had to get home. But she had nothing in her pocket. It was gone as soon as she got paid.

Yes, the money white people paid in Birmingham was better than the money they paid in Johnson Creek, but it flew out of your pocket a whole lot faster. She had to pay for the room. And food. And clothes for a child that seemed to be doubling in size every month. She couldn't get back home. And she longed to get back home and look into the face of such a woman as Eva had become.

Jimmie stirred on the narrow bed. She had to get to work and it was time to get him up and dressed. He was coming with her today. He always played quietly and hardly ever cried. It wasn't bad. Just her and Jimmie. And Mrs. Steepe was nicer than Mrs. Ward. She had to try and pinch a little more money back, though. Because she had to get home. She had to see this new child and look into its eyes so that she would know it was another bit of devilry.

39

WILLOW SAT ON THE PORCH STEPS watching Eva walk down the road, carrying the baby. She was going to visit the neighbors, show off little Patricia. Eddie Adam walked with her a little piece and came back to sit beside her on the steps.

"She all right, ain't she Grammy? Eva, I mean," he said.

"Why wouldn't she be? She fine far as I know."

Eddie Adam sighed. Willow knew something else was coming.

"Well, she don't seem to . . . to like me as much as she used to. Not since she found out she was having a baby."

Willow smiled, but she didn't let him see.

"Womens get that way sometime after a baby come," she said, reassuringly. "The baby still sucklin'. Eva ain't gon' want to be with you for a while. 'Sides, it wear a woman out, nursing a baby and taking care of a baby and a man and everything else she got to do. Don't be after her. Leave her 'lone for a bit."

But even she began to wonder as months went by and the baby was weaned and Eva still seemed far away from the two of them. She helped with the cooking. She made sure Eddie Adam's clothes were clean and pressed. She took care of him in every way except one. Willow could see that. He wandered around like a boy with a schoolyard crush instead of a young man with a new wife and baby.

Again, he came to Willow one day, while she was out in the woods digging around with her stick.

She just shook her head when he brought it up. She was gathering plants and roots. When she found something she wanted, she put them in the bag she wore slung across her body.

"There's a lot goin' on inside a her that you ain't never gon' understand. That man took somethin' 'way from her, and then her sister, the one she closest to, her other half, took 'way the rest."

She leaned on the stick and wiped the beads of sweat from her face with the hem of her apron.

"Some days, I wanna kill him," Eddie Adam said. "Naw, make that every day, Grammy."

"How that gon' help you? It sho ain't gon' do your wife and chile no good to have you sittin' in the jail. Sittin' in the jail for the likes of Lou Evans!" Willow raised her hands to the heavens as if asking the gods for explanations. "No, baby. That won't make it right. You just love her. That the only thing that gon' help that girl. But even if that ain't enough, you ain't got no reason to be surprised."

40

Summer 1925
᳁᳁

THE PROMISE OF RAIN HAD EVAPORATED underneath the late July sun. Lou Henry's hoe slipped easily through the dry, sandy hills of dirt piled up around his cotton plants. As usual, the weeds were stronger than the cotton and were thriving, even in the heat. He had rejoiced at the appearance of a momentary darkness to the sky. But the storm cloud had drifted off and he continued to chop away. He was quite a ways from his house, but he could see it well enough, and beyond it the road that curved past, and soon he noticed a large cloud of dust traveling along that road. He stopped for a moment and leaned on the hoe, squinting and adjusting his hat for more shade against the glare. Even from here he could make out who was driving that wagon. Will, probably on the way back from the store. He could see his characteristic posture, his bent back making a C over the seat.

But someone else was there beside Will. Shorter and slighter. Lou Henry straightened up when he saw that it was a woman. And when the wagon stopped in front of his house, he could only stare with his mouth open. Will got down and when he came around to the side of the wagon, she handed down something and then climbed down herself. By the time Will started unloading the trunk from the back of the wagon, Lou Henry's hoe was lying in the dust and he was stumbling over the dirt hills toward home.

The wagon pulled off and she stood there watching it leave. And then she put what she was carrying down and he saw that it was a child. He stopped for a moment then and maybe there was something that told her he was there, because she turned toward him, grasping the child's hand and he saw, though he had known from the first moment that the wagon had stopped in front of his house, that it was Mary Nell.

What could she want now? After three years? He had made up his mind that she was gone for good. He had lain in bed at night and cursed himself for being the man that he was. After Mary Nell left, so had his desire for Eva. And Eddie Adam's decision to marry the girl had been the nail in that coffin. He was proud of himself for keeping up a good front. Nobody knew he even thought a thought about Mary Nell. And here she was with a boy child holding tightly to her fingers.

He started again toward the yard. She hadn't moved. She stood quietly, wearing a dark gray dress, a gray and white hat and black shoes. She looked like she might have been in mourning. A widow. The child was quiet also. He chewed thoughtfully on his own fist, but other than that there was no movement. Except for his eyes, which followed Lou Henry's progress.

He felt old and tired and dirty beside the two of them. For some odd reason he worried about the condition of the house. Was it clean? He couldn't remember. He didn't know if she was there to stay anyway. Cleanliness might not even matter.

Finally, he was standing before them. She looked up at him calmly. He thought she even smiled a little. But it was not a happy smile.

"Here is your son," she said, thrusting the boy's hand toward him.

"Son?" He stared down at the small hand, then into the child's face.

"Don't know why men always think they can do whatever they want and nothin' gon' touch them atall," Mary Nell sneered, and he took a step back. "You knew you little girlfriend was gon' have a baby . . . where you think the baby went?"

"Pearl . . ." he said faintly, still staring down at the small hand. "I thought she had 'im."

"I'm his mama, now," she said with satisfaction. "And ain't nobody gon' dare say different. Least of all you. Pick that up." She gestured toward the trunk and box that was sitting in the dirt yard. Lou Henry blinked twice, trying to find his brain inside his skull, and moved to lift the trunk.

Mary Nell took the child's hand again and strode toward the house. He hadn't laid eyes on her since 1922, and she acted like her absence had been nothing at all.

"His name Jimmie," she said over her shoulder, "just in case you interested."

41

THOSE EVENINGS WHEN EVA hauled bucket after bucket to the stove to warm water for a bath, Eddie Adam would leave the house, taking the long road down to the creek to smoke his pipe. He would feel his grandmother's eyes on him as he stepped down off the porch and went off, but Willow never said a thing. Patricia would try to follow him, and sometimes he'd take the little girl with him, letting her toss stones in the water while he stood on the north bank of Johnson Creek, breathing smoke in and out. He'd only begun smoking a few years ago, not long after the baby was born.

Eva had stood at the front window all day looking at nothing that he could see. In the fading light, they sat at supper with his older brother shifting uncomfortably in his seat and only Patricia saying anything at all. Baby talk.

After supper, Willow built up the fire and set the kettle on the stove, thinking Eva would be taking her bath that night. She heated the water and the sky turned golden while Eva sat, her forehead leaning against the glass.

Finally she got up from her chair and went out to the back porch and got down the tin tub. Eddie Adam got up then. That was his habit when Eva started readying her bath. He went out.

He left Patricia at home this time, took his lantern and went down to the bridge. The sun was nearly gone, and already the moon was rising. There was nearly enough moonlight to see by without his light, but he didn't want to take a chance stepping on something that didn't want to be stepped on. The noises coming out of the woods were enough to make a man half crazy if he stopped and really listened. Crickets and the hoots and calls of unseen birds. Bullfrogs giving a deep-throated chorus.

Not long after he lit his pipe, he heard rapid footsteps coming down the road. Someone was running, by the sound of it. And when he backtracked a little ways so that he could view more of the road and the bridge, he could see a figure approaching with some speed.

"Grace!" he called out, as soon as he recognized her, and she let out a startled cry.

"Lord, man, don't do that to a person!" she said, stopping short, panting. She had her hand over her heart.

Eddie Adam lifted the lantern so that he could see her face. He thought she looked frightened.

"What done happened? You look scairt to death."

"She back. Came back this afternoon. With the chile."

Eddie Adam didn't have to ask whom she meant. He lowered the lantern, letting the night surround them both again for a moment. His body was still, but his mind raced, trying out several scenarios in his head, because he had to be prepared when Mary Nell and Eva met again.

So she was here. The boy was here. He had no way of knowing how Eva would react. He would see soon enough, he supposed.

"She ain't back with Lou Henry?" he asked now.

"That's the thing, Eddie. She sho is back there at they ole house. With the boy. I ain't even seen her. Will tole me, 'cause he the one brought her from town. He came straight to Mama after he dropped her off."

"Let's go," he said, dumping out the contents of his pipe and stomping on it.

They didn't say anything to each other as they made their way to his back door. Eva was there on the porch beside the steaming tub of water. But she stood looking out into the darkness. She started as they approached. Already she had been leaning forward. She visibly relaxed as Grace spoke.

"Eva."

"I thought . . ." Eva started to say, but didn't finish.

"I got somethin' to tell you," Grace said, coming up to the bottom of the steps and looking up at Eva. Eva stood there nodding.

"You think she gon' come over here?" Eva asked.

Grace smiled slightly, bowing her head and shaking it a little.

"I felt her sometimes even when she was away and I didn't know where she had taken him. And I could feel her gettin' closer and closer, Grace. And the boy. I can feel him, too, now that he's here. It's a strange feelin' suddenly being close to somebody that way."

Eva came down the steps until she was standing right in front of her sister. Eddie Adam hung back, trying to stomp on that little bit of fear that was creeping up inside him. Who were they, these women? He watched Grace hug Eva, murmuring in a comforting manner. They looked like two ordinary women, pretty to look at, but just women. But when Eva had said that she had felt Mary Nell coming, Eddie Adam had felt a chill. What if this thing *was* evil? Mary Nell had already hurt Eva, and he couldn't help but think that if the two of them had just been ordinary women that never could have happened.

He looked at Eva. She didn't seem upset. But then, like she said, she had known Mary Nell was coming and maybe had prepared herself for the moment. Still, there was a tension about her, a stiffness in her body that had not been there that morning.

Eddie Adam climbed the steps and stood beside her.

"If you don't want to see her, I can go and tell her," he said. "At least give you a chance to get yourself ready for . . ."

"For what, Eddie Adam?" Eva asked softly. "Gotta see her sooner or later. And I can't see him without her. She got a hold on him now that I don't think I can break. I don't know if I want to . . . that little boy ain't really mine now, is he?" She stared down at the cooling bathwater, looking at her reflection in it. "I ain't sure about nothin', but I feel I gotta get it over with, seein' her and the boy."

Eddie Adam slipped an arm around her shoulders and she leaned her head against his. She hadn't leaned on him like that in a long time, and even this moment was brief, because she straightened up and went into the house, saying, "The water's gettin' cold. I need to pour in another kettle-full."

Grace stood there frowning after Eva had gone into the house.

"Eddie Adam, you or Willow gotta stay with her," she said. "One of us need to be with her when Mary Nell and Eva see one t'nother again."

He nodded. Eva came back out with the kettle.

"You still here, Grace?" she asked. "Better get on back home to George now."

Mary Nell felt around with her mind for Eva. She did this while she was sitting at the kitchen table, pretending to be listening to Lou Henry. Well, she was listening with maybe one ear. And Jimmie was listening to him with rapt attention, even though the man was ignoring him and had been for the past day or so.

"I really done missed you all this time, Mary Nell," Lou Henry was saying earnestly. This was the tune he'd been playing for the past twenty-four hours, ever since she'd come in and sat down and asked if there was anything to eat. Surprisingly, there was. And even more surprising to her was the fact that he scrambled to get together dinner himself. She realized then that in all the time she had been away, she had rarely thought about Lou Henry, at least not about him in particular. She'd thought about the humiliation of what he'd done to her. She'd thought about whether or not you could be a respectable married woman if your husband did the kinds of things Lou Henry had done. He had robbed her of her respectability, she thought. She'd thought about the child and how he needed to know his father.

But not once had she thought about whether she loved him or not.

Even now, she could not think about him too much, her mind was so bent on seeking out Eva. It traveled across the dust of

Johnson Creek looking for her. She hadn't thought out, either, what she was going to say to Eva. She'd just known she had to come home and see her and see what she had become. She knew about the marriage to Eddie Adam. Will had told her that. He'd gone on and on about their little girl. Beautiful child, he'd said. Lanky, like their sister Grace.

She wondered if the child was Eddie Adam's. When she saw Eva, maybe she'd know.

"I guess what I'm wonderin' is, if you here to stay," said Lou Henry, glancing at Jimmie. "You ain't goin' off again? Things been mighty hard 'round here without you. Things been mighty lonely for me."

"I can't imagine you being lonely," Mary Nell said quietly. Her mind searched and searched for her little sister. Yes, there she was. She was different, Mary Nell thought. Joyless. The thought of it didn't bother Mary Nell at all.

"Well, I have been."

"I don't know yet 'bout stayin'," Mary Nell said. "I just wanted you to meet your son."

Lou Henry looked at the boy, and again looked away.

"No use you pretendin' he ain't there. If I stay, he sho gon' stay with me. He's mine. So you better get used to him sittin' there. 'Sides, he be a help to you down the road when he's older."

"So you stayin'?"

"I don't know. That depends on some things." Like whether she could live so near to Eva. Would they share dreams again? Mary Nell didn't think she could stand such closeness again.

There was a knock at the door and when Lou Henry opened it, Grace stepped in. Her eyes swept the room, taking in Mary Nell and the boy in one glance.

"Well, it didn't seem like you were gonna come to us, so I came to you first," she said.

Mary Nell stood up and walked quickly over to Grace, almost throwing herself into her arms. "You all right?" Mary Nell asked. "You all right?"

"Well, baby, I'm glad to see you." Grace drew back and looked at her sister. "Though it look like you been livin' a little rough."

"You all right?" Mary Nell asked again, insistently.

"I'm all right—some of the time." Grace dropped her arms. "I had to almost throw myself in front of Mama to keep her from marchin' over here. But I wanted to see you first."

"This here is my son, Jimmie," Mary Nell said, going over and putting a hand on the little boy's shoulder.

Grace frowned at her. "I was there, remember? I know whose son he is," she said.

Mary Nell only smiled and said to the little boy, "Go on and give your Aunt Grace a hug, chile. She my big sister."

Jimmie came hesitantly over to Grace and slowly wrapped his arms around her legs. She bent down and looked into his soft, brown face, then squatted to embrace him.

She looked back and forth between Lou Henry and Mary Nell, shaking her head slowly. "Don't do this, Mary Nell," she whispered. "Surely, the good Lord knows who belongs to who. You can't pretend otherwise."

"But it's God that done give him to me, Grace. He made me barren, but He gave me Jimmie to make up for it. He's mine, mine and my husband's. Who's gon' tell me different? You? Eva?"

"Mama and Papa know'd what you done."

"So? I don't think they gon' say different either. I'm the only mama he knows, anyway. It's too late for anything else now."

Grace just shook her head, stroking the boy's small head. He looked up and smiled at her.

"We gon' go over later today and meet your grandmama and grandpapa, Jimmie," Mary Nell said. Lou Henry looked pained, but Mary Nell noticed that he didn't protest anything she said. She gave him a small smile and he looked startled. She felt more sure that she could stay. Yes, she could stay and live in this house with her husband and son. There was only Eva to see. Get that over, and her life was set.

Eva was startled by the sound of squeaking. Behind her, Eddie Adam was hanging a kerosene lamp from a hook.

She had been sitting on the porch for hours, it seemed. Now she absently noted the sun leaving the sky. Dusk lay as heavy as a blanket. And *she* was coming. Eva had felt it all day.

"If you gon' be out here, have some light," Eddie Adam said. She looked up at him, knowing well that worried look he wore.

"Don't let Patricia come out here," she said.

The child's incomprehensible chatter came floating out, riding on the backs of evening breezes and lightning bugs, and Willow's voice, low and slow, answered. But Eva couldn't make out the words.

All her attention was focused on the mind that now opened itself to her. For three years she had groped with her thoughts for Mary Nell, and a dark curtain had blocked out all light between them.

Two days ago the curtain had lifted. Mary Nell was coming home. She no longer feared her own anger. It was safely obscured behind a shimmering hard shell, but Eva felt it there still. It screamed inside her head. Her sister had not come home for reconciliation.

Eva heard a sound, and turned her head to glance up at Eddie Adam. But he had gone inside without her noticing.

She looked back out into the approaching night, feeling Mary Nell. But it was not her that Eva saw first. It was the child, pattering down the road way ahead of the light—the lamp Grace carried—that feebly poked a hole in the gray dark.

Eva didn't even see Mary Nell until Grace was striding into the yard, with Mary Nell walking in her wake. And by then, the child was standing at the bottom of the steps gazing up at her uncertainly. He had been singing a little nonsense song. But he stopped when he reached the steps and now only the night—close all around them—spoke through the voices of things unseen.

Eva stood up quickly, in one sure motion. Dimly, she was aware that Eddie Adam had returned to the doorway and that Patricia continued to talk baby-talk inside the house, but Willow was now silent. Eva waited to fall apart as she came to the edge of the porch and looked down at the boy's face, gleaming in the light of the lamp. But she didn't. She could still breathe and stand.

He smiled, and Eva felt her heart lurch. She put a foot forward, ready to step down, and a wave of angry indignation swept over her, traveling across the dirt yard from Mary Nell, who now pushed Grace aside and surged forward. But her expression was bland as she took the child's hand.

Grace sighed, coming forward to place the lamp she was carrying on the bottom step.

"Here," she said wearily, to neither of them and to both of them, "is your sister."

Eva stepped down until she was eye level with Mary Nell, planting both feet on the bottom step. Mary Nell stared at her defiantly, squeezing that child's hand so hard that he winced. Much that Eva had forgotten came rushing back. The sharp sense of duality, of being partway inside another person's skin and skull, came back to her entering her body it seemed through the very air. As Mary Nell exhaled, Eva inhaled, and in that way she again reconnected the tattered ends between them. But it wasn't the same, of course. It was as if, as Mary Nell looked at her, the deep well Eva had fallen into three years ago became bottomless. She was forever falling, adrift in the moist air, wanting more than anything to hit the bottom and know no more of life.

Grace sat on the steps and looked up at the two of them as they stood there. She couldn't say anything more; Ayo was coming. Even as she watched Eva and Mary Nell's stare-down, her grandmother was arriving, as she had so many other times. She was arriving and planting her mind on top of Grace's. Ayo's consciousness grew like a weed, steadily smothering that part of Grace that she recognized as herself.

She rarely fought it anymore and usually, luckily, Ayo chose to emerge when Grace was alone. Not tonight, however. Her headache had been building since last night's visit to Eva; a tension had been tightening the screws.

Grace had a way, though, of ignoring her. The old woman whispered loudly to her with the voice of a child, and Grace made her body very still and limp. She breathed as deeply and evenly as possible.

What to do? Them two can't be without each other, if they

could only see that. They gon' live a hellish life without each other.

Grace tried not to think. Because if she answered Ayo with her thoughts, she responded by speaking even more. So Grace just put her hands between her knees and breathed until everything in front of her eyes blurred and she couldn't see anything, though she knew her eyes were still open. She just breathed. She imagined the air leaving her body and turning into a night bird and flying high, high until it touched the roof of the surrounding forest.

Mary Nell and Eva still said nothing and then Ayo's voice came into the silence, echoing her own fears.

They don' understand. They don' understand what they got. If they knew how wide the world was and how few people could do the things they do, they wouldn't be standing there, silent and angry.

Grace felt herself nodding, but she didn't dare put any words in her head. She let her hands go limp, resting them in the folds of her dress. Ayo became silent.

After a few moments, she saw a light in the distance. Even as it caught her attention, it grew. Then the night was before her again. And so were her sisters, Mary Nell bending over her frowning, one hand stroking her arm. Eva standing there, on the verge of tears, with the boy clutching her skirts. She absently had an arm around his little shoulders. Mary Nell sighed and smiled.

"Still scarin' folk, I see," she said. "Thought you might be over that by now."

Grace shook her head. Inside she was listening. Ayo was still silent. She didn't feel that peculiar sensation, like two people in one body. Eva had once described the same feeling when trying to explain about herself and Mary Nell. Why does Eva get to share everything with a real, live person and I have to endure this spirit? she thought. And even as the thought flickered in her mind, she sensed a weak response, from somewhere deep down, but then Mary Nell grasped her arm to pull her up and whatever answer was forming never materialized.

"Come on in the house for a minute, Grace," Eva said. She then seemed to become aware that she was holding Jimmie's shoulders and started, moving away to look down at him. Mary Nell looked from Eva to Jimmie, unsmilingly. But she didn't say anything.

"Yeah, let's go on in and get you some water," she said.

Grace's legs felt shaky as she stood. The boy stared up at her and she tried to smile. Looking up, she saw that Willow had joined Eddie Adam at the door and now as she made her way up the steps, she went back inside.

As soon as Grace sat down, Willow came forward with a glass of water, but she wasn't looking at Grace. She couldn't keep her eyes off Mary Nell, who had come to stand inside the door. Jimmie was beside her again, clutching her hand. Little Patricia, who had been hovering around the stove, came over and planted herself in front of him and just stared.

"You want somethin' girl?" Willow asked Mary Nell.

"No, I just stopped by to speak to y'all. And to . . . bring my son by to meet y'all."

Eva sucked in her breath and turned away, her face to the wall. Willow smiled wryly.

"Now, Mary Nell. You ain't foolin' nobody here in this room, 'cept maybe that there child." She nodded at Jimmie. "Pro'bly you won't be foolin' anybody . . ."

"Why not?" Mary Nell lifted her chin a little higher. "Far as anybody know he my son. I'm the only mama he know. You can't go 'round tellin' on me without tellin' on her." She waved her hand briefly at Eva. "You want everybody to know what she done?"

"She ain't done nothin' wrong!" Eddie Adam burst out. Patricia started and looked up at her father in wonder and fear. Grace had never seen him angry before, but now his head was thrust out toward Mary Nell. His clenched fists beat against the tops of his thighs. Eva went quietly over to him, putting a hand around his waist and whispering. Eddie Adam made a disgusted sound and stomped around the table and out the back door.

"Mary Nell," Grace said, her voice sounding strange to herself, "you know this is wrong. And you without Eva is wrong. How you gon' live here in Johnson Creek and with all this hangin' between you? How you gon' just steal a woman's chile and expect to live in peace?"

"He mine. God gave him to me. He mine and Lou's," Mary Nell said in a low, quiet voice that scared Grace. Her face was like stone. "Ain't no more to say. I done already started tellin' folk he mine. How you gon' come along behind me and say somethin' else? Then what you gon' say? That she laid down with my husband like a whore? You can't say the truth. Anyway, he mine now."

Eva sank down on a chair, her back to Mary Nell and the door. Grace saw that she was quietly crying. Willow came over and put a hand on her shoulder.

"Get out of this house," Willow said. When Mary Nell didn't move, Willow approached her. "Don't make me do nothin' in front of the boy."

"What you gon' do, cuss me? I'm already cursed, and Eva the one that done it. This boy all I got left. You ain't got enough roots in the world to worry me, old woman!"

"It ain't me you gotta worry about," Willow said quietly. "There's Him that knows everything, even that sad, black place deep down inside of you. That's what's gon' get you, girl."

Mary Nell glared at her and without saying anything else, grabbed Jimmie's hand and went through the front door. Patricia stood staring after them, waving.

42

Spring 1934

GRACE DIDN'T HAVE A DAY OF nausea. She felt good, full and clear-headed. Moving around was awkward, but still it was a wonderful time.

This pregnancy was so much easier than her first. Giving George those twin sons had been the hardest thing she had ever done in her life. After they were born, it seemed as if God had said she'd done enough. But then you couldn't know the mind of God, could you? Ten years later, here she was, again waiting. Her father was convinced that it was another boy.

Ayo hadn't spoken for many long months. She was silent and Grace laughed so much that George often said he wasn't sure it was his wife. But he loved it, he drank her laughter.

She didn't want the child to be born. She liked the feeling of someone tumbling around inside of her. Even when it was uncomfortable, it was comforting. The soft presence of the child was different from the urgency, pain, loss and fear that Ayo seemed to bring with her. And while the baby was there, Ayo was gone. That in itself was a miracle.

"Uh-huh," Willow said one day, as she bent her head and pressed an ear to Grace's swollen belly. "Girl."

"What you doin'?" Joy had asked, frowning.

"Listenin'. Sound like a girl."

"That's crazy. You don't know." Joy came over and actually pushed Willow's head away from Grace's belly. "I know you too old now to stop your devilish ways, but I wish you wouldn't bring it to my doorstep!"

Willow caught Grace's eye and smiled. Grace simply laughed out loud and Joy squeezed her lips together in a straight line and turned her back.

"I hear her! I hear my baby laughin'!" George called from the porch. Grace heard his heavy boots and then he was in the doorway.

"Your baby in here," she said, smiling and pointing at her belly.

"Two babies," he said. He came over and touched Grace's cheek briefly.

He had come to walk her back home after she'd spent the day at Joy's, supposedly helping her with a quilt top, but mostly just sitting there watching her sort pieces of fabric and listening to her talk and talk the way she did.

"I'm ready," Grace said, holding on to his arm to get up.

"Oh, here, darlin'," Joy said, getting up quickly. "You said you wanted to make a quilt for the baby, though I wish you had started long before this. You really ain't got any more time. Here, take these." She handed Grace a large bundle of rags tied together with a string.

"I think the colors will go together well," she said. "And I got plenty to use."

"Thank you, Mama," Grace said, delighted and eager to get started.

"Thing is, you better at sewing than I am, and that ain't an easy thing for a proud woman like me to own up to." Joy smiled, even as Grace opened her mouth to deny it. "Don't bother, baby, you know you can quilt better'n me. Lord knows I don't see how you make them stitches so little. I guess you inherited that from my mama. She was good with sewing or anything to do with cloth. You seen her quilts. Matter of fact, I put some of her left-over pieces—you know, what was in that old trunk—in with what I done gave you. Might as well use everything up before it get too old and falls apart."

Grace was struck dumb for a moment, even as Joy pushed the bundle into her hands. She felt a little pang go through her. *Is it me that sews or is it Ayo?* Her grandmother was silent, but still there, guiding her hands. She was there in Grace's fingertips. She turned the cloth over in her hands, recognizing the older pieces from the trunk, although she hadn't seen them for a long time.

Grace started to hand that bundle right back, right there in that room. She thought about it, she even moved her arm as if to hold it out. But Joy was smiling and George was smiling. He had his hand pressed against Grace's back, rubbing gently. Willow was making for the door and talking up a storm.

"Now, George, when the water break, you just send some-body. Send one of the twins. Don't *you* leave her, now, send somebody else. I'll be ready." Willow was halfway out the door now and Grace heard her say on her way down the stairs, "Got my bag ready to grab and go . . ."

So Grace just took the bundle of cloth. Tucked it under her arm. Ignored the mental discomfort that settled around her, even then in the midst of one of the happiest times of her life.

They ate supper early and Grace sat out afterward with a basket full of the cloth scraps on the porch beside her feet. She had put in there all the pieces she thought might work for the quilt. Just a little quilt, she thought. A child's quilt.

The boys were arguing in their room. George was somewhere in the back of the house, worrying with the dogs, maybe, and the evening was moving in fast. Soon she wouldn't be able to see the cloth in the basket on her lap. Or maybe she would. Grace noticed that the full moon had already appeared in the eastern sky.

With some difficulty, she bent down and sifted through the basket's contents until she found that old piece of blue cloth she had noticed earlier. It seemed light as air, almost transparent, but still colored a deep mysterious blue. That was certainly one of Ayo's pieces. Grace had seen it before. Too dark, surely, for anything for a child, especially for a girl, if Willow was right.

Grace held it absently in her hand. She could just go with a nine-patch. Simple. But somehow she needed it to be a little fancier for her baby. Not just a plain old nine-patch pattern that any child could make. Maybe a basket pattern that would be nice for a girl.

The evening seemed very loud. The crickets were going to town. She seemed to hear everything and anything that was out there beyond the porch, beyond the yard, on the edge of the night that approached. From out back, she heard George singing to himself, then banging something, then muttering. Some animal was walking around in the bushes on the other side of the road, sniffing and snuffling. If the possum was going to be that loud, it would be a dead possum soon, Grace thought.

The moon rode up in the sky, soft and full. It seemed to be racing and she felt as if she had let the day slip from her fingers. She had spent nearly all day at her mother's house and now the light had faded on her as she sat there trying to picture what the quilt should look like.

She bent down again and ran her hands over the cloth, looking for something. She had just thought of a bird, a dove maybe. And she'd seen some white muslin there in the bottom of the basket. There it was and in her mind's eye she pictured pure white wings fluttering across a field of sky blue. They grew and grew in her mind into the largest bird she'd ever seen.

I thought at first it was a big bird. See, I just could see out the corner of my eye. I'm lying there with my face in the sand and one eye closed shut and off in the distance these huge white fluttering things.

"No," Grace whispered aloud. She saw them, too, the large white sails and the ship rolling on top of the waves. She only saw the ocean in Ayo's nightmares, waking or otherwise, and she knew that her grandmother had returned. The child stirred within her, restless and straining. She'll be here soon, Grace thought. And I can't be in a state when she comes.

She'll remember. If you show her, Ayo whispered. *Mama and me carrying the basket. The market and him what carried me off. The ship on the water.*

Each scene Ayo laid out leapt to life in front of her eyes. She rocked the chair back and forth on the porch boards, her hand on her belly, and Ayo gave it all to her, as if she were turning the pages of some frightful book.

The sound of the ocean was in her ears, though she had never heard it for herself. And she was on that sand, trying to stand.

"All right, them dogs are set for the night!" George came out on the porch, wiping his hands on a towel, and Grace blinked. The sound of the ocean still lingered in her ears, but she was there again in Johnson Creek, on the porch of their house, rocking and putting out an arm to George so that he could help her up and into the house.

"I'm almost afraid to touch you these days, honey," he said, smiling. "You might pop!"

"I might," she said, trying to recapture the lightness that her voice had had earlier in the day. But it was gone.

"Don't worry," George said, looking down at her as he shut the door behind them. When he did, she didn't hear the ocean anymore.

She nodded. "Everything's gon' be fine."

The next morning after George had gone out to the field with the two boys, Frank and Phillip, and she had cleaned up the dishes, she sat at the kitchen table cutting the cloth. She had decided on a simple, colorful nine-patch that could be made quick. But as she held the scrap of blue cloth in her hand, the only shape she saw was a female figure. The waist and hips. She found a sheet of old newspaper and drew the shape on there. Just chest, waist and hips—no head. Then she laid the newspaper on top of the blue cloth and cut around it, leaving a little cloth for seams, and folded the edges of the cloth over the paper.

When she turned it over, she smiled. A shapely figure in a blue dress.

The cloth basket yielded a good sized piece of green cloth for background, and Grace placed the blue figure on it tentatively, moving it several times before it seemed to rest in the right spot. Putting that aside, she cut another smaller figure from the blue, just as she had done before and placed it beside the larger one.

"Mama and child," she murmured. "Maybe I can put this square in the middle and use a nine-patch border."

But the next day, as she sat there at the table, watching her husband walking through the field working, she cut out three sails from white cloth. The next day she cut out the boat, and pinned them down on a gray background. All through the week, a variety of pictures emerged from the basket, and as she wielded her scissors, Grace was no longer smiling. She felt like crying all the time, actually, and she hid the scraps of cloth away when George came home.

She knew that Ayo was speaking again, this time through the cloth, giving her those horrible pictures to show to the world. But she didn't stop, because as long as she had the quilt to work on, the voice of Ayo that usually took up residence in her mind was quiet. But still, she showed Grace what she wanted her to know. And the pictures that came into her mind, the ones she tried to translate to the cloth, were often too horrible to speak of anyway.

So she just sat and worked. She didn't do much of anything except cook and cut cloth for that whole week. Late on Friday, she began having little twinges of pain, but she said nothing to George.

On Sunday after church, as she sat down to dinner at her mother's table, she felt something in her belly give. And then there was womb water soaking through her best dress and George standing there looking dumbstruck and Eva running home to get Willow and her father, Frank, dancing gleefully and shouting something about grandchildren. "A boy this time, a grandboy!" he shouted.

Everyone was flying all different directions except her boys, who happily took care of the abandoned meal.

She remembered her mother pushing her father out of the way playfully, in order to help Grace to the bedroom. Then the pain that washed over her at regular intervals made the room look hazy. It was hard to see. She thought Mary Nell was there for a while and for a moment, Ayo, Ayo herself stood at the foot of the bed, passively looking. She was an old woman, her head swathed in a red rag, her hands lined and knotted. Grace propped herself up on her elbows to look at her. Sweat slid down her forehead and into her eyes, blurring everything for a moment, but Ayo still stood there.

"What is it, chile?" Willow asked, looking at the place where Grace was staring so intently.

"I have to get up," Grace said wearily.

"What you mean, you gotta get up?" her mother squeaked.

"Help me," Grace gasped, beginning to move to the side of the bed. "She's comin'!"

"What?" Willow asked, even as she helped Grace to sit on the edge of the bed.

"Sarah's comin'!" Grace began gesturing. "Put something down, something soft, on the floor. I have to squat." She looked back to where Ayo was standing. The old woman was smiling now.

"You gotta what?" her mother gasped. "Listen, now, we ain't slaves squattin' in the cotton field. You lay down now. You gon' hurt yourself and the baby . . ."

"Be quiet now, Joy, she ain't gon' hurt nothin'. If the mother got a mind to do somethin', you let her. That's how you had yours, remember? Yo' mama made you and it was a whole lot easier." Joy snorted and rolled her eyes, while Willow threw some bedclothes on the floor. "Get over here! Get behind her and hold her under the arms."

Willow caught baby Sarah; she didn't let her hit the floor. Grace leaned back in her mother's arms and Joy gently wiped the sweat from her face with a clean towel.

Sarah didn't cry. She lay there in Willow's arms wiggling.

"She all right?" Grace asked. "She breathin'? She ain't cryin'!"

"She fine. She a beauty." Willow smiled as she cleaned the baby. "She say she ain't got no reason to cry. It's a beautiful birthday and she glad to be here."

Grace took a deep breath and laughed. When she looked back at the foot of the bed, Ayo was gone. For now.

43

THE STORM RUSHED UP FROM THE southeast and Eva, walking from the church to her parents' house, came to that place in the road.

The wind flogged the bushes and small trees off to the side of the path, making their thin branches whine with pain. Eva put a hand to her throat where the memory of bruises lingered. And then she ran toward home, trying to stay ahead of the wind, only stopping when she reached her grandmother Bessie's back porch, gulping damp air.

One day, it wouldn't be so, she thought. I'll pass this way, storm or no storm, without a thought. I won't frown and I won't flinch.

Eva hadn't been here in awhile. Not since that day she and Grace had looked through the trunk for linens. Her mother used to talk of living in this house and about how Grandmama had spoken often of slavery time before she died. Sometimes she talked, too, about Africa. Joy said she had written down a lot of her mother's stories, but when they asked to hear them, she would just bend back over her sewing. Papa would look up from whatever he was doing and a certain hardness would descend on his features, half anger, half fear.

"No need to listen to Bessie's old stories," he would say, his usual pleasant expression replaced by an unhappy shadow.

And Grace would shiver there by the fire.

Eva, breathing heavily, sat down on an overturned tin tub, half rusted through, in the yard. She wondered if Bessie had left it there. Maybe she'd done the washing one day, and just put it down and went inside, and never walked outside again.

She wrapped her arms around her shaking body, knowing she ought to keep going on, but thinking it might be better to wait until the rain passed. It was surely coming. But Eddie Adam and Willow would worry if she wasn't there soon. And her daughter would ask for her. The church's ladies' aid meetings were not long. Everybody got nervous when Eva was gone for long periods of time. They would remember a Sunday in June that she'd never made it to church and they'd come to look for her.

The sky, dark and pregnant with heavy water, stepped down from heaven to speak to the land in anger, and then caressed it with electric fingers. That first flash of lightning threw shadows all about the woods and in one patch of gray, a figure moving slowly, coming closer with each illumination. Eva saw a shadow thrown out against the bushes that grew beside the narrow road.

By the time Willow was close enough to speak, the rain was falling fast and Eva was standing.

"Crazy will save you."

That's what Eva's mother-in-law said, standing there with the clouds dumping their sorrow on her, making her clothes stick slickly to her body. Mud dissolved into little red pools around her bare feet, as if they bled.

"Miz Willow," Eva sighed in relief. "You scared me half outta my head, sneaking round the corner like that. Why ain't you back at the house? Where's Patricia?"

"Now—" Willow stopped at the bottom of the porch steps and pointed her stick upward "—is good a time as any."

Eva's arms tightened around her body. She said nothing, but looked up at the iron gray clouds. She thought maybe she should try to escape from the rain, at least seek whatever shelter the patchwork porch could give her. But she made no move. Her body didn't want it. Behind her, Ayo's old house creaked as the air moved through the many spaces in the boards and Eva took a step or two backward, upward on the steps, looking down into Willow's eyes, which gave off their own, faint light as the sky darkened.

"If I was near the real water, the sea, I'd take you there. I seen it befo'. Down in Mobile. She was big, big, chile. She rolled back and forth, licking the land. Oh, she make you real right, the sea. But a storm next best thing. Hard rain—that's the sea for sinners. Baptize you in new water from heaven. Make you clean," Willow said.

Cold fear gripped Eva. "Why'd you follow me? When I left, you said you was busy making a dress. Where's my chile?"

Willow glanced back over her shoulder. "Patricia is fine. She with her daddy. God put me on the path behind you 'cause He know'd it was time. When people hurts you, they leaves a stain.

I see it. I see it all over you. I see that man's evil self stand where you are, and you carry his sin 'round with you."

"Who you talkin' 'bout, old lady?" Anger and fear crumpled Eva's voice into a tight fist. She didn't want Willow to speak of it. Already, she felt as if her shame must be riding around on the air. People must be breathing it in and then breathing it out as they whispered in each other's ears.

"You think I don't know he squeezed the life out of you with his lust? You 'bout old as me now. Older. And I'm a very old woman." Willow smiled gently. "But it ain't just years make you old. You was old always, and on Second Sunday you got older. If you mama and papa had let you, I could have helped you, made you strong, strong as old Bessie . . ." She sighed, looking past Eva at the house.

"You crazy. I never believed Mama when she said so, but you is crazy!" Eva tried to laugh, but it came out as a snort.

"You need crazy. Come on and get some. Crazy gon' save you."

Eva stared at Willow, leaning there on her walking stick with her bare head and the wet wind winding and unwinding her long gray naps around her neck. Willow smiled and turned around to walk back down the road in the direction of the church. As she came to the curve, just before she was lost from sight, she turned all the way around and gestured to Eva with her stick, motioning her to follow. Then she disappeared around the curve in the road.

Eva went down the porch steps, stopping at the bottom. Could Willow have done what she said? Kept Lou Henry away? Turned his eye so that it fell on some other unfortunate soul? Kept his heart with her sister?

The lightning flashed and Eva thought for a moment that she was back there in Willow's yard, looking at the charm bag being held out to her. And then she was there in the kitchen with the cup of herb tea in front of her, begging for some way to erase her shame. She thought of little Jimmie and the last time she had seen him, playing in her own yard with Patricia until they were both covered with red-gold dust. Again she shivered, and Willow's voice came to her.

"He gon' die," she heard her say. "He gon' die in pain and fear." Who? Eva asked silently. Who? Was she talking about Lou Henry? But all Eva's mind saw was Jimmie's little face, round and happy. It was as if he was standing right there in front of her, where he hadn't been a moment before. And he was beckoning to her to go somewhere. Pointing to where Willow had gone down the road.

"Jimmie!" She felt as if she were screaming. She turned around and around in the rain-soaked yard, but she was the only one there.

"Come on chile. Now is the time." It was Willow's voice, coming from far ahead on the road. Eva couldn't be hearing her this clearly, not with the howling wind trying to compete with the thunder. But she found herself moving, slowly at first but then faster as lightning burned the sky.

They had turned off the road long ago, and Willow now led the way through thick pine trees whose tops spiraled in the wind in some kind of drunken shimmy. They were on old Johnson's land, once part of his vast fields. But the woods had waited and taken the place back. After the war, when Johnson had more land than people to work it, he had just let more and more of it lay. And the trees and weeds had edged over the old rows of dirt, burying the cotton field.

There was an old shack back there, the one that overlooked the creek. It once had stood on the back edge of a field. Now it slumbered amidst the trees, tumbling down around itself. Only half of it was standing, and when they arrived there a deer was inside, shaking the water off her mottled coat. The doe took off through the driving rain as they came crashing through the bushes.

"What we here for?" Eva cried.

"We need to be 'way from the road. So's folks cain't see."

"See what? What you doin'?" Eva turned to leave, but Willow put a gentle hand on her arm.

"I'm gon' make it so the Lord touch you as he would a new-born chile. Take off your dress."

"I ain't!"

"Lord, wash this chile clean of the touch of sin!"

"You must be outta yo' head. I sho ain't taking off my dress."

"Take it off." Willow came and grasped Eva's head and looked at her hard. "You have to do it now, while you still remember what it's like to be whole. I been waiting for a day like this. A stormy day in May, in spring. May rain makes everything clean. It makes everything grow. Wash the evil off your body and outta your heart, and become a chile again. The little one needs someone who ain't dead inside. My grandson he love you with all his heart and he need you, the real you, the live one. Not this dead thing that goes 'round walkin' and talkin' like a woman."

Eva almost gave in right there and then, under the weight of Willow's tumble of words. The old woman's rock-hard will seemed unnatural coming from so thin a body. This was a woman she had grown to love and respect, but there, surrounded by grayness, noise and rain, the whisperings about witches and root workings came back to her. Eva wrenched herself from Willow's grasp without a word, picked up the tail of her skirt and walked past Willow.

"I'll be waitin'," Willow said, loudly to be heard over the wind. She thumped her stick on the ground.

Eva didn't answer. She kept stepping through the wet weeds toward the road. Glancing back, she saw that Willow had taken a seat in the dirt next to the shack's one good wall. The rain was starting to make her clothes cling. She propped her walking stick against the wall, where it stood like a sentinel.

Damn that old woman, Eva thought. Now I gotta go and get Eddie Adam to fetch her.

The wailing sound that began to come up through the trees could have been the wind, it was so lonely. A howl almost. But it was Willow, singing.

"Oh, Freedom! Oh, Freedom! Oh, Freedom, over me, over me . . ."

Now what was she up to? Eva stopped walking, looking back again. She couldn't see Willow anymore, but the song made her present in a large way.

"And befo' I'll be a slave, I'll be buried in my grave and go home to my Lord and be free!"

"Yeah," she heard Willow say, so clearly that Eva spun around to see if she had somehow snuck up next to her. "I used to work here. Right here, for Johnson. There was a cotton field right in this spot, where I'm sittin'. I was on Johnson's, Bessie was on Ward's. Them days, them days! All we talked 'bout was what it would be like to be our own selves in our own skins. What it would be like to own our chillun. When the day finally come, we was as lost as newborn babies, some of us. We hadn't been fed freedom; we'd grown up in slavery's land. But Bessie, she knew what to do. She knew what freedom was 'spose to feel like, she ain't forgot. She was always free, I 'spect."

Eva found herself moving. Willow's voice wasn't much more than a whisper, and it never got any louder. She was nowhere in sight, but her voice sat right close to Eva's ear.

"Ummp!" Willow was saying. "Lot of them folks back then became free in body, but in they hearts . . . in they souls . . . it took a long time for them to get comfortable with that, see. Didn't know that they didn't have to go runnin' to a white man for every little question 'bout life. Some ran to the white man, some ran away from him. Mostly, they just didn't know how to get free all the way through. But they learnt. Bessie—her and her man—never did have no such problem with that thing freedom. They knew how to get free. We's all gots to know how to free ourselfs."

By now, Eva had stumbled her way back to the ruined shack. The rain, falling in big hard drops, had made a total mess of her dress. Her white head rag, which had been clean and starched this morning, hung limply half on, half off her head.

Willow hadn't moved a muscle it seemed. But when she saw that Eva had come back, she stood up slowly and took her staff in hand.

"No powders or potions or roots here, baby," she said. "Just freedom. Just you and me and God. Only us to see you as you are. You ain't got to be scairt. When you walk outta these here woods amidst God's glory, that Lou Henry gon' be scairt of you. For the rest of his life, he gon' look at you and see his damnation."

The sky was nearly black, as night had suddenly fallen, and a torrent of rain came hard and fast. It seemed to Eva that the world had closed into a little circle that included just her and

Willow and this suddenly angry God that was trying to beat her clothes off her with wind and rain.

"So you tell me," Willow said, as she held one hand out to Eva. "Tell me and tell God the way it went. And then give it to the wind. Get it from buried so deep down, so you can dig it out. Dig it out."

A few more halting steps and she felt the old woman's hand even before Willow grasped Eva's and looked into her eyes.

Willow smiled, even as her legs were crumpling. She fell to her knees, her mouth moving. Eva could not hear her over the wind, and bent down beside her.

"Willow!"

"Never mind. I'm doin' fine, chile. Now, take off your dress. It's all right." Her voice was weak and her body burned like fire.

Eva stood up again and began unbuttoning at the collar of her dress. She let it fall, and as wet as it already was, it became a dingy mass at her feet as soon as she let it go. She stood shivering in her worn white underslip.

"The underclothes. The shoes. Everything," Willow whispered.

Afraid not to go on, Eva did as she said, trying to pile everything neatly and watching the rain quickly create a puddle inside her shoes. She wrapped her arms around her body, trying to cover her full breasts.

"Now," Willow motioned Eva to kneel beside her. When she didn't move, Willow grabbed her wrist and pulled Eva down. She snatched the limp, soaking head rag off Eva's head and flung it on the ground. Eva felt something like a scream positioning itself in the back of her throat, moving forward, choking off her breath.

"You tell me. But you know you ain't really tellin' me. You tellin' Him. You telling God."

Eva shook her head.

"Don't you want to be a real woman again? Not a ghost woman? Don't you want to go home to your husband and chile whole? I ain't sayin' this here gon' fix it all. But you got to put a crack in that stone fence you got 'round you. And you best make it a big one."

She couldn't tell if the old woman was weeping or whether that was rain running down her face. Could have been either one.

It had been a long time since Eva had been this open. And everything came at her at once. Her mother, back at home, going from the kitchen table to the window to look out at the storm, to the table again. Mary Nell surely was in her barn; Eva felt her brush up against the mule she was leading out of the storm, felt the stiff hairs on the animal's hide and heard Mary Nell's voice trying to soothe it. And Lou Henry called out to her from outside, sending a shiver through Eva. And Grace lying spread eagle on her bed, her eyes staring up at the stained ceiling, in another world. And George coming to gaze at her in fearful incomprehension. And Patricia, beginning that whine that would soon turn into a cry. And Eddie Adam. Eddie Adam, gazing sadly into the fire as the little girl squirmed on his lap.

Eva let go of Willow's hands and held them up to her ears. The pine needles slipped and slid under her knees, as if the earth was moving.

Willow put her hands over Eva's and forced them down. She put an arm around her and rocked her like a baby there in the howling wind and rain. They were both shivering, but Eva began to feel calmer.

"I was late," she whispered. "Like usual, I was slow. And they all went on to church without me. So I had to hurry. I didn't want to get my dress dirty." She hesitated and Willow squeezed her shoulders. "I musta done something," Eva continued. "I don't know. But I don't remember doing anything bad. I didn't do nothin'! I was on the road, just tryin' to get to church, tryin' to get there before the song started. It was like they had already started. I thought I could hear the singin' and I was mad with myself. And he stepped out into the road. And he had me. God, Willow, he had me. He threw me down in the mud . . . !"

She stopped. The rain had begun to let up a little, but she felt none of it anyway. Willow shivered, but held on to her tightly.

"You go on, baby . . ." she said. "It's all right. Nobody got to hear 'cept me and God."

"God don't want to hear nothin' from me . . . can't just unmake somethin' by talkin'."

"Maybe you ain't never told God your side of things. All you been doin' is listenin' to your sister maybe. Even after she left, you listened to her voice in your head and turned your face from God. You cain't do that, baby! God knows who you are. Take all your pain to Him."

Eva tried to remember everything she'd ever heard about God. Kneeling there, she tried to remember. Sin was sin, wasn't it?

"Sin is sin," she whispered.

"Listen to me," Willow said, shaking her and placing her palms on either side of Eva's face, turning her head so that she could look directly into her eyes. Willow was soaked to the skin. She kneeled there with Eva, blinking rain out of her eyes. "Yes, sin is sin. But it's his sin, not yours. It's his evil that you carryin' around like you done bought and paid for it."

Eva shivered.

"He pulled . . . me . . . down . . . I saw the trees . . . then he was rippin' everythang, rippin' me apart and I couldn't stop him . . . dear God, I couldn't stop him . . . I couldn't . . ." She shook with fear and anger and the white-hot pain tore into her. But only for a moment. She shuddered and slipped out of Willow's arms onto the soggy ground and the lightning continued to illuminate the cloud-gray sky. Willow stood, holding out her hands.

"You stand up now and be a woman," she said. She looked strange and ghostly, swaying there, and Eva reached up to grasp her hands. They stood for a moment. The lightning flashed and Eva saw Willow's smile.

"You on the road now," she said. "You still got a ways to go. But you on the road.

"Here now," Willow said, dropping her hands and going over to where Eva's dress lay in the mud. "It's too wet to put back on. Just wrap it 'round you and go home to him that love you."

"What you gon' tell him 'bout what we did?" Eva said, trying to straighten out the dress enough to get the cloth around her body.

"You gon' tell him. You should be the one. Just remember how you feel right now. Clean. You feel clean, don't you?"

Eva didn't know how she felt. Different. Wide open. And that made her afraid. Tomorrow the storm would be gone, but she would still be stumbling in the dark. She didn't want all of Willow's effort to come to nothing, but she didn't know where this moment would take her. She was simply naked before God.

She sighed, holding the dress around her with one arm and starting off in the direction of the road. Willow stayed planted in the same spot.

"Ain't you comin', Miz Willow?" Eva asked, stopping. "You gon' catch your death out here in the wet. What you gon' stay out here for?"

"Don't worry 'bout me," the old woman said. "I got business."

Eva nodded and walked home alone under the clearing sky. By the time she came to their back door, stars were showing themselves through a soft veil of clouds and she paused there for a moment.

"Eva?"

Eddie Adam stood there on the porch, his arms down at his sides, staring at the state she was in. She tried to smile and found that it wasn't so hard, that her smile grew. She climbed the steps until she stood in front of him. And she put out one mud-covered hand and cupped his cheek, as he looked at her in uncertain wonder.

"How you, Eddie Adam?" she asked softly. "Is Patricia sleep?"

"I don't know, Ayo, my friend," Willow murmured. She walked slowly back to the roofless hut and sank wearily down onto the ground. "I think it took, but I don't know. May be I'll never know if I helped her. But I did all I could. And she stronger than she know, I think."

The clouds rolled away. The stars were appearing and the air was washed clean. She leaned her head back. The rough, old boards of the cabin seemed to give a little, and she looked up at the shining sky.

Just before she closed her eyes, she thought she saw Grace, standing like a statue in the broken-down doorway of the cabin. "Oh, my friend," Willow whispered. And Grace smiled at her with Ayo's smile.

It was Grace who told them about Willow. She appeared at the back door late that night, clutching her baby, trailed by an anxious George. Asking for Willow, then placing the child in Eva's arms and leading Eddie Adam and George to the little cabin. They found the old woman propped up against the wall of the shack, eyes wide and staring. Grace knelt and took her arm and Willow turned toward her touch. She looked without seeing.

"My friend . . ." Grace barely heard the wisp of breath that traveled between Willow's lips. ". . . I been here too long. Or maybe just long enough. Just long enough . . ."

Grace bent her ear close to Willow's lips, but she said nothing else.

MARY NELL WATCHED THE END OF summer and the plants grow increasing heavy with their fruit. As the pods on the field peas began to bend toward the ground, she started gathering her fortitude, because the day would come when her mother wanted help shelling the peas that inevitably grew in her father's fields. But she dreaded seeing Eva, who would also be there.

The pictures that often flashed in her mind of her younger sister seemed to mock her attempts at avoiding Eva during the past few weeks. It did not matter that the girl wasn't there; her presence was so acute that Mary Nell often turned around—in the house, in the barn, and especially at a certain spot in the woods—expecting Eva to be standing just over her shoulder.

1938

THE QUIET IN THE ROOM UNNERVED EVA. She didn't know quite what to make of it. Outside the open windows of the school, birds were calling to each other. Inside, twenty children sat clutching the copybooks she had just passed out. And for the first time in four years, she wondered if she was doing the right thing.

She didn't know when the thought first entered her head. After that terrible time sixteen years ago, when she had left Tuskegee with her arms empty and her heart hard, Eva could no longer remember what she had meant to do with her life. She must have had something she wanted before all of that, some dream or wish for the rest of her days, but after the train pulled into Union Springs and she had climbed into the back of her father's wagon and ridden home over the rutted road to Johnson Creek, every thought she had ever had about what would become the rest of her life left her.

It was only when she saw Eddie Adam standing there in the yard of her parents' house, waiting, that she had any idea what would happen to her.

But after that rain-soaked night when Willow died, a little thought had crept in, a little glimmer of a wish.

She had left school before finishing. Johnson Creek School only went to the sixth grade anyway. She had thought no more about it until recently. She was already married and a mother and . . . what more could there be now? She could barely keep her mind on anything.

She sat at night by the firelight with her daughter, Patricia, missing Willow, sitting with old books crumbling in her lap, going over and over the words with her, and the light in the little girl's eyes ignited a tiny something inside Eva.

As soon as she glimpsed that something, she tried to push it aside. She had a daughter to raise, a husband and house to take care of and Willow was gone. They both needed her now. She didn't need any second sight these days to see what was ahead of her.

But the thought grew and visited her mind more and more often, until once again she found herself at the train station in Union Springs, on her way to Tuskegee. Eddie Adam had looked sad as he held their daughter's hand. Patricia was crying. Mama, Papa and Grace were beaming, although Eva thought, as she looked back out of the window of the train, that Grace's smile had faded into something else. She looked very slender, almost thin, and very much alone standing there on the platform. Eva had almost wanted to get off, but it was too late for that. She was on her way to college and to long hours working in the school's kitchen to pay her way. Mary Nell, of course, had not come to the station. She tried, most of the time, to always be where Eva was not.

She felt a pang as she thought of Mary Nell and a flash of something white outside the windows caught her eye. She heard soft footsteps crunching the gravel out where the churchgoers on Sunday parked their wagons. She felt uneasy. She heard—and recognized—the ragged breathing of the person lurking.

"I'll be right back," she said to the children. "Don't get up from your seats!"

Still, they swiveled their heads and turned around in their desks as she strode down the aisle and opened one side of the church doors. Closing it quietly behind her, Eva said, "Is there something you need, Mary Nell?"

"No." Mary Nell stood in front of her. "I don't need a thing. Just passing."

"Shouldn't you be at the Wards'?" Eva asked.

Mary Nell didn't answer this question.

"How's school then?" Mary Nell asked, and Eva sighed, turning back.

"We haven't started. But I think it will be fine."

Mary Nell nodded. She sighed, glancing back at the door. "I don't know how you can keep all them things in your head long enough to teach nobody. And how you gon' keep all them chillun quiet long enough."

Eva found herself smiling a little. "We'll see soon, I suppose," she said.

"Now, if it had been me what went up there to Tuskegee, I

would have gone in for nursin'." Mary Nell, just for a moment, let drop the hard mask she always presented to Eva and an expression of profound melancholy settled over her face, over her whole body really. "Always planned that . . ."

"You would have been a good nurse," Eva said, softly. "You still could go, you know."

The mask quickly came up again.

"I ain't got time for that now. And I'm a bit old to be going up there."

"No, no, Mary Nell," Eva took a step forward and involuntarily grasped Mary Nell's forearm, ignoring the stiffening of the muscles under her fingers. "There were plenty of people our age there at the school. And older. You can still go . . ."

Mary Nell jerked her arm away, her eyes hard. Then she smiled a little, but Eva could see no joy there.

"Look at ya!" Mary Nell said. It was almost a sneer and Eva took a step back in the face of her scorn. "Went on up there to Tuskegee to try and clean yourself up, huh? Took all the country out of your voice. Walkin' a little different now, huh, since you come back? You think bein' a teacher gon' make you into a respectable person? The only reason I don't tell everybody what you really is, is 'cause I ain't gon' hurt our mama."

"How can you tell everybody what I really am, without telling what you really are," said Eva quietly. "A woman who steals other people's babies out of their birthin' bed."

Mary Nell took a step toward her, her face flashing a number of different emotions: hatred, anger, fear.

"God has a way of makin' things right," she said. "And He made things right when He gave Jimmie to me, and everybody in Johnson Creek know he my son. Naw, naw, little sister. I ain't got no time to be goin' up to no fancy school in Tuskegee or nowhere else. I got a family to take care of. I got a son."

Eva stood there shaking. She had tried for so long to put away her anger. Since Willow had died, she had tried to live up to her silent promise to the old woman: to keep on living and keep her heart open. Mary Nell made it hard. Her older sister still had an outpost in Eva's own head, making her acutely aware of exactly how Mary Nell felt about her. She felt all of her anger, malice, fear, regret and loneliness. If there was any love left, it had been smothered by these. Every attempt that Eva had made at reaching out had been rebuffed. She could stand even to see Lou Henry these days more than she could Mary Nell. He had retreated into himself and went about like a hollow man. But Mary Nell was actively cold and hard toward her, and Eva couldn't help but wonder, again and again, how they had gotten here.

She heard the children moving around inside, and faint whispers and small giggles. Without saying anything more to Mary Nell, without looking at her, Eva opened the door and went inside.

Spring 1940

A SOUND MADE ITS WAY TO GRACE'S EAR; something outside the window. Maybe a twig tossed by the wind. But maybe, the heavy breathing of ghosts coming to share their agonies with her at the very moment when such a thing would break her down. It was all leading to the crazy house, one way or the other.

"You know how it is with me now." Eva paused and put her hand on the back of the chair, slowly sitting. "I *feel* things more than I see them."

Grace stared at the window. She heard Eva, but at the same time her mind was turning over any number of options. She always came back to the same thing.

"I don't know how to help you, Grace. I love you, but I don't know how to help you. Damnation, girl. I'm just getting ahead of crazy myself—God bless Willow! But Mary Nell . . . well, Mary Nell's already there. And I just don't know how to help. I don't know how. I wish I knew how to make us all free of this . . . whatever it is."

"Gift?" Grace smiled slightly, then gave a snorting laugh.

"You leaving, then?"

Grace nodded, looking at her wonderingly. "I'm still surprised that you know these things. You've never stopped surprising me, not since the day you were born. But yes, I think . . . I can't hold nothin' in no more. She comes, the spirit, and talks to me wakin' or sleepin'. I think she's here, right here on the roads and in the woods. And if it was just her thoughts gettin' into my head, I know I could carry that burden. But she shows me things, Eva, that I don't think I can stand to look at, and yet there I am seein' it all. And the pain that she brings to me, I can't describe that to you. It's too hard."

"You should have let Willow help you," Eva said.

"She couldn't."

Eva looked down at Grace's hands lying in her lap. She took one in her own and pushed up the sleeve of Grace's blouse.

"George seen that?" she asked, tracing the line of a scar that wrapped all the way around Grace's wrist like a bracelet.

"He think I got it tangled in some barbed wire. But Ayo got it on that slave ship. That and more."

Eva rubbed the scar gingerly, closing her eyes. "More of that coming, maybe. I can see blood. I don't know whose. But when I touch you there, I see it."

Grace gently grasped Eva's fingers and removed her hand from her arm, pulling the sleeve back in place. "I ain't gon' burden you with the when," she said. "I don't rightly know when I'm goin'. I almost can't stand to think it. When my mind is clear, I put it away back in my head, 'cause I think maybe it be over, you know? Maybe that last time was the last time. But it ain't ever, Eva. It ain't ever the last time. Even when them visions gone, she's there. Inside of me, looking out on the world. Giving me her pain to keep for her. Oh, Lord . . ." Grace balled up a fist and pressed it to her chest, her head dropping so that her hair fell over her face. Through that veil of curls, Eva heard her say, "Maybe if I go away from this place, she'll stay here."

Eva was silent, and Grace jerked her head up, trying to meet the younger woman's eyes. But Eva wouldn't let Grace see into her.

"You know something."

"I don't know anything, Grace. All I got is shadows and voices up there in my head. I recognize you sometimes. And it feels sad. But that's just about all I got. If me and Mary Nell . . ." She paused and shook her head slightly. "Well . . . it just ain't the way it used to be."

"The chillun . . . Sarah and the twins . . ."

"Yes?"

"Are they gon' be all right?"

"I don't feel nothin' about them. But I think that's good."

Grace sighed. "You'll help him, Eva? Please. George. I don't think it's gon' be for long. I'll be back when things get better."

Eva was silent.

"The other night," Grace said softly, "I was in here and one of them fits came over me. A bad one. And I didn't really know where I was. But I did see George come in, happy. And he pulled me up and threw his arms around me to hug me, and I felt this awful, awful pain all over my back, like it was covered with raw welts. And I knew what it was from—when they beat her. Our grandmother was beaten worse than a mule. And it was like them scars were there, just made . . . when he touched me."

Eva buried her face in her hands, but Grace continued.

"And I just fell down. My legs went right out from under me when the pain hit. I was down here right on the floor screamin' and when I knew anything again and could think again I was layin' on my stomach on a bed and someone was there. I knew, I knew, that I'd gone back. Back to when she got them whip marks. And there was blood everywhere.

"I woke up sometime that night, early mornin' really, just before the sun, lying in there on the bed where George had put me. And he's sittin' there staring at me, so scairt, so scairt. I could see it in his eyes. I was on the bed and he wasn't touchin' me. I don't never want to see that look on his face again, like he was looking at the devil himself or some demon or some witch. And he ain't been back in our bed since that night."

Eva shook her head, her eyes full of tears and just visible over her fingers.

"Before then, I had already reckoned on going. That same day, I had taken the suitcase down. But I was hurtin' so. And I just didn't want to leave George with that look on his face. I didn't want that to follow me. But, I know I have to. I have to." Grace looked down at her hands in her lap. "She won't leave," she whispered. "So I gotta leave her."

"Where will you go?" Eva asked hoarsely.

"North. Everybody goin' north these days. Why not?"

THERE WAS EVA AT HER DOOR with so much sadness on her face that Mary Nell forgot what she was going to say. Her face was made gray by the new screen door Jimmie had put up just yesterday.

"It's Grace, ain't it?" she asked.

Eva nodded, and Mary Nell silently swung the door open. Eva hadn't been inside her house for many years, and she came in slowly, cautiously, looking around.

"Don't worry. Lou ain't here," Mary Nell said, seeing a startled look on Eva's face that dissipated quickly.

"She say she goin'," Eva said. "I thought maybe the two of us could talk her into not leavin'. She says her mind's made up, but every time she mentions the children, I can see ... she ain't sure. She might not go."

"What can we do?"

"You seen some things about her, haven't you?"

"Yes. And we can't change what we see," Mary Nell said.

"But what we see is only what might come, it's not for sure. That was why we was given it, I suppose, to help hold off some of the bad things that happen. We certainly haven't been using it right."

"You got somethin' in mind?"

"Go to her, the two of us together, and talk to her. If we can do that, maybe she'll find the strength to stay. Maybe she'll remember the way it was once, before things got away from us."

"You mean before you and Lou . . ."

"That's a dead mule you're beating, Mary Nell," Eva interrupted, drawing herself up a little taller. "You know what's true."

Mary Nell found that she didn't have anything to say to that. She opened her mouth to say something and nothing happened.

"I don't think us being suddenly nice to each other is gon' make her ghosts go away," said Mary Nell, finally.

"We have to try. We have to do something. I don't want to lose another sister."

Mary Nell sighed.

"I gotta think about it," she said, turning back toward the door. And there was Jimmie at the back door. He had heard some of it. It was there on his face. Mary Nell tried to quickly herd Eva out. She pushed her out, slamming the new screen door as soon as Eva's feet touched the porch boards.

While Mary Nell was thinking, Grace left.

Eva was at their parents' house two days later with Patricia. Mary Nell was there. As they sat on the porch, a commotion reached them from the direction of the road, the chug of a motor and the grinding of gears. The noisy black Ford came barreling down in a cloud of dust, turning into their drive and sending chickens flying and squawking in all directions when it came to a halt. George leapt out, nearly dragging Sarah and the twins with him. He'd hardly gotten out before Son Jackson, at the wheel, began turning the car around.

"She gone!" George said without preamble. Eva stood up, letting the book on her lap fall to the floor. She shot an angry glance at Mary Nell, who, for the first time in a long time, looked unsure.

"What you talkin' 'bout, George?" Joy asked. "Why you haulin' them chillun 'round like they was sacks of flour?"

"Grace gone, I say! I gotta go to Union Springs. To the station. Can you keep the chillun?" He deposited the bewildered boys on the porch.

"What?!" Now Joy stood up, but George was already stumbling down the steps, with little Sarah and the rest of them following close behind him. Son Jackson had kept the motor running.

"You can't come, baby," George said to Sarah, shooting a glance at Joy, who immediately grabbed the little girl's hand.

"I'm going!" Eva said, looking at Mary Nell. Without another word she climbed into the backseat of the car. Mary Nell hesitated for just a moment, before getting in after her. Patricia started crying.

"It's all right, baby, I'll be back soon," Eva called out of the window. "Tell Eddie Adam where I am, Mama?"

Joy nodded. Sarah peeped out from behind her skirt.

Eva watched them disappear behind a curve in the road.

"She left this," George said. Eva took the piece of paper from his hand.

My dear George

It hurts me to leave you and sarah and the boys. It hurts more than I can say. But it ain't because of you that I go. This sickness in my mind won't leave me, it won't let me be your wife. I'm afraid to stay and hurt you all and I'm gon try and get back to you someday soon.
Your loving and beloved wife
Grace Mobley Lancaster

Eva passed the note to Mary Nell.

"Did she say anything to y'all?" George said. He didn't wait for an answer. He hurried the words out of his mouth, like he was afraid of any kind of silence in the car. Son drove hard. The church passed now like a dream, the gape-mouthed stare of the deacons outside—they were spending the day cleaning up around the building—barely registering before they were gone.

"She been sad lately, I guess," George was now saying, as Eva watched the deacons grow smaller out of the back window. Son didn't even try to avoid the road's many holes and Mary Nell and Eva got tossed around the backseat.

"She been sad a long time. And cryin' a lot. And sometime I come into the room and she just sit there starin' at the wall."

Son glanced over at him nervously. "Starin' at what, man?"

"I don't know," George said. He turned around in his seat to look back at the two women. "Bet they know, though."

Eva stared helplessly into his anguished eyes. Grace's secrets were not hers to give away. Mary Nell just looked out of the window.

The train was long gone by the time they got there, despite the fact that Son had attacked the road between Union Springs and Johnson Creek. Eva thought he was going to rattle the old car all the way apart. And all the time she knew Grace was gone. Grace was throwing herself away from Johnson Creek as fast as they were throwing themselves at that train station. They got out of the car and while George went over to the platform and then to the ticket office, Mary Nell and Eva stood there beside the car, watching people mill about.

"You remember, Eva," Mary Nell said softly. "We saw her on the train. And that little girl was with her."

"Ayo," Eva nodded.

"She ain't comin' back."

Eva put her hand on Mary Nell's arm. She took Eva's hand and drew it through the crook in her elbow.

"She ain't comin' back," Mary Nell said again. "It's almost like I can feel her dyin'. Oh!" She began to cry and Eva put her arm all the way around her waist now. Eva opened the car door and put her inside just as George came back, looking pretty shaky himself.

He just shook his head, and they got in the car, too, though it was a long time before Son Jackson cranked it up and turned it around.

$\ll$48$\gg$

Detroit

Nothing had bothered Grace since she'd shaken the dust of Johnson Creek off her shoes. Even in the midst of her pain and her longing, that silence had been like heaven. She had been told that heaven was filled with singing. But maybe it was filled with silence.

Maybe she's gone, she thought. But it had only been a few days.

She had washed out a few things last night, and now, as the sun set behind the gray clouds, she folded the last bit of her laundry and put it in her trunk. The room didn't have much furniture, just the bed, a table and a chair. She kept all her things in the trunk, even the orange-stained stockings that she'd unsuccessfully tried to get clean. They hung limply on the back of the chair and she sighed as she gathered them up.

"Alabama mud," she said. "Ain't nothin' like it."

She tossed them into the open trunk. It had rained for days and days, all the way from Alabama to Michigan. The low-hanging clouds still dumped their contents on the dirty gray city buildings, buildings like nothing she had even imagined before. They were tall and tightly built, and Grace didn't see how anybody could live a real life here. But a real life was not what she wanted, at least not at the moment. She wanted something that didn't feel, look or smell like that life she had left behind. So when she looked out at the Detroit landscape she felt a something that could only be hope. Because since she'd stepped on that train, they had left her alone—the voices, the visions.

Please, please let her be gone, she thought.

She looked down at the stained stockings. That's one thing I ain't gon' miss, she thought, that mud, sticking to everything, lookin' like old, faded blood. People gon' think I got bleedin' feet.

Grace closed the trunk lid, laughing to herself. She sat down in the chair to remove the stockings she was wearing, white ones. They were still damp. Detroit puddles were as deep as ponds, and she'd stepped in every one, walking around looking for work. She pulled off one stocking and then the other, wondering at their sticky wetness.

"What is that?" she said, though she was alone and there was no one to answer. When she looked down, she had to grab the chair back for support when she saw the blood seeping from her ankles.

"No." She stood up and began to turn around and around in the small room. "No! I didn't leave my home and my husband and . . ." her voice broke on a sob, ". . . my chillun for this! You 'sposed to be gone. Gone! Left back there in Alabama. Hoverin' 'round your grave or somethin'. Not here! How far I got to go?"

There was nothing but the sound of rain against the glass and Grace trailed blood over the worn wood floor, her flesh aching in a new way. Now the silence cursed her; there was no answer to her questions. She closed her eyes and then opened them, but the blood continued to flow. A red ring adorned her bare ankle.

She sat down hard on the floor, feeling too weak to stand. Metal clinked as her body met the wood. The rain came down on the deck, whipped into razor sharpness by the wind, and there was her blood still seeping from under the leg irons and washing away.

Grace heard someone whimpering and pitifully moaning and realized it was herself.

"Not here. I can't go here no more. Please." She lay down, pressing her body to the ship's deck, trying to stop it from rolling. "I'm tired, Ayo," she said. "I'm tired." Again that silence, except for the rain. Grace wept into the wood, mingling her tears with water and blood.

When she opened her eyes she didn't know where she was. She turned over and over, her whole body aching.

She remembered packing up her life in a box and going away. She remembered brown skin and beautiful eyes and voices that carried Alabama through the streets of Detroit, voices that sometimes sounded like the voices of lost children. She had the familiar taste of the sea air in her mouth and the sound of waves in her ears.

But all around her was just a room. Just a room in a rooming house in a city full of rooming houses, a city full of lost people. Grace cried. This was all she had now, this room and Ayo's memories.

❦49❧

Johnson Creek 1945

ONE DAY IN 1940, not long after Grace left, Frank Mobley sat down in his rocking chair and didn't get up. Just like that. Strong and full of laughter one day and silent the next. Mary Nell had never thought of him as old. He was just Papa. She looked at his face in his casket and didn't recognize what was lying there. There was his thick, straight gray hair, but his beautiful red-brown skin just looked like old leather stretched over a frame.

Joy lost a little bit of herself then. She told Mary Nell that she had put off thinking about being old and dying until that very moment when she had woken up on that pale morning to find Frank slumped in his chair, his pipe still in his hand. Then it was on her mind a lot.

But still she seemed content, melancholy but not deeply unhappy. She worked and played with her grandchildren and went to church and shook her fists at the Japs when they bombed Pearl Harbor the next year, even though she said she couldn't even form a picture in her mind of where and what Hawaii was.

"Etta Mae say it's just like Florida, but better. And they got womens there that dance naked in public," she said one day in late October. The war was over, but Hawaii was the one thing that Joy remembered most about it. "You think that's true, Mary Nell?"

Mary Nell said she was sure Etta Mae wouldn't lie.

Joy died a few weeks later with the taste of Christmas oranges on her lips.

At the end of the year, around about the last Saturday in December, Lou Henry came back from town with a steamer trunk that had been left at the station for Mary Nell.

Mary Nell asked Eva to be there when she opened it. They recognized it as the one that used to be in Grace's bedroom. She had kept it at the foot of her bed. Mr. Johnson, who had been the one to give her a ride to the train station, had mentioned that she had a trunk and suitcase with her. Mary Nell's heart fell to the bottom of her being when she saw it. She wasn't coming back.

There was a letter.

Dearest Mary Nell,

The strangeness has dogged me north and I know to learn all I can about past days.

I took Mama's papers with me as you said I should, hope they would help me sort things out and they have. It pains me that I missed Mama's funeral but I had a

sickness on me at that time that would not let me travel.
I send the papers back to you with the other things.
Things that belong with the family. I also have sent that
quilt I was working on when I left. It's finished and
Ayo's whole story is set on it. I feel better now it's
through. No telling where I might end up so it be safe
with you.

Now Mary please do not show these to my baby
girl Sarah. Well I reckon she aint such a baby no more.
She will ask questions that you cannot answer that I'm
not sure I can anser. And I could never burden her with
the thought that her mother is crazy. I could not curse
her with these things that are happening to me. I
thought getting all that down on the quilt in front of me
out of me would get rid of it somehow. I don't know
about that. But I know I cant pass it on to her this
craziness. So save it but not for Sarah. Maybe Sarah will
be safe.

I feel that others after us will need to know. Our
grands maybe will need to get these things. Please leave
these for my granddaughter. I know she aint here yet.
But I have faith that you and Eva will know when the
time is right and when it is she will be waiting.

Please dont worry. I am well. Somehow it is all eas-
ier to bear without being around the pity of your loved
ones but is harder too. My poor George would have
done something about it. I am glad I saved him the
trouble.

Kiss Eva and Sarah and my twin boys for me.
Your sister Grace.

Mary Nell let the letter fall on the kitchen table. Eva picked it up and looked at the words.

"Her granddaughter?" she asked. Mary Nell had a brief flash of memory. Children, little girls, playing. Had it been a dream?

But she merely shrugged as she bent over the trunk. She took the trunk key from her apron pocket and in a few moments the lid was open and she was pulling out one thing and then another.

First a stack of papers. Eva began reading them while Mary Nell continued to explore the depths of the trunk.

"This is what Mama wrote about Grandmama," Eva said. Mary Nell saw a shudder ripple through Eva's body. "Remember that?"

"Yeah, and I remember that after Grace read them she started to lose her mind," Mary Nell said, taking out a small box and opening it. There was a gold pendant necklace in it.

"George gave her this," she whispered. "She loved that, Eva! How could she give it up?"

"That ain't all she gave up, it seems," Eva said, now noticing some other things. "There's her marriage license, those pretty little crocheted gloves she made and these handkerchiefs. Mama made those edgings, I think. And, oh, Mary Nell, look at this!"

Mary Nell looked at what Eva held in her hand and started laughing. The sound startled Eva, and Mary Nell realized that it had been many years since she'd really laughed in Eva's presence. She stopped when she noticed Eva staring at her, but the smile lingered as Mary Nell took the little grass doll Eva was holding.

"I can't believe Grace would keep one of Mama's grass dolls! Ours would fall apart soon as we started playing with them."

Eva smiled, too. When they were little and got to buzzing

around their mother's skirt tails too much she would sometimes go out and pull up large handfuls of long grass and make these dolls with roots for hair.

"Grace was much more careful with her things than we were," Eva said. "She was more careful with everything. We were wild little things!"

"Eva—look . . ." Mary Nell's head was back in the trunk and this time she pulled out Grace's quilt. They both sat staring at the dazzling colors and patterns and without a word stood up to spread it out on Mary Nell's freshly scrubbed floor.

"I ain't never seen nothin' like that," Mary Nell muttered.

The quilt top was full of pictures. Boats and water. People and houses.

"She said it was Ayo's story," Mary Nell said. Eva glanced back at the sheaf of papers she'd left on the table. Sitting down and quietly flipping through, she came to a page and read out loud, "I think when that man grab me in the market I kick him but he put his hand over my mouth and nose and I cant get no air."

Mary Nell gave a swift intake of air and pointed silently to a spot on the quilt. There it was, that same thing Eva had just read, but there it was a picture. The little black girl dressed in blue cloth was being held by a large man, her feet suspended above the ground, her eyes round with fear.

"That's her gettin' kidnapped. That's Bessie in Africa," Eva said. She thumbed through the pages, her eyes going from the quilt on the floor to the words in front of her.

"Is that what she been seeing? All this time?" Mary Nell whispered.

"Listen," Eva said, reading again. "'She's carryin' a whip and them two mens hold my arms while she whip me cross the back. Oh daughter, she was laughin' while she done it . . . her pink dress was all spattered.'"

Mary Nell was already staring at the scene on the quilt. The red cloth that Grace had used for blood seemed redder than the real thing to her. "She talkin' 'bout that time old Miz Ward split open Grandmama's back with that whip . . . oh, my Lord." Mary Nell sat down on the floor on the edge of the quilt and they both looked at it for a long time, Mary Nell tracing the edges of the cloth with her forefinger and Eva bent over the diary pages, glancing back and forth from the paper to the quilt.

"What we gon' do?" Mary Nell asked. "Where is she?" She picked up the letter again from the floor where she'd let it drop. "Detroit, Michigan. We should go. We should go and get her, Eva. What she doin' way up there?"

"Let's write her. Let's both write," Eva said. Mary Nell nodded, her eyes still on the quilt.

She didn't remember what else was in that trunk after that remarkable piece of cloth came out of it. Mary Nell stopped emptying it. And eventually she put everything she had taken out back in, adding the letter, folding the quilt carefully and placing it on top. Eva helped her take it in the bedroom, where she shoved it under the bed.

They stood rather uneasily in that room. Mary Nell knew Eva wanted to leave before Lou Henry and Jimmie came back from wherever they had gotten to. But something had changed for Mary Nell and Eva when she opened her mouth and laughed, when they stared down together at their grandmother's sorrow all laid out before them on the floor. They knew they would dream together again, dream about those pictures and those words.

Mary Nell struggled to find something to say that would tighten the tentative bond that held them together in that room. She was surprised that it was something she even wanted. But all that came out was, "I guess I'll see you at church." Eva just nodded and Mary Nell walked her to the door.

"They cried at first. But the chillun don't talk 'bout her no more."

George folded and unfolded the brim of his hat as he stood on the church step looking up at Eva. It was his good hat, she could tell.

"Detroit, you say?" He looked confused.

Eva nodded. She handed him the letter. He opened it slowly and read it even more slowly, his mouth moving over every word at least twice. Then he folded it again and gave it back to Eva.

"I would never have done it," he said.

"Done what?" It was Mary Nell who asked the question. She had come up behind him.

"Done somethin' 'bout it, like she say," he answered. "She my wife. Thick and thin, ain't that how it's 'sposed to be? She just didn't want to be here. Some women's like that. She tried real hard not to marry me, but I just kept at her."

"George . . ." Eva put a hand on his arm. "She loves you. She loves her children. It's just that . . . those other things wouldn't let her rest."

"Other things. Hearin' voices and such? I knew 'bout all that long befo' we got married. That weren't nothin' to me," George said. Then he said, "I should go. I know some folk up there."

"What about the children?" Eva asked.

"I won't be gone long."

"Where you gon' look? There ain't no address on the letter."

"I don't know. I should go."

"She might not come back," Eva said softly. "She thought being in Johnson Creek made things worse."

George's handsome jaw was set in a stubborn line and Eva sighed. She tried to think what Grace would want. She looked at Mary Nell, who shook her head. If they tried to talk him out of it, he would be more determined to go. Let him go home and look into the faces of his children. He wouldn't leave them.

"How 'bout you, George?" Mary Nell asked. "You all right?"

"What kind of fool question is that?" George scowled at her. "I ain't got no wife no more. My chil'ren ain't got no mama. What kind of fool question is that?" His expression became sad, defeated and his voice low. "She just shoulda asked me, talked to me. I would never have let nobody hurt her."

"It was all just too much," Eva said. "Trying to be a wife and mama. Trying to get away from the world that Ayo keeps drawing her into. Don't you see? It was all too much."

"I should go," George said again. "I wonder how far Detroit is?"

SOMETIME IN AUGUST, JIMMIE WENT OFF. At least Eva thought it was sometime in August, because Mary Nell didn't mention it until he had been gone quite some time and only because Eva ventured to ask why she hadn't seen him. Even then Eva thought that Mary Nell only answered because Son Jackson was standing there in the yard of the church with Eva, passing the time of day. Otherwise she probably would have ignored the question or said that it wasn't any of Eva's business where her son was. Because after all, she still called him her son.

They were at the church with the rest of the ladies, cleaning. Eva was standing there holding a broom, which she had been using to sweep the leaves and debris out of the yard. Son had stopped on his way somewhere else to ask if he could help. Eva had just said no, she didn't believe so, when Mary Nell came out carrying a rag rug that was used in the pulpit. When Eva caught her eye, she asked her. It had been on her mind, about Jimmie.

Mary Nell started to fling the rug around, shaking out dust, but she didn't say anything. Son stared at her, and she looked sorry that she'd even stepped out of the door of the church.

"Mary Nell?" Eva said.

She made a noise with her tongue, an impatient clucking. Eva thought of that day she had sat on the floor of Mary Nell's house laughing, holding Grace's grass doll in her hand.

"He ain't been 'round here for a while," she said.

"Where he gone?" Son asked.

"Said he was going to Birmingham. Don't want to work on shares, he say." Her voiced dropped into a near-whisper. "Why should he? Work and work for nothin'?"

"How long he been gone, Mary Nell?" Eva asked. "Why didn't you—" Mary Nell cut her off.

"Oh, Eva, you know how people talk 'round here. They would have been makin' up all kinds of reasons why he went. Ain't really nobody's business now is it?"

Considering the kind of relationship they had now, the tentative peace they cultivated but so far removed from the closeness of childhood, Eva was sure that she was the "nobody" Mary Nell was referring to. Eva tried to picture Birmingham and then she tried to picture Jimmie in it. Nothing came to mind, and that was the first thing that frightened her. She looked over at Mary Nell, surprising a scared look that seemed to go with what Eva was feeling. Mary Nell continued to shake the rug, even though no more dust came out of it.

"What's he going to do up there?" Eva asked.

"He lookin' for work. He gon' try to get on as a porter, he say, travel all over the place." She tried to smile.

Jimmie, a porter? Jimmie bowing and smiling false smiles at white people? No, he'd never even try that. He never bowed to them. And he had been lucky so far that no white person had ever taken offense.

"I don't bow to nobody but God," he had said to Eva once. "And I tell ya, Aunt Eva, even the Almighty might have to show me His papers." She had laughed when he said it, but now when she thought of what he'd said, she felt chilled, right there in that dusty yard, and her womb flipped over with longing to see him again.

Patricia came out of the church, covered with dust.

"Ma!" she called. Eva answered "Yes?" without taking her gaze away from Mary Nell.

"Can I go? Everybody just about to leave anyhow."

Eva nodded and listened to her daughter's feet on the wooden steps. She saw her racing down the road out of the corner of her eye, flinging off her apron and balling it up as she ran.

"Very ladylike," Mary Nell said softly.

"I can't see Jimmie being a porter," Eva said.

"Why not? They make good money, too. Travel. He gon' send me postcards from all them places he gon' get to see. What he gon' be a ole dusty farmer for?"

"It was good enough for Papa."

"Well, Papa didn't have no other prospects now, did he? 'Sides, Papa had his own land to work."

"His land Jimmie's, too. I wouldn't have been mad if he lived in our old house and worked it. Be good for the place. It's lonely since they passed. Somebody ought to live there."

Mary Nell nodded, lowering her head. But then she said, "I don't think Jimmie gon' want it. Ever." She looked off down the road. "Can't keep that boy at home."

"He grown now, sister," Eva said softly. "And we can't turn back the clock."

Mary Nell gave her a sharp look. "Who wants to?" she said. "I don't."

How many times Mary Nell must have held that boy in her lap, Eva thought, kissed that boy and bent close to him while he slept to see if he still breathed. Eva had done the same many times with Patricia. Every time she had taken her daughter in her arms, she thought of Jimmie, maybe sitting in Mary Nell's lap, too. And the thought of him pained Eva and gladdened her all at the same time. It was her fervent wish that he'd never come. But her heart was joyful every time he walked into a room.

Now, as she stood looking down at her sister, Eva tried to picture him in a place that was not Johnson Creek. She tried to find him with her mind. Mary Nell looked at Eva, shaking her head discouragingly.

Eva closed her eyes. He was excited and afraid. His heart beat fast.

"Don't you do that!" Mary Nell whispered fiercely. "He's all right. He's all right."

Eva wasn't sure. But she opened her eyes and turned away from Mary Nell, going into the church and leaving her standing in the yard.

New York 1949

"YOU A CRAZY MAN, MARTIN," GRACE said, unfolding herself from the sofa with a sigh. "You know I can't do that. We can't do that."

The tall, lanky man holding out her coat just shrugged. "Why not?"

"I'm married, for one thing."

"So you say. But I don't see any husband here. I don't see anybody but you and me."

"Not to mention I'm too old to be thinkin' 'bout that. Almost fifty." Grace laughed, but her throat was tight and dry. She thought about what the doctor had told her just yesterday.

"Most women I know would be glad to get a marriage proposal," said Martin. "And we act like we married anyway."

"I'm already married." She drew deeply on the cigarette she was holding, thinking of George. She certainly had been gone long enough now for him to get a divorce. For desertion.

"I couldn't blame him," she murmured.

"What?" Martin was still holding the coat. Grace stubbed out the cigarette and walked over to him, pushing her arms into the sleeves.

"Nothin'," she said. "We fine like this, right? You can't be tryin' to make me respectable." She grinned. "I long ago stopped being respectable."

Martin frowned at her, but didn't reply to that. Instead, he picked up his hat and her gloves from the table by the apartment door and said, "I told Dusty to save a table for us down front."

The club wasn't crowded tonight, because it was Tuesday. Grace had Wednesdays off, so she and Martin often went out the night before. She enjoyed the relaxed smokiness, the empty tables scattered here and there, the band that seemed to be playing just for them. There were always other people sitting at some of the tables, but it was a quieter crowd. Martin just did this for her. He preferred Saturday nights, when it always felt like the roof was about to jump off the place.

The small combo was playing without a singer tonight. Grace and Martin had hardly sat down when somebody set glasses and plates in front of them: gin and barbecue. But Grace pushed her plate away, lit another cigarette and considered the glass of gin.

"Are you up for dancing?" Martin asked.

She shook her head. A man two, no three, tables over had

caught her eye. He was in his early twenties, she thought. Tall and lanky. She could tell that even though he was slouched down a little in his chair. He seemed to be almost half-drowsing, his fingers loosely wrapped around a bottle of beer. His face was turned away, but still he was familiar. She smiled wryly. She could tell, by the way a man held his body, by the out-of-date clothing, that he was a Southerner. A Bama, she thought, amusedly. She stared at the back of his neck, remembering George and feeling homesick.

The man seemed to be in deep thought, not paying attention to the band. Just as Grace was about to turn away, another man approached the table. Same lanky build, slim hands. He turned.

She let out a little gasp and half turned away.

"What?" Martin looked up.

Grace didn't answer. She looked over his right shoulder at the two men. The second one was sitting now, too, his face toward hers.

Her mouth formed the word. "George . . . ?" But it didn't really come out of her mouth. And it wasn't George. He was too young and not as dark. But the face was right. She tried not to look, but she couldn't help it. It was like a little bit of home had landed right here in Harlem.

He caught her staring and nudged his companion. When the other man turned, too, Grace nearly choked on her cigarette.

The two men pointed at her now.

"Martin . . ." Grace stood up abruptly. "I have to go. Now!"

Martin stood up, too, quickly following her gaze to the other table. The two young men were both standing, pushing chairs aside. Grace moved swiftly toward the door, leaving Martin gaping for a moment. Then he followed her.

"Twins," he murmured. "I'll be damned . . . !"

"Martin . . . come on!"

"What's wrong with you?" He frowned, even as he collected her coat. She was looking over her shoulder. The two men were moving toward the door.

"That would be right . . . just about . . ." Grace murmured. She hurried out the door, around the corner and to the alley where Martin had parked.

"Come on, Grace!" Martin's expression cleared, his frown was replaced by an incredulous look. "They can't be yours!"

"Just get in the car, will ya!?"

She didn't see the two men come out of the door. Martin screeched down the alley. He kept saying her name over and over. "Grace? Grace! Talk to me, girl!" She couldn't.

Back at the apartment she shrugged off the coat and let it drop on the floor. She lit another cigarette and went over to the window.

"My boys. That was them. I ain't seen them since they was sixteen, but that was them, Martin. Damn, if they don't look just like George . . . !"

"Come on now, Grace. You just said you ain't seem them in what . . . nine, ten years?"

"They look the same. Taller. I'm sure that was them. What they doin' here?"

"Looking for you, maybe," Martin said. He plopped down in the armchair. "Or maybe they came up here like thousands of people do every day."

"They could ask Dusty 'bout us. They could find me."

"Would that be so bad?"

She turned abruptly, looking stricken. Then she turned again to the window.

"I want to take a trip," she said.

"What? Now?"

"I wanna see the mountains. Real mountains, Martin. Let's go. Let's go out west."

"What? What for?"

"I'm sick."

Grace heard Martin move quickly across the room. His arms came around her.

"Tell me," he said softly.

"Cancer. He wants to operate."

"When?"

"Next week."

Martin turned her around to face him. She didn't like seeing that expression on his face. Fear and love. Something about it reminded her of the last time she'd seen George.

"Why do I get the feeling that you weren't going to tell me?"

"I did tell you. Just now." She pulled away and sat down in the armchair, still clutching the lighted cigarette between her fingers.

"Grace," Martin said, coming to stand in front of her, "maybe you ought to think about goin' home?"

She shook her head. She had felt pretty good up until now. Now with the thought that the twins might be right here in Harlem and with Martin looking down at her, she was shaky.

"No," she said. "I don't belong there no more. Suppose them was my boys, Martin. They saw me sittin' in there next to you. What kind of woman can I be to them now? They must hate me now."

"Maybe not," he whispered. "Your sisters. Don't you want to see them again?"

"Mountains," she whispered. "The Rockies. It's beautiful there. I've seen the pictures. It's beautiful and clean."

"But don't you need to be here near the doctor? Hospitals . . ."

"After the operation, I'll be better and we can go then."

"But . . ."

"They got doctors out there, don't they?"

"But what kind of people, Grace? You get out there and maybe the Klan be at the station to meet you."

"Please!" She put her head in her hands. He knelt down in front of her and took the cigarette from between her fingers. He held both her hands in his. "Martin . . . I want to be far away. Just for a while. I don't want them to ever find me."

He stared at her, stroking her fingers. He looked at her bent head for a long time.

"Fine," he said, sighing. "Whatever you want. I promise we'll go. Baby, whatever you want."

1950

MARY NELL TRIED TO IMAGINE WHERE Montana was. Eva had gotten the school globe and pointed to somewhere in the middle of the country, and then they had sat there, wondering how it had all come to this. How their Grace had died so far from home.

"Martin? Who is he?" Mary Nell had asked. Eva just shrugged. Grace had never mentioned him in the few letters that she sent. For the past few years those letters had come postmarked New York, New York. Not long after the first New York letter, the twins had gone up there. But they had not found Grace. How could they possibly think they'd find her in a place like that?

After Martin's telegram and letter had come, Mary Nell had gone over to tell Eva and the two of them sat there.

"What happened to her, Eva? Did you see anything?"

Eva sighed. "I haven't seen anything about Grace in a long time. She's in my dreams sometimes. But there wasn't anything about them that made me think . . ." she nodded at the papers in Mary Nell's hand, ". . . something like this."

"We better send for the twins," Mary Nell whispered and Eva nodded.

"I don't know how they thought they was gon' find her in a place like New York, anyway."

"Montana . . ." Eva whispered. "It's just us now, Mary Nell."

Mary Nell didn't answer.

Eva walked into the Evans' barn looking for Mary Nell, startled to find Lou Henry in there raking hay out of the stalls. When he saw her, he stopped, leaning against the pitchfork.

She realized that the last time she'd been alone with him was many, many years ago, in this same barn. The last time she'd been alone with him, he'd had his hand around her throat and his body in her body, tearing her all apart. Trying, that second time, to finish her off.

She didn't know what to do with herself. Eva turned her head to the left and then to the right more than one time. She took a few steps back, tried to back out of there. She backed into Son Jackson, coming in. When his arms came around to steady her, she struggled for a moment, crying out.

"Eva!" Son laughed, dropping his arms and putting them up in front of his face in mock defense. "Just me! What . . ."

Lou laughed then and she stopped flailing her arms. Son's

laughter stopped, hung in midair for a moment and then sunk into oblivion. She turned to go, trying to get past him, but this time, he did catch her, not letting her go. He grasped her upper arms and looked down into her face and back over to where Lou Henry was. When Eva looked up at Son, finally, she saw horror there. She saw horror and recognition. And when she looked back over her shoulder at Lou, she saw smug satisfaction. The tired discontent that had been his expression for years was momentarily replaced by the old cockiness.

"Eva," Son said curtly. "You go on. I'm sorry. I didn't mean to startle you. You go on, now."

"What you gon' do?"

"I just came over here to see Lou Henry about helping me with my crop," Son said quietly. Eva didn't like his voice. She didn't move.

"I got my own to worry 'bout," Lou Henry said. "What you come in here for, Eva? Been a long time since you came out to the barn."

Her body sort of froze then, tensed up. The tension was contagious. Son's grip on her upper arms tightened. She felt his thumbs marking her. She looked over at Lou Henry and he had that expression on his face. Something in her fell away, years of her life fell away from her and she was frightened again, numb with fright. By the time Son was looking at her, her eyes were wide with the knowledge of her shame and he saw it. He saw it and a veil of pain and sorrow came over his face, turning his skin a strange, grayish color. In that moment they became older than they really were, just as Eva had become something other than a child when Lou Henry dragged her down in the dust on that June Sunday long ago.

"You said on the road," Son whispered to her hoarsely. "On the road was where he did it."

"The first time," she said, wondering at the new voice she was using. Quiet, like her real one, but firmer. As frightened as she was, Son knowing and believing sent a surge of strength through her.

"The first . . ." He shook. He began to shake all over. She made a feeble attempt to break free of his hold, but he held her there not only with his strength, but with the force of his rage. It was pure and undeniable. Eva hadn't seen Son's temper in years. As he got older and worked that land and watched his mother wither and die, he had become quieter. He had become a quiet man.

"I see it," he said. Tears gleamed in his eyes, but they were not tears of sadness. "I see it all now. I wasn't enough of a man to see it then."

"What y'all talkin' 'bout?" Lou Henry said, beginning to come over to where they were standing.

Son Jackson stood stone still, his gaze on her unwavering.

"What's your problem?" Lou Henry said. "I can't help you, now. I got too much to do my own self."

"You tell me," Son said to her, as if Lou hadn't spoken.

"Not here," Eva whispered desperately, glancing over at Lou, who had begun pitching hay again. "Please . . ."

"Here," Son Jackson said nodding.

"I tried to tell you that one time, Son, and you . . ."

"I was a fool," he said. "Nah, you don't have to tell me. I know what I need to."

Lou Henry came up behind Son, but Son didn't turn his head.

"Let's go now, Son," she said, her fear returning in a rush.

But he didn't move at all. Then Lou Henry put a hand on his

shoulder and the expression Eva saw in Son Jackson's eyes made her reel back. He let her go, turned and rammed his fist into Lou Henry's jaw, all in one smooth dance-like motion.

Lou hit the hay, the pitchfork flying out of his hand. He lay stunned on the ground for a moment. Then he was up again, wiping a trickle of blood from his chin, his eyes wide with fear and anger and utter confusion.

"What the hell is wrong with you?!" he screamed. "I told you I can't help . . ." But he never finished that sentence, because Son moved and Lou Henry was on his back again.

"What kind of creature is you?" Son said, grinding out every word through clenched teeth. "You defile a little girl and then walk 'round for years and years like you still a decent human being? Smilin' and talkin' and makin' like you got the right to be here with the rest of us?"

Eva couldn't take her eyes off Lou Henry's face. His brow was puckered for the longest time and she could see he was try-ing to work through what Son had just said. Son just stood over him and waited, while Lou Henry looked back and forth, from Son's face to hers. They all stayed like that for a very long time, it seemed, while the pucker left Lou's forehead and the light of comprehension lit his face. Then he laughed.

"Man! Man!" he said, scrambling to his feet. "You mean to tell me you been listenin' to her talk 'bout somethin' from a mil-lion years ago?" He laughed. He laughed and laughed, with much delight. "So I humped her . . . every woman got to have a first time, ain't she? And a second . . . !" He laughed again.

Lou Henry didn't move. After his initial burst of anger, he seemed quite calm now. "And you . . . you were somethin' comin' up to the house and questionin' me. I didn't want to tell you then how it was. You were angry. So I just told you it wasn't true. Better for ev'rybody that way. If I had told you what your little sweetheart had done, no tellin' what that would have done to your little mind! And I'm sorry I couldn't save her for you, man!"

Eva felt her body move toward him, and Son moved aside as she came.

"Don't you do it, Lou," Eva said quietly. "Don't you stand there and act like I asked you to do it, like I wanted you to do it. Don't you stand there and pretend to anyone here that you didn't force me. There on that road. Here in this very place where we're standing."

"Just 'cause you fought me don't mean you didn't want me there," Lou said confidently. Son, behind her now, took a step forward. She put her hand on his arm. "I knows a girl gots to fight sometime. That just how it works, right? But I was givin' off signals and you was gettin' them, I know'd you was. Right there under Mary Nell's nose. And when the time was right . . . ooh, whee!! I ain't never forgot it, you twistin' and turnin' under me. She was good, Brother Son." Lou laughed again looking over Eva's shoulder at Son. "Tender and good. Just thinkin' 'bout it . . ." He slid his hand down to his crotch.

"Nah," Lou said. "Man don't forget somethin' like that."

"You muthafucker," Son bit out, lunging past Eva and throwing all his weight at Lou Henry.

"No use gettin' mad now, Son Jackson. Ain't no use gettin' worked up over an old woman just 'cause I rolled her once."

Son's head made contact with Lou Henry's stomach and the two of them landed on the hard-packed dirt floor. Eva found herself leaping around to avoid them as they rolled around through the hay and manure. Their grunting sounds filled the whole barn and Lou's mule began to bray in his stall and kick the wooden door enthusiastically.

Son finally dragged Lou Henry up from the ground and hit him hard, making him stagger. Lou now had his back to Eva and as he reeled toward her, she stepped back and back until she was pressed against the barn wall. When she looked up again, a flash of metal caught her eye.

The knife Lou was holding was big. It was the big hunting knife her father used to carry and that Joy had given to Lou Henry after her husband died. Lou slashed the air in front of him with it, causing Son to retreat. Lou laughed now, coming up on Son fast. Son was running out of barn.

The knife flashed and there was the sound of ripped fabric. Son grabbed his arm, but not before Eva saw blood oozing from the wound her papa's knife had made.

Eva groped around with her hand and her fingers found a wooden handle. She breathed hard as she lifted the axe with both hands. It was heavy and comforting to hold as she watched Son back away from Papa's knife until his shoulder blades were touching the far wall.

She and Lou Henry raised their arms at the same time, but his never came down. The force of the axe hitting the side of his head spun him around and he faced Eva, his face alight with an expression of quaint surprise, his mouth working, but no words emerging from the lips that were already turning blue.

Eva dropped the axe in the hay. Lou Henry stumbled toward her one, two times and toppled like a tree, knocking her over in the process. She heard Son Jackson cry out as she fell and she again was in the barn with Lou Henry's weight pressing her into the hard floor. His head was heavy on her thighs, his blood soaking the white apron. Eva looked up at the barn's holey ceiling, praying—for what she didn't know—until Son Jackson's head appeared above her and he was pulling Lou away.

They sat on the porch and waited for the sheriff and for Mary Nell. Son slowly rolled a cigarette, taking the tobacco tin out of the pocket of his checked shirt and then the papers. He placed the thin cigarette paper on his lap and pinched a bit of tobacco onto it, then rolled it caressingly with his long fingers. Eva watched him, and after he lit the cigarette, she took his hand. Son sighed.

Even after Eddie Adam came up the path to the house looking for her, she didn't let go of Son's hand. Eddie Adam stared at the large, still-wet patch of blood on her dress.

"Somethin' happened," Son said.

Eddie Adam just stared.

"Lou Henry's in the barn," Son said, and Eddie Adam went off to see.

Son drew long on his cigarette.

"When the sheriff get here, I'm the one that did it," he said quietly. "Understand?"

"What you mean?" Eva asked, knowing what he meant. Out of the corner of her eye, she saw Eddie Adam stumbling out of the barn with his palm pressed to the back of his head.

"We had a misunderstandin' and I lost my temper and I killed him," Son said. "That's all the white man need to know."

After a few moments Eddie Adam came and sat on the steps at Eva's feet. He didn't seem to notice that she held Son's hand.

"I done called the sheriff, Brother Davidson," Son said.

Eddie Adam nodded, then croaked, "Eva . . ."

"Eva gon' go on in the house and find something else to wear," Son said calmly. "All the sheriff got to know is that I defended your wife's honor. He was talkin' too much and I stopped his talk. That all he need to know." He drew once more on the homemade cigarette and dropped it off the porch and into the dust.

Eddie Adam looked at Son and then at the ground.

"I should have set him straight years ago," Eddie Adam said.

"You wouldn't have been able to," Son answered. "He might have killed you. And where would your wife and child be then? I ain't got nobody dependin' on me, see. So it's all right."

"You be goin' in my place, I reckon," Eddie Adam said slowly after a moment, not looking at Son and Eva, just drawing a circle in the dust with the toe of his boot.

"Nah," said Son. He looked out across Lou Henry's corn. "I owed her."

Every story Eva had ever heard about what happened to colored men in jail came rushing back to her and she gripped Son's hand like a vise. "You don't owe me nothin', Son Jackson, you hear? Nothin'."

"Nah, girl. That was my own shame that killed that man in there. I shoulda minded what you told me about him back then. It was so long ago, wasn't it? And Eddie Adam here believed you and I didn't. I ran away from you and put all the shame on you. That weren't right, Eva. And I think I done knowed it for a long time now, I just swallowed my shame. Until today."

"Son . . ."

He dropped her hand. "Go on in the house and find another

dress. I'm sure Mary Nell got somethin' in there you can wear," he said.

When Eva came out again, no one said another word. She sat there in the fading light of day, between the two of them, until a bone-weary Mary Nell came home, her face a question.

53

Murder makes men famous. Lou Henry became known
in two counties just because he was a dead man and Son Jackson
became known as a man who makes men dead. And although it
got out that the whole thing was over a woman, Eva could tell by
the way people talked that they didn't guess the real story.

They all assumed it was all about Mary Nell. To Eva's surprise, her sister didn't try to set anyone straight. If anyone dared
to try and get her to tell her story, she assumed an air of mystery.
Oddly, she seemed a bit more light-hearted, especially after the
funeral. That day, she went home from the cemetery and ever
after Lou Henry's grave sprouted weeds all year long until that
one day a year when the Eastern Star ladies cleaned the graves of
everyone, both the beloved and the forgotten.

Sept. 19, 1953

Dear Eva

Cant remember that I ever write a letter befo. Aint that strange. Here I am bout old and this the first one. I hope your man wont be mad cause Im writin you but because of what happened I just don't want you to worry bout nothin. The judge say 10 year but that may be cut to seven or so if I play it write. And it aint so bad Eva not as bad as you think. Some boys are into some awful things here, but I aint with that. So don't worry. God got his ways and all we got is faith in him. So be glad cause there is things to be glad about. I will go now. But if Eddie Adam don't mind I will write again. You write and let me now.

Your friend and servant

Isaiah Jackson

54

EVA DREAMED THAT SHE SAW JIMMIE asleep in a rowboat with no oars that was floating down the Pea River. He frowned in his sleep, but didn't stir, even when she thought she heard his voice. *Mama?* His voice was a whisper through closed lips as he went past. When she looked downriver, following the play of water over rocks and sandy little islands, she saw it widen and disappear into swamp and even farther she saw an endless shimmering water that went right up to the horizon. Out where the marsh met this sea, a huge boat was bobbing up and down on the waves. It was a sailing ship like she'd seen many times in pictures. There were many, many people on it, too far away to see any faces. She wanted to go closer to the big boat to see, but she didn't—couldn't—will her body to move. Jimmie's little boat drifted, going down to the sea.

Eva knew she was overfeeding the chickens, because she was listening to her grandson, John, talk as he walked around the yard. She didn't like what he was saying.

"I'm thinking 'bout goin' up to Atlanta. Some people are organizing up there."

"You already put off school a year," she said. "You transferring to a school up there?"

"Nah, nah, Grandmama," he said. "I'm still going to Tuskegee. Just next year."

"Hasn't the 'movement' had enough of your time? It seems to me you're getting real accustomed to not being in school. Too accustomed. What all y'all gonna do when it's over?"

"Gran . . ."

"Move on and let some other boy get his chance with Martin Luther King and all of 'em."

"They won't even let niggers ride the bus no more in Montgomery, I hear," said Son Jackson, who was perched on the back steps. "Not since they arrested that lady."

"Coloreds stopped riding on purpose, fool!" Eddie Adam said, laughing. "And that was years ago!"

"Not that long," Eva said softly.

Son stared at Eddie Adam so incredulously that Eddie Adam just laughed more.

"What you mean, on purpose?" asked Son.

"It was a protest, Mr. Jackson," said John. "Don't you know what a protest is?"

"Well, you got to remember I was away for a while back then. We didn't always get the news direct, you might say."

"They treated Negroes bad on the buses so we stopped riding. Why give your money to somebody that treat you bad?"

"Well, I guess I ain't never thought about no protest," said Son. "If I had protested every time some white folk treated me wrong, you and me would have never met. I would have never made it without my neck gettin' stretched."

Eddie Adam stopped laughing rather abruptly. He sat there wiping tears from his eyes, although Eva didn't know if he was crying from laughing so hard or from something else.

"Well, there's a time for everything, I guess," said John. He stood up and came toward Son, holding out his hand. "And it sure is nice to know you, Mr. Jackson."

Son smiled slightly, as if trying to catch some joke. But as John continued to stand there, he stood up too and solemnly shook his hand. "Sho is nice to be here," he said.

Mary Nell was at Eva's door the next morning.

Eva had given up on ever seeing Mary Nell at that door, although it had been on the tip of Eva's tongue many times to ask her, maybe when they passed each other in the church aisle and she saw and felt, just in a moment that came and went in the time it took to breathe in and out, some soft memory of the two little girls they had once been. But Eva never did ask her. She just asked her about Jimmie, more and more frequently over the past six months.

It was because of Jimmie that Mary Nell was here now, hesitating on Eva's doorstep, twisting a red piece of cloth in her hands. Her knuckles were scraped raw.

"She always makes me wear this," she said in annoyance,

finally walking through the doorway into the front room, gesturing with the red rag.

It was the first time Mary Nell had ever set foot in the house Eddie Adam had built for Eva. She stood on the front hall rug nervously mangling her rag.

"I gotta make sure it's all starched and everything. Here I am, halfway to my eternal rest, and she still walkin' 'round there like there ain't never been no Civil War. Three or four other wars done come and gone, and I'm still paradin' 'round the big house in a red head rag.

"I wouldn't mind it if it was my own idea. But it wouldn't be red. I used to like red, but not now."

"Mary Nell . . ." Eva started talking, but couldn't stop her flow. Mary Nell walked into the parlor, surveying the furniture.

". . . She think I like red. Always givin' me somethin' red. Glass candy dish, old tablecloths. I just throw it all in an old box. Gonna burn it one day."

She didn't seem able to think of anything else to say at this point, so she took a seat.

"You're worried," Eva said.

"Patricia all right?" she asked.

"She's fine, Mary Nell."

"I don't know what I should do," she said quietly. "What can I do but wait to hear something terrible."

Eva sat down, too, in the chair opposite her. She stared at the door as if she expected bad news to arrive right away.

"Now, Mary Nell, you know as well as I how this thing works. Nothing is that clear. May be something far off. May only be something that *might* happen."

"I ain't never seen the ocean," Mary Nell said. "You?"

"No." Eva thought of how Grace had described it to her once. How Ayo had stood at the rail of the slave ship and looked down at the gray waves. "But thinking about it scares me."

Mary Nell nodded. Then she sighed.

"That dream mean he dead, don't it?" She twisted the rag between two fists. "Dead or close to it."

"We don't know that," Eva whispered.

"We do. I ain't got no letter from him in five months. He always write me, even when he don't want me to know what he been up to. You got a letter?"

She looked at Eva, who shook her head. Then she got up abruptly. "I don't even know why I came here," she said sourly. Eva heard the screen door flap noisily behind her as she left and sat there for a moment in the brilliant morning light tasting Mary Nell's lingering bitterness.

Then Eva heard the door again and stood up just in time to see Mary Nell step back through the doorway, backward, with Eddie Adam coming in behind her.

"There's a telegram for you at the store," he said to Mary Nell. "You gotta sign somethin' for it, Mary Nell."

She turned around, all the way around, and looked at Eva. Very slowly, her eyes widened and her hands crept up to her face. It seemed to Eva as if both their hearts had stopped. Eva knew her eyes were as wide as Mary Nell's. Then Mary Nell spun around and pushed past Eddie Adam and out the door.

For a few moments, he and Eva stared at each other in tense silence. Then Eddie Adam stepped aside and pushed open the screen.

"Well?" he asked.

Eva found her slumped on the bottom step leading up to

Johnson's Store. She sat beside Mary Nell and took the little piece of paper from her dead fingers. And she read, as big-booted men stepped over and around them and cursed their presence, the words "son," "jail," "dead," "hanged."

When Eva put her arm around Mary Nell she realized that it was only the second time she'd touched Mary Nell in more than thirty years. It was a shock to touch her and to sit there together becoming a bundle of human grief.

Without much discussion, they decided to go to Montgomery together. Eva called the Negro funeral home in Union Springs to ask them to go and get Jimmie. Son drove Eddie Adam and the two women to the jailhouse.

The white men showed them the cell where Jimmie had died. Eva found herself clutching Mary Nell's arm as they stood in the small square of sunshine that ventured through the window. It was cold.

"That there is where we found 'im," said the man, pointing to the ceiling and a pipe that ran the whole length of the cell. He had no expression on his face as he pointed. "Don't know why he went and done that. We just picked him up for hangin' 'round on the street. Loiterin'. And he said he didn't have no place to go. Had a real big mouth, that one."

Eva stared at the pipe.

"He pulled the bed over," the man continued, lowering his arm and scratching a bit underneath it. "Used the sheet."

No he didn't, Eva thought. She saw him swinging there, his face an ugly shade of dark purple, his hands and arms and feet dangling. Mary Nell shuddered. And they just stood there staring, while the white policeman shuffled from one foot to the other.

The funeral home did a good job on him, but there wasn't enough paste and powder in the world that could hide the bruises on Jimmie. People filed past the casket set up in Mary Nell's narrow front room, looking and shaking their heads but saying nothing of how he came to be there.

The next day they sat under a cloudy sky while he was put in the ground. Then a procession of people made their way to Mary Nell's house.

Eva slumped in an armchair and pushed away the plate that Patricia waved under her nose. She watched people filing in and bending over Mary Nell as she sat by the door. She didn't even look sorry, Eva thought. After all we went through, my son is gone and she ain't even sorry.

"Eva." Eddie Adam sat next to her. "Maybe we should go on home."

"Look at her, Eddie Adam," she said. "Accepting everybody's consolations. I made up my mind a long time ago to just let things lie. I thought maybe God had stepped in and Jimmie was with Mary Nell because that was the better thing. I don't know if I could have loved him the way a mother did. But now I feel . . ."

"Honey?"

Eva shook her head. "I remember how it felt that first time he lay in my arms. I remember waking up to see that he was gone." She turned to Eddie Adam, touching the gray hair at his temples.

"I love you, you know that don't you?" Eva said. She had never said that to him before. He nodded, swallowing hard as he looked at her.

"But I keep losing these parts of myself. Mary Nell, Grace, Jimmie. And I'm losing them in the most unnatural ways. The world is crooked and I don't know how it started, how it got that way." She looked over at Mary Nell, who must have felt her gaze, because she turned briefly to lock eyes with Eva.

"That's the person who always used to love me the most and understand me best," said Eva. "I lost me first when Lou Henry did what he did. And I lost her the same day."

"Eva," Eddie Adam said. "Let's go on, now." He stood up and held out his hand to her.

"I tell you, Eddie Adam," Eva said, ignoring his hand. "I'm tired of losing."

THE NIGHT WAS LOUD, WITH THE clouds finally giving way, seemingly ripping apart to release the storm. Mary Nell silently thanked God that the rain had waited until after the funeral and the receiving of guests was over. After everyone had gone, she had slipped into her most comfortable dress and shoes and wrapped all the leftover food. She could barely fit the dishes in the Frigidaire. She tried not to think of the rain watering the bare earth over Jimmie's grave. She wondered why, in the end, she was here, alone.

"You need to come, Mary Nell."

The voice so startled Mary Nell that she dropped the glass dish she was carrying on her foot, but when she cried out it wasn't in pain, it was in terror.

Whipping around, she turned to face Eva, who had come into her house and her kitchen without Mary Nell hearing a thing. But then it was a noisy night.

"What?"

"I have to show you something."

"No you don't. Not this time of night."

Eva didn't move. Mary Nell saw that she was wet from head to toe. She had planted herself there in the kitchen as if she was a tree that had grown up there while Mary Nell's back was turned.

"Back when I was a shell of a person, after Lou Henry had jerked my guts out and you stomped on them, after you stole my son and my sanity—" Eva took a breath. "Somebody rescued me."

Mary Nell didn't like the low tone Eva was using. She tried to block out her voice and just concentrate on the feelings she was giving off. What she felt frightened her, because Eva was angry and Mary Nell realized she had never seen Eva angry before. Happy, frightened, confused or numb, but never angry. And there was something else that reached across the small space of the kitchen and hit Mary Nell in the face. Determination.

"There was a storm like tonight, and Willow took me out there and helped me. She helped me to know myself again. She helped me to know the person I am when it's just me and God and I ain't never been hurt by nobody. Because she did that, I can go to that place any time I want. Because of that, I can love my husband and my daughter and I can look you in the face every day and not rip your eyes out."

"Oh, my God . . ." Mary Nell took a step backward.

"But one thing I don't have," Eva said, moving forward. "I

don't have you. I don't have my sister. The one who loved me best. The one who shared my dreams, my mind." She reached out a hand.

"What, have you lost your mind? Don't you touch me!"

Eva laughed and Mary Nell didn't like the sound of it. She should run. She glanced at the back door. She should run, but she didn't. Underneath Eva's anger she felt a hint of old feeling.

"You come with me, Mary Nell."

Mary Nell shook her head. "No."

"This is the only way I can think of." Eva grabbed her wrist. "When the storm blew up, I thought about it. It was like Willow was there in my mind, telling me what to do. We're going to the place she took me. You gon' stand underneath that wet sky and let it wash you clean and tell the truth before God!"

There was a fire in Eva's eyes.

"You have just gone on past crazy!" Mary Nell screamed, even as Eva jerked her out the door, leaving it wide open and banging in the wind.

"I want to know just what you think you gon' do!" Mary Nell screamed. "I just gotta see this!"

They trudged out of the yard and down the main road, over the bridge and then along the creek. There was no lightning or thunder, just wind and rain. Their shoes sloshed in the thick red mud on the creek bank.

"Got me out here in the wet!" Mary Nell said loudly. But Eva noticed that she didn't try to pull away from her grip. "Don't you think you can work some of Willow's hoodoo on me!"

"It ain't hoodoo!" Eva said, raising her voice to be heard over the wind.

"Where the hell . . ."

Eva had stopped. They stood on the creek bank just below a little cliff. The old tumbledown cabin still stood there. After a moment's pause, Eva began moving up toward it. She was breathing hard.

"Umm . . . ain't that where Willow . . . ?" Mary Nell said tentatively.

Eva didn't answer, jerking Mary Nell's arm when she threatened to stand still and not go any farther.

Then they were standing where the door used to be. Eva finally let go of Mary Nell, putting a hand out to lean against one of the rough walls, trying to catch her breath.

"What you gon' do now?" Mary Nell asked. She stared Eva down, shaking her head. "Damn if Willow didn't make you into some kind of root woman, witch woman or whatever! This just the kind of thing she would do, bringing somebody out in the woods at night and do God knows what."

"Yes," Eva said, nodding. "That's right. God knows. But I still want to hear you say it."

"Say what?"

"Tell me, tell Him"—Eva pointed to the heavens—"that you was wrong. You been wrong for all these years. Blamin' me for what Lou did. And Jimmie . . . !" Eva felt as if a great, evil clot had become dislodged from somewhere inside her body and was traveling, struggling, to leave it. She looked at Mary Nell standing there, her drenched face set in a hard frown and she wanted to wipe it off.

"My baby—" Eva whispered. She felt her hand come up over her head. She meant to hit Mary Nell. She thought she saw the glimmer of tears in her sister's eyes, but she couldn't be sure. It might be just the rain.

"Eva!" Mary Nell called out, half in command, half in fear, and Eva lowered her hand.

"Just what did Willow do to you out here?" Mary Nell asked.

"She brought me out. She made me take all my clothes off and we stood together while I told her everything that he had done to me. I told it to God. And she looked at me and said it wasn't my fault. She said that I could be whole and learn to love people again. And after awhile, I saw that she was right." Eva ran her hands over her wet hair. "It was from that moment on that I started to hope that you and I could love each other again. It was so hard holding on to that hope. And since Grace died, I thought I saw something in you change. I began to think it could happen . . ."

Mary Nell folded her arms and leaned back on one foot. Eva had seen their mother in just that pose hundreds of times, usually when she was somewhat amused by something. Sure enough, when Eva looked at Mary Nell now, there was a little smile playing about her lips.

"She made you take off your clothes, huh?" Mary Nell snorted. "You must be crazy if you think I'm gon' do that! Surely there's a better way to make peace than me standing here buck naked in the Alabama woods."

Eva hadn't heard that note of amusement in Mary Nell's voice for a very long time.

"Well," Eva tried to muster a smile of her own. "I don't really care to see you naked either." Then Eva's smile faded. "I don't care about that."

She stepped carefully over and laid a hand on Mary Nell's arm.

"I just want you . . . I just want you back. I want my sister. And I guess I want to hear you say that you know what happened back there on that road that day."

"I know what happened," said Mary Nell. She unfolded her arms. "And the day Lou Henry Evans died was emancipation day for me."

Eva stared at her.

"Then why? All these years, we could have been sisters," she said, dropping her hands and letting her knees buckle until she was kneeling on the wet leaves. She couldn't hold her head up anymore. She let it fall down into her open palms and gave in to tears.

"I don't know," Mary Nell said. "I didn't know what to do. He was my husband."

She paused and the wind skipped through the trees, whistling. The rain was slowing, turning into a fine mist. Eva could feel Mary Nell's eyes on her.

"After awhile," Mary Nell said, "you don't know how to go back. You don't know how to say you was wrong. 'Specially after puttin' out so much to make yourself be right, and make the world the way you thought it ought to be, instead of lookin' right at the way the world really was." She sighed heavily, turning so that Eva couldn't see her face. "Ain't no point in comin' out here and tellin' God about it all, Eva. He know and He don' acted. He took Jimmie."

"I don't know about that, sister," Eva said. "It seems to me that them white men at the jailhouse took Jimmie. And if God made that as punishment, then He wanted me to suffer, too. Because he was my son. He was my son." She put her head in her hands and let the tears come.

"He was your son," Mary Nell whispered.